The Man Upstairs

Mary Swift

To Libby and Jessica

for countless hours spent reading

To Christine

for her unwavering support

And to my mother

for always believing I could

.

Chapter 1

Fox Cove, Maine

1784

Hugh MacPherson had been a thief for fifteen years when he came upon the Winslow House late one evening. He was coming to the end of a particularly successful crime spree, five houses in the last week, and all ripe with booty.

He had nabbed and fenced a silver tea set that afternoon and treated himself to a hearty dinner. It was his thirtieth birthday. He celebrated in the tavern, eating and getting drunk, all in the company of some lovely ladies. At least he assumed they were lovely, he had had a lot to drink that night. It didn't matter, it was time he was on his way. The sheriff would be looking for him. Five houses was pushing his luck, even for someone as talented as himself. Three was his usual limit in one town. Once he had gone for four and it had cost him six months in a stinking jail. He was lucky he hadn't been hanged.

He was walking into the woods looking for a place to sleep when he first saw the house. It was well after two o'clock in the morning. It was called the Winslow House because a couple named Winslow lived there with their grown son. They had built it less than a year before after moving from the city where Mr. Winslow had been a blacksmith. His health had taken a turn for the worse and his doctor advised him to seek cleaner air and settle in the country.

Hugh knew none of this family history, nor would it have interested him very much. His main objective was to try the front door and see if it was locked. As he stumbled up the narrow path something in the back of his mind told him he shouldn't be doing this in his condition. He ignored his instincts and pressed on. He pushed on the front door, it swung open revealing a pitch black hallway. People ought to lock their doors he thought to himself, anyone can just walk right in. He smiled at his own joke and pulled his shoes off, leaving them on the front step. This was going to be a cinch.

He crept into the dark hallway in his stocking feet. A room to the left looked like a parlor. As he entered a sliver of moonlight coming from the window helped to reveal a pair of silver candlesticks on the mantle. He quickly snatched them up, it occurred to him that he hadn't brought a bag for the loot. That was the problem with spur of the moment crimes, there was always something missing. He took a look around as best he could in the dark but there didn't appear to be anything else of value.

His gut told him to leave, this place clearly didn't have much to offer. But the alcohol and the compliments from the women had left him feeling confident. Besides he was Hugh MacPherson, professional thief. This wasn't just some idle hobby, he had supported himself since the age of fourteen by breaking and entering and other petty crimes. He was in now, he might as well have a go at the place.

On the other side of the hallway was a long dining room, a pewter bowl was on the table. He quickly grabbed it. Beyond the dining room was a kitchen and larder. Not much to see in there, although a half eaten blueberry pie did look tempting. Beyond the larder was another small room. Inside a boy was sleeping peacefully on a narrow wooden cot. The sound of his breathing made a soft whistle in the air. Hugh wanted to laugh out loud. Even half drunk he could still pull it off. He was tempted to creep in and have a look around. No. It was better to go upstairs where there were probably adults with more valuable possessions.

As he walked back through the dining room he felt a slight wave of nausea. He stumbled and stubbed his toe on a chair, it scraped loudly against the stone floor. He froze in place and waited. Nothing. He smiled to himself in the dark.

The staircase began in the front hallway. Hugh set the candlesticks and pewter bowl by the front door and ventured up. The first six steps led to a wide landing, the stairs then turned right and continued to the second floor. Hugh paused momentarily on the landing, he thought he had heard a noise. He waited a few more seconds before continuing on. The wood still smelled fresh, the house must be new.

"Hold it right there." said a voice.

Hugh stopped. Standing at the top of the stairs was a man in a white nightshirt, he was holding a rifle. This was not good.

"I, I must be in the wrong house." Hugh said. His voice was shaking, his words slurring ever so slightly from the ale.

"Quiet." ordered the man.

"But I can explain-" He put up his hands to show he was unarmed and tried to take a step backwards but instead he stumbled and fell against the wall.

The man with the rifle took a step down. Hugh heard a voice behind him. "Father don't." It was the last words he would hear alive. A flash of light illuminated the stairwell followed by a tremendous bang. He was aware for a split second of a strange feeling in his chest, falling backwards onto something soft and then another flash of the purest white light he had ever seen.

A second later Hugh found himself standing upright. He looked down and saw his body staring up at him, the light was gone from his eyes. There was someone lying underneath him. It was the boy who had been sleeping in the room behind the larder. He must have been in back of Hugh when the man fired his rifle. Hugh backed down the stairs and stood in the front hallway trying to figure out what was going on.

The boy was dead. Mr. Winslow dropped his rifle and rushed down the stairs followed closely by his wife. They pushed Hugh's body aside, it fell haphazardly down the steps, landing in a sprawl on the floor. He could see the small hole in his shirt where the bullet had passed through him and into the boy standing directly behind.

Mr. Winslow let out an anguished howl. He pulled the boy's body to him, rocking him back and forth as he sobbed. Mrs. Winslow sat next to them and hugged her knees to her chest. She ventured a glance at the body of Hugh MacPherson, a look of disgust passed over her face.

It began to occur to Hugh that he must be dead. He had been threatened with the gallows several times in his long criminal career, but he had always managed to escape the worst. It seemed unbelievable that his life could suddenly be over, but here he was staring at the destruction he had created.

"I told you not to come in here Hugh." a voice said next to him. He turned his head and found a man standing next to him. He was dressed all in black with dark hair and piercing blue eyes.

"Who are you?" Hugh focused his attention on this newcomer. Was this man dead or alive? What was happening to him?

"I'm Mika." he said as though Hugh should already know it. Mika stared at him so intensely that Hugh began to wonder if they hadn't met somewhere and he had forgotten. "I'm your Watcher."

"Are you my guardian angel?"

"I am no Angel, don't insult me. My job is to Watch over you, to guide you. I am your protector."

"Then why didn't you protect me just now? Why am I dead? Why is that boy dead?"

"That boy is dead because of you, don't blame me." Mika said sharply. "And as for your pitiful life, I told you plenty of times to get out of here. You hesitated when you first came in. Remember? And then I stopped you when you were all set to go into that boy's room and snoop around. That was me again. Do you really think you had those thoughts yourself? You would steal anything that wasn't nailed down. I am your conscience, although you rarely listen to me. I've been telling you for days to get out of this town. Thirty years I've been putting up with you and for what? You go and get yourself shot and take someone else with you."

"Why didn't his Watcher save him?" Hugh asked quietly. Mr. Winslow's hands and arms were covered in blood. He was muttering something as he held his son. Mrs. Winslow's face was gray.

"I am sure his Watcher told him that some fool of a criminal was in his house and he should beware, just as his father felt compelled to protect the family. A Watcher can only advise, nothing more. You chose to ignore me and got yourself and that boy killed."

"It's not my fault. I didn't mean for it to happen."

Mika's blue eyes flashed. "If you hadn't been so intent on stealing a pair of candlesticks while you're half drunk that boy would still be alive. It was only a matter of time before something like this happened. I have been warning you for years, but you never listen to anything I tell you. Now you're responsible for the end of a life. You might as well have fired the rifle yourself."

"What happens to me now?" Just then a man walked by him. No. A man walked *through* him. He felt a momentary surge of warmth. He hadn't realized how cold he had become. Two more people came in, one walked through Hugh and the other through Mika. They both looked at Hugh's body in disgust.

Mika stared at the scene on the landing. "The boy will be taken care of, he's already there. His parents will suffer the rest of their lives."

"What about me?" Three more people arrived including the sheriff. Hugh had seen enough lawmen in his days to catch the flash of a gold star pinned underneath a coat collar.

"What about you?"

"Are you going to take me to heaven?" He hesitated. "Or somewhere else?"

"Heaven? What makes you think you belong there? Sometimes I just can't believe I got stuck with you. What a way to occupy my eternity. You're staying right here."

"Here? Here in this house? Why?"

"To Torment, what else?" Mika said. "You've got to pay for what you've done."

"Torment? For how long?"

"You don't know what forever means?"

"You can't be serious."

"Dead serious." Mika replied smirking. "Oh, that was funny."

"What am I supposed to do here?" A man with a doctor's bag rushed through him. He took a quick look at both bodies and shook his head. Meanwhile the sheriff was poking his hands into Hugh's pockets. He held up the gold pocket watch Hugh always carried.

"That's mine!" Hugh shouted. The sheriff turned the watch over in his hands. "That's mine." he repeated to Mika. "My father gave me that watch. I didn't steal it."

"I know. I was there when he gave it to you. Look in your pocket."

Hugh was wearing the same clothes he had died in. He looked down at his bloodied shirt with disappointment. A brand new shirt ruined. He reached his hand in his pocket and pulled out the watch.

"Try dropping it on the floor."

Hugh opened his hand, the watch stayed on his palm as though it were glued in place. "What?" he mumbled. He shook his hand but the watch remained.

"Now put it in your pocket"

Hugh put his hand in his pocket, he felt the watch slide away.

"It can't leave your body. Nothing you're wearing can." Mika looked past Hugh's shoulder as though he saw something there. "I've got to be going now."

"What? You can't leave me. I thought you were my Watcher." A gripping fear was coming over him. He didn't want to be left alone with these strangers. He didn't want to see what they did with his body.

"You're dead. What am I protecting you from? Besides there's a new life coming into the world and I have to be there to start my Watch."

"So I'll never see you again?"

"If only." Mika said. "No, once a Watcher, always a Watcher. But I can't be here all the time, I have others to look after. If you need me just call out my name and I will come. But don't do it all the time. And don't do it five minutes from now just to see if it works. And only if it's really important, not just because you want someone to talk to. I'll check in on you from time to time."

"What am I supposed to do here?"

"I want you to think about what you've done. Think about what kind of life you have led up until now." Mika looked into the distance and smiled.

"I have to go. Don't forget I can still hear and see everything you do, so don't be a jackass like you usually are."

Hugh began to feel afraid.

"I am going to disappear now. I just wanted to give a warning so you're not surprised. I'll see you later Hugh." Mika slowly dissolved into the air until there was nothing left of him.

Hugh stood in the hallway not wanting to look at the destruction he had caused. "Happy birthday." he whispered to himself as his body was carried past him and dumped outside.

Chapter 2

Augusta, Maine

1889

I was happy in Augusta. The thought of living anywhere else had never even crossed my mind. Our small apartment in the heart of town was all I needed. My father Edward worked at a barber shop down the street while my mother Elsay kept house and tended to me and my older siblings Eve and Ethan. One evening in September Father came home in a very excited state and everything changed.

"Wife, children." he began. "I have the most wonderful news. I have an opportunity to own my own barber shop."

Mother looked nervous. "How is this possible Edward? We haven't the money for such a venture."

Father rubbed his hands together. "You remember Senator Hershival Brown don't you?"

Mother frowned. "I don't think so."

"Of course you do Mother." Eve said. "He has those awful mutton chops and he always smells like maple syrup."

I tried not to giggle.

"Oh yes. Him." Mother said. "Why does he smell like maple syrup?"

"Ah, well, that's uh." Father stammered and scratched his nose. "Anyhow, I have always had a certain touch with Senator Brown's hair, other barbers just don't appreciate its unique properties. And his beard, I am very good with his beard too. He says no one else understands his hair the way I do."

"You're very gifted Edward." Mother said admiringly.

"Thank you dear. Now this morning ole' Brownie asked me why I didn't have a shop of my own." He stopped to let the question hang mysteriously in the air.

We all stared at him. We knew why he didn't have a shop of his own, we were not wealthy. We lived modestly at best and there were no expectations that our circumstances would change.

Father waited another second before continuing. "So I said, Senator Brown I would love nothing more than to have my own name hanging over the door, but I've got a wife and three children to support. I can't chase a dream."

"Oh Edward, have you really wanted your own shop all this time?" Mother asked.

"Now Elsay, I have you and the children to think of. Mr. Blake's shop is good enough for me. But Brown did get me thinking." There was a sparkle in his eye I hadn't seen before. "Now I am just getting to the good part. Senator Brown lives in Fox Cove and-"

"Where on earth is Fox Cove?" Mother asked.

"On the coast, near a small inlet." Ethan said.

"Very good my boy." Father nodded.

Ethan peered over his glasses. "It's in our new atlas."

"What does all of this have to do with us Father?" Eve asked.

"I am trying to tell you that. Now Senator Brown says that back in Fox Cove there isn't a decent barber to be found. He's going to put up the money to have my own shop."

"What does this Fox Cove have to do with your barber shop?" Mother asked. "He still won't get a proper haircut when he's home."

"Dearest, the shop will be in Fox Cove. Brown is looking for families to populate the town. Decent, hardworking folks. He said we are just the sort he's after."

"Move! Move to this Fox Cove place?" Mother stood up and paced about the room wringing her hands. "We can't move there, where will we live? Oh Edward I can't believe you've done this."

"Don't worry Elsay. Brown has already found us a house, one of the oldest in town. He says it has real character, and we can buy it over time, imagine us homeowners."

Mother's faced relaxed a bit. She had always wanted a home of her own. "One of the oldest homes you say?"

"Yes. A *historic* home. And there's room enough for each of us to have our own bedroom." Father glanced at Eve.

"Really Father? My own room? I wouldn't have to share with Emma?"

My very own bedroom. I could put my telescope anywhere without Eve hanging her clothes on it, and I would finally have some privacy. There was something important to consider however.

"You don't think there's a chance of any dead people being there do you?" I whispered to Ethan.

"I doubt it. Let's wait and see when we get there. I'm sure we have nothing to worry about."

Chapter 3

Edward Hollis came to look at the house first. He was slim with salty gray hair and a neatly trimmed beard. His brown eyes were lively, darting to and fro, taking in every detail.

Edward was accompanied by Senator Hershival Brown. He was a tall man in his fifties with brown and gray hair and a long bushy gray beard. Hugh noticed the distinct smell of maple syrup wafting from him. They walked from room to room talking of "the shop". Hugh loved the company of the living. It gave him a chance to listen to conversations, to walk through warm bodies, and for a brief second to feel alive.

He was well behaved that day. If he started making trouble he would scare them away and he would be alone once again. Not that it made much of a difference, in the end they would leave, everyone did. Within a few months this family would be gone just like all the others. But he could revel in the moments when he had been part of a family. And all wasn't lost, someone new always came along. The house was dirt cheap.

Hugh had been dead for one hundred and five years. Mika had said the first two hundred are the hardest. In those first few weeks after he died he had attempted to escape. He tried the door, windows and even in desperation the chimney, but he could not leave. When he neared the front door it felt as though he was walking through mud, the air was thick and impenetrable. There was nothing he could do, he was eternally stuck.

The parents left a few months after their son was killed. His name had been Charles, but everyone called him Charlie. His funeral had been in the front parlor. Mika and Hugh stood and watched while Mrs. Winslow sobbed on her husband's shoulder. Hugh couldn't bear to look at the pine casket Mr. Winslow had made himself.

Mika came barely once a year. Hugh could call him, but he would only come after several pleas. Loneliness, according to Mika, was part of Torment, perhaps the most important part. "I told you not to come in here." he would say angrily.

But now here was Edward Hollis to follow about and study. "Yes I think this will do. It will indeed." Edward said to Senator Brown.

Senator Brown nodded. "I thought you would like it. It's one of the oldest houses in Fox Cove you know, you're quite lucky it's become available."

"It's always available." Hugh said aloud. He enjoyed making comments to the living as they spoke to one another, it was almost like being part of the conversation.

"Yes it will do just fine Brown. I can't thank you enough for this."

Senator Brown shuffled his feet and looked at the floor. "It's my pleasure Hollis. Fox Cove needs a decent barber shop, and more importantly it needs decent folk like you and your family." He let out a puff of air and rocked back on his heels.

"Elsay and the children will be very happy here, I know it. And as for the shop, you won't regret it. I'll pay back every penny with interest." He laughed nervously and glanced over his shoulder, mumbling something under his breath.

Senator Brown chewed on his bottom lip. An awkward moment of silence developed. "I should tell you something about this place Hollis." Brown finally said.

"Oh no, don't." Hugh muttered.

"What is it?"

"There are some in town who say this place, well I don't believe it, but some say this place is haunted." Senator Brown stuffed his hands in his pockets.

"Haunted you say?"

"Yes, there was a murder here, it was years ago, and I mean a long time. A thief broke in and murdered a youngster in the parlor."

"How do these rumors persist?" Hugh cried. "I didn't murder anyone! *I* was murdered! Why doesn't anyone remember that?"

"A murder you say?" Edward asked.

"Yes, some say that the ghost of that poor boy haunts the house. Of course it's utter nonsense but-"

"There's a ghost you say?"

"Some people in town think so, it's just gossip and rumor. Utter nonsense. Why? Does that bother you?"

"He's got it all wrong!" Hugh shouted at Edward.

"No, I am sure it's just a story. It's just that my-" He stopped. "Never mind Brown. I am sure my family will be very happy here." Edward smiled nervously. The two men shook hands and slapped each other on the back before they each lit a cigar.

Hugh sat on the stairs watching and listening to everything. They left a half hour later. He was getting a new family.

Chapter 4

 Senator Brown had arranged everything for our move to Fox Cove, including several wagons to bring our furniture and belongings to our new home. It was a two day journey and by the time we arrived that foggy afternoon in April we were all cranky and tired.

 Father did his best to cheer us. "Just think, our new house is waiting for us. Tonight you will sleep in your very own room Eve."

 "Uh huh." Eve muttered as she nodded off.

 We were crammed into a restored stagecoach owned by the Senator. It was painted with red lacquer, the letter "B" featured prominently on the side in gold paint. The previous day it had seemed like a luxury, now it was just a stuffy, bouncing box. I looked out the window but there was little to see except fog.

 "Just how much are we indebted to the Senator?" Mother asked.

 "Don't worry dear. I have it all calculated. In ten years I will have paid him back and I will own the shop and house free and clear." Father said.

 Mother snorted. "Ten years? Emma will be twenty two by then. I don't want to think of how old you and I will be Edward."

 "It will be fine Elsay." Father patted her hand and smiled. "Here's the town now."

 At that moment we turned a corner and the seaside town of Fox Cove came into view. The town was built into the side of a hill, one main road cut across the land, zigzagging its way down to the sea. The cove was a small horseshoe carved into the rocky shore. A dozen or so fishing trawlers bobbed on the water. One was pulling up to the wharf as Ethan and I gazed out the window. It was the first time Ethan or I had seen the ocean. Both of us took turns looking out the window. The road we were on had many new houses, some were still being built. People stopped to stare at the coach and two wagons following us.

 "Do you like it Emma?" Father asked.

I nodded enthusiastically. Ethan was taking far too long at the window. I tugged on his sleeve. He pulled his head inside, his face was pale. I knew immediately what was happening.

"Outside?" I whispered.

"Yes."

I stuck my head out of the window and saw a man with dusty clothes walking back and forth in front of a new house. Blood was running down the side of his face. "Blasted chimney." he said aloud. "My mother warned me not to become a bricklayer." A second later a little girl skipping down the street passed through him. I shut my eyes before he had a chance to make eye contact.

"Is there someone there?" Ethan whispered in my ear. I nodded.

"What are you two whispering about?" Mother demanded. She tugged at my elbow and pulled me back inside.

"Nothing." I said. Ethan took a book out of his pocket and began reading.

"It had better be nothing. I won't tolerate any of your fantasies Emma. Not today."

"It's nothing Mother, really. I was just showing Ethan the boats in the water."

"That's right." Ethan said looking over his glasses. "I was wondering if we might be able to take a ride on one."

"Since when are you interested in boats?" Mother asked.

"I may be a ship's surgeon one day." he said earnestly.

Ethan wanted to become a doctor. He was always reading medical journals and textbooks on every part of the human body. It was unclear to any of us how he could achieve this dream, we hadn't the money for college. His only hope would be a scholarship.

"Let's just enjoy the ride." Father said. "There's not much farther now." The coach jerked as the road took a sharp turn to the left, winding its way down the bluff towards the sea.

I didn't dare look out the window again. I leaned back on my seat and watched Ethan read a book called *Wonders of the Eye*. I could feel my mother's stare. She was angry with me. I couldn't help it if I sometimes saw dead people, it was not as though I wanted to.

I had seen a lady in the park when I was five, she was walking with a knife sticking out of her back and blood dripping from the corner of her mouth. When I screamed Mother told me I was embarrassing her. The lady with the knife looked at me and said, "She can't see me, I'm dead."

I didn't realize this strange talent was going to be a problem until one day at my Aunt Linda's house. I was eight and Ethan was ten. As we sat in the parlor with Mother and Aunt Linda a little boy walked into the room, his clothes were old fashioned and his face was gaunt.

I looked at Ethan. He appeared to be staring right at the boy. "Can you see him?" I whispered.

"Sort of, the air is shiny. Is someone there?" He glanced anxiously at my mother who was deeply engrossed in conversation with Aunt Linda.

"Yes there's a boy, I think he's dead."

"What are you two conspiring about over there?" Mother asked.

"It's nothing." Ethan replied.

"There's a dead boy in the corner." I said pointing.

"Emma, please don't. You don't see anything."

Aunt Linda looked at me. "Is it Hubert?" she asked with a hint of desperation in her voice. Hubert was her son, he had died almost twenty years before, but I had no idea what he had looked like.

"I don't know. Are you?" I asked the boy. He stared at me for a minute and then walked through the wall and disappeared. "He's gone."

"For shame Emma, stop this nonsense." Mother said. "Can't you see you're upsetting your aunt? What a mean trick to play. I'm ashamed of you."

"It's not a trick Mother. Emma can see them, and I can-" Ethan began.

"Quiet Ethan!" Mother's voice was full of anger. "Your father will hear about this."

"But Mother-" I said trying not to cry.

"We are leaving." She grabbed my arm. "I am terribly sorry Linda. I assure you they will both be punished severely."

Aunt Linda's face was pale. "Elsay, they may be telling you the truth."

"Nonsense. I have never heard of such utter nonsense. They are spoiled children who will be taught a lesson."

"Please Elsay, they are just children." Aunt Linda smiled weakly at me.

Mother squeezed my arm tighter. "You will be receiving a written apology dear sister." She dragged Ethan and me straight home. That night my father heard the whole story. He did not ask us any questions. Ethan and I both took separate trips to the woodshed. We wrote letters of apology to Aunt Linda, and bought flowers for Hubert's grave with our own money.

Now Fox Cove had its own ghostly entity. I would have to avoid him. If the dead discovered you could see them they almost always wanted to talk, usually about how they died. There was also the danger of being seen talking into the air, and therefore thought of as the local lunatic.

"This town is so small." Eve said looking out the other side of the coach.

"There will be more to see." Father said. "Remember Eve, we are country folk now."

"Ugh."

We rode in silence for the next few minutes. The coach creaked slowly along the road. It was not the main street we were used to in Augusta. The buildings and the sidewalks were made of wood. There were two general stores, a grain and livery store, one hotel and a number of dark looking taverns.

Looking out I could see a small shop with a sign reading "Hollis Barber Shop." It was tucked between a store with ladies hats in the windows and a pub with red fringe curtains.

"That's the shop. We open tomorrow. Brownie has everything set." Father said proudly.

"I like those hats next door." Eve said.

"And you'll be able to buy one Eve, as soon as the shop takes off, we will have everything we have ever wanted."

Several smaller roads led off from the main street including a short road called Brown Lane. At the end was a large three story stone house.

"That's Brownie's place." Father said. "He's done quite well for himself."

"Where's our house?" Ethan asked.

"Just a little further."

Main Street ended at the mouth of the cove. There was a great amount of noise as the last of the fishing boats were coming in for the day. Men were shouting back and forth as the catch was being hauled onto the wharf. The cove was dotted with structures of every shape and description. Nets and lobster traps were stacked in neat piles among the buildings. The air was thick with the smell of salt and fresh fish. The main road had ended, but a small rutted lane forked slightly to the left. The coach lurched as the wheels settled into worn tracks.

"Oh Edward, where are we going?" Mother held onto him to prevent herself from falling off the seat.

"We're nearly there dearest."

Ethan put his book away. It was impossible to do anything except try to hang on to each other and hope there wasn't much further to go.

The road was very narrow and well shaded by a number of white pines, oaks, and maples. There was an old peeling wooden fence on our left. In the distance was a white house with black shutters.

"Is that it?" Eve cried.

"No." Father said. "Old man Johnson lives there. I met him last time I was here. He's quite elderly."

Another house came up on the right. It was a ramshackle affair with a sagging porch.

"That's not it is it?" Eve said looking glum.

"Heavens no. A family named Cooper lives there."

A third house came into view. It was neither left nor right but straight ahead.

"Is this the end of the road?" Ethan asked.

"Yes, it's a dead end. The road used to continue another few miles, but there was a fire some forty years back, it burned everything in its path until it got to our house. They never rebuilt this part of town, they started moving everything up on the hill. Here we are." The carriage came to a sudden stop. "Everyone out."

We flung open the doors of the carriage and one by one stumbled out. Our new house stood before us. It was two stories with battered siding that looked as if it had been painted several different colors in its long existence. The majority of the paint had peeled off exposing gray weather beaten clapboards. The windows were small and dingy.

"Edward, did you look at this house before you bought it?" I heard Mother say.

"We can't live here." Eve moaned.

"Of course I looked at it. Brownie found it for us. It needs a little work, but it's one of the oldest houses in town." Father said.

"Clearly." Mother muttered.

In one corner of the house was an oak tree. It was growing crooked from having been planted too close to the house, or perhaps the house came later for the trunk was a foot and a half across. As I looked up I noticed an attic window tucked under the peak of the roof. It was the perfect place for my telescope. There was a flash of color in the window.

"Ethan, look at-"

"What?" He had returned to his book.

"Oh nothing." I couldn't constantly interrupt his studies and it was probably just a trick of the light filtering through the tree, it had to be.

My parents and Eve had already gone inside. Ethan followed them while I stopped to check the attic window again. There was nothing there, it must have been my imagination. It had been a long day.

I walked through the front door. Ethan was standing in the middle of the hall with his book in front of his face while Father looked about and then ducked into a doorway on the left. Mother and Eve were nowhere to be seen.

I was about to ask Father if I could pick out my bedroom when I first saw him. A man was creeping down the stairs, his skin pale as moonlight. He was wearing a bloodied shirt with a small hole near his heart.

This was going to be a problem.

Chapter 5

Hugh had been waiting all day for the Hollis family to arrive. He remembered the date from the last time Edward had been there. Since dying he was aware of the date and time instinctively even though there were no calendars or clocks in the house. Mika said it was called Time Awareness and that nearly everyone had it when they died.

He waited for them in the attic. There was a small window under the peak of the roof that had a good view of the road. He stayed there all day until finally, during the last hour of daylight, a coach and two wagons approached. Hugh felt his dead heart skip a beat. Even from the third story he could feel their energy. Life was so powerful, he had never realized that when he was alive. He had taken everything for granted back then.

The coach lurched to a stop, the doors flung open and five weary passengers got out. Edward yawned and pulled at the seat of his trousers. Hugh smiled. Dear Edward. He was already quite fond of him. He strolled towards the front door looking more than a little pleased with himself.

Beside Edward was a woman Hugh presumed to be Mrs. Hollis. She was pretty with dark blond hair streaked with gray and a generous bosom. She was wrinkling her nose as she looked up at the house. He could see the disappointment in her eyes.

The oldest child was not exactly a child, but a young woman. She was extremely attractive with her mother's blond hair and more delicate features than either parent. As she walked her dress swayed to and fro accentuating her slim hips, and from Hugh's high vantage point, her also generous bosom. Oh, to be alive again.

The other two children were far less interesting. One was a boy of about fifteen. He was walking and reading a book at the same time. An intellectual. There was a little girl behind him who couldn't have been more than twelve. Both had dark brown hair like their father.

Hugh rushed downstairs and stood on the landing close to where he had died. He loved being there when new people arrived. The door opened and with it a jumble of voices came inside. Edward walked in nodding his head approvingly now and then. The mother followed and went into the next room, women always liked to see the kitchens first. The attractive daughter was twirling a bit of honey colored hair in her fingers. Her eyes swept past him as she gazed around the hallway. She said something to her father and then dashed upstairs, walking through Hugh. Her body was warm and scented with lavender.

Finally the boy arrived. As Hugh suspected he was dull. He didn't even put his book down. He merely stopped in the middle of the hallway and kept on reading. A second later the little girl came in. At last they were all there. These were his new people.

Hugh started down the stairs. He was going to follow each one of them in turn, perhaps allowing them to walk through him and warm his cold body. It was going to be a wonderful day. He would be able to relive it over and over in his mind for years to come. It was at that moment that something remarkable happened. Something that had never happened in the one hundred and five years he had been Tormenting in the Winslow House, something he never expected. The little girl looked him dead in the eye.

Hugh stopped in his tracks. Could she see him? He took another step. The girl tugged on her brother's sleeve. The boy closed his book and looked searchingly towards Hugh. He nodded ever so slightly. He didn't look directly at him, but Hugh had a feeling that the boy knew he was there.

"Can you see me?" Hugh asked.

The girl kept watching him while the boy stared vaguely into Hugh's direction. Hugh didn't know what to do. There had been perceptive ones before, people that looked over their shoulders when he passed by or woke up in the middle of the night as he breezed through their rooms. But none of them had acted like this.

"You can see me can't you? Both of you."

"Emma and Ethan, what are you two staring at?" The mother suddenly emerged from the kitchen looking cross. She looked at where Hugh was standing, but it was clear she didn't see a darn thing. She grabbed Emma's arm and bent over. "None of this. I will have none of this. This is our new house, you are not going to start this again. I won't allow it."

"Mother-" Ethan began.

"That goes for you too Ethan." Her face was tense and her lips were drawn into a tight line. She was still holding Emma's arm.

Hugh didn't say anything. Emma stared at him.

Edward came out of the parlor. "What do you think Elsay?" he said patting his stomach. He stopped and stared at the three of them. "Is everything all right?"

Elsay let go of Emma's arm, her face relaxed. "Of course Edward. The house needs work, but it will do." It was obvious it wasn't what she wanted. Not that he blamed her, the house was old and it was haunted. Hugh would never have bought it.

"Children, why don't you go upstairs and pick out your bedroom before Eve gets the best one." Edward said.

Ethan walked through Hugh while Emma followed close behind. Hugh didn't bother to move out of the way, he was used to people walking through him. As Emma passed her arm brushed his hand, his skin tingled.

She had not passed through him. She could touch him. Hugh had learned long ago that he could either pass through objects or people, or he could choose to touch them. It took more concentration to touch or hold something than to simply walk through it. But the living could not choose, it wasn't possible. Emma could do the impossible.

"Emma, can you see me?" He followed her upstairs. She didn't react. It occurred to him that perhaps she could see but not hear him. "Can you hear me?" he asked as they rounded the landing. Again she ignored him.

Eve was at the top of the stairs exactly where Mr. Winslow had stood the night he shot Hugh. "What took you two so long? I've already picked out my room."

"That's not fair Eve. Emma and I haven't even seen them yet." Ethan said.

Eve shrugged. "I'm the oldest, I should get to pick first. Do you want to see mine?" She opened the door at the top of the stairs. "Here it is."

Hugh knew the room. It was the best bedroom in the house. It had three large windows. They all stepped inside.

"Are the other rooms like this?" Ethan asked.

"No." Hugh said aloud. Emma stood a few feet away but she made no indication that she could hear him. Maybe it had been his imagination or wishful thinking.

"These windows would be perfect for Emma's telescope." Ethan said.

Eve rolled her eyes. "That." she said dismissively.

"The attic stairs are nearby, awfully drafty for a delicate young woman." Hugh said.

Emma rubbed her arms. "Isn't it cold in here?"

"I don't feel anything."

Emma poked her head into the hallway and then came back in. "The attic stairs would be right outside your door Eve, they feel drafty."

"You can hear me! I knew you could. How? How?" he cried. She ignored him.

"Oh you're just saying that because you want this room. Let me show you yours." Eve said.

"Are you ignoring me because of them?" Hugh asked as he followed them down the hallway.

The next bedroom was small and narrow with two windows that overlooked the backyard. "This is your room Ethan." Eve announced.

Ethan straightened his glasses and looked about. "That's fine. I will be studying most of the time anyway."

"And this is your room Emma." Eve said as she pushed open the door to the corner bedroom. Hugh had never cared for that room. It was el shaped with a small fireplace that smoked and narrow windows which didn't get much sun. "See, this is fine for you."

"There's a panel to the left of the fireplace. Push on it." Hugh said.

Emma moved her head slightly in his direction. Casually she walked towards the fireplace and leaned on the panel next to it. Hugh heard the familiar click as the panel sprung open. Emma's eyes widened as she discovered the secret door.

"What's that?" Eve asked. All three looked curiously into the dark recess behind the door.

"It's a staircase that leads down to the parlor." Hugh said. He had used it more times than he could count.

"Maybe it goes to the parlor?" Emma suggested.

Eve rushed headlong down the rickety steps. She came back a few seconds later pulling a cobweb out of her hair. "It leads to a door in the parlor. I couldn't open it though, Mother and Father were in there."

"Why shouldn't you tell them about it?" Ethan asked.

Eve smiled coyly. "I think you should have the other room Emma."

"Really?" Emma's face lit up. "Thank you Eve."

"It's me you should be thanking." Hugh said.

"I should bring my books inside." Ethan said.

Emma and Ethan left Eve to contemplate how best to use the secret door. Hugh followed Emma as she walked into her new bedroom. She looked over her shoulder and then shut the door in his face.

He walked through the door and found her on the other side with her arms folded across her chest, her face was red. "I would appreciate it if you would just go away!"

Chapter 6

"I would appreciate it if you would just go away!"

"That's a fine way to act after I helped you get the best bedroom in the house."

"I didn't ask you to do that." In another minute the whole family would be in here wondering who I was talking to.

"I know." he said. "But I heard you mention a telescope. I thought you would like it."

"I like this room very much. But I can't keep talking to you."

"Why not?"

"Because you'll talk all day and night and you'll want to tell me about how you died. And because my mother doesn't believe in ghosts and she doesn't believe I can see them. She would be so angry if she could see me now. I'm supposed to pretend this type of thing doesn't happen."

"Oh." He looked severely disappointed. "I could do something to make her believe, you know, make things fly in the air and such."

"No! That will frighten her and somehow I'll end up getting punished."

He strolled towards the windows looking dejected. "You can't stop me from talking you know. I do it all the time. There has never been anyone here to listen before."

"You can talk all you want but I won't answer you."

"Fine." he said angrily. He walked past me and vanished through the bedroom door.

A second later there was a knock. Ethan poked his head inside. "Was someone here? I thought I heard you talking."

I nodded. "Come in."

Ethan stepped inside and shut the door behind him.

"There's a ghost here Ethan. He's haunting the house."

"He told you about that secret door, didn't he?"

"Yes. But I told him I can't talk to him. If Mother catches me-"

"Did you tell him about Mother?"

"Yes, but I don't think he understands. He wants someone to talk to, he's going to be a problem Ethan. You can't let on that you sense anything unusual. Don't look in his direction."

"What does he look like?"

I paused for a minute, thinking I heard something outside the door. "He's old, at least thirty. His clothes are really old fashioned, he wears knee breeches and one of those white shirts with the fancy collars that tie at the throat."

"A cravat?"

"A what? I guess so. His shirt has some blood on it, and a small hole too, right near his heart."

"What's his name?" Ethan asked.

"I didn't ask. You don't know what they're like, if I ask his name he'll never stop talking and Mother is bound to catch me."

"But-"

Eve opened the door, the ghost was standing behind her grinning. "You two are always whispering. Mother has supper ready, she wants you out of these rooms so the men can bring up the furniture."

We followed Eve downstairs with the ghost behind us. The kitchen was a long room with five windows and a large fireplace. The men had already brought in our pine table and chairs. We took our usual places. The ghost circled around us looking at the plates of cold meat and bread that Mother had brought with her in the coach.

"Our first night in our new home." Father said.

"Never thought I would see the day." Mother's eyes were watering.

"My new family." the ghost said. I couldn't help glancing at him out of the corner of my eye.

"Tomorrow I will be at the shop all day. Children you'll be off to school in the morning. Brownie has already spoken to the schoolmaster and told him to expect three new students." Father said.

"School already!" Eve cried. "We just got here. Can't we wait a few days?"

"I would like to begin right away." Ethan said. "I wonder what sort of man this schoolmaster is. I hope he's well acquainted with current scientific theory."

"Just as I thought, an intellectual." said the ghost.

"And I ought to invite Brownie to dinner sometime this week." Father said.

"Oh yes, the maple syrup man."

I set my fork down and coughed to keep from laughing.

"This week!" Mother cried. "We just moved in, the house is in such a state. I can't begin receiving company so soon."

"Now Elsay, let's remember what this man has done for us." Father said. They both looked at us. "We will discuss this later."

"I can fill you in Emma." the ghost said behind me.

The commentary continued until supper was over. We were all tired and everyone was more than ready for bed. The men had brought our trunks upstairs. I couldn't wait to put on my nightgown and go to sleep. There was a bedroom on the first floor behind the pantry. My parents had chosen it for their room.

"Goodnight children." Mother took Father's arm and they disappeared into the darkened pantry.

"That's a well used room you know." the ghost said as he trailed behind me. "You wouldn't believe the things I've seen going on in there. Actually you're too young to hear about it. Let's just say even I was blushing. Oh that's probably still too much. I never did know when to stop talking. Mika says my brain and my mouth work independently from each other. That is something he would say. You don't know about him yet, but I'll fill you in as we go along. I wonder if he can see your Watcher? Now that would be interesting."

I followed Eve and Ethan upstairs. Eve quickly dashed down the hall to her room.

"I bet she's going to use the secret staircase to get out. There used to be this one boy who would sneak out every night, of course he was going to meet a girl and you know it, she ended up, well you know. So anyway, her father was so furious he took a branding iron and gave the boy the letter G, that was the first letter of the father's last name, right on his backside. They shipped the girl off up north somewhere to have the baby. But oh boy did I laugh every time I saw his bare ass. Oh that story probably wasn't suitable for someone your age. Sorry."

"He's still there isn't he?" Ethan asked.

"Yes and he never stops talking."

"Just ignore him, he's bound to get tired of it. Goodnight Emma." Ethan went into his bedroom and shut the door.

"I haven't talked *that* much."

"Yes you have."

"I'm sorry. I know you don't want me around but-"

"I didn't say that." I paused. "I know it sounded like that before. I just don't want my parents to know about you, to know about what I can do."

"That you talk to dead people?"

"I've tried to tell them before, but they don't believe me, they just punish me. So I can't do this." I turned on my heel and went into my bedroom, shutting the door behind me.

"Why can't we just talk now and then?" he said as he walked through my door.

"Are you going to just walk into my room anytime you feel like it?"

He smiled slyly. "Would you rather I do this?" He winked and then opened the door and went back into the hallway. A second later there was a soft knock. I opened the door. He was standing there grinning like a fool.

"You are determined aren't you?"

"I haven't had a conversation with anyone except Mika in one hundred and five years, and if you knew him you'd know that wasn't saying much." I noticed for the first time that his eyes were green. "I'm lonely Emma. I've been alone for so long sometimes I think I'll go crazy. You're so young, I don't expect you to understand-"

"I understand." I sat on the edge of the bed and swung my legs. "Ever since I can remember I've seen people like you. No one except my brother is like me and he can't really understand what I see. He hasn't seen people who have been hacked by an axe or fallen onto a saw blade. Everyone I see has been injured or is suffering somehow. And Ethan is the only one who believes me. I feel alone lots of times." I yawned.

"You're exhausted. Go to sleep, we can talk tomorrow. I forget about sleep. I don't need any. It's kind of handy not getting tired, but it's hard to think of enough activities to fill the hours. That's usually why I start misbehaving."

"I am tired."

"I will say goodnight then. If you need me I'll be in the attic, that's sort of my room. Mika says I should stay on the stair landing but that's boring."

"Why the landing?"

"Because that's where I died." He opened the door and closed it quietly behind him.

"Um, sir." I hoped he could still hear me.

He stuck his head through the bedroom door. "Yes? Oh sorry about this but it sounded like it might be important."

"I was just wondering what to call you."

He grinned, a twinkle of light came into his green eyes. "My name is Hugh. Hugh MacPherson. Goodnight Emma." He pulled his head out of the door. As I started to open my trunk I heard him calling out loudly. "Mika, Mika, Mika!"

Chapter 7

Hugh ran up the attic stairs calling Mika's name. He had never felt so alive since the day he died. He had just had a real conversation. Emma looked him in eye, she was aware of his presence. She didn't look through him as the others had.

"Mika!" he called again. He never came on the first try. He had so many questions. How was she able to do it? Why now? Was his Torment over? Mika would have the answers, if only he would appear.

"Damn it Mika, I need to talk to you!"

"I can hear you all the way in Copenhagen. And you needn't swear."

Hugh spun around. Mika was standing behind him with his arms crossed.

"I need to talk to you." Hugh said excitedly.

"Well, go ahead. I haven't got all night. I'm busy."

"A new family moved in and one of them can see me."

"I know." Mika looked out the window.

"She can talk to me and I can talk to her and she can even touch me. She accidentally touched my hand and it sort of tingled, you might even say burned, but in a good way. And her brother can see some things but not everything. And there's an older sister, fine looking although a bit brainless, she reminds me of the Wilson girl who lived here maybe seventy years ago? The years all run together I'm afraid. Anyway there's a mother and father too, but they don't seem to see me either." Hugh stopped. Mika was still looking out the window.

"It's too bad the Coopers haven't fixed that place up yet."

Hugh coughed even though his throat was clear. "Did you hear what I just said? There's a little girl here who can see me. Don't you think that is remarkable?"

Mika turned away from the window and sighed. "For the thousandth time Hugh I know everything that you do, no matter where I am. I am quite aware we have a Seer in the house. I knew it the minute she crossed the threshold."

"How is she able to do it?"

"She was born that way. Some are and some are not."

"Why?" Hugh asked. "And what about her brother?"

Mika seemed more annoyed that usual. "She's a Torment Seer, she sees souls in Torment, nothing else. It's a rare ability, but not very useful. Her brother has the greater gift, he sees all of us. He can see our energy."

"Could he see you?"

Mika hesitated. "Yes."

"Her mother doesn't like her talking to dead people."

Mika nodded. "Smart woman. Would you want your child talking to a dead man? I certainly wouldn't. Besides her mother is afraid. She has her reasons."

"I want to talk to her. It's so lonely here."

"It's supposed to be lonely."

"I know." Hugh said. Mika walked to the opposite side of the attic and looked out the other window. "You seem angry."

"Old man Johnson doesn't have much time left."

"I shouldn't have called you."

"You were right to call me. I needed to come here and assess the danger."

"Emma isn't dangerous, she's just a girl. As for the boy, he's a bit dull perhaps. I'm sure they won't harm me."

"Harm you?" Outside the wind began blowing against the clapboards. "You're already dead, they could ram a shovel through your head and it wouldn't matter."

"That wouldn't be nice." Hugh said trying to lighten the mood. He had never seen Mika like this before. They had never had a friendly relationship, but he had never been frightened of him until now.

"Stop making jokes. You've been doing that since you were a boy, trying to make everyone laugh when it's a serious occasion. I have had enough of it." His foot tapped angrily on the wood floor.

"Sorry."

"A Torment Seer." Mika sneered. "Just as you are beginning your Torment she comes along. How will you suffer now?"

"Actually I've been here a long time-"

"A long time? What do you know about a long time? You are responsible for that boy dying. You are to suffer!" Mika shouted. "And instead you're going to be chatting with *her*." The windows rattled, somewhere a shutter was flapping against the house.

"Maybe I've suffered enough now?" Hugh ventured.

"Ha!" Mika said pacing. "You're still feeling sorry for yourself. Give it another two hundred years, then you'll start to realize what you've done. But this girl is going to ruin everything. I should just stir up a hurricane and blow the house down."

"I won't talk to her."

Mika turned his head, his face was inches from Hugh. "You know you will. You can't help yourself Hugh, you never could." Mika backed away and looked out the attic window once again. The wind outside diminished. "I've said too much."

"No you haven't. You never tell me anything. What do you really know about Seers anyway?"

Mika gave him an ironic smile. "Hugh, I am one." he said before vanishing.

Chapter 8

I expected to see Hugh first thing in the morning. I waited for him to tap on my bedroom door, but he did not. He was nowhere to be seen. I was considering venturing up the attic stairs when Mother mentioned that we should start walking to school.

"It's your first day, better to be early than late." she said. "Father will go with you."

"Ah yes." Father said smoothing his beard. "I will shepherd you there, got to get to the shop you know."

It was a bright morning, sun filtered through the canopy of leaves overhead. Broken branches littered the front yard and road.

"I think there was a storm last night." Father said as he tossed a small limb out of our way. "The wind was blowing something awful. I suppose that's something we will have to get used to now that we live close to the sea."

Ahead of us was the Coopers' house. As we approached the rickety porch a procession of red haired children filed out of the front door.

"Hello!" shouted one of the boys. "See you at school!"

The other children waved enthusiastically as they followed their brother. Their tattered clothes hung loosely on their thin frames. The second to last child, a girl, grinned as she started skipping down the road, her copper hair catching the sunlight as it swung from side to side.

The school was just off the main road heading into town. It was built in a grassy field overlooking the sea. Mr. Burns, the teacher, was an amiable man in his thirties. He asked Eve, Ethan and myself a little bit about what we had been learning at our old school and then assigned us a seat. The other students stared suspiciously at us.

The school day was quite like any other I had experienced. Mr. Burns was an uninteresting teacher and I found my mind frequently drifting back to Hugh. I wondered what he did all day to occupy his time. As I started the walk home after school I found the Cooper girl who had skipped by us in the morning suddenly next to me.

"Hello." she said airily.

"Hello." I answered. She smiled revealing a large gap between her two front teeth. She wore a shabby dress with holes at the elbows and two shoes that did not appear to match. Her red hair was tangled, a green bow that had begun its day on the top of her head was dangling at the end of one strand.

"You are Emma, right?"

"Yes."

Eve was ahead of me in a tight group of girls, they were giggling incessantly while several boys walked in front of them. Ethan was somewhere nearby reading a book as he walked.

"Was that your father with you this morning?" she asked.

"Yes."

"He's handsome, for an old man."

"Thanks."

"Is he a drunk?"

"What? No."

"Oh that's too bad. My Pa is a real drunk, spends most of his time in that tavern over there." She pointed. "Ma says it's better that way, keeps him out of her hair." She swung her books by a worn leather strap.

"I never thought of it that way."

"Oh sure. Anyway I forgot to say my name is Candace Cooper, although you can call me Candy, all of my friends do. I'm thirteen."

"I'm twelve."

"You're just a kid." she said. "I had to stay out of school last year when Ma got sick and needed tending. She had twins but one of them died. Is that your brother back there?"

I looked behind us and saw Ethan deep into his copy of *Functions of the Human Lung*.

"Yes. He's studying to be a doctor."

"Impressive."

We walked a few minutes in silence. The busy noises of the cove drifted up the bluff along with a pungent fish smell.

"So what do you think of the ole' murder house?" Candy asked.

My pulse quickened. "The what?"

"That's what folks call your place, the murder house. Didn't you know? There was a murder there years ago. A thief broke in and hacked up a whole family with an axe. Boy I would have loved to have seen that. It must have been terribly gruesome." Candy's eyes widened.

"I didn't know that."

"Oh sure, everyone knows the place is haunted. You know some people say it's one of the victims out for revenge. Some say it's the thief whose soul returned to the house where he died to suffer eternal damnation. I prefer that one myself. Too bad we couldn't know for sure. The last family tried a séance and they said the devil himself appeared right in the parlor. Oh I would sleep with one eye open if I were you."

I didn't say anything. I couldn't tell her I had already spoken to the ghost the prior evening.

"I didn't mean to scare you or anything. Whatever is in the house, it's never killed anyone, yet. I am sure you'll be gone by the end of the year anyway. No one lives there for too long. That's why the house is so cheap. I always wished we could live there. I'd love to be haunted day and night, it certainly would keep things from getting boring. But we'll never have the money to buy the place, Pa drinks most everything he earns."

Another red haired child ran up behind Candy and whispered something in her ear. "I better run. Maddy split her lip open again. See you soon!" she cried as she turned and ran back towards the schoolhouse.

Ethan closed his book and caught up with me. "Did you hear what she said?" I asked him.

He nodded. "Most of it. So, he's a murderer."

"We don't know that. It might just be rumors."

"Have you been talking to him?" He looked over his glasses.

"I can't help it. I feel sorry for him."

"I thought we had a rule that you don't talk to them. If Mother finds out-" his voice trailed off. "Can't you just ignore him? You've always done that before." We turned into our narrow lane, old man Johnson's house stood quietly nearby.

"I never had to live with one before. It's easy to ignore them when you're passing on the street. You don't know what it's like Ethan. He hasn't spoken to a soul in ages."

"I don't want you to get in trouble Emma." Ethan lowered his voice as we passed by the Cooper house. A beleaguered looking woman with dark blonde hair and a stained dress was on the porch shaking out a rug.

"Afternoon." she said.

Ethan and I both said hello as we continued home. The front door was open. As we stepped inside we could hear Mother and Eve in the parlor discussing the day's events. Mother was questioning Eve quite extensively about Mr. Burns and what he looked like.

We ran upstairs. Ethan went straight into his bedroom and shut the door behind him. I put my books in my room and went to look for Hugh. I treaded quietly up the attic stairs.

The attic was large and airy. Light came from two windows that were set under the peak of the roof at either end of the room. In the corner were a few crates the men had brought up last night. A ghost was sitting cross legged on the floor staring straight ahead.

"Hugh?"

Chapter 9

"Hugh?" Emma whispered. She was standing at the top of the attic stairs.

"I didn't expect to see you here."

"I know. I wanted to ask you something." She took a few cautious steps forward.

"Oh?"

"Um, yes."

"Go ahead then." he said coolly. He hadn't meant to sound angry but he was having a lousy day.

"All right." She stood awkwardly in the middle of the attic. "It's just that someone told me today, well they told me that, they told me-"

"Yes?" he asked impatiently.

"They told me that someone broke into this house a long time ago and murdered five people with an axe and that the murderer is haunting the place. I was just wondering if that was true?"

Hugh gritted his teeth. He stood up and paced a few times. "Does this look like an axe did it?" He pointed to the hole in his shirt, he moved the fabric so she could see the tiny pinpoint of light that radiated through his body.

"No it doesn't."

"I don't know how these stories get started."

"Candy Cooper said-"

"Candy Cooper? Who is that? I've never heard of her."

Emma's eyes followed him as he continued to pace. It was strange to be watched, he had been invisible for so many years.

"She lives next door." she said

"I know who the Coopers are, just not her. There used to be a Matt Cooper who would come up here years ago to pee on the oak tree. Oh, I shouldn't have said that. Sorry."

He shouldn't be so cranky, here was an opportunity to talk and he was ruining it. He wouldn't blame Emma if she never spoke to him again. It was all Mika's fault, if he hadn't started talking about Seers and how Emma was going to ruin his Torment he would have thoroughly enjoyed himself instead of worrying that the house might blow apart at any second. He hadn't even begun to contemplate Mika's comment about being a Seer himself. He was always doing that, making remarks and then leaving before Hugh could ask any questions.

"Candy says the house is haunted by a murderer. Is it you?" Emma's voice was small. She was frightened.

He reached into his pocket and felt for his watch. Hugh could still picture the look on his father's face the day he gave it to him. He sat on the floor and sighed.

"I'm not a murderer. That is the absolute truth."

"But you did die here?"

"Yes. But my presence, no my intrusion, caused another person to die, so I am responsible for the ending of a life. But I never wielded an axe, I was shot with a rifle. Only a bullet would cause a hole like this." He pointed to his shirt.

Emma wrinkled her brow and sat on the floor opposite him. He smiled as he watched her. She was so young. He had been her age once, but it felt like a million years ago.

"I came here-" he stopped. She wouldn't understand. If she knew what he had been she would hate him.

"Go ahead."

Hugh shook his head. "You won't like it."

"Just tell me. You said you weren't a murderer, how can anything be worse than that?" She gave him a little smile of encouragement.

"I came to this house to rob it. I was a thief Emma. A criminal."

She nodded. "All right then. What happened?"

"I, I was drunk and clumsy, not like myself at all. I made too much noise and it woke up the family. The man of the house, Mr. Winslow, cornered me as I was going upstairs and shot me. I didn't feel anything. I died instantly. What we both didn't know was that his son was behind me. I guess he was planning on tackling me or something like that, the bullet passed through me and into him. His name was Charlie, he died at the same time I did." He felt a sense of relief as he told her what had happened. He had never been able to talk to anyone about it.

"Then *you* were the one who was murdered?"

"I suppose, but it was justified."

"Perhaps." she said. "Were you carrying a pistol?"

"No. I never did. I didn't have to. I was a professional and I was good at it, except for that night. I had been celebrating too much. I was walking by the house and I thought why not go in and take a look around? I knew I shouldn't have. I told myself the minute I walked through the front door, or rather Mika told me. But then as he says I never listened to him. He's right."

"Now who is this Mika? You've mentioned him before."

"Wait a second. You're not bothered by the fact that I told you I was a thief? I really was. That's all I did from the age of fourteen until I died. I broke into houses and shops and took things and then sold them. Of course I got caught more than a few times, but I always managed just a few months in jail. Then I was on the road again. I was lucky that way."

Emma's brown eyes glittered in the afternoon sun that came in the window. "Did you rob stagecoaches or banks?"

"No. I was what you might call a sneak thief. But I still broke the law."

"I know." she nodded. "I think people do things for a reason. You must have had a reason why you didn't take a job."

"Because I was good at thieving, and I was lazy." He felt in his pocket again. "Actually by the time I truly understood what I was doing it was too late to change my ways. Oh I could have if I really tried. Mika kept telling me to, but I was only just beginning to listen to him and then I was dead."

"Mika. Now, tell me who-"

"Sh. Someone is coming up the stairs." Since dying his hearing had been greatly enhanced.

Emma stood up. A second later Elsay was at the top of the attic steps looking irritated.

"Emma Hollis I have been looking all over for you. What are you doing up here by yourself?"

"I was just checking to see if this would be a good place for my telescope." Emma replied. Hugh was impressed, she lied quite well.

Elsay frowned. Hugh stood up and waved at her. "I don't like you being up here alone. If you must erect that telescope you will do so in your bedroom."

"Yes Mother."

"And another thing." Elsay grabbed Emma's sleeve and bent down to speak into her ear. "Don't let me catch you claiming to have seen or have spoken to any dead people. That business in the coach yesterday was the last time. We are in a new town, with new people and I don't want the kind of nonsense that happened back in Augusta. Is that understood?"

"Yes."

"Now let's go downstairs and have dinner and you can tell me about your day at school." Elsay said, her voice turning a shade sweeter.

They started for the stairs. Emma suddenly turned back to look at him. "Come on." she mouthed.

"No, I'll get you in trouble."

She reached for his hand. Their skin touched for a split second. Hugh pulled away, a current of energy, life itself, ran up his finger and into his hand. It tingled and twitched in the most pleasant way.

It was over in a second. Emma dashed down the stairs. Hugh hesitated and then hurried after her. There had to be more where that came from.

Chapter 10

The rest of the family was already downstairs. Father was at the dining table drinking a glass of wine with a look of satisfaction on his face. Eve was staring out the window towards the Coopers' house while Ethan read a book at the table.

"I found her in the attic." Mother said under her breath.

"Whatever were you doing up there?" Father asked.

"Looking for a place for my telescope."

"Yep, that's right." Hugh said next to me.

Ethan looked at me and then to the bit of air Hugh was occupying. He shook his head and went back to his book.

"I thought you were keeping it in your room." Father said.

"I was, I mean I am. I was just checking." I stammered.

Father nodded and took another sip of wine.

"Eve come away from that window, it's time to eat." Mother said.

Eve sighed and slid into a chair. Hugh circled the table and stopped behind Father. Meanwhile Mother bustled about from the stove to the table, putting dish after dish in front of us. She put out a final basket of bread and sat down.

"Everything looks delicious Elsay." Father said looking at each steaming hot bowl and platter.

"It should. I worked very hard today."

"That's true. She did." Hugh confirmed.

"I know how you feel." Father said. "Honestly I've never known such a taxing day. I know you're all dying to hear how it went."

Our hands stopped in midair as we were reaching for the serving spoons and forks.

"Go on then Edward. *I* would like to know." Hugh said.

"I had seven customers. Seven. Ole Brownie was there most of the day. What a man he is, just kept driving them in. I believe I will have a regular clientele before the month is out."

"That's wonderful Edward."

"Indeed. I've asked Brownie to dinner tomorrow night. Eve you might think of wearing your Sunday best." Father said with a twinkle in his eye.

Eve's mouth dropped open. "Wear my Sunday best for old Mr. Brown?"

"You would sacrifice a young attractive girl like Eve to that old man?" Hugh cried.

"Now Eve it was just a suggestion. Ole Brownie is a rich man. Imagine the sort of life you would have." Father said.

"I don't have to imagine it. I've seen it." Hugh said. "We once had a ninety year old living here, he was married to a girl not more than twenty and-" Our eyes met and he smiled. "Never mind then."

"Don't be upset with your father, he was just trying to be helpful." Mother said. "Now tell me about school."

Eve sighed. "It was fine."

"Mr. Burns is a capable teacher." Ethan said. "Although I am not clear on what he knows of current scientific theory. I expect I will learn much this year."

"And what does Emma think?" Father asked.

"I had a very nice day." I said glancing at Hugh.

After dinner Ethan, Eve and I were excused to go upstairs to our bedrooms. Hugh tagged along behind us.

As we got to the top of the stairs Eve grabbed my arm. "Emma. Did you notice Scott Cooper today?" Her cheeks turned pink as she spoke.

"No. I met a Candy Cooper."

She rolled her eyes. "He was that tall boy at the back of the class with red hair. You can't have missed him, he's got to be the most handsome boy in school."

I shook my head. "Sorry I didn't see him. Why?"

"Never mind." she said dashing off to her bedroom.

Ethan looked over my shoulder where Hugh was lingering. "I wish you wouldn't bring him along."

"I can't help it if he follows me. Besides he is not a murderer. I asked him about it this afternoon."

"He probably lied to you. That's what a murderer would do." Ethan said glaring in Hugh's direction.

"I am not a murderer you little toad."

"Stop it Ethan, you're upsetting him."

"You are going to get us both in trouble you know." Ethan said. "Listen Emma, you and I are different than the rest of the family. Mother and Father don't like us to talk about it, we've always kept it between the two of us. But if you start doing what he wants you're bound to be found out."

"But he's lonely."

"Damn right."

"If Mother finds out what you're doing she will insist that we move, probably to another town, and then your new friend will be all alone." Ethan said.

"He has a point." Hugh said.

"You're not going to tell on me are you?"

"Of course not. Just be careful not to be seen talking to yourself." Ethan said. "Now if you will excuse me I have to study the inner workings of the digestive system. By the way, what's his name?"

"Hugh." we both said at once.

Chapter 11

Ethan went into his room and closed the door. Hugh supposed he was all right as brothers went. He had had two brothers of his own, Patrick and Connelly. He had last seen Patrick when he was twenty four and it wasn't under the best circumstances. Hugh had been the defendant and Patrick the prosecutor. The whole thing was better off forgotten.

"Do you want to help me put my telescope together?" Emma asked.

"Oh yes." he said excitedly. He was being asked to help do something, he was needed again. He suddenly felt giddy. They went into her bedroom and shut the door.

"It's over here." she said pointing to a large box underneath the windows.

"I have to tell you I don't know much about telescopes."

"That's all right. You can just hand me things out of the box." She opened the case. A myriad of brass tubes lay neatly in the remnants of an old blanket. It would have been a good prize back in the old days of thievery.

"When did you get this?" he asked as she dug into the box and pulled out a black wooden tripod.

"A few years ago." She fixed the legs of the tripod, tightening each one with a tiny brass screw. "I never expected to have one on account that they are so expensive. Then one day Ethan and I got a beating for seeing a dead man at the butcher shop. I wouldn't have said anything except the man walked out from behind the counter with a big meat cleaver in his chest. He said one of the other men there had done it to him. So I had to say something, I couldn't just walk out of the shop and let a murderer run free. I saw a policeman outside so I told him. Mother was so angry I thought her head would blow up. That night she told Father and the next day Ethan and I both got beat with a switch."

"What happened to the man in the butcher shop?"

Emma shrugged and picked up another part from her telescope case. "Nothing I suppose. I never went there again. Mother probably told the police I was her crazy daughter who sees things that aren't there. I can understand her not believing me, but Ethan is a scientist, he wouldn't make things up. Anyway after Father took the switch to us he must have felt bad because he bought me this telescope and he bought Ethan a stack of medical books. It's not new, see?" She pointed to a brass plate on one of the tripod legs. It was inscribed, *Property of E.V. Scribner.*

"It's really not fair that Ethan has to get punished every time. I am the one who always talks to them, I can't help it. Ethan only sees shimmers and shadows and sometimes other things that I can't. I don't understand it."

She seemed to have forgotten to let him help as she busily put together the rest of the telescope. He didn't mind. It gave him a chance to watch her, he liked watching people, it was a pleasure he didn't discover until after he died. He hadn't taken much time to observe Emma since he had spent most of his time talking.

She would be pretty, he was a good judge of things like that, with her smooth porcelain skin, brown eyes, and a bit of a turned up nose. Her brown hair hung in a long braid down her back instead of put up. He liked that. What he liked most about her was that she wasn't phony. He had met a lot of pretenders in his life and death, including himself, and he knew Emma was not one of them.

She carefully picked out each part of the telescope and attached it. As the last few pieces went on she leaned over and looked into the eyepiece. Her fingers went automatically to a worn brass dial. She spent a few minutes making adjustments before looking up at Hugh and smiling. "All done. Oh, I forgot to let you help." she said laughing softly.

"It's all right. Can you see anything?"

"Do you want to look at the moon?" She checked the eyepiece one more time and then motioned for him to take a look. He had of course seen the moon before, but never through a telescope. "You adjust the focus like this." She guided his hand to a dial near the eyepiece. His hand tingled. The sensation was starting to travel up his arm when she stepped away and everything went cold again.

"Do you see it?"

He did see the moon magnified in its creamy brilliance. The stars twinkled brightly in the sky. It had been so long since he had seen anything except the view from the windows. He longed to be walking under that sky.

"What do you think?" she asked. "Can't you just imagine what the moon is like? Or the planets? There must be so many other worlds out there."

"The house next door is like another world to me." With that thought he swung the telescope around and found he had a perfect view of the Coopers' front porch. "This could be handy."

"It's not used for spying."

Hugh stepped away from the telescope. "Skyward only?"

"That's the idea. But I suppose I can't stop you from using it during the day."

"How do-" he stopped. "Your mother is coming upstairs."

Emma's face went white. "You better go." she whispered. "Goodnight."

Hugh passed silently through her door. Elsay was at the top of the stairs looking cross. He ran downstairs to see what Edward was up to.

Chapter 12

The next day was like the one before. I awoke early and went to school. It was to be my routine for many years to come. Father did not walk us to school, he had already gone to the shop by the time we woke up. As we passed by the Coopers Candy and several of her siblings ran out of the front door past their mother who was throwing out a pot of water.

Candy joined me. "Good morning! Did you sleep well or did the ghost get you?"

"I slept fine. I haven't heard or seen anything unusual so far." I felt my face turn red. There was no way she could possibly know that I spoke to dead people, but I felt as though it was somehow printed on my forehead.

"Oh that's too bad. I was hoping you might have had to call a priest or something."

Ahead of us Eve was walking with Scott Cooper. She tipped her head back and laughed, pushing a blond curl neatly behind her ear. Scott nervously shifted his books from one arm to the other.

"Looks like your sister is going to marry my brother." Candy said.

"They just met yesterday."

"Oh that doesn't matter. Ma said she only knew Pa a month when they got married. Of course she had to cause-" Candy stopped. "Oh I better not say. Boy your brother sure likes to read. Doesn't he ever talk to anyone?" She looked at Ethan who was walking behind us.

"He's very serious."

"I'll say. He should put down his books once in a while and make some friends. He's sort of cute in a book reading kind of way."

Ethan paid no attention to her.

"I don't think anyone has ever called Ethan cute." I said. "Not even my mother."

"My Ma has had so many babies she just says here's another Cooper and gets back to her work. Say, why don't you come over after supper? You can meet my Ma and my Pa too if he isn't drunk, you can meet him when he's not drunk but he ain't so much fun."

"I would love to Candy. But we are having Senator Brown over for supper and I have to be there."

"Senator Brown? You mean Hershival Brown? The man who smells like maple syrup?"

"Yes. Do you know him?"

"Oh sure. He tried to buy our house and run us out of town. Ma says he doesn't like our sort, whatever that is. She says he's trying to bring in new people from other places to clean the town up."

"Do you know why he smells like syrup?"

"Everyone knows that. He uses it like cologne. He's looking for a wife you know and whatever woman falls for the scent of maple will be his bride. Pretty romantic huh?"

I wrinkled my nose. I had never thought of maple syrup being romantic. A bell began to peal. I gathered my books to my chest and raced towards the schoolhouse.

Chapter 13

Hugh had spent a lot of time with housewives over the last century. His favorite had been Hester Vipens. Once her husband left to work on the fishing boats she would take off all her clothes and do her housework naked. Hugh never missed a morning with her. After a few months Hester's husband realized something funny was going on while he was away and they moved out.

He doubted very much that Elsay was going to take her clothes off anywhere except her bedroom, but it was still more entertaining watching her cook dinner than sitting in the attic staring at the walls.

Senator Brown was coming for dinner that evening. Elsay divided her time between unpacking the rest of their belongings and running into the kitchen to check on various pots on and inside the stove.

It was clear to Hugh that the family didn't have much money. The plain stoneware dishes and pewter cups, the lack of fancy candlesticks and porcelain figures gave it away. Not that Hugh minded, material things were useless to him now.

Edward had the potential to be a wealthy man. He was hard working and determined and that was all it took nowadays. Back in Hugh's time you either were born to money or you married into it. There were so few opportunities to make something of oneself, that's what he used to tell himself. Thieving had not been a choice but a means of survival. He preferred that view to the truth. A sharp knock on the front door interrupted his internal musings on wealth and brought him back to the present.

"Who on earth?" Elsay muttered as she stopped slicing a loaf of bread and wiped her hands on her apron. She pushed her hair into place and opened the door. A shabbily dressed blonde woman stood on the doorstep.

"Good morning." the woman said. She was holding a jar of honey in her hands.

Elsay took a step backwards. "Good morning."

The woman looked at her worn dress and blushed. "I'm Margaret Cooper, I live just over there." She turned and pointed to the house next door. "I wanted to welcome you to Fox Cove and give you this." She held out the honey.

"Thank you." Elsay took the jar with two fingers and held it up to the light.

"I make it myself." Margaret said.

"You made this?"

"Invite her in." Hugh said.

"Yes, I make most everything myself. If your children are ever sick come and see me. I make all kinds of remedies. I've cured my little ones many times."

"Doesn't this town have a doctor?"

"Yes, there's old doc Butler. He's expensive and quite frankly I don't think he knows what he's doing. Most ailments you can take care of at home."

"I see. I am sorry Mrs. Cooper I would invite you in but I am expecting Senator Hershival Brown for dinner."

"Oh that's fine Mrs.- I am sorry I don't recall your name."

"My name is Mrs. Hollis."

"Oh yes, Mrs. Hollis. I will let you get back to work." Margaret turned to leave and then stopped. "I should tell you Mrs. Hollis, Senator Brown is in pursuit of a wife and-"

"I am a married woman Mrs. Cooper."

"I meant he is actively looking for a wife. It's been said that he prefers younger women. I know you have two daughters, I thought it best to warn you. Mother to mother."

"Mrs. Cooper! Are you accusing a fine, upstanding senator of un-gentlemanlike behavior?"

"Un-gentlemanlike?" said Hugh. "What century are we in?"

"No, it's just that I have heard rumors-" Margaret began.

"I don't listen to rumors Mrs. Cooper."

Margaret took a deep breath and smiled. "It was nice to have met you Mrs. Hollis." She turned on her heel and strode back towards home.

Elsay shook her head and shut the front door. "Good heavens."

"What a snob you are." Hugh said.

Elsay looked at the jar of honey. Hugh followed her into the pantry where she stuck it on a high shelf out of sight.

"I can't believe how rude you were." he told her.

Elsay straightened her apron and went back into the kitchen. Hugh lingered for a moment and then headed into the room behind the pantry, the one that now served as Edward and Elsay's bedroom. It was a place he generally avoided. It had been Charlie's room once, and it was a reminder of Hugh's past.

There wasn't much to look at besides a bed, wardrobe and nightstand. Hugh eased open the wardrobe and immediately was confronted with a pair of Edward's underpants draped over a clothes hanger. He quickly shut the door.

He didn't know what he was looking for, but Elsay's dismissal of Margaret Cooper had left a bad taste in his mouth. He hated snobbery, he had been looked down upon plenty of times in his life. At that moment he would rather snoop around in her bedroom than watch her cook dinner.

He opened the nightstand drawer. Inside was a cheap novel with a sensational cover. Hugh smiled, he hadn't read a book in a long time. There was a scrap of paper halfway through. He would have to keep his eye on it, as soon as the book was set aside he would discreetly take it up to the attic. Underneath the book was a new pack of playing cards still in the box.

Cards! Hugh loved cards. He had had several decks over the years, the last one had been taken by a preacher when he tried to exorcise Hugh from the house. What a ridiculous day that had been. Mika had conjured blue fires in every hearth and spoke in a loud evil voice until the man finally left. He had felt sorry for him until he pocketed Hugh's well worn deck of cards. He had kept that pack for nearly thirty years.

But here was a new deck sitting right in this drawer. It didn't even look like it had been opened. The thief in his mind was waking up. This was easy pickings. He doubted that Edward and Elsay played cards very often. Edward was busy with his shop and Elsay had the house to look after. Somewhere in the back of his mind Mika was warning him to shut the drawer and find something else to do.

He started to close the drawer. Emma. He could play with Emma. He could teach her the games he knew and the ones he had made up. He glanced at the doorway to make sure Elsay wasn't standing by watching her nightstand drawer open and close by itself. He slipped the cards in his pocket and quietly shut the drawer. He would just borrow them for a while.

Elsay was in the kitchen staring into a steaming pot on the stove as Hugh ran past her and upstairs to the attic. He cracked open the deck and busied himself for the rest of the afternoon playing cards on the attic floor.

Chapter 14

Hugh was nowhere to be found when I came home from school that afternoon and there was no time to look for him. Mother sent us upstairs to change before Senator Brown arrived. My best was nothing more than one of Eve's old dresses that hung loosely from my shoulders. Eve said it was hopelessly out of date, but I doubted the Senator would care much.

Once dressed we went back downstairs so Mother could inspect us. After a few minor adjustments we were deemed fit to be seen and arranged ourselves in the parlor to await Father and Senator Brown. They were planning to meet at Father's shop and walk home together.

"Let Father do most of the talking." Mother said as she smoothed the folds of her skirt. "Eve, you and I will add to the conversation as needed. Ethan and Emma, it's best if you don't say anything unless spoken to. I don't know if the Senator likes children. He is a bachelor after all."

"They say he's looking for a wife." I said.

"Who says? Where did you hear such nonsense?" Mother asked.

I hesitated. "Candy Cooper told me. She says he puts maple syrup on himself so he will smell better and attract a wife."

"That's the most absurd thing I have ever heard Emma Hollis."

We could hear male voices outside. A second later the front door opened and Father and Senator Brown came into the parlor.

"Ah, what a nice family scene." The Senator stroked his beard.

"Just a typical night at home in the Hollis family." Father patted his stomach. "I think you know my wife Elsay." Father took the Senator by the arm to begin his introductions.

"Yes, yes Elsay."

"And my eldest daughter Eve."

"Eve? Oh yes, I haven't seen you for so long. My how you have grown."
The Senator took Eve's hand. As he held her small fingers I noticed his
thumb caressing the back of her hand. Eve curled her lip and pulled away.

"Um yes." Father said.

At the back of the parlor Hugh walked through the secret door. "Oh no
I'm late. I got caught up in- Oh never mind. Please continue."

I couldn't smile or make any acknowledgement towards him because
Father was introducing Ethan and me. Senator Brown nodded and tried to
look interested, the scent of maple wafted strongly in the air.

"Ethan hopes to be a doctor." Father said.

"Really?" The Senator raised his eyebrows. "Fox Cove could use a good
doctor. I might be inclined to help you with your tuition, provided you
return here and set up a practice. Ole' Doc Butler isn't going to live
forever, bless him."

Father's face dropped to the floor. "Oh that would be more than generous
Brown. I have always encouraged Ethan to pursue medicine. It's just that
people in our position can hardly think of sending a son to college."

Senator Brown nodded and stroked his beard. "Education is very
important these days Edward. I would have gone to college myself if I had
the chance, a brilliant mind such as mine would have no doubt flourished,
but anyway. I would like to finance the boy's education, of course I will
expect a few concessions from you."

"Naturally." Father agreed.

"Be careful of those concessions Edward." Hugh warned.

Ethan's face was beaming. "Thank you so much Senator, I won't
disappoint you." He shook Brown's hand.

"I know you won't. Keep your grades up, and remember I expect you to
return and practice medicine here in Fox Cove. Don't think you're going
to run off to the big city."

"I wouldn't think of it." Ethan was still shaking the Senator's hand.
"Mother, may I go upstairs and study?"

"Certainly not Ethan. We haven't even had dinner yet."

"And you remember Emma?" Father said. He was still trying to introduce the family.

"Emma?" The Senator searched the corners of his mind. "Oh yes I do remember you. Nice to see you dear." He patted the top of my head.

"Thank you."

Father produced a small glass of sherry from somewhere and handed it to Brown.

"Thank you old boy." The Senator sat down. His hand shook slightly as he watched Eve over the top of the glass.

"The shop went well today." Father fidgeted on the edge of his chair.

"People are talking." said the Senator.

"Really?" Father slid another inch forward. "What are they saying?"

"Easy there Edward." Hugh said.

"Oh just that there's a new barber from Augusta come to town. City haircuts, that sort of thing."

"You should probably try and keep up on the latest styles Father." Eve suggested.

Senator Brown set his sherry on his knee and turned his attention to Eve. "You seem to be a fashionable young lady." His eyes drifted down the front of her dress.

"Take a good look why don't you?" Hugh said.

"Thank you." Eve said flatly. The Senator licked his bottom lip as his eyes remained on her bosom. She shifted uncomfortably.

"I've seen that look before." Hugh said. "Ugh. Disgusting."

Mother cleared her throat and announced that dinner was ready. Eve jumped to her feet. The Senator rose and offered her his arm. She looked desperately at our parents who quickly linked arms and proceeded towards the kitchen. Eve sighed and reluctantly took the Senator's arm. This was something I had never seen before. We were hardly the type of family that walked arm and arm to dinner on any given night.

"Oh I love formality, this is how we used to do it." Hugh walked through two chairs and the Senator to offer me his arm. "Shall we?"

I hesitated. I couldn't chance being seen holding an invisible arm. But my parents, Eve and the Senator were already on their way across the hall. They would never know.

"Emma what are you doing?" Ethan whispered. "Why does he always have to be here?"

"What else does he have to do?"

"That's right." Hugh sniffed.

Ethan sighed and followed the others.

I looked up and found Hugh grinning. I took his arm, his skin felt cold through the fabric of his shirt. I felt myself blushing, he was so much older than me. His green eyes sparkled in the candlelight. I didn't know if anyone else would think him handsome with his dark shaggy hair and brush of stubble on his face. He was shorter and leaner than most of the men I knew. There was something else too, something in the way he moved. He was elegant, or maybe it was just the clothes he wore that made him appear that way.

We followed the rest into the kitchen which also served as our dining room, as we had no formal dining table or china. No one noticed my arm hanging mysteriously in space. They were all too busy trying to follow Mother's instructions on where to sit. I let go of Hugh's arm as I took my place at the table.

"I miss eating." he sighed. "Hmm, nowhere for me to sit." He ended up crouching next to my chair, his shoulders level with the table. "I don't want to miss anything."

Ethan scowled and poked me in the side with his elbow. I took my eyes away from Hugh and realized Senator Brown was saying grace.

Chapter 15

"Amen." Hugh said trying to follow the Senator's blessing. He had his doubts that the old man really meant it. Hugh had seen his type before, leering old goats who liked younger women. He noticed the Senator trying to catch Eve's eye. Eve seemed aware of it too, she busied herself with her dinner and didn't look in his direction.

He considered pulling on one of the Senator's chair legs or something else subtle enough to put a scare in him without attracting too much attention. But there was always Elsay watching Emma and Ethan for signs of the unknown. He didn't want to drive the family away.

He couldn't risk Emma leaving. For the first time in a very long time he felt hope, even joy. He knew he should feel guilty for those emotions, he was a tormented soul after all. But he had someone to talk to, someone who saw and acknowledged him and someone who could even touch him. His arm still felt warm from where she had held it for those few seconds. His entire existence had changed. He supposed that was why Mika was so angry, he was no longer suffering.

He stuck his elbow on the table while he thought of the coming years with Emma and what it would be like. His thoughts were far away when she crashed her elbow into his arm. Her fork flew out of her hand and onto the table. The conversation ceased.

"Emma good heavens what is the matter with you?" Elsay cried. Her face blushed with embarrassment.

"Sorry." Emma said sheepishly. Edward picked up her fork and handed it to her.

"That was quite funny." Hugh said. Emma gave him a cross look as she wiped the fork on her napkin.

"Now what were you saying Senator?" Elsay asked. Senator Brown continued his boring tangent on the state of politics in Maine. Hugh certainly could not be bothered with such a trivial topic as politics. Dead men couldn't vote.

Dinner passed without another incident. Hugh made sure he stayed safely away from Emma's elbows. Afterwards the family was forced back into the parlor for more time with the Senator. Eve was allowed to recite some poetry and Ethan gave a little talk on the liver. All in all it was a bore and without being able to talk to anyone Hugh found his mind wandering. He was grateful that they didn't own a piano, he had heard far too many supposedly accomplished girls screeching out melancholy tunes in his years of Torment. He was recalling one particularly untalented lady when he noticed Brown's arm nudge Edward. He made a quick motion with his head. Edward nodded in agreement and stood up.

"If you will excuse me, Brownie and I are going to take a bit of fresh air." Edward laughed nervously.

Senator Brown rose from his seat, groaning as he did. "I always think it's best to take an evening constitutional after such a filling supper." He tipped his head and smiled at Elsay.

"Thank you Senator."

The two men went into the hallway. "I'll be right back." Hugh whispered in Emma's ear.

By the time he caught up Brown and Edward they were at the front door. "Don't go out there!"

"I could do with a little fresh air." Senator Brown was saying.

"So could I." Edward said.

"No! I won't be able to follow you." Hugh shouted. Every time something interesting happened it was always outside.

"I'd like to discuss something with you Edward."

"All right." Edward started to open the front door and then closed it. "I've got some fine whiskey in the pantry, would you care for some?"

Brown stroked his beard and smiled. "I never pass up a drink."

"Oh yes, that's a much better idea." Hugh said.

The three of them went into the kitchen. Brown took a seat while Edward disappeared into the pantry. Hugh sat opposite the Senator in a chair that was already pulled away from the table. He stared at him until Edward returned.

"Here we are." Edward put the bottle of whiskey and two glasses on the table. He sat next to Hugh and poured both men a drink.

Brownie tipped his head back and swallowed his in one gulp. "Good stuff." he said squinting at Edward.

Edward nodded and took a little sip while the Senator poured himself another. "You wanted to discuss something with me?"

"Ah yes." Brownie nodded, his eyes searching Edward's face. He shifted in his seat and licked his lips. "As I said earlier I would be happy to pay for Ethan's education."

"You don't know what that means to me."

"Yes, well I meant it. As everyone knows around here I have done everything I can to improve this little town and the quality of the people in it. A decent well educated young doctor would serve us well. Of course I did mention there would be concessions."

"Here it comes." Hugh muttered.

"Concessions? Yes, I suppose I could pay you back, in installments naturally." Edward gripped his glass nervously.

"Installments?" the Senator chuckled. "It's not about money Edward, heaven knows I have plenty of that. No, I was thinking of something else you could do for me."

"Oh?"

"You see, I've been a lifelong bachelor. I've always put the interests of the town and my constituents above all else. But now as I am entering my prime-"

"Your prime?" Hugh exclaimed. "You're a lot older than me. Sort of."

"I am thinking of settling down." the Senator continued. "I want to find a wife right here in Fox Cove, but so far I haven't seen anyone to my liking, or to my standards, but tonight all that changed."

"Really?" Edward swallowed hard.

"Yes." Brown nodded. "I think you understand me?"

"Ah well yes. I mean I guess I see your point." Edward fidgeted in his chair. "It's just that Eve is strong willed and she should make up her own mind."

The Senator laughed. "Of course she should make up her own mind. Did you think I wanted you to hand her over like a prize donkey? Good heavens Edward. I think with the gentle persuasion of yourself and your wife and my continued presence in your home, there is no reason for her to say no. She doesn't have a beau does she?"

Edward hesitated. "No she doesn't, we've only been here a few days. But it's Eve's decision."

A flicker of annoyance crossed the Senator's face, but Hugh wasn't sure if Edward noticed. "Of course it's her decision. But what reason would she have to say no?"

"Because you're a creaky old goat." Hugh said.

Edward coughed and drank the rest of his whiskey. "I suppose she wouldn't have a reason to object." he said meekly.

Hugh resisted the urge to slam his fist on the table. "Edward you should tell him to take his generosity and stick it somewhere. Eve isn't going to want to marry him ever. Stand up for yourself."

Edward watched the Senator finish his third drink. Brown dropped the glass on the table and burped.

"Ugh, disgusting. I am so sick of hearing people burp. That was unthinkable in my day. No one has any manners in this century." Hugh said.

"Shall we rejoin the ladies?" the Senator asked. He stood up and left the kitchen with Edward following quietly behind.

Chapter 16

"That was just awful." Eve whispered as we headed upstairs to bed. Senator Brown had departed an hour before. She was still wiping the back of her hand where he had kissed it as he bid her goodnight.

"You don't want to marry him then?" Ethan teased.

"Of course not!" Eve hurried into her room and shut the door.

"I guess she really doesn't like him." Ethan straightened his glasses and looked towards Hugh. "What does he have to say about it?"

"I thought he didn't want me around." Hugh pouted. "Now that he's realized I can serve as his spy he doesn't mind."

"It's not that." I said.

"Is he complaining about me?" Ethan pointed a finger at Hugh.

"Yes." Hugh said.

"No. He was just about to tell us what he heard when he followed Father and the Senator."

"I was?" Hugh asked. "I suppose I could. But do you really want to discuss this here?"

"No. Let's go in my room." I opened my bedroom door, Ethan and Hugh stepped inside.

"Ugh, I think he walked through me." Ethan said as I shut the door.

"I did. That hallway is awfully drafty. I had to warm up somehow." Hugh smiled and ran to the telescope. "I wonder what's going on at the Coopers." He moved it from its skyward position straight towards the Coopers' front porch. "Nothing so far."

"You shouldn't let him use that." Ethan said.

I shrugged. I really didn't mind. No one was ever interested in my telescope. It didn't matter if Hugh only used it to spy on the neighbors, at least I had someone to share it with.

"So does he want to hear what happened? He's so grouchy." Hugh asked.

"Stop complaining Ethan. Let him speak."

Ethan folded his arms across his chest. "Very well. Speak Hugh."

Hugh stepped away from the telescope. "It's very simple. The Senator wants Eve, and your father is going to help him get her."

"No!" I cried. "Father wouldn't do that." I couldn't believe my father would help persuade Eve to marry that old man.

"What? What is he saying?"

"Think about it Emma." Hugh said. "The Senator has paid for the barber shop, this house and now Ethan's education. Don't you think he expects something in return?"

"Father is going to pay him back."

"Yes, eventually he will. But the Senator is not going to wait that long."

"What are you two talking about?" Ethan demanded.

"Senator Brown wants Father to help him win over Eve." I said.

"What? Why? Because he's going to pay for my college?"

"Yes and for all the other things."

"That's crazy!" Ethan cried. "I won't let him."

"That's ridiculous. Where else is he going to get a chance like that?" Hugh said. "If someone had offered to pay for me to go to college I wouldn't have ended up a criminal. Tell him that."

"Hugh says you should take the offer."

Ethan rolled his eyes. "I should take advice from the family ghost now?"

"Oh, am I the family ghost? I quite like the sound of that. It makes me sound important."

"I don't know what to do." Ethan said.

"Sleep on it." Hugh said.

"Hugh says to sleep on it."

"Maybe I should." Ethan turned to leave then looked hesitantly towards Hugh. "Is it okay to leave you alone with him?"

"I beg your pardon!" Hugh stared Ethan in the face. "Do I look like someone who can't be trusted with your sister?"

"He can't hear you." I said.

"He's mad isn't he?"

"Of course I am." Hugh grabbed Ethan's suspenders and gave them a good hard snap.

"Ouch!" Ethan crossed his arms over his chest.

"Sorry. I couldn't help myself."

"Hugh says he's sorry."

"I'll bet."

"No, really I am." Hugh tried not to giggle as Ethan winced.

"He really is sorry Ethan."

"Very well. I was just trying to protect my sister." Ethan looked warily towards Hugh. "I don't know what you find so interesting about him."

"I like talking to him."

Ethan shook his head. "I have studying to do." He turned and left the room, closing the door quietly behind him.

"He's not usually like that." I said.

"I shouldn't have snapped his suspenders."

"Probably not. Still you had your reasons."

"Exactly." Hugh rushed back to the telescope. I started brushing my hair. "Oh boy, come and look at this." He stepped aside so I could look into the telescope. Thankfully the Coopers kept a lamp in the window next to the porch, it allowed me to see Eve talking closely to someone who was lost in the shadows. She pushed her hair off her shoulders and laughed. "Bet you a nickel that's Scott Cooper she's talking to."

"Do you think she used the secret door?"

"Of course she used the secret door. It's good for letting people in too."

"She wouldn't sneak him in here."

"Ha. We shall see. That just goes to show that she has no interest in old maple drawers."

I turned away from the telescope. "Why would Father help him? I know he has done a lot for our family and he's going to pay for Ethan to go to college, but why wouldn't Father just say no?" I closed the curtains and sat down on the edge of my bed.

Hugh sighed and grabbed a chair from my desk. He sat down. "Fathers disappoint us sometimes."

"He's always so smart and knows what to do to take care of us. And now-" I stopped. I didn't know what I was saying.

"And now he's come up against someone who is stronger than he is. That's all." He took a gold watch out of his pocket. "I used to think my father was invincible."

"Really?"

"Yes." he said smiling sadly. He opened the watch and snapped it shut, he put it back in his pocket. "But he wasn't."

"What happened?"

"He was a judge, a well respected one too. He was presiding over this big case. A little girl was kidnapped and-" He looked at me and scratched his chin. "She was killed in the end. There had been some witnesses and anyway they figured out who had done it. So when it was time for my father, the judge, to announce his verdict it was not guilty.

"The town was in an uproar of course. A few days later it came out that my father had taken a bribe to find the defendants not guilty. When I heard that I felt like someone had punched me in the stomach. I couldn't understand why he had done it. My father! He had been perfect to me. He had created the happiest of homes for me and my brothers and sister. When someone heard I was his son they would always tell me how much they admired him, how lucky I was. Then they would ask me if I was going to follow in his footsteps and of course I would respond yes, naturally. In one day he ruined it." Hugh stared at the floor, his jaw was clenched tightly.

"Why did he take the bribe?"

"I don't know. I never found out. The father of the girl who was killed was furious of course. People started to rally around him, demanding justice. Then word started to spread to other towns. Father was arrested but we had money and he was able to post his bail the same day. When people saw him back in his home something just broke in town. One night they came, I don't know maybe fifty or sixty of them, mostly men but some women. They started throwing bricks and rocks in the windows. I don't know if they set the house on fire or if one of our own lamps started it, but the house began to burn.

"It was so smoky I couldn't see anything. I heard my parents' voices once or twice, but I couldn't find them. I should have tried to find them, to get them out, but something kept telling me, actually it was Mika telling me to get out. I ran from the house and into the woods. The house burned all night. In the morning there was nothing left but the foundation and the chimneys. When I came out of the woods after dawn the bastards that had done it were all gone. My parents' bodies were there, they had been shot. I ran after I saw that. I just started running and I never looked back."

"You said you had brothers and a sister. What happened to them?"

"I had two brothers, Patrick and Connelly and a sister Laura. Patrick survived. I saw him years later under not so favorable circumstances. Connelly went down the same path I did, I used to see him from time to time. But Laura, I never knew what happened to her. I hope she survived."

I didn't know what to say. I felt foolish complaining about my father and Eve's romantic drama. Hugh took out the watch again and looked at it. "How old were you when all this happened?" I asked.

"Fourteen. The month before I got this for my birthday." He held up the watch. "It was a present from my father. I was so happy, he carried one just like it. I was going to be just like him. A month later he was dead and a month after that I was a criminal." He put it back in his pocket.

"I'm so sorry Hugh."

He nodded and stood up. "I should go up to the attic now. I'm sure you're tired." He wiped his eyes and tried to force a smile.

"Yes." I said even though I was wide awake.

"All right. Goodnight then."

"Goodnight and thank you for telling me."

"I've never told anyone that, ever."

"I won't tell anyone else."

"I know. I'll be upstairs if you need me." He drifted effortlessly through the door. I stayed awake for a long time that night thinking of everything he had said.

Chapter 17

Hugh sat against the attic wall and shuffled his newly acquired playing cards. He had not meant to tell Emma the whole story. He had only wanted to illustrate to her that loved ones, especially parents, disappoint in the end. That night was never far from his mind, even after more than a century had past.

No one had ever known where he had come from when he was alive. He never made any true friends that he confided in. Occasionally he did get to talking, either during his stints in jail or when he had too much to drink. Few knew he was from a wealthy, educated family. Better to think he had come up the hard way than tell them he was the infamous Judge MacPherson's son.

He shuffled the cards again. Out of the corner of his eye he saw something move.

"I can't believe you told her." Mika said. He was standing over Hugh looking grim as usual.

"I wasn't planning to, it all just came tumbling out. Am I in trouble now?"

Mika's expression didn't change. "Why should you be in trouble? You told the truth. That's all I have ever asked of you. Of course the same can't be said for that deck of cards in your hand. You just couldn't resist could you?"

"I am just borrowing these." Hugh said. "I could have saved them you know."

"What? The cards?"

"No, my parents. I heard their voices that night, but instead I ran out of the house and saved myself."

"That's what I told you to do."

"The one time I really listen to you my parents end up dead and my sister, who knows what became of her."

"They're all dead now, including you."

Hugh tossed the cards away, sending them skittering across the attic floor. "You know Mika I can't stand it when you're like this. Do you even have an ounce of feeling inside of you? Or is whatever you're made of, or wherever you've been, washed it all out of you? You said you were a Seer so you must have been human once. There must have been someone you cared about. Why can't you just show a little compassion?"

Mika didn't move. A blinding white light began to grow out of nothing. It illuminated the entire attic in a blazing hot glow, becoming stronger and stronger until Hugh had to squint and then finally shut his eyes.

"Stop!" he shouted. He cracked one eye open and found things were back to normal. "I'm sorry."

"I'm still human and you know nothing about what I've been through." Mika said coldly.

"I'm sorry."

Mika glared at him and sat on the floor.

"I didn't know you could sit down." Hugh said.

"Of course I can sit down. What an absurd comment. If you insist on speaking constantly at least say something intelligent."

"I'll try."

"Please do. I'm very smart you know, smarter than you'll ever be." There was almost a tone of laughter in his voice. Hugh shifted his legs and swallowed. Mika was staring at him with his intensely blue eyes.

"I'm sure I could never be as smart as you."

"That's true. Am I making you nervous?"

"Sort of."

"I've always made people nervous. I really don't know why."

"You don't?"

Mika smirked. "All right maybe I do. I am quite extraordinary you know."

"I suppose."

"Now listen to me. I am only going to say this once. I am not having this conversation three hundred years from now because you want to hear it again."

Hugh nodded to show he was paying attention.

"My job is and has always been to guide you and protect you. When your house was burning it was my job to get you out of there alive. It was not the responsibility of a fourteen year old boy to save everyone else. Yes your parents died, but that is not your fault. You and your brothers lived."

"And my sister? You never told me anything about her. You must know."

"Knowing won't change anything."

Hugh shook his head in disgust. "I should have known you would say that."

"As I just said two seconds ago my job is to protect *you*. You're a complete wreck right now. I hate it when you're like this." He paused. "What was the name your brother Connelly used to use as a criminal?"

"The Scarlet Highwayman." He always felt a pang of embarrassment when he said it aloud.

Mika started laughing. Hugh couldn't believe his eyes and ears. Mika did not laugh. This was a peculiar night.

"Why the *Scarlet* Highwayman?" Mika asked although Hugh believed he already knew the answer.

"Because he wore scarlet red gloves and a scarlet red mask."

"And?"

Hugh sighed. "And a scarlet red sash."

Mika laughed again. "That was the most incredible outfit."

"Yes it was." Hugh said smiling. The last time he had seen Connelly he had been riding away on a horse, his sash billowing romantically behind him. He started to snicker.

"Do you feel better now?" Mika asked. The smile was already fading from his face.

"You know I do."

"Good then I have done my job."

"I didn't know you could laugh."

"Of course I can laugh. I just can't tell a joke." Mika said. "I am human. I thought tonight you needed to know that."

"Will you tell me about your life before you died?"

Mika's mouth twitched. "Don't you have someone to talk to now? The Torment Seer?"

"Yes but-"

"Talk to her then."

"Can I tell Emma about you?" Hugh asked.

"I don't know why you're asking since you've already said my name in front of her more than once."

"I have?"

"Yes." Mika stood up. "I have other souls to tend." He raised his hand, a sign he planned to disappear. "Goodnight Hugh. And don't snap any more suspenders." he added before he vanished.

Darkness settled into the room. Hugh began picking up his cards. It had been a most unusual day.

Chapter 18

It was Saturday morning. Hugh was already in the kitchen when I came down to breakfast. "Good morning!" he called out. I nodded slightly and slid into a seat next to Eve who was yawning repeatedly.

"Eve, did you not sleep well last night?" Mother asked.

"She wasn't even here last night." Hugh said smiling delightedly.

"I did not." Eve said crossly. Her eyes were puffy and red. "Just the fact that he kissed my hand is enough to make any girl stay awake at night."

Hugh laughed out loud.

"Who are you talking about?" Mother looked perplexed.

"Senator Brown of course."

"Good morning all." Father walked into the kitchen scratching his stomach.

"Morning." we all mumbled at different intervals. Father wrinkled his forehead and sat down.

"That was a most pathetic greeting." Hugh said. "When I was a boy I was taught to say good morning father."

"Are you ready for this most wonderful day?" Father asked, looking around the table.

"I am planning to start a model of the inner ear." Ethan said.

"I'm sorry son but I think you've forgotten we are all going to walk into town to see the shop this morning."

"What's this Edward?" Mother asked. "We've had a very busy week."

"Darling I mentioned it in the coach on our way here." Father checked his watch. "I have to open the shop today, and none of you have seen it. Besides it would be good for people to get a sense of who the Hollis family is. I am afraid your model will have to wait Ethan."

Ethan sighed.

"I have things to discuss with Emma." Hugh said. "It's about Mika."

"Father-" I was thinking I might tell him I had a headache. Whatever Hugh had to say sounded more interesting than looking at a barber shop. I had been waiting to find out about Mika.

"I can't wait for you to see the shop Emma." Father said smiling at me.

My courage left me, despite his unsettling plan to marry off Eve he was still my father and the shop was his greatest dream. Hugh would have to wait until later.

"I can't either." I said trying to look excited.

"Excellent. As soon as you're all done eating we will leave."

We finished breakfast quickly mostly due to Father constantly checking his watch. Hugh was waiting as we filed out the door. He stepped aside for Ethan who treaded nervously past hugging his hands to his chest in case Hugh got hold of his suspenders. Hugh allowed Mother and Eve to walk through him. "I never get tired of that." he said closing his eyes.

I was the last one out the door as usual. "Goodbye Emma." he said. "I will be waiting in the attic for you when you get home."

"I'll be there." I whispered.

"Hurry up Emma." I heard Father's voice outside.

"She's coming!" Hugh shouted. "Goodbye for now." I stepped outside and shut the front door.

"What were you doing in there?" Mother eyed me suspiciously.

"Nothing."

"Nothing is not an answer."

"It could be an answer, scientifically speaking." Ethan said as he took a book from his pocket.

"Is everyone ready?" Father looked at his watch again. "It's nearly time for me to open."

"Yes let's go." Mother said.

Eve yawned and we started off towards town. Father had somehow acquired a walking stick and was already striding jauntily along at the front while the rest of us lagged behind. Next door Margaret Cooper was on her front porch. She was smoking a cigarette while two toddlers played at her feet.

"Good morning Mrs. Cooper." Father called out.

"Good morning Mr. Hollis." she said blowing smoke into the air.

"Stay close children." Mother whispered. Margaret shifted her weight as Mother approached, she took one last puff on her cigarette and tossed it into the bushes.

"Good morning Mrs. Hollis."

"Good morning Mrs. Cooper." Mother tugged hard on my sleeve. I found myself stuck to her side.

There was a commotion in the house. The Coopers' front door opened and several red headed children burst out including Candy and Scott.

"Hi Emma!" Candy waved her hands frantically. "Where are you going? Can I come?"

"Hi Candy." I said feeling my mother bristle next to me. "We are going to see my father's new barber shop."

"Oh that sounds really interesting. My father could use a good haircut, couldn't he Ma?" She tugged at Margaret's arm. "You're always saying he's such a mess."

"Candy, go back in the house and get Dylan dressed."

"Oh well. See ya at school Emma!" Candy turned and ran back into the house, her red hair swinging behind her.

Scott remained on the porch, leaning casually against the wall. He looked like all the other Coopers with red hair and freckles. His eyes were dark brown and set far apart. He barely noticed the rest of us, his gaze focused entirely on Eve. As she walked by Eve's eyes flicked constantly to him and then back to the ground. She pushed a strand of hair behind her ear and bit her lip.

Mother quickened her pace and the rest of us followed. The Coopers were soon behind us. We passed by old Mr. Johnson's house, the rusty front gate was shut, weeds had completely taken over the front yard. The doors and windows looked like they were never opened. Father was ahead of us, heading towards Main Street. Once we passed the Coopers Mother let go of my sleeve. I let myself fall back until I was walking in stride with Eve.

"Do you like Scott Cooper?" I whispered to her. "He was looking at you when we walked by his house."

"He was, wasn't he?" She blushed. "But I don't really know him that well. I only met him this week."

"Candy says that's long enough."

"That little sister of his says a lot more than she should. But did she really say that?"

"Yes. She thinks you're going to marry him."

A smile spread over Eve's face. "I don't know about that, but I really, really like him Emma."

Father looked back at us. "Elsay do catch up. I'm sure to have customers waiting."

"Good heavens Edward do you really need to shout so?" She picked up her skirts and began hustling up the hill. "Come children."

"I think Father would like it if you married Senator Brown." I told Eve.

Eve screwed her face up. "*Him.* He's old enough to be my father, maybe even my grandfather. Why would I want to marry him?"

"He has a lot of money."

"Who cares?" She rolled her eyes.

"He's really important in town, what do they call it? Prominent?" I ventured.

"I don't care about any of that. I don't like him and he smells." We looked ahead and found our parents far in the distance. "We better catch up." She began to jog up the hill towards the center of town.

I stayed in place while Ethan caught up to me. He closed his book and stuck it in his pocket. "You should have told her the real reason. She is Father's payment back to the Senator."

"Don't say it like that Ethan."

"Why not? It's true. Why shouldn't she know?"

"I don't know. I just couldn't tell her." Mother was motioning for us to hurry up. "We'll just have to make sure it doesn't happen. Hugh can help us."

"Splendid. I thought you weren't going to talk to him."

"I'm not." I lied.

We stopped talking and hurried into town. To my surprise there were already customers waiting when we arrived at the shop.

"There he is!" cried one elderly man.

"Not to worry gentlemen, everything is under control now." Father fished his keys out of his pocket. "I've brought my family with me this morning to keep us company."

"Good day." Mother said stiffly. "I am Mrs. Hollis. These are our children. Eve, Ethan and Emma." She pointed to each of us as she said our names. The men were mostly interested in Eve.

We went inside the shop. It was one long room with two barber chairs on one side and a long wooden bench on the other. The elderly man went straight to Father's chair while the others filled up the bench.

"Looks like it's going to be a busy day." Father beamed.

"What are we supposed to do?" Mother whispered.

"Oh just wander about and talk with people."

"How can I wander here?"

Father grimaced. "Elsay." A look passed between them.

"Very well." Mother sighed and crossed the room to speak to one of the men. "I am sorry to keep you waiting." Father said to the old man in the barber chair.

The man chuckled. "Oh that's all right, I used to be married."

The next few hours the four of us mingled with Father's customers. I had never seen my father at work. He was always a friendly person, but with his customers he seemed to be able to find something to talk about with each one, whether it was the weather, politics, farming, or fishing.

Just before noon the door opened and Senator Brown walked in with another man. Everyone in the shop stopped talking while a few stood up and shook the Senator's hand.

"Good day everyone." Brown said stroking his beard. "Carry on, carry on." The mood in the shop relaxed. "This is Jeremy White, as some of you may recall. Another one of my success stories."

Jeremy White was tall and lanky, standing a few inches above the Senator, with pale blonde hair and blue eyes. He looked about twenty five years old. "Nice to see all of you."

"I took this young lad from the orphanage in Augusta and put him through college. He's a lawyer now." Brown said. As he spoke his eyes kept wandering towards Eve. She avoided his glance and stared at her hands.

"That was very kind of you Senator." Father said as he finished with his customer.

The Senator nodded in agreement. "Yes, I know. I'll be doing the same for this young man soon." He slapped Ethan on the back. "This is going to be our next town doctor."

Jeremy stepped forward and shook Ethan's hand. "Glad to know you young man. Senator Brown is just about the most generous person I know. Now that I'm finished with school I will be working as his personal lawyer."

"I'm very grateful for his generosity." Ethan said.

"Tell me," Jeremy began. "How do you like living in the Winslow House? Senator Brown told me about the tragedy that happened there years ago. How many were killed? Four or five?"

From somewhere in the shop Mother gasped.

"I don't really know what you're talking about. I haven't heard anything." Ethan stammered.

"Really? I thought it was common knowledge. The murder house-" Jeremy looked questioningly at Brown. The Senator shrugged his shoulders casually.

"What is common knowledge young man?" Mother was suddenly in the center of the room. Her face was red, her eyes narrowed to tiny slits.

"Oh. Well I'm sure I don't know everything. But-" Jeremy wiped his forehead with his handkerchief.

"Elsay, don't-" Father began. His scissors were frozen in mid-air.

Mother's nostrils flared. "I want to know about my house. What happened there?"

It was clear she wasn't leaving without an answer. Two men waiting on the bench shifted nervously and looked liked they wished they were somewhere else. The man in Father's barber chair watched anxiously in the mirror.

"I don't really know that much." Jeremy said.

Mother took a deep breath and turned her attention to Senator Brown. "You must know something. You who proclaim to know everything about this town." she said frostily.

Senator Brown took a step backwards. "Mrs. Hollis!"

"I want to know."

Senator Brown rubbed his round stomach and started to laugh. "You've got a spirited filly here Edward"

Mother's mouth twitched. Apparently she didn't like to be compared to a horse.

"It's really nothing Mrs. Hollis. Many years ago, before you or I or even our grandparents were born there was a family who was killed in your house. A criminal of the lowest kind broke in and killed them with an axe. I believe the story goes that the youngest son killed the varmint by splitting his head open with a butcher knife before the young hero died himself. It's just gossip. Some say the place is haunted but I've never seen any evidence of it." The Senator smoothed his beard and rocked back on his heels.

"Thank you." Mother said coldly. She shot Father an icy glance. "I think I will be going now."

"Elsay don't. It's just gossip." Father began. "Nothing will happen. I promise you."

Mother ignored him and picked up her hat. "Let's go home children."

Senator Brown cleared his throat. "Mrs. Hollis, I was hoping to take the children back to my house and show them around. I have my coach outside. I could drop you off at home if you like."

"You can take Eve and Ethan. Emma and I will walk home, thank you." At the back of the room Eve's face dropped.

Mother grabbed my hand and dragged me out of the shop. We raced down the street towards the cove. I didn't dare ask her to slow down. The smell of saltwater and fish hung in the air. As we entered the narrow road to home she stopped in front of old Mr. Johnson's place.

"Is it true?" she asked.

"Is what true?"

"Is the house haunted?" Her lower lip quivered.

"No." I said shaking my head. She couldn't tolerate the answer and I knew it.

"Are you sure?" There was a flicker of hope in her eyes.

"Yes. I'm positive." It was a necessary lie.

Mother closed her eyes and took a deep breath. "Thank you Emma." She gently took my hand. "Let's go home. I'll deal with your father tonight."

Chapter 19

Hugh waited anxiously for the sound of the latch on the front door. The empty house was unbearable without Emma. He was working on making up a new card game when he heard the familiar click. He put the cards on the windowsill and raced downstairs.

Elsay was taking off her hat while Emma was fiddling with the strings on her bonnet. She looked at him and turned to her mother. "Do you want me to help you with supper?"

Elsay looked tired. "No, you can go and play Emma. I'm going to lie down for a while. I imagine Eve and Ethan will have supper with the Senator and your father can get his own." She sighed and patted Emma on the shoulder.

"Are you going to be all right?"

Elsay smiled sadly. "Yes I will be fine. I've just had a difficult day. Don't worry about me." She strode off towards her bedroom.

Hugh waited until Elsay was out of sight before speaking. "What's wrong with her?"

Emma put a finger to her lips and pointed upstairs. They didn't speak again until they were safely in the attic.

"What happened?"

Emma sat on the floor. "We were in Father's shop today when someone told her that this house was haunted."

"They didn't tell the old axe story did they?"

"Yes, but that's not important-"

"Of course it's important. I am remembered as some axe wielding maniac. As though I would break in with an axe. That is so impractical."

"I know it's wrong, but that's the story Senator Brown told her."

"Ugh." Hugh muttered in disgust. "*Him.*"

"Yes him. Anyway, Mother knows about the house."

"She looked upset."

"Of course she's upset. She asked me on the way home if I had seen any ghosts."

"Really? What did you tell her?"

"I lied of course. I told her I hadn't seen anything. I couldn't tell her about you. She would never set foot in here again."

"And then you would have to leave." Hugh said slowly. He sat down and leaned against the wall. "Mika says she has a reason to be afraid."

"You still haven't told me about Mika. Is he another ghost?" Emma scooted across the floor and sat next to him.

Hugh scratched his stubbly chin. "Who is Mika? That's a good question. I don't know much about him except he's my Watcher."

"A Watcher? Is that like a guardian angel?"

"That's funny, that's one of the first things I asked when I met him. He's not an angel, he's always sure to tell me that." Hugh paused. "You know that little voice in the back of your head, the one that tells you what you should do, even when you don't want to?"

Emma nodded.

"That's your Watcher. Their job is to protect you, to guide you through life. We all have one, and when you die they are there to meet you. That's how I found out about Mika. When I was killed he was standing next to me."

Emma wrinkled her nose. "If it's his job to protect you then why did he let you die that night? Why doesn't everyone just die of old age?"

"When I came here that night I was drunk. I wanted to steal something to prove to myself that I could. I was arrogant. Mika kept telling me to turn around and leave. He told me over and over again that I was too drunk. But I didn't listen. I rarely listened to him then, I thought I knew better."

"You didn't know he existed then."

"No, I didn't. But that's not an excuse. No one else knows they have a Watcher but they still heed those warnings in their mind, if they're smart. I wasn't that smart, and then it was too late and I was dead."

"So is he here right now?"

"Mika? Oh no, he only shows up when he feels like it, or if I scream at the top of my lungs for him. He doesn't have to be here. He can see and hear everything I do anyway."

"So he knows we are having this conversation?"

"Yes. And so does your Watcher."

"Oh." Emma said quietly. She glanced around the attic as though something might jump out at her. "That's really strange."

"I know. I can't get away with anything." he laughed.

"So-" Emma stopped and stared at him. "I have so many questions. Are you supposed to be telling me this?"

Hugh laughed again. "Probably not. But Mika is part of my life, whether I like it or not. I would never be able to keep him a secret from you."

"So you won't get in trouble?"

"Trouble? Oh, most likely. But I am used to his scolding. He's not happy that you're here."

"Why not?"

"He doesn't like Seers."

"What's a Seer?"

"That's you."

"That's me?" Emma pointed to herself. "What does that mean?"

"Mika says you're a Torment Seer. You just see souls in Torment. He says Ethan has the greater gift. He can see everything, just not in the same way."

"He sees shapes and shadows but he can't talk to any of them like I can. He can't touch them either. Why can I see only Torment?"

Hugh shrugged. "I don't know. You just can."

Emma was quiet. She stared at the floor. "That does explain a lot. So he doesn't like that I am here?"

"No."

"But why? He doesn't even know me."

"You're a Seer, that's all he cares about. That's how Mika is. He's peculiar. He says he was a Seer when he was alive, but I guess he doesn't like them anymore."

"Was he like me or Ethan?"

Hugh thought for a moment. "I don't think he said. Mika's not the kind of person you ask a lot of questions."

"I guess I wouldn't be able to see him then?"

"You're not missing much."

Emma was quiet again. Hugh could see a dozen thoughts flickering across her face. "So when are you done Tormenting? Do you have to stay here forever?"

Hugh smiled. How many times had he asked himself that? "Mika says Torment is a long process. I guess that means forever, or nearly forever."

"So you could be here long after I'm gone?"

"I suppose so." He shrugged, pretending it wasn't important. Emma didn't seem to notice the dark cloud that came over him. She had spied the deck of cards on the windowsill.

He had watched people in the house come and go for years. He had barely blinked an eye when old lady Cronkite died in her sleep. When Billy Barker fell out of the oak tree and broke his neck Hugh was not concerned about never seeing him again. They were just amusements to him. He had no real connection with any of those people.

Emma was different. She was his friend. He knew she would grow up and move away. And even if by some chance she stayed in the house for her entire life, she would die. Emma was not the type of girl who was going to spend her afterlife Tormenting in an attic. She was going straight up as Mika would say. How was he going to bear it when she was gone?

"Where did you get these?" She was holding up the cards.

"Oh." he said absently. He was still thinking about the day she would leave. He would have to teach himself not to think about it. He had learned to put away his feelings before, he could do it again. He would enjoy this time with Emma while he could and not think of the inevitability of the future.

Chapter 20

I turned the cards over in my hands. They were practically brand new. "Where did you get these?"

Hugh looked melancholy. "Oh. I stole them. I'm a thief you know."

His mood had turned suddenly. "What kind of games do you play?"

"All kinds."

"Like what?"

"Whist, Cracker, the usual ones. My father taught me a game called Tribute. That's my favorite."

"I've never heard of it."

"It's old. Like me."

"Will you teach me how to play?"

"Do you really want me to?" A flicker of a smile spread across his face.

"Yes." I tried to shuffle the cards like I had seen my father do, but I didn't know how.

"Let me see." he said holding out his hand. As I gave him the cards my fingers brushed his skin. He flinched.

"This is how to do it." Hugh took the deck and expertly shuffled them. He brushed the dark hair out of his eyes. "I wish I had gotten a haircut before I was shot to death."

"Why? I like it."

"I'm afraid I'm hopelessly old fashioned looking."

"Wasn't that how men wore their hair back then?" I asked. "I've seen pictures in books."

"Yes it was."

"I think it's just fine and besides why would you want to look like anyone else?"

"I suppose."

"You don't see clothes like that today either. They're much nicer."

"You really like them? You understand this isn't nearly my best."

"I know."

"Men did know how to dress in my day. Nowadays they wear those hideous long pants. Ugh. There's nothing worse than seeing a man in a pair of long wool pants, it looks like he's wearing a couple of stovepipes on his legs."

"They all wear those." I laughed.

"Indeed. Mika wears them too, although his clothes are even worse than what you see around here. Fashion has taken a dreadful turn I'm afraid. I was never a dandy but I never went out of doors looking like a milkmaid's donkey either."

I laughed again. "I thought you were going to teach me to play."

Hugh smiled. "I was, wasn't I?"

"Yes. I want to learn this Tribute."

He shuffled again and dealt me eleven cards face up. "We'll do the first few hands together until you get the idea." He finished dealing and put the remainder of the cards face down on the floor.

It took me five hands before I really understood the game. I had never played cards before. Hugh was patient and explained the rules at least three times. He won each hand easily.

"This is fun!" he cried as he dealt again. I looked at my cards and tried to figure out what to do. What had he said? What was an ace worth?

A few minutes later Hugh giggled and called "Tribute!"

"What?" I cried. "You're done already? We just started."

He laughed again and spread his cards out so I could see them. "Always play jacks and eights, that's what my father used to say."

"Jacks and eights?"

"If you can get them, and I usually do." he said with glee.

"How?"

"I have my ways." he said with a wink.

"I'm never going to get this."

"You forget I've been playing for the last one hundred and thirty years, give or take. That gives me a slight advantage."

"So maybe in one hundred and thirty years I can beat you?"

He looked up from shuffling and smiled. "Maybe." Sunlight from the far window shone on his face. If it was blinding him he didn't seem to mind. The light illuminated his skin, taking it from ghostly white to almost peachy. He looked nearly alive. We played a few more hands until a chorus of voices from downstairs caught our attention.

"I think Eve and Ethan are back." He put the cards on the windowsill. We hurried downstairs. Eve was in the hallway stamping her feet. Her face was red.

"I've never had such a dreadful evening." she said to no one in particular. I looked in the parlor and found Ethan settled into Father's chair reading a book.

"What happened?"

Eve pouted. "What do you think happened Emma? The old goat breathed down my neck the whole time. He kept dropping hints about how much money he had and how he was still looking for a wife. And-"

"And what?" Hugh said.

"And what?" I asked.

"And he mentioned how he wanted a son. That's why he wants a young wife so she can give him a son. It's disgusting." She muttered something and threw her bonnet on the floor.

I picked up the bonnet and hung it up. "You don't have to marry him Eve."

"I know I don't. I have no intention of it. It's just that Father thinks it's a good idea." she said hiccupping.

"He's a dope." Hugh said.

"Father feels obligated that's all."

"Obligated to just hand me over?"

"That's how it works." Hugh said.

"Where's Mother?" she asked. "I can't believe she just left us there in the barber shop. And you, you got to come home. Why? You don't know how lucky you are."

"And she got to spend the afternoon with me. That's extra lucky." Hugh said.

"Mother is sleeping. She was upset by what she heard today."

Eve frowned. "Why? Because of that nonsense about the house being haunted?"

"Yes."

"That's just gossip. I haven't noticed anything odd here. And besides you and Ethan are always going on about seeing things, you would have said something right?"

"Of course. There's nothing odd about this place."

"Oh, I have such a headache." Eve rubbed her temples. "I'm going to bed. Maybe when I wake up this whole day will be nothing but a bad dream."

"Don't bet on it." Hugh said.

Eve walked past me and through Hugh. Once I heard her bedroom door close I poked Hugh in the arm. "Do they have to walk through you every time?"

"Why not? They don't know any better. And besides *I* like it, you don't realize how cold I am."

"I know. I'm just afraid they might sense something."

"Eve? I assure you she's never going to notice my presence, it isn't in her nature."

"Are you sure? It's just that I wouldn't want her to find out about you."

"Because of your mother?"

I turned away and looked at the wall, embarrassed by what was about to come out of my mouth. "No, because of me. I don't want to leave this place, and you."

Chapter 21

"Oh." Hugh said, trying not to show how pleased he was.

Emma's face was burning red.

"I'm sure you're tired."

"Yes I am."

"Goodnight then."

"Goodnight." She hurried upstairs.

She was so young. He had forgotten what it was like to be embarrassed by such a little thing like telling someone how you felt. He wished he had been better at it when he was alive. But like Emma he had been taught to keep his real feelings to himself.

He went upstairs and passed idly through Eve's wall. He found her in a serious state of undress. "Oh boy." he said aloud. These were the moments he typically longed for. But now that he was friends with Emma it seemed almost sinister to be spying on her sister. Regrettably he averted his eyes and left for the attic.

He shuffled his cards and listened to the house settle for the night. He let his mind drift to thoughts of his brothers, Senator Brown and his peculiar odor, and even Mika.

It was nearly midnight when he heard a door open. It wasn't the front door, he knew the sound of the latch by heart. He listened closely. It was the secret door. Hugh hurried downstairs into Eve's room. The secret door was just shutting, he ran through it and found Eve walking gingerly down the narrow staircase. He followed close behind her, taking in the sweet smell of her perfume.

At the bottom of the steps she paused. He could have told her that no one was coming. Slowly she opened the door and crept into the parlor shutting the door in his face. He walked through it. Eve was nervously adjusting her collar and smoothing her skirt. She was on her way out. Hugh followed her to the front door. She eased it open and looked outside. He thought he heard footfall on the other side.

"Oh." Eve said softly. She crept outside closing the door gently behind her. Hugh could not open the front door, it was physically impossible for him. Instead he stepped into the kitchen and looked out the window. He caught a glimpse of Eve linking arms with a young man. As they walked away the boy ventured a glance backwards. He was a Cooper, although Hugh wasn't sure which one.

"You're meddling." Mika's voice was behind him. Hugh turned around. He was sitting at the kitchen table. "What business do you have with the living?"

Hugh hesitated. "I don't want Eve to marry that old man."

"Who cares about what you want?" Mika stood up. His chair made no sound on the floor. The air in the room seemed to suddenly drop twenty degrees. The glass on the kitchen window frosted over obstructing Hugh's view outside. "And you are sure she belongs with that silly boy?"

"Isn't it better than the old man?"

"Isn't that for Eve's Watcher to decide?"

"If Eve knows she doesn't want to be with the Senator then isn't that what her Watcher is telling her?"

"Don't make a pest of yourself." he said crossly.

"You don't seem to be in the same mood as the last time. Don't you remember? We were talking about my crazy brother Connelly, the Scarlett Highwayman."

"My moods change."

"I thought it was nice. You know we don't really have proper conversations. I enjoyed it." Hugh swallowed. The air was blistering cold. His dead breath drifted around him in nervous puffs.

"Thank you for your seal of approval. I have had a difficult day and then I find you sneaking around playing matchmaker. Be careful of what you meddle in. The result might not be what you want."

"It's about what Eve wants."

"No, it's about what you think she wants."

"I think I've learned a thing or two in the years I've been dead."

Mika snorted. "Just a fountain of wisdom, aren't you?"

"I have been dead for over one hundred years."

"So what?"

"I suppose you probably know more than I do." Hugh conceded.

"You think?"

"I don't like arguing." Hugh shivered.

"Why not?"

"Because you can be scary as hell." It wasn't a lie. He was now certain that Mika could destroy the house and everyone with it if he wanted to.

"I scare you?"

"Sometimes." The air in the kitchen fell a few more degrees. Hugh's teeth started chattering.

Hugh heard a noise in the pantry. He and Mika both turned and saw Elsay in her nightgown. She was rubbing her arms from the cold.

"What on earth is going on in here?" She poked the coals in the fireplace. "It's freezing."

"What is it?" Edward called from the bedroom.

Elsay threw another log on the fire. "Just the fire."

"Do you want me to get up?" Edward asked.

Elsay shook her head. "No." she cried. "Heaven forbid you have to get out of bed." she muttered to herself. She poked the fire one more time and shuffled back into the darkness.

The fire roared to life and the temperature in the room returned to normal. The ice on the windows faded and Hugh's teeth stopped chattering.

"I have to go." Mika said suddenly.

"All right."

"I won't be around for a while, I have things to do."

"When will you be back? What if I need you?" Hugh asked.

"You just said I scared you. What do you care if I ever come back?"

"I don't want to be alone."

"You have *her* don't you?"

"She doesn't know where I've come from, you do."

"From the sound of your constant yammering she'll soon know everything I do." Mika said.

"Where are you going?"

"That's none of your concern."

"I suppose someone as powerful as you doesn't have to answer to someone like me."

Mika smiled. "Powerful huh? Faster than a speeding bullet? Able to leap tall buildings in a single bound?"

Hugh frowned. "What does that mean?"

"I forgot where I was. Never mind. I'll let you know when I return." He vanished.

Chapter 22

The town of Fox Cove had a fine church built high on the bluff overlooking the ocean. I wasn't sure I wanted to go. The church in Augusta had a grotesque ghost near the altar that used to scream during the sermons. There was no telling what would be lurking in this building.

"I'm quite looking forward to this." Ethan said on the way there. "You see the most interesting shapes and colors in churches, there are all sorts of beings moving around, especially near the ceiling."

"Lucky you. I only see tormented souls." I whispered.

We passed by the Coopers. The oft forgotten Mr. Cooper was sitting on the porch with a toddler wriggling in his lap.

"Morning." he said nodding his head.

We each greeted him in turn. Mother tightened her grip on Father's arm. Candy told me that the Coopers didn't go to church. Mother said they were heathens, each and every one of them.

When we arrived the churchyard was already crowded. Father was greeted by several men who shook his hands and slapped him heartily on the back. He laughed and broke away from Mother and the rest of us who were left standing awkwardly side by side.

"Father already knows so many people in town." Eve lamented.

"Of course, he's a man." Mother said.

We stood off to one side while more and more of the congregation arrived. I recognized some of the boys and girls from school, but no one came over to talk to us. A group of older boys had noticed Eve twirling her hair in her fingers.

"Well this is just fine Edward Hollis." Mother said under her breath. A few minutes later Father returned accompanied by the dreaded Senator Brown.

"Good morning all." he said looking at Eve.

"Good morning." we mumbled with various degrees of enthusiasm. Eve stopped twirling her hair and folded her arms across her chest.

"We're sitting with the Senator this morning." Father said excitedly.

"Yes, I thought it best, give you folks a chance to get to know everyone." The Senator suppressed a burp and carried on. "Naturally I sit in front. Best chance to hear ole' Reverend Monk, a fine speaker he is. I put him through college you know, found him begging on the streets in Augusta, brought him right up. The sermon is on the importance of marriage and family I believe." He smiled and offered his arm to Eve. "Shall we?"

Eve sighed and took his arm. The rest of us followed in a loose collection behind them. I took a deep breath as we entered the church, my eyes swept over the large space and quickly found there were no tormented souls. I breathed a sigh of relief.

Ethan stared up at the ceiling. "It's beautiful." he whispered. "It looks like it's painted in swirls with a thousand different colors."

I looked at the dull white ceiling in disappointment. Ethan had all the luck. I had to see tormented souls while he looked at heavenly visions. But I had Hugh. I smiled to myself wondering what he might be doing back at the house.

As we walked towards our seats people took notice of Senator Brown and the pretty young girl on his arm. One man even stood up and shook the Senator's hand vigorously. "Congratulations."

The first congratulations sparked off a flurry of well wishers jumping in front of the couple as they tried to take their seat.

"Best wishes."

"Best of luck."

"I didn't realize Senator, capital idea. Good luck."

Eve's face was burning when we finally arrived at the front pew. She sat down and stared at the floor. The Senator hitched up his pants and looked back at the congregation. He gave them a little wave before sitting next to her. I was forced into the corner near the wall which gave me a limited view of anything.

"Are they engaged?" I whispered to Ethan.

"Not that I know of." he said shrugging.

"Thank you all for coming." Reverend Monk said from the pulpit. He was a wiry little man with a shriveled face and small hands that shook as he spoke. "This morning I want to focus on the importance of marriage." He smiled and looked at the Senator. Eve buried her face in her hands.

"Ugh. I bet he planned this." I said to Ethan.

"Probably."

There wasn't much else to say. Reverend Monk launched into his sermon, speaking loudly and with gusto. I barely listened, all I could think about was getting back to Hugh.

Eve and Father argued all the way home from church. I had never seen her in such a state. She and Father had had disagreements before, but never like this. Eve was shaking as she walked through the front door, tears staining her face, she blindly tried to hang her hat up. It fell onto the floor along with her shawl.

"Paraded through church as though I was his fiancé!" she cried. "I am not and never will be."

"Stop it Eve, please stop!" Father said. He was pacing nervously and wringing his hands. He looked exhausted.

"I will not stop it. You are allowing it to happen. You expect me to marry him as payment for all he's done for you." She wiped the tears from her eyes.

"Only if you want to."

"Ha!" Eve cried. Mother, Ethan, and I stood trapped in the front doorway. None of us dared to pass Father and Eve as they circled each other.

"He is a very rich man Eve. You'll have everything you want." Father said.

"No, you'll have everything you want!" She pointed a finger at him. "If I am his wife you'll have him and his money at your disposal."

"She's right Edward." Hugh said from the stair landing.

"You're wrong Eve. I want you to be happy."

"No you don't. Otherwise you wouldn't be doing this to me."

"Doing this to you? Who do you think all this is for?" he said looking around. "I've done everything for you and this family. Where would we be if we were still in Augusta? I would be just another working barber living in an apartment. Now I am a business owner and we own this house. You three have a chance at respectability now. You couldn't have even dreamed of marrying a man like Brown back home. We were beneath him, now we are his equals."

"Don't be so dramatic Edward." Hugh said. "No person is better than another."

"I don't care about marrying a man like him. I never have." Eve sniffed.

"You've never talked like this before." Father said. "You were all for coming here, you said it would change our fortunes. Don't you remember saying that Eve? Now that Cooper boy has you thinking differently."

"It's not him, it's you. You've changed since you came here."

"I have not."

"Yes you have. I'm sorry you can't see it." She hiccupped and ran upstairs through Hugh.

Father watched her go. He stood motionless in the hallway with his back to us, his shoulders slumped as the fight drained out of him.

"You're being an ass Edward." Hugh said from the landing. "Do you want her to hate you? Let her marry the Cooper boy if she wants. That Brown is a letch and he smells like maple syrup."

Father remained still for a moment, he then turned to the three of us in the open doorway. "Ethan and Emma, go upstairs to your room. I want to talk to your mother."

"Yes Father." Ethan said. Both of us moved quickly towards the stairs. Ethan went up first, breezing through Hugh's left side. I didn't notice

Hugh's foot sticking out as he leaned on the stair railing. My foot caught his and I fell with a loud thump.

"Oh, I forgot again." he said. "The worst things happen on this landing."

"Emma you've gotten awfully clumsy since we got here, watch where you walk." Mother told me.

"Yes Mother."

"Don't worry Elsay, I'll look after her." Hugh waved at my unknowing parents and followed me upstairs.

Chapter 23

It wasn't until the end of the following week that a real opportunity to help Eve presented itself. After saying goodnight to Emma, Hugh slipped into Eve's room to see what she was up to. She had taken to using the secret staircase quite often, and tonight appeared to be no exception. She was spraying lavender scented cologne on her neck when he entered her room. She smiled at herself in the mirror and tossed her hair playfully over her shoulder

She slipped a shawl over her shoulders and hurried downstairs, cautiously crossing the parlor like she had done many times before. Hugh watched as she gently opened the front door. Scott Cooper was standing on the doorstep. Eve jumped.

"Scott! What are you doing?"

He wrung his hands nervously. "My Pa is drunk. I don't want him to see us. You don't know what he can be like."

Eve glanced over her shoulder. "Why don't you come in?"

"I don't know. What if your parents catch us?"

"Oh please Scott. When a girl invites you in, you go in." Hugh said.

"They sleep like bears, they'll never know." she said.

"That's true." Hugh remarked. He could hear Edward and Elsay snoring away.

Scott looked back at his house. Hugh heard someone shouting obscenities.

"All right, but just for a minute." Scott said. Eve giggled. She took Scott's arm and led him through the parlor and into the secret door. Hugh followed them up the narrow staircase.

"You can't imagine how many people have used this staircase. You wouldn't believe how much infidelity goes on in this world, or at least in this house." Hugh said aloud.

Once safely upstairs Scott kissed Eve gently on the mouth. She grinned and sighed. "Have you seen the old man again?" he asked.

Eve rolled her eyes. "God yes. They put him in front of me every chance they get."

"Don't they know you don't like him?"

"They don't care. My Father thinks it's my duty to him."

"I'm sorry Eve. I really am." Scott took her hand. She leaned into him, her bosom resting ever so slightly on his chest. Hugh knew where this was going.

Scott coughed and took a step backwards. His face was red.

"Oh come on. You've got to be jesting." Hugh said. "When a girl did that to me I knew what to do."

"Scott." Eve took a step closer.

"Yes?" His voice was shaking.

"Will your parents be looking for you?"

"No. They don't keep tabs on me. It's just that Pa is so drunk tonight."

Hugh waited a second longer. It was becoming clear that he was going to have to do something to help things along. He pushed Scott lightly on the shoulder blades. He stumbled and stepped on Eve's toes, when he looked down at her feet his forehead crashed into hers.

"Ouch." they both said clutching their heads.

"What's the matter with you?" Eve hopped on one foot and rubbed her forehead.

"I don't know." He glanced nervously behind him as though he expected someone to be there. "Are you all right?"

"I'm fine."

"I should go."

"No, not yet!" Hugh shouted. Scott couldn't leave, nothing had been accomplished.

"With all this noise we're making someone is bound to wake up." Eve said. She kissed Scott's cheek, her fingers lingered on his coat sleeve.

"Goodnight." he said.

"Goodnight."

They started towards the secret door. Hugh panicked and ran through both of them in order to get there first. He threw himself against the door, pushing with all his strength to keep it shut.

Eve tapped the door and waited to hear the quiet ping of the latch. She looked confused as nothing happened, the force of Hugh's weight was keeping the mechanism from working. Eve looked at Scott and tried again, her hand passed through Hugh's chest warming him. He enjoyed being so close to her. She was remarkably pretty, her blond curls danced playfully in his face. He couldn't help but smile.

"It's not working."

"Let me try." Scott said. Eve stepped away and Scott took her place. He tried opening the door but Hugh remained steadfast. "Something's wrong."

"Why don't you take her in your arms?" Hugh said. "Do something. In my day we hardly needed little more than a nod to get things started. The youth of today."

"What are we going to do?" Eve bit her bottom lip.

"I don't know. Maybe I should try your bedroom door? I can slip out quietly enough."

"I don't know, my father has really good hearing."

Hugh laughed. He could still hear Edward and Elsay snoring below. He listened again. There was a sound coming from Ethan's bedroom, the pages of a book turning, he was studying. That could be a problem. He would hear Scott coming out of Eve's room.

The second Eve and Scott started for the other door Hugh dashed across the room. Eve always left the key in the lock. He quickly locked the door and held the key tightly in his closed fist. He only hoped the room was dark enough that they wouldn't notice it appearing to float in midair. He ducked into the corner where the candlelight barely reached.

Eve got there a second later. She tugged on the doorknob and then bent down to look at the lock. "What on earth? It's locked and the key is gone." She looked at Scott.

"It wasn't me." He showed her his empty hands.

"We're locked in." Eve said. Hugh smiled to himself in the dark, finally something was going right.

"Maybe we should try the other door again." Scott suggested.

Eve shrugged. "Why? It's obviously stuck. We can try later." Hugh was impressed and a little surprised. For a girl her age she seemed quite able to handle the situation.

"What if your parents find me here?" Scott played nervously with one of the buttons on his jacket.

"I'm starting to think you don't like me." Eve pouted. She crossed her arms and blew a stray hair out of her eyes.

"No! It's not that at all. It's just that your parents don't really like me and then there's Senator Brown."

"Him again! I am not engaged to him Scott. And I am not promised to him either. They can drag me up to the altar with a team of horses but I am not marrying him!" Eve's voice rose. Hugh sensed that Ethan had heard something.

"Be quiet you two." Hugh said despite its uselessness. A few seconds passed and the pages of Ethan's book began to turn again.

"I'm glad to hear that." Scott smiled and put his arms around Eve's waist. He kissed her tenderly. "I'll stay a little longer."

Eve hooked her fingers behind his neck. "I love you Scott."

"Well done Eve." Hugh said. This was just what he had in mind.

Scott looked surprised, but a smile soon spread across his face. "I love you too." He pulled her close to him. They kissed again, this time for much longer. Hugh considered giving Scott another push but it seemed unnecessary.

Hugh thought it was probably time to leave. He had done his part. The secret door would now open anytime they wanted to try it. He glided through Eve's bedroom door and into the upstairs hallway, slipping her key into his pocket as he left. He could make objects as liquid as he was if he wanted to.

He could still hear the pages of Ethan's book turning quietly. Downstairs Edward and Elsay were gloriously oblivious to it all. He paused at Emma's door and then passed through. She was sleeping peacefully, the soft moonlight gave her face a silver glow, her eyelashes cast a faint shadow on her cheeks.

Satisfied she was safe and comfortable he left her room and headed up to his unofficial room, the attic. Without much thought he put Eve's key on the windowsill with his cards. He would put it back in the morning.

He sat on the floor and took out his watch. Scott and Eve's declaration of love played over and over again in his head. Part of him was envious, no one had ever said those things to him and meant it. He sighed and put the watch away. He leaned against the attic wall and stared into space. There were times he longed to sleep like the rest of the world instead of sitting alone.

Chapter 24

I was awoken early the next morning by shouting coming from downstairs. I pulled on my robe and ran out into the hallway. Ethan was coming out of his room looking equally perplexed. Without saying a word the two of us hurried downstairs. Father's voice was coming from the parlor in loud, angry bursts. We rounded the corner and found our parents in their nightclothes looking at Eve and Scott who were both fully dressed. Behind them the secret door was open.

"I assure you my intentions are honorable." Scott was stammering. The time on the mantle clock said it was 5:14.

"Young man there is nothing you could say to make up for the fact that I find you and my daughter sneaking out of the house at this hour." Father's face was red. Mother stood next to him, her hands in her pockets, her lips tightly pressed together. "And to make matters worse I come to find there is some sort of secret entrance to your bedroom."

"Father, I only invited Scott in for a minute, to say goodnight, when he went to leave the door wouldn't open. He tried leaving through my bedroom door but it was locked and the key was missing." Eve said. Her eyes were watery and pleading.

"And may I ask what you were doing with him last night in the first place, when you should have been in bed?"

Eve looked at the floor. "I snuck out. I admit that, but only because you insist on trading me to the Senator. I don't like him. I like Scott."

"And what-" Father began. He stopped and looked over his shoulder at Ethan and me. "What are you two doing here? Get back upstairs."

"Oh come Edward let them stay." Hugh said strolling through the parlor door. "I plan on watching the whole argument." He smiled and leaned against the wall behind me.

"We love each other and we want to get married." Eve told them.

"Married?" Mother cried as though she had never heard of such a thing.

"Don't change the subject Eve, we are talking about last night." Father said. "You still haven't explained why you never showed us this door before."

"Good God Edward didn't you notice the outline in the paneling? *I* found it straight off." Hugh said.

"I should have told you. I didn't at first because I thought I might have some fun with it, you know, surprise you sometime, or sneak into the kitchen at night for a snack, but then you started pushing me towards Mr. Brown. I knew you didn't like Scott. I just wanted to be with him."

"And you young man, what do your parents say about you sneaking around at night? Don't you think they're looking for you right now?" Father asked.

Scott swallowed and pushed back his shoulders. "No sir, they won't be looking for me. We're a large family and there are little ones that need tending. My Ma and Pa consider me an adult. I'm eighteen you know."

"So you come and go as you please?"

"Yes. But they know I am responsible and can take care of myself."

My parents exchanged glances. Mother looked down at the floor while Father shuffled his feet. "Are you planning to finish school in the spring?"

"Why yes sir."

"And what will you do after that? Where will you work?"

"Here in town. I have already inquired about an apprenticeship with a carpenter. Do you know Mr. Lloyd? He is building those houses up on the hill."

"Yes I know him. Course hair. Black with some gray. Three cowlicks." Father said. "And this is enough to support yourself and a wife?"

Scott looked at Eve with a glimmer of hope in his eyes. "Yes sir, it won't be much to start with but Mr. Lloyd owns some of the buildings up there. He would rent to us, I mean me, well us, and anyway he would rent one of the houses to me and take the money out of my pay."

"So you've looked into this?" Father asked.

"Yes sir. I knew you would ask these sorts of questions. Any father would sir."

"Hmm." Father murmured. He looked at Mother again. She gave him a slight, barely perceptible nod.

"If I were to give my permission for you two to marry there would be conditions."

"Thank you-" Eve began.

Father put up his hand. "Wait and listen Eve. You might not like the conditions."

Her faced dropped a little. She sighed and took Scott's hand.

"First off you are not to announce your engagement until after Christmas." Father began.

"After Christmas? That's two months away." Eve said.

"Eve, these are my conditions." Father said firmly. "You will make the announcement after Christmas. Moreover, I want both of you to finish school. I also would like for Scott to be a few months into his apprenticeship to make sure it's a good fit. Once he is settled in his job you may marry. That would bring us to about next August or September."

"That's almost a year from now!" Eve cried.

"Those are my terms." Father said flatly.

Scott smiled and looked at Eve. "We agree Mr. Hollis. I think you are most generous sir."

"Don't thank me. You should be thanking your fiancé. If it weren't for this little stunt of hers I would have not considered it. Under the circumstances, the two of you spending the entire evening together, I see no other choice than for you to marry." Father sighed and folded his arms across his chest.

"Father, I swear you have nothing to worry about." Eve said.

Father shook his head. "I don't want to hear about it. There are some things a father doesn't need to know. I just hope that circumstances do not precipitate an earlier marriage date."

"I swear sir I have been nothing but a gentlemen with your daughter." Scott said.

"I should hope so."

"The door really wouldn't open. And my bedroom door was locked and the key was gone. I don't understand it." Eve said.

"Oh I do." Hugh laughed. "I made sure both doors were shut tight." I looked at him in surprise.

"Before the end of the day that door will be nailed shut." Father said wagging his finger. "And you will stay in your room at night. No matter what."

"Yes Father."

"And I have already unlocked and returned the key to her bedroom door." Hugh said triumphantly.

"Thank you so much Father." Eve put her arms around him.

"Your mother had something to do with it too."

Eve smiled and took Mother's hands. "Thank you Mother. Are you angry I am not marrying Mr. Brown?"

Mother smiled and smoothed Eve's hair. She looked wistfully at Scott. "I expected more of you Eve. However, believe it or not I was your age once and I know what it's like to be in love. I just hope this is really what you want."

"It is."

"Very well, it's settled. I suppose with so much time until the wedding we can make you a proper wedding dress."

"Really? Oh Mother I would love that."

"I love a good wedding. Hugh said. "And I am a terrific wedding guest."

"Young man you best be getting home to your folks." Father said to Scott. "And if you want to see Eve from now on you will knock on the front door, is that understood?"

"Yes sir."

"And if I were you I wouldn't go out of your way to talk or engage the Senator in any way."

Scott shook his head. "No sir. He doesn't exactly like our family."

"Oh God Ethan, does this mean Mr. Brown won't pay for your schooling?" Eve asked.

Ethan smiled and shook his head. "Don't worry about that. I got him to sign a paper the other day while we were at his house. If he doesn't pay he's breaking our contract and I can sue him."

"Ethan Hollis!" Mother cried. "What possessed you?"

Father began to laugh. "That's my son. A Hollis to the bone. Good boy Ethan."

Ethan's news lightened the mood considerably. Father shook Scott's hand and then showed him to the door. Mother and Eve began chatting about the wedding dress.

Father looked down at me as if he was noticing my presence for the first time. "Emma, are you still here? I thought I told you to go to your room." He bent down and winked. "Don't you ever put your old father through this."

"I won't."

"Go upstairs and back to bed, both of you."

"Yes Father." Ethan and I returned to our rooms with Hugh following us.

"I suppose he had something to do with the doors not opening." Ethan asked when we were safely out of earshot.

"Yes I did." Hugh said.

"Yes." I answered.

"I'm glad. Thank you." he said looking in Hugh's general direction.

"Glad I could help." Hugh said bowing politely.

Ethan returned to his room, shutting the door quietly behind him.

"I can't believe you did that." I said.

He shrugged. "The idea just came to me."

"I am glad it did." Without thinking about it I stood on my tiptoes and kissed him on the cheek.

He took a step backwards and put his fingers to his face. I felt my own face turning crimson in the darkness of the hallway.

"Sorry."

"Don't be."

I pretended to yawn. "I think I will go back to sleep for a bit." I rushed into my room. I dove headfirst onto the bed and pulled the covers over my red face.

Chapter 25

Hugh felt a little dizzy as he sat in the attic shuffling his cards. He couldn't remember the last time he had been kissed by someone who meant it. He had spent a decent amount of time with women when he was alive. They were never serious relationships, the type of women he met were similar to him, nameless and constantly on the move. The last truly sincere kiss was from his mother the night before she died. She had said goodnight to him outside his bedroom door, the next time he saw her she was dead.

He had never had a chance to truly fall in love. There had been a few minor attachments, but looking back he realized they were mostly one sided. He had once thought himself to be in love with an innkeeper's daughter. He spent an entire six months in one town courting her. It turned out that she was working with the sheriff, he didn't find that part out until he was in the courtroom being tried. Best not to think of the past he told himself.

His cheek still burned, his skin felt warm and alive. He knew Emma had embarrassed herself so he didn't linger in front of her door. He would have felt the same way at her age. She had no idea that there was very little that could embarrass or shock him now, he had seen it all over the last century.

The day was going splendidly so far. Eve was engaged and Senator Brown was out of the picture. He could not wait to see that old man's face when he found out Eve was taken. Hugh wasn't sure why Edward wanted to wait until after Christmas but he must have a good reason. The nailing of the secret door was a tragedy. Of course it had been closed off before, a secret door is never a good idea in any home.

The attic filled with bright morning light. A shadow suddenly fell over the day. Hugh knew without looking up that Mika had arrived.

"I thought you were going away for a while." Hugh said.

"I did."

"That was just a few weeks ago." he said looking up. Mika was standing in the middle of the attic staring at him.

"Not long enough for you?"

Not by a long shot Hugh thought to himself. "I thought you meant a *really* long time."

"Time is irrelevant." Mika said with a wave of his hand. "At least to me." He had a faint smile at the corner of his mouth, as though he knew something Hugh didn't. "How long do you plan on shuffling those stolen cards?"

Hugh stopped and looked guiltily at Edward's brand new cards. "I don't know. Do you want me to put them back?"

"As though you really would. You've stolen every deck of cards that has ever been in this house." He sat on the floor opposite Hugh. "Why don't you deal them out?"

Hugh shifted uncomfortably. "You want to play?"

"Why not? What's that game you've been teaching the Torment Seer?"

"Uh, Tribute?"

"Yes, deal that out."

Hugh dealt the cards. "Do you know how to play?"

"Of course I do." Mika picked up his cards without looking at them. He put them on the floor face down and fanned them out. "I start?" Hugh nodded. Mika picked up the top card from the reserve pile, he didn't look at it, but simply added it to his cards on the floor. He then discarded one of his own.

They played several turns in silence. Mika never looked at his cards, but it was clear to Hugh he was winning the game. They continued on until Hugh couldn't stand the silence any longer.

"Did you have a nice trip?"

"What?" Mika asked as though Hugh had broken his train of thought.

"You said you were going somewhere."

"Yes I did, didn't I? It was fine, nothing you need to concern yourself with. I am allowed to conduct some personal errands you know."

"Of course." Hugh looked at his cards, he was hopelessly losing.

"Ah ha!" Mika cried. He put his cards face up on the floor. "Tribute!"

"Ugh."

"What's the matter? Not used to losing?" Mika smirked.

"You're a cheater. You obviously know what the cards are without looking at them. You must be able to see what I have."

"Maybe I'm just really smart. Besides, I can't help it." Mika shrugged. "The same way you can't help interfering with that girl Eve."

Hugh swallowed. He knew this was coming. "I just didn't think it was fair that her father was pushing her to marry the old man."

"You're here to Torment, not to help a teenage girl get engaged. Do you even remember Charlie? He lost his life because of you."

"I remember." Hugh knew he hadn't been thinking of Charlie. Since Emma and her family had moved in he had scarcely thought about his death at all.

"As I suspected you've forgotten your purpose here."

"It's hard to when I have someone to talk to."

"Oh yes I know. You follow her around like a lost puppy. You're still dead you know. That will never change."

"I know."

"Torment Seers." Mika sneered.

"I thought you said you were a Seer."

"Yes, but not like her. That's little better than a parlor magician." He picked up the cards and began shuffling. "Shall we play again?"

"Aren't you going to tell me more? What kind of Seer were you? Like Ethan or Emma?"

"What do you care what kind of Seer I was? A month or two ago you didn't even know we existed."

"You never tell me anything about yourself."

"I don't have to tell you anything. You're supposed to listen to my guidance not my life story."

"But wouldn't part of your guidance come from your own life experience? Isn't that how it works?"

Mika put down the cards. "I was not a nice person when I was alive."

"I wasn't either."

"No, you were a thief. That was your profession. You were never a cruel person, you never harmed anyone." There was a softness to his voice that Hugh rarely heard. "I used people. I did whatever it took to get what I wanted and it worked. I became rich and successful and had everything I desired in life."

"But you were miserable?"

"Yes. I couldn't understand why I was so unhappy. You name it, I had it. But I wasn't satisfied, it was never enough. Then one day someone decided to murder me."

"You were murdered too?"

"Yes. But you're not seeing my point."

"What is it then?" Hugh asked. "I know that money and power corrupt. Just because I lived long ago doesn't mean I don't understand how the world works."

"I wanted money and especially power so I could feel acceptable. I always felt different, abnormal. My brother used to call me a freak."

"Brothers can be like that. Was it because you could see dead people?"

"Yes dead souls and other things. But I didn't see it as a gift then. It just set me apart from everyone else. People could sense something in me, but they didn't know what it was. I didn't know anyone who was like me, and I was already different enough in other ways."

"Like what?"

Mika stared at him. Hugh half expected him to get up and leave. "My name is Mikhail Valerevich Vernikov and-"

"I thought I had a long name."

Mika looked annoyed at being interrupted. "You do. As I was trying to say that is my name. I was born in Russia, I moved to America when I was five. I grew up in a time when Russians were hated. I was called names every day in school. I didn't have many friends."

"Russia is so far away. What a long journey. Why did you leave?"

"Do you really want to hear this?"

"Yes."

"We left because my family was in danger of being sent to the Gulag."

"What's that?"

"It's a prison work camp."

"Prison." Hugh could relate to that. "Was your family doing something illegal?"

Mika looked insulted. "Of course not. My father is a physicist and my mother has a PhD in botany. They wanted to send us there because we're Jewish."

"You're Jewish? Since when?"

"Since I was born." Mika snapped. "Stalin was sending Jewish intellectuals to the camps and my father was sure that we were next. That's why we left."

"Was Stalin the czar?"

"Sort of."

Hugh was confused. "You come here every Christmas to see me."

"So?"

"So, you don't celebrate Christmas."

"Is this a problem for you?"

"No. I used to live across the street from a rabbi. Remember? I was quite enamored with his daughter. I think her name was Amelia."

Mika looked disgusted. "What's wrong with you? She had horse teeth."

"She did not. She was pretty." Hugh insisted. He couldn't exactly remember Amelia, but he was certain she had nothing in common with a horse. "What else?"

"What?"

"Tell me something else."

"Like what?"

Hugh tried to think. "Were you married?"

"Yes."

"What was your profession?"

"You won't understand it."

"Why? Do you think I'm that unsophisticated?"

Mika sighed. "I have degrees in aerospace engineering, and physics. I owned my own technology firm and we specialized in-"

"You're right. I don't understand." Hugh admitted. "Did you have any children?"

A strange look crossed his face. "Enough questions. Do you want to play again or what?"

Hugh would have preferred to hear more about Mika. "I don't suppose I have a chance of winning?"

"Not really. I rarely lose at anything." He dealt out the cards, once again not looking at his own. They began another game in silence. "Will you just play your king already?"

Hugh realized he was holding up the game. "Yes, I think I will." He tossed the king on the discard pile.

Mika smirked and threw his cards down. "Tribute!"

"This is pointless."

"Don't feel bad, technically I'm a genius."

"I thought you weren't going to tell me anything else."

"You should have figured that one out for yourself." Mika said. "Had enough of cards?"

"Yes."

"What else shall we talk about?"

"Shouldn't you be going?"

Mika shrugged. "I have nowhere to be." He tapped his fingers on the floor. "I know. Let's talk about you. You got kissed tonight."

"It's not like that. Emma is a little girl. She was thanking me for helping Eve. What's wrong with that?"

"Nothing. Don't get so defensive Hugh. You haven't been kissed for a very long time, especially by someone who meant it. I thought you might have liked it. When a living person touches you it's quite a shock. Literally."

"I've noticed." Hugh said squirming.

"It can be quite addicting."

"Is that so?"

"Oh yes. Lifeforce is more powerful than we can ever understand when we're alive. It can do things you can't even imagine."

"And how do you know all this? That must mean you've been touched by someone who is alive."

Mika smiled. "I'm not sure you're old enough to hear that story. You might get embarrassed. Maybe in another hundred years."

"Oh come now."

Mika suddenly held up his hand. "I have to go." he said darkly. "Something's wrong." Before Hugh could respond he was gone.

Chapter 26

As I opened my eyes the next morning it all came back to me in a sudden burst of memory. I kissed Hugh. I pulled the covers over my face. What on earth must he think of me? How was I going to face him? I wondered how long I could stay in my room. Eventually he and the rest of my family would come looking for me. Already there were noises coming from the kitchen below.

I waited a few more minutes and then climbed out of bed. The floor boards were cold. I hurried to my bureau and got dressed. I put on a pair of woolen socks and carefully opened my bedroom door. Thankfully Hugh was not there.

I breathed a sigh of relief and treaded quietly downstairs. The rest of the family was already in the kitchen. Hugh was lingering by the window. He looked up and smiled. I felt my face getting hot as I slid into my chair.

"Good morning Emma." Eve said. Her face was beaming as she spoke. It was the happiest I had seen her in weeks.

"We were just talking about church this morning." Father said.

"Oh?" I had forgotten it was Sunday.

"Yes, about Senator Brown actually." He looked sideways at Eve.

Hugh remained quiet as he peered out the window.

"I can do it." Eve said. "Now that I know I don't have to marry him I can put up with his attention for one morning."

"Not a word from anyone about Scott Cooper." Father warned. We all agreed, even Ethan who was busy eating his oatmeal and reading a book.

Hugh was silent all through breakfast. It began to trouble me. Maybe he was angry. Perhaps ghosts weren't supposed to be kissed by the living, it was certainly a first for me. Or maybe he just didn't like me being that affectionate. I was after all just a girl and he was a grown man.

As soon as breakfast ended we went our separate ways to begin getting ready for church. I ran upstairs to get my shoes expecting Hugh to follow me, but he did not. I came back downstairs looking for him, my stomach felt heavy. I didn't want him to be upset. I didn't want him not speaking to me. He was in the parlor sitting on the sofa, no one else seemed to be around.

"Good morning." There was a strain of caution in his voice.

"Good morning." I took a small step forward.

"Off to church then?"

"Yes."

"Emma-"

"I am so sorry about what I did last night. I don't know what I was thinking. I was so grateful to you for helping Eve and then I went and acted so stupidly. I don't know why I did it. Just forget about it." I stammered, my face burning hotly. I had never felt so foolish.

Hugh smiled gently. "You don't need to apologize Emma."

"I don't? Aren't you angry with me? You've hardly said a word." The pressure in the pit of my stomach began to lessen.

He stretched his legs out in front of him. "I knew you were embarrassed."

I nodded, feeling even more humiliated at his noticing my embarrassment. "Thanks." I mumbled. I began to wish that one of my family members would appear and end this mortifying conversation.

"Come here." he said. I glanced over my shoulder. No one was coming. I sat on the couch next to him. He held out his pale hand, his skin was bluish and almost translucent. "Take it."

His fingers were icy. His arm jerked as I touched him. I pulled my hand away.

"Don't." he said shaking his head. I took his hand again, his cold fingers wrapped around mine. His arm moved slightly but he seemed able to control it this time.

I wasn't sure what was supposed to be happening. My fingertips felt cold as I held his hand. He closed his eyes and kept his body still.

We sat like that for a minute or two then he opened his eyes and smiled. "Look." Our skin tones were nearly the same, his hand looked peachy and warm.

"How?" I asked looking from his flushed hand to his pale face.

"It's you. It's life."

"I'm doing that?"

"Yes."

"How does it feel?" I asked.

"It's-"

"Emma! Are you ready?" Father was standing in the door of the parlor. I dropped my hand to my side and ran into the hall without looking back.

Everyone except me walked to church with a spring in their step. I would have preferred to spend the day with Hugh. But family duty called so there I was heading into town.

Shortly we passed the Coopers. Margaret was on the porch smoking a cigarette, a toddler played quietly at her feet. Scott was next to her reading a book, as we approached he stood up. "Good morning." He ran down the steps and stopped in front of Eve. "For my fiancé." he said handing her a small nosegay of wildflowers.

Eve held them to her nose, breathing in the sweet scent. "Thank you."

"I'll see you later?" Scott asked.

Eve bit her lip and looked at Father. He nodded.

"Yes."

"Thank you." Scott vigorously shook Father's hand.

"Not at all young man." Father said patting his stomach. "And how are you Mrs. Cooper?"

Margaret took a puff on her cigarette. "I am fine Mr. Hollis. We will be family soon." Mother started to cough.

We continued on towards town passing old man Johnson's house which looked abandoned as usual. "They say he doesn't have much time left now." Father said quietly. The curtains were closed and weeds had grown through the brick path out front. I had never seen anyone visit old man Johnson, but everyone seemed to know his daily condition.

Senator Brown was waiting for us in front of the church. His face lit up behind his bushy beard as we came up the walk. Mr. White was standing at his side. Both of their eyes followed Eve as she carried her flowers in her hand.

"Senator Brown!" Eve cried. "And Mr. White, what a pleasant surprise to see you here."

"Thank you Miss Hollis, you look lovely." Mr. White said sheepishly.

"Really?" Eve asked as though she had never received a compliment before.

"Yes indeed." said the Senator. "And who did you get that from?" He pointed to the flowers. "An admirer I suppose."

"A hopeless admirer I am afraid." Eve looked helplessly into the Senator's face. "I told him my heart is regrettably taken by another."

"Oh my." said Senator Brown, his voice rising up as though someone had tickled him.

"Perhaps we should go inside." Father suggested.

"Shall we?" The Senator held his arm out.

"Oh yes." Eve took his arm and they went into the church followed by Mr. White.

Ethan and I lagged behind the rest of the group. Senator Brown and Eve were watched closely by the congregation. "Isn't she lovely?", "What a striking couple." I heard whispered as we walked to the front row.

"Good grief." Ethan muttered under his breath.

The service was the same as all the others I had attended so far. Reverend Monk talked endlessly. I only listened when he mentioned something about dying and then again when he said the word "afterlife". I wondered if he saw things the way Ethan and I did. Was it a prerequisite for being a man of God? Maybe I would ask Hugh.

Eve sat snugly next to Senator Brown, she appeared to listen carefully as he leaned in and whispered something in her ear. Father fidgeted in his seat as he watched them. As soon as the service ended he stood up and suggested we all get some fresh air.

We filed back outside into the sunlight. Father shook the Senator's hand. "Best to be off."

"What's the hurry? Good heavens Edward you're as jumpy as a cat in a room full of rocking chairs." He looked at Eve and smiled. She nodded in approval of his quick wit.

"Ah yes. I think my wife is not feeling well." Father looked desperately at Mother.

"I am a bit tired." Mother confirmed.

"Nonsense. I've arranged to have luncheon prepared. You need to do nothing more than sit Mrs. Hollis, that's far better than having to go home and prepare a meal."

"Um." Father began.

"Oh do come." said Mr. White. "The Senator has the most delightful cook. I eat there every Sunday and any other chance I get."

"He does too." Brown poked Mr. White in the stomach. "Someday we'll find him a wife and I'll never see him. What do you say Edward? I am sure we are all hungry."

"I think it's a splendid idea." Eve said suddenly.

"You do?" Father raised his eyebrows.

"Yes."

Father nodded meekly and took Mother's arm. "Let's go then."

"Excellent! Right this way young lady." The Senator said to Eve. She turned her head and looked at me, she rolled her eyes and grinned.

I had never visited Senator Brown's house but I had seen it many times. It was called Brown Park and was located on Brown Lane, built high on a bluff overlooking the ocean. It was three stories made of a gray stone. The windows were tall with a stained glass design featuring a brown "B". An odd looking flag flew from the highest peak. Ethan said it was a coat of arms.

Besides the entry on Brown Lane the house could be reached by a small footpath running from behind the church and across the open bluff. We had to walk single file on the uneven path, the wind coming off the ocean blew fiercely at us. More than once my foot turned and I nearly tumbled down the steep hill. Ethan caught my arm and shook his head in frustration.

"This walk will be the death of us." he said.

We all survived and shortly arrived at a plain oak door on the side of the house.

"Welcome. Welcome." Brown said as he opened the door. We filed inside windblown and hungry.

He brought us down a wide hall that opened to a large foyer. It was painted a dark shade of green, the walls were covered with several large paintings. A staircase with a highly polished banister stood nearby. I noticed even the steps were carpeted. I had never been in such a fancy house.

"Dinner awaits." said the Senator. He ushered us into another room which turned out to be the dining room. It was painted blue and white with a large gilded mirror on one wall and a window looking out on the garden on the other. The table was set for dinner with shiny white and gold plates. Two men dressed in matching outfits were standing at the end of the room with their hands behind their backs. Father was right, the Senator had a lot of money.

Next to each plate was a little card with a name on it. I found mine and sat down. I was glad to find I was far away from the Senator. As soon as we were seated the two men went to work serving us an endless array of food. For a long time I paid little attention to anything else, there were far too many good things to eat.

As my belly filled I became aware of a lot of dull conversation. Senator Brown, Mr. White and Father were discussing politics. Eve and Ethan were quietly talking about something that had happened at school last week while Mother stared at her plate. She looked up and gave me a weak smile.

I snapped a piece of bacon in half. I was about to eat it when I heard a voice behind me. "Damned people cluttering up my house. Gobbling like hogs too." I looked over my shoulder and saw an old woman shuffling through the wall. She had no obvious physical injuries however the fact that she was passing through the dining room wall confirmed she was dead. I turned my head hoping she wouldn't notice I could see her.

I kept my head down as she passed by Senator Brown's chair. "Dregs of society, that's what they are." Her clothes were soiled and torn, her silvery hair stuck out at odd angles.

Out of the corner of my eye I saw her coming towards me. Still mumbling she passed a hand through Mr. White's head, and then Mother's. They ate their meal unaware. Don't, I thought. Don't try it with me.

The old woman continued towards me, her hand outstretched. I almost shouted for her to stop, but I could not. I waited, holding my breath. As her hand came near me I bent over as if to check my shoe. She barely missed me. Barely. Her hand brushed the top of my head. If I had only ducked a little farther we would have never made contact.

"What's this?" She stopped behind my chair. I looked straight ahead as she poked the back of my head. By now Ethan, who was across the table, realized what was happening. He swallowed nervously.

"Hey you." She poked me again. I held as still as I could, hoping no one would notice my head pitching back and forth. "You're a Seer, ain't you? I've seen your kind before. And you're not the only one in the room, are you?"

I looked desperately at Ethan. He put down his fork. "Senator, if I might interrupt. I was wondering if I could show Emma the library."

Senator Brown stopped mid chew. "What my boy?"

"I thought I might show Emma the library."

"Ethan we are still eating." Mother protested.

"Oh, so you're trying to get away from me, eh?" said the old woman. "No one gets away from Ma Granger." She grabbed one of my braids and yanked on it.

"Ouch!" I cried, grabbing my head.

Everyone stopped eating and stared at me. "What on earth is wrong with you?" Mother said. She nudged me under the table with her foot.

"I, I-" There was no time to finish as Ma Granger took my other braid in her hand and proceeded to pull me off my chair and onto the floor.

"That'll teach you to sass Ma Granger."

By now dinner was completely disrupted. Everyone was out of their seats. Mr. White helped me to my feet while Mother scowled at me. A beating was in my future.

"Stop this right now." She hissed under her breath.

"Is that your Ma?" Ma Granger shouted in my ear. "I'll fix her for you. I don't like the looks of her anyway, looks like a painted woman I used to know."

"Don't do anything. Please." I said aloud.

Mother's face went red. "I can't believe you're doing this again."

"Your Ma's not a believer eh?"

"No." I answered. I glanced at Senator Brown and Mr. White. They looked completely baffled.

"I could show her a thing or two."

"It's time for you to go home young lady." Mother said. I nodded in agreement.

"I have to admit I am a bit confused." Mr. White said.

"My sister sometimes has episodes like this." Eve told him.

"Let's go shall we?" Father said. "I think we are all tired."

"If you must." The Senator threw his napkin on the table and glared at me. "Let me show you out."

"Don't trouble yourself Hershival. We can find our way." Father circled around the table and took my arm.

"Going so soon?" Ma Granger said. "I've haven't even had a chance to tell you how I died. It was ever so gruesome."

Father guided me out of the dining room towards the front door with the rest of the family and Ma Granger following.

"I hope you feel better." Mr. White said as we left.

"You must come back again Seer." Ma Granger called out. She passed through Eve and Mother and stood behind me in the front hall. "He's lying to you. He's not what he appears."

"Who is?"

"Emma, stop this!" Mother cried.

"Him." Ma Granger said vaguely.

"Hugh?"

"Who's that? I don't know anyone called Hugh. The liar is in this house right now, he's a liar and he knows it." Her wrinkled face lit up as she laughed. She clapped her hands together and passed through the wall and out of sight.

Chapter 27

Hugh spent the morning reading. The book that had been in Edward and Elsay's bedside table had finally found its way onto a small shelf in the corner of their bedroom. Hugh swiped it after they left for church. It was the usual sort of cheap overdramatic piffle, but he loved to read and it was a diversion from the monotony of Torment.

It was mid-afternoon when he heard the latch on the front door. He dropped the book on the floor and ran downstairs. The Hollis family ambled through the door looking weary and cross.

"Upstairs. All of you." Elsay said.

"I didn't do anything." Eve moaned.

"I don't care. I need to talk with your father. Upstairs, now." Elsay pulled her hat off.

"Do as your mother tells you." Edward said.

"Bad morning in church?" Hugh asked as Emma trudged up the stairs followed by Ethan and Eve. Once they were on the second floor and out of their parents earshot Eve ripped into Emma.

"Why do you always do that?" she said coldly.

"I can't help it." Emma said hiccupping. She was on the verge of tears.

"It's not her fault." Ethan said.

Eve rolled her eyes. "Come on Ethan she's been doing this since she was little. Claiming to see things that aren't there, and she's got you doing it too."

"You don't believe either of us?" Ethan asked.

Eve crossed her arms. "No, frankly I don't."

"I could make her believe in two seconds." Hugh said feeling his temper rise. Emma's shoulders were shaking. She wiped her eyes and took a deep breath.

"Why would we make this up?" Emma sniffed. "I'm probably going to be whipped or worse."

Eve shrugged. "Attention. You have a sister who's engaged and a brother who's going to medical school. Why shouldn't you feel like you have to work extra hard to get noticed?"

There was a tone of superiority that Hugh recognized. Patrick used to talk to him like that. He used to accuse Hugh of trying to be like him, or being envious of him. Older siblings, he thought grumpily. As though he would be jealous of a prattling lawyer like Patrick.

"How can you say that to her after all we've done for you?" Ethan asked.

"That's right." Hugh said. "And I did the most of all."

"All you've done for me? You haven't done anything for me."

"Ha." Ethan laughed. "And besides what do you care if Senator Brown thinks we're both crazy? You can't stand him. I would think you would be thanking us for getting you out of there so soon."

"I can't stand him, but that doesn't mean I want to be completely humiliated in front of him. What must Mr. White think of us?" Eve shook her head.

"Who cares what he thinks?" Ethan said.

"That's right." Hugh agreed, although he had no idea who this Mr. White was.

Eve ignored his question. "I'm going to meet Scott."

"You're supposed to stay here." Ethan said.

"I am not in trouble, you are." She smirked and turned on her heel, passing quickly through Hugh. He couldn't help but notice her lavender perfume. She ran downstairs and out the front door.

"I can't believe her." Ethan said hotly.

"She's just embarrassed." Emma said quietly.

"You're being too nice. Now I wish she was marrying Senator Brown."

"Me too." Hugh agreed.

"Don't say that." Emma dried her eyes. "She just likes being the center of attention, that's all, she's used to it. I have a headache."

"What on earth happened today?" Hugh asked.

Emma rubbed her forehead. "There's a ghost, a Tormented Soul in Senator Brown's house."

"Really?" He felt a thrill run through his dead body. He wasn't the only one.

"She took hold of my braids and pulled me off my chair and onto the floor, right in the middle of dinner."

"I haven't used that trick in decades. There was this rotten little girl who lived here and once I- Oh never mind."

"I hate it when you two start talking. How am I supposed to follow along?" Ethan asked.

"Sorry Ethan."

"You can fill me in later Emma. It's impossible to talk to him. I'll be in my room studying." Ethan took a book from his coat pocket and went into his bedroom.

Emma continued to rub her head as she walked into her room. Hugh followed her, shutting the door politely behind him. "Who was she? Did she say her name?"

"What?" Emma sat on the edge of her bed.

"Did the dead person give you a name?"

"Oh. Ma Granger. She was an old woman in really tattered clothes."

"Ma Granger huh?" Hugh rubbed his chin and looked thoughtfully into the air.

"Do you know her?"

"No."

"It sounded like you did."

"I know, didn't it?" Hugh chuckled. He was still a pretty good liar.

"She mentioned something else too." Emma said, ignoring his clever fibbing.

"What's that?" He was intrigued by the possibility of gossip. He sat on a stiff horsehair chair in the corner. It was the type of chair that the living typically avoided, it was as uncomfortable as hell. Hugh didn't mind however as he had no need for comfort.

"She said that he was lying and he knew it."

"He who?"

Emma shrugged. "I don't know."

"She definitely said the word he?"

"Yes."

"Who were the males in the room?" he asked.

"There was Father, Ethan, Senator Brown and Mr. White."

"Who is this Mr. White?"

"He's a lawyer."

"Well there you have it."

Emma's face clouded. "I don't know. It was really strange."

"She was probably just saying that to upset you. Who knows how many blows to the head this woman took before she died."

"I don't know."

"Oh forget about it. Let's go upstairs and play cards." he said trying to lighten her mood.

"They still haven't decided on my punishment."

"Punishment? For what?"

"For falling off the chair, for talking to Ma Granger when I was supposed to pretend she wasn't there." Emma sniffed.

"How can they? It wasn't your fault."

"They always do." A single tear ran down her cheek.

Hugh remained in his chair. He wasn't sure what he should do. Comforting women, or more precisely girls, was beyond his scope. Most of the women he had known were skilled in comforting him. Still he had to do something, he couldn't let her just sit there and cry. Suddenly the door opened and Edward walked in looking grim.

"At least I knock on the door." Hugh told him.

"Emma." Edward said gravely.

"I know." She got up and followed her father out of the door.

"This is completely ludicrous." Hugh said. It was time to give Edward Hollis a good hard kick in the behind.

Chapter 28

There was no use fighting. When my parents made up their minds about a punishment they stuck to it. It was best to get it over with.

Father followed me downstairs with Hugh close behind. I heard a strange noise followed by a muttered swear.

"That serves you right." Hugh said.

"Move a little faster Emma." Father told me.

"What's the matter?" I stopped on the landing. Father wiped his brow with his handkerchief. Hugh was lurking behind him looking gleeful.

"Let's get this over with. Straight to the parlor for you young lady."

"Edward, you are an ass." Hugh exclaimed.

I continued downstairs and into the parlor. Mother was there with a wood switch in her hand.

"You are not going to hit her with that!" Hugh cried. "I'm going to stop this."

I kept silent. If Hugh wanted to try something I would have to let him.

"Emma you know your mother and I don't want to do this, but you've left us no choice." Father said. "You have continued to disobey us year after year."

"Something has to be done." Mother tapped the switch nervously on her other hand.

"I know you believe me. You asked me if there were any ghosts in this house just the other day. You wouldn't have done that if you didn't believe me." I said swallowing hard and holding my breath.

Mother's face went white. A minute passed in awkward silence.

Finally Father spoke. "Did you ask her that Elsay?"

"Yes."

"Elsay-"

"Edward, don't say it." She threw the switch on the sofa and folded her arms across her chest.

Father looked at me. "Go upstairs."

"Am I still going to be punished?"

Father knelt down and looked me in the eyes. "You're going to have to pretend you don't see anything. I know you can do it."

"How?" I asked, automatically looking at Hugh.

"What are you looking at?" Mother cried.

"Emma, you're going to have to pretend." Father said. "No matter what."

I nodded.

"Now go upstairs." He squeezed my shoulders and kissed me on the forehead.

"Yes Father."

"It's about time that you two straightened up." Hugh said looking at my parents. He leaned over the back of the sofa and took the discarded switch. My parents were too busy watching me to notice. Hugh laughed and vanished through the blocked secret door.

"Upstairs Emma. Now." Mother said avoiding my eyes. "And tell Ethan to come down here, we need to talk to him."

"Yes Mother." I went upstairs and knocked on Ethan's door. He was lying on his bed reading. Hugh was nearby twirling the switch in his hand.

"Guess who's here?" Ethan took off his glasses. "Can you tell him to stop fiddling with that stick, it's driving me crazy." He rubbed his eyes and put his glasses back on. I realized that to Ethan's eyes the switch appeared to be dancing in midair.

"Very well." Hugh set it aside. "I was having fun."

"They want to see you downstairs."

"How bad was it?" Ethan asked.

"I didn't get punished. I have to ignore the dead people when I see them."

"Except for me." Hugh added.

"And how are you supposed to do that? That thing pulled you by the hair." Ethan said.

"I don't know. I just have to."

"I wish I could go over there. I would tell this Ma Granger a thing or two." Hugh said.

"Hopefully that's the last time you'll ever have to set foot in that house."

"I hope so. I don't see any reason to go back. Ethan, Ma Granger said something funny today."

"Who is Ma Granger?"

"The ghost in Senator Brown's house. She said that one of the men in the room was a liar."

"Really? What could that mean?"

"I don't know."

Hugh picked up a book and began thumbing through the pages.

"Which one of them would be lying? Maybe Senator Brown or Mr. White?"

"Ah, the mysterious Mr. White." Hugh said from behind the book.

"Say, does he have to look at my books?" Ethan asked.

"What do you want him to do? He's got a lot of time on his hands and he likes to read."

"That's right." Hugh agreed.

Ethan sighed. "The only other two were Father and I. Father has nothing to hide and I am certainly no liar."

"My boy when I was your age I excelled at lying." Hugh clapped the book shut. "This is awful, who wants to read about the digestive system? I'll take a cheap novel any day."

"He's got to study, he's going to be a doctor." I said to Hugh. "You should go Ethan."

"All right." Ethan stood up and left the room.

"You don't think Ethan is hiding something do you?" I asked Hugh.

He looked at me for a second and then smiled. "Let's go upstairs so I can beat you at Tribute."

"I might win."

"Perhaps." he shrugged. "I got beaten horribly by Mika the other day. My ego is still a bit bruised."

"Mika plays cards?"

"Oh yes, he's doing all sorts of unusual things these days. Come upstairs and I'll tell you all about it." He held out his pale hand.

It was like holding a block of ice. His arm jerked, he shut his eyes for a second and then smiled. "I'm sorry." I said.

"It's just life." He laughed and ran out of Ethan's bedroom with me following close behind.

Chapter 29

Hugh was happier than he had ever been. It was mostly because of Emma, but each one of the Hollis family played their own part. Hugh had come to enjoy spending his days with Elsay. He liked following her from room to room, she accomplished her tasks with such tidy efficiency that Hugh found it soothing. Proof of her dedication was everywhere. The windows were now hung with cheery curtains and the tables and dressers were topped in fancy crocheted doilies. The walls had been whitewashed and the floor covered in homemade rugs. He couldn't remember the last time the house was so snug.

Edward was away a good deal of the time. But when he was home Hugh liked to watch him strut about like a proud rooster watching over his hens. He was apparently making a success of the barber shop. Hugh was reminded of his own father when Edward came home and lined his shoes up perfectly by the front door, hung his hat carefully on the hook and straightened his hair before he called out to the family to announce his arrival. Elsay and the children would gather in the front hall and ask him about his day, just as Hugh's own family had done years before.

Hugh rarely saw Eve anymore. She spent afternoons at the Coopers and after supper she actually studied in her room before going to bed. The closing of the secret door had severely curtailed her nighttime activities. He missed following her down the stairs to rendezvous with Scott, her perfume wafting behind her, the folds of her skirt swinging gently with her hips.

Hugh didn't bother following Ethan anywhere. He was usually reading and other than the occasional bump into a wall when he wasn't looking where he was going, there was little enjoyment in watching a future doctor study.

Then there was Emma. She was the best friend he had ever had. He had never had many friends growing up. Usually he stuck with his brother Connelly, both of them ended up criminals so perhaps that had never been a good idea. After the fire he had been on his own, it was a risk to form friendships, people could never be trusted, it was better to go it alone.

But now he had Emma right under his roof. She was a patient listener, especially when he droned on about all the years he spent in the house and the people who lived there. He sometimes had to edit certain stories due to her age, but he would retell them later with all the details when she was older. She always seemed glad to see him and wanted to know what his day had been like.

He was glad she was young. She still had the optimism for life that comes with youth. She hadn't experienced real disappointment yet, the kind that changes and hardens the shell we all have around us. It made him think back to before the fire, when he had a family, how different his life was then. Her enthusiasm was infectious, he felt young again at one hundred and thirty five.

He couldn't wait for her to get home each day and come upstairs. She would drop her school books and immediately they would begin a game of Tribute while he told her about his day. Then it would be her turn to give him a detailed account of what happened at school complete with direct quotes and town gossip from Candy Cooper. Later there would be a family dinner followed by studying in the parlor where Hugh would sit on a chair in the corner and pretend he was one of them.

Occasionally Emma would be allowed to go to her room early. They would take turns using the telescope. She did most of the actual stargazing while he generally waited and watched for a drunken Michael Cooper to stumble onto his front porch. When Emma was ready for bed Hugh would return to the attic and his lone book, he had already read it twice.

His blissful existence was interrupted one day in December when Elsay went up to the attic. He was lying on the floor staring up at the ceiling thinking about nothing in particular.

"Humph." she muttered. He sat up and watched as her eyes scanned the room. Suddenly her gaze settled on the book Hugh had taken from her bedroom. He had carelessly tossed it in the corner.

"Ah ha." she said licking her lips. She snatched the book and opened it to where Hugh had folded the corner of the page down. "Emma." she muttered, slamming the book shut. She started to leave when she suddenly spied the cards lying on the windowsill. "What's this?" She picked them up. "You'll pay for this girl."

"No, wait!" Hugh cried to no effect. "It was me, your resident thief, not Emma."

He followed Elsay downstairs where she put the book and the cards on the kitchen table. She folded her arms and looked out the window. Emma would be home soon.

"You've got it all wrong." Hugh moaned. There was nothing he could do. He stood behind Elsay and watched out the window with her.

A half hour passed. Elsay paced back and forth muttering to herself. Finally Eve came into view with her books tucked under her arm. Her golden hair was loose and shone like straw in the mid-afternoon sun. Hugh couldn't help but be impressed.

"Where's Emma?" Elsay called out as Eve walked in the front door.

"What?" Eve put her books down and pulled her coat off.

"Where's Emma?" Elsay repeated.

"I don't know. She's coming. What's wrong?"

"Never mind. Go to your room. Or better yet go and see Scott."

"Really?" Eve asked, her eyes wide with delight. "Oh thank you Mother." She pulled her coat back on and ran out the door. From the window Hugh watched her hurry to the Coopers' house. As Eve passed by the window Ethan came into the view, surprisingly he was not reading a book but simply staring straight ahead. He looked annoyed. A second later Hugh discovered why. He was being followed by a red haired girl that he now knew was Candy Cooper. Emma was right behind them.

Ethan came in the house. "I don't think she ever stops talking." He took off his wool cap and gloves. "I'll be upstairs."

Elsay pulled back her shoulders and stared into the front hallway. Emma arrived with Candy.

"And then Pa threw up all over the table, it was so awful, but then Ma says better at home than in the gutter." Candy was saying. Emma nodded and took off her coat. She hung it next to Ethan's cap. She turned around and found her mother staring at her.

"Hello." She glanced nervously at Hugh.

"Greetings Mrs. Hollis." Candy said smiling widely. Her coat was far too big for her and came almost to her ankles. She wore one white mitten and one green glove, her fiery red hair hung limply down her back.

"I need to speak with you Emma. Now." Elsay crossed her arms.

"Oh I know that look." Candy said. "My Ma looks like that just before she's about to give us a walloping. My Pa gets that look too, but he's usually too drunk to do much walloping. Ma says liquor makes him cross eyed, one time he tried to hit me and he ended up socking Scott. Lucky for me."

"Candy I think you should go home." Elsay said.

"What's wrong?" Emma asked.

"Goodbye Candy." Elsay said sharply.

Candy shrugged and pushed up the sleeves on her coat. "Oh well. I guess you're gettin' a lickin' Emma. See you later!" She skipped out the door.

"What's the matter? What did I do?" Emma's eyes wandered to the kitchen table with the book and the cards. Hugh could tell she was thinking of an explanation.

"Would you like to tell me what these were doing in the attic?"

"I, I took them."

"Where did you get them from?"

Emma looked at him for help. He pointed towards the back bedroom.

"Your bedroom."

Elsay drew in a quick breath. "I knew someone had been in there. Emma Hollis you should be ashamed of yourself, sneaking around your parents' bedroom thieving. Wait until your father hears about this. What did you need with a deck of cards and this book?"

"I wanted to play with the cards."

"Do you know any games?"

Emma glanced at Hugh again. She ought to stop doing that or her mother might notice. A flicker of a smile crossed her face.

"Do you find this funny?"

"No."

"And how do you explain this book?" Elsay held up the cheap novel, its lurid cover screaming out in the conservative kitchen.

"I wanted to see what it was like."

"This is not the type of book a girl your age should be reading."

"Then why do you leave it lying around?" Hugh asked.

"I'm sorry Mother. I won't do it again." She wiped her eyes. Hugh wasn't sure if she was really crying or pretending.

Elsay nodded and reached for something on the windowsill, something Hugh hadn't noticed before. It was a ruler. "Oh come on Elsay. It was me, it was me."

"Hold out your hands." Emma did as she was told. "Will you go into my bedroom and steal again?"

"No." Emma said, her lips quivering.

"Of course not." Elsay slammed the ruler down on Emma's hands. She shut her eyes but not before a tear escaped and ran down her cheek.

"Say it." Elsay said.

"I won't go into your bedroom and steal."

Elsay nodded and raised the ruler again.

"No, I won't let this happen. I can't. You will not take a punishment for me." Hugh put his own hands over Emma's. Elsay lowered the ruler and unknowingly struck Hugh's knuckles. He stepped on Emma's toe and she cried out. She opened her eyes and looked up at him in surprise.

Emma's outburst seemed to convince Elsay that she had been struck. "Say it again."

"Cry out this time and rub your hands together so she doesn't see they're not getting red." Hugh told Emma.

"I won't go into your bedroom and steal." Once again Elsay slammed the ruler down on the back of Hugh's hands. He was grateful he felt no physical pain, she was giving it all she had. Emma cried out and clasped her hands together.

Elsay nodded satisfactorily. "Now if you promise to stay out of my bedroom I won't tell your father about this."

"I'll tell him about it, even if he can't hear me." Hugh said.

"Thank you Mother."

"Don't thank me. Stay out of places you don't belong." Elsay pointed the ruler in Emma's face. She scooped up the cards and the book and slipped them into her apron pocket.

Hugh sighed. How many years would it be before he had a chance at another deck of cards? "Nothing is my own."

Chapter 30

My hands stung despite being struck only once. Mother put the ruler away and started working at the stove.

"Nothing is my own." I heard Hugh say.

I didn't want to look at him. I felt terrible he had lost his cards and the book too.

"Go to your room." Mother said over her shoulder.

I turned and left the kitchen. Hugh didn't follow me. He was quiet the next few days. It was easy to see he was bored again. I noticed he had taken to opening and closing the doors downstairs and rearranging the pots and pans in the kitchen. If he kept that up it wouldn't be long before Mother would start to suspect the rumors about the house were true.

The week before Christmas I got an idea. We were finishing breakfast on a Saturday morning when Father suddenly stood up and stuck his thumbs in his vest pockets. He cleared his throat. "Children, I have an announcement. I am giving each of you five dollars to spend for Christmas."

"Five dollars! That could feed and clothe a village in my day" Hugh said. He was moping by the pantry door.

"Oh Father!" Eve clapped her hands together.

"Now this is to be spent on others, not yourself Eve."

"I knew that."

"Edward don't you think *five dollars* is a little excessive?" Mother asked.

"I do." Hugh said.

"Not to worry my dear. Old Brownie gave me a little bonus money today." Father patted his stomach. He reached into his pocket and took out three five dollar bills. He handed one to each of us. I had never had so much money in my life. "Spend it wisely children."

The three of us could not get out the door quick enough. It had snowed the night before. As I walked into town snow trickled down the top of my boots and melted around my toes. Once we were on Main Street Eve disappeared into a shop. Ethan and I walked for a little while together.

"What are you going to buy?" he asked.

"I'm not sure yet." I said vaguely.

"We really should do this separately. I might see something I want to get you."

"Yes, I think that's a good idea." I was relieved. I had a plan of my own and I didn't want to be seen, even by Ethan.

"I'll meet you at home then?"

"All right." He crossed the muddy street looking back over his shoulder. He watched me for a second. I realized he didn't want me to see where he was going. I smiled and set off towards a fancy shop for ladies that I had passed many times but never gone into.

Mother and Eve were easy to buy for. I had their gifts picked out right away, a hair comb for Eve and a lace collar for Mother. In the next shop I found quills and paper for Ethan. Father was the most difficult to buy for. I finally settled on a coin pouch.

I had just enough money left over to do what I had planned. I headed to Jennings' Emporium. Cole Jennings was a big man with a square head and tiny pinpoint eyes. He sweated profusely as he hustled around the store. "Can I help you Miss?" he asked as I stepped inside.

"Yes, um. I would like a deck of cards please."

"Cards, huh?" He scratched his square head and looked around the store. His eyes stopped on a particular shelf. He grabbed a pack of cards and slapped them on the counter. "Anything else?"

"Um, yes do you have any books?"

"Yup. Right over there." He motioned to a nearby shelf. I wandered over and looked at the titles. Half were different versions of the Bible, the others consisted of manuals on housekeeping and a few recipe books.

I turned back to Mr. Jennings who was mopping his brow with a cotton rag. "Do you have anything else?"

"Like what?"

"Novels?" Several customers stopped what they were doing and turned to look at me.

"Novels? What in God's name are those?" Mr. Jennings looked puzzled. "Oh you mean like the cheap trash they sell over there." He jerked his thumb towards the window. Across the street was another store, Thalberg's, I had never been in there.

"I don't know. I wanted something different than this."

"How old are you?"

"Twelve."

"What does a God fearing little girl want with cheap novels and playing cards?" He leaned over the counter and stared down at me. His square head was getting redder and redder.

"It's not for me, it's a Christmas present for someone else." I heard one of the customers snicker.

Mr. Jennings shook his head and put the cards away. "You're not getting these. You're not getting anything here. I want you out of this store now."

"What?"

"You heard me. I have two little girls living upstairs and I don't want your dark little soul corrupting them. Get out of here and don't come back." He pointed at the door.

"You don't want me coming back here?"

"No. Who's your father anyway? I want to warn him about you." He picked up a pencil and paper.

"I don't have one." I moved towards the door.

"Wait a minute!" He came out from behind the counter. "What's your name?"

I bolted out the door and ran across the road narrowly missing a team of horses coming up the street. The driver yelled at me. I leaned against the window of Thalberg's and caught my breath.

I was tempted to go home and forget the whole thing, but I couldn't. I wanted Hugh to have something of his own. I stamped the snow and mud off my boots and turned to look in Thalberg's window. A man looked back out at me with dark hair and eyes. He had a course black beard that equaled Senator Brown's. He nodded and motioned for me to come in.

I pulled open the door and stepped into the warm shop. There were no other customers inside. The man who had looked out the window was sitting behind a counter. "Good morning." he said with a slight accent. "Did Mr. Jennings ask you to leave?"

"Yes. How did you know?"

"You ran across the street like a scared goat."

"He said I can't go in there again." I stepped further inside. It was so different than Jennings'. The floors, walls and shelves were a dark stained wood that had been polished to a sheen. The air was warm and smelled faintly of spices.

"That's how I get most of my customers." The man laughed and came out from behind the counter. "What are you looking to buy?"

"Um." I stammered, hoping he wasn't going to stop being nice as soon as I told him my requests. "I wanted a deck of playing cards."

He nodded and went to a shelf behind the counter. "One or two?"

"Two please." I said suddenly feeling decadent.

He put two decks on the counter. "What else?"

"Books. Novels actually. They are for a friend, he has a lot of time on his hands."

"Of course. Follow me." He took off towards the back of the shop. I was surprised to see his store was actually larger than Jennings'. Near the very back, after the canned foods and dry goods, were several tall bookcases. "I always have books."

"I will have to tell my brother."

"He likes to read?"

"Oh yes." I said reading the spines. "But right now I'm looking for some really cheap novels."

He laughed and picked five books off the shelf. "Ten cents each. Cheap enough?"

"I think so." I noticed one was called *The Murdering Menace*.

"Has your friend read Dickens?"

"I don't know." It was impossible to know what books had passed through Hugh's hands over the years.

"Maybe try a couple? If he has read them you can bring them back." He took two more books off the shelf and handed them to me. "Anything else?"

"No, not today."

He led me back to the counter and added up my purchases on a small piece of paper. After I paid him I began to think of how I was going to bring them into the house without Hugh noticing.

"Can you hold them until Christmas eve?"

"Of course. You don't want him to see?"

"No." I said feeling suddenly embarrassed.

"What is your name?"

"Emma Hollis."

He wrote my name on a slip of paper and stuck it inside one of the books.

"Thank you. What is your name?"

The man laughed and looked up at the large window next to the counter. "Did you not see the window? Thalberg."

"Of course. Thank you Mr. Thalberg."

"It was my pleasure Miss Hollis." We shook hands and I set off for home. It had started snowing again. I turned up my coat collar and put on my gloves. I never set foot in Jennings' ever again.

Chapter 31

Hugh had very few happy Christmas memories. When his family was together they had attended church at midnight and then the next day there was a large dinner and a few gifts. Although they were wealthy his father had never believed in spending a lot of money. He and his siblings would usually receive a book and some candy.

Once he was on his own he spent most holidays holed up in a tavern or sometimes in jail. There had been many celebrations throughout the time he had spent in the house, some were grand, some small, and some non-existent. He was not looking forward to watching the Hollis family celebrate, as much as he cared for them. It was a reminder of everything he had lost.

He watched with little interest as Elsay went over her menu on Christmas Eve. He had been ordered downstairs by Emma who had come lumbering into her room with a mysterious package wrapped in brown paper. She said it was a surprise for Ethan. He assumed it was some kind of medical thing.

"Elsay, I shouldn't worry too much about dinner tomorrow." Edward said strutting into the kitchen. He was wearing a tapestry vest with a holly berry pattern.

"Good grief, that waistcoat is revolting." Hugh muttered.

"That's easy for you to say."

"What I mean is that ole' Brownie is bringing the dinner." Father said. "I just saw him before I closed up the shop."

"I'm not letting him into my kitchen."

Edward smiled. "His servants are doing it all."

Elsay set her list aside. "Edward, do you really think we should be taking things from him now that Eve is engaged to Scott? When are you planning on telling him?"

Edward put his hands in his pockets. "After the new year."

"Are you waiting just so you can get something from him?"

"Of course. I had a feeling he was going to do something special for our first Christmas in town."

"Edward! I can't believe you would take advantage like that."

Edward shrugged and rocked back on his heels.

"Take him for all you can." Hugh said.

"You ought to be ashamed of yourself." Elsay said. "What do you think he's going to do when he finds out you've allowed Eve to become engaged?

Edward looked completely unconcerned. "Let me worry about that Elsay."

Elsay started to respond but Ethan stepped into the kitchen with his hat on. "We'll be late for church."

Elsay hustled into the hallway. "Eve, Emma time to go!" she called up the stairs. "Honestly what can those girls be doing up there?"

A minute later both girls came rushing down the stairs. Emma was smiling strangely. She looked at Hugh and giggled. What was wrong with her? There was nothing to be cheerful about.

"We're going to be late." Edward said. There was a mad rush for coats, boots, hats and gloves. They filed out the front door one at a time. Emma was the last to go, she seemed to be purposely hanging back. As she left she turned around and waved.

They didn't come home until one thirty in the morning. Hugh stayed in the attic, it hardly seemed the time to be wandering around downstairs. There was little to do but stare into space and think about his death.

The next morning was a flurry of activity. Senator Brown came at the inconvenient hour of nine o'clock and stayed all day. He brought with him a cook, a maid and a wagon load of packages.

Elsay was overcome when she opened a crate and found a new set of red patterned china dishes. "Oh Senator I don't know what to say."

149

"It's nothing at all." Senator Brown took a puff on his pipe and blew a ring of smoke into the air. "And what do you think of your present young lady?" He looked at Eve.

Eve's present was in her lap. It was a new hat all the way from New York City. She smiled wistfully and sighed. "It's lovely Senator."

"You might want to reconsider this whole deal Edward." Hugh said. "You're all making out like bandits."

"The pleasure will be all mine when I see you wearing it in church." The Senator brushed his whiskers and tilted his head into the air. "Smells like dinner is nearly ready. Elsay, your husband and I will carry your new dishes into the kitchen and we shall dine on them straight away."

"Oh yes. Thank you so much." Elsay said beaming. "Do be careful."

The two men got to their feet and picked up the crate. The Senator grunted far more than necessary in Hugh's opinion as they carried the box into the kitchen. He was growing tired of the merriment and good cheer, he slipped quietly upstairs to the attic. He sat on the floor and stared at his stocking feet. He was figuring out how many hours were left in the day when a black shoe kicked his leg.

"When you feel sorry for yourself you really do it in style." Mika said.

"I am not feeling sorry for myself. I just don't like Christmas."

"You never minded it when you were a child."

"I had a family then. It isn't the same now."

Mika shrugged. "How could it be the same?" He sat on the floor. "You're missing quite a celebration down there. Senator Brown has had a few too many I'm afraid. It could be quite entertaining."

Hugh was enjoying his moping and he didn't want anything to interrupt it. "Where have you been?"

Mika smirked. "Been missing me, have you?"

"I didn't say that."

"Then why do you always ask where I've been?"

"Just being polite."

"If you're going to be like this I might as well leave. What a grouch. I came here because I know how you get on this day. But if you're going to act like this I'll leave."

"Fine with me." Hugh said.

"Me too."

"Wait a minute. I want to ask you something."

"What?" Mika said crossly.

"Have you ever heard of a Ma Granger?"

"Who's that?"

"A Tormented Soul that lives in Senator Brown's house."

Mika frowned. "Why would I know about her? Or for that matter care?"

"I thought you might know, with you being a Watcher and all."

"As a rule I am only interested in souls that I Watch. How do you know about her?"

"Emma saw her when she was at Senator Brown's house. She told Emma that one of the men in the room was a liar."

"Really?" Mika suddenly appeared interested. "Who was there?"

"Just Senator Brown, somebody called Mr. White, Edward and Ethan."

"Oh I see."

Hugh leaned forward. "So is one of them a liar?"

"All four of them have been liars at some point in their lives. But one of them is keeping a secret. It's old news though, I've known it for quite some time."

"Are you going to tell me?" Hugh asked.

"Of course not. Why should you know?"

"I'm curious. Say, didn't you hear Emma and me talking about this?"

"I might have."

"So you're not going to tell me?"

"A smart boy like you should be able to figure it out." Mika smiled slyly. "I'm going. The Torment Seer is coming. Merry Christmas Hugh." He was gone.

Emma appeared at the top of the stairs. "Hello. Are you still in a bad mood?"

"Yes. Mika was just here. So it's even worse now."

"I have something that might cheer you up. It's in my room, come and see." Her brown eyes were dancing as she spoke. He noticed she had a red velvet ribbon in her hair.

"Is that new?" He touched the ends of the ribbon.

Emma reached up to see what he was doing. She touched his hand sending a shock through him. "Yes, from Eve."

"Nice." Hugh admired.

"Thanks. Now come on. I want to show you something."

He followed her downstairs to her bedroom. Emma dragged her telescope case into the middle of the room. When she was done she pointed at the box and said. "Open it."

Hugh looked at her curiously. He had no idea what she was up to. He sat on the floor and unlatched the box. As he pulled back the lid he found the contents covered with a blue cloth.

"What is it?"

"Take a look." Her face was beaming as she knelt next to him.

He pulled back the cloth. A row of books were laid neatly in the case so he could read the titles on the bindings. Next to the books were two brand new decks of cards.

"This was certainly an odd gift." he said quietly. "Who gave you these?"

"They're not mine." she said giggling. "They're yours."

"What do you mean?" There was a feeling of excitement stirring in him.

"I mean that I bought them for you. It's my Christmas present to you. I thought you could keep everything here in my telescope case. Mother will never think to look in here and there's room for more too."

"These are mine?"

"Yes. Don't you like them?"

Hugh looked over the books. They were cheap all right, just like he preferred. His. He kept repeating it in his mind. These belonged to him. They were not stolen, borrowed or sneaked out of a bedroom while no one was looking. They were *his things*.

It was then that a feeling of joy came over him that he had never known in life or death. He was completely happy. Tears started at the corner of his eyes. He wiped them away quickly, he hadn't cried real tears since his parents had died. He had wept many times in the courtroom but it never did any good.

"Are you all right Hugh?" she asked quietly.

"This is the nicest thing anyone has ever done for me." He didn't know what else to say, how else to explain his gratitude. He had been on his own for so long he had forgotten what it was like to be cared about by someone else.

"I couldn't wait to show you."

He could see her grinning through his tears. "Thank you Emma. Thank you so much." He wiped his eyes on his sleeve and took a deep breath. Then without regards to her personal embarrassment or the shocking jolt of Lifeforce he was about to endure he grabbed her arm and pulled her towards him, hugging her tightly.

Her arms wrapped snugly around his neck. Lifeforce pummeled his body like a hail storm. "Thank you." he whispered in her ear. It had been possibly the best day of his whole existence. He loved Christmas.

Chapter 32

Reverend Monk had said something in a sermon a few weeks before, during one of the times I was paying attention. He said the act of giving was divine. I didn't feel exactly divine, but giving Hugh those presents was the best thing I had ever done.

He had taken time to look at each book, he had not read any of them. Then he carefully wrote his name in pencil on the inside covers. The cards went immediately into play and I lost five games of Tribute in a row.

It was the dead of winter and there was little to do but stay inside and watch the snow fall. After the first of the year Father announced at breakfast that he was going to speak with Senator Brown that morning about Eve's engagement.

"The time has come." he said grimly.

"Oh Father, I am so nervous for you. Do you want me to come with you?" Eve asked.

Father smiled and patted her arm. "Thank you dear that won't be necessary. I have it all planned out up here." He pointed to his temple.

"I'm worried too Father. I think I should go." Ethan said.

"No, no. I will do this on my own." He took a deep breath and looked nervously at Mother.

"Maybe you should take something with you just in case."

"Like what?"

"A pistol." Hugh commented from the back of the room.

"No, that won't be necessary. Senator Brown is a reasonable man. I will just calmly explain the situation."

"But he gave us all those gifts at Christmas, don't you think he will realize you waited until now just so you could get them for us?" Eve asked.

Father rubbed his whiskers and sighed. "My family had the best Christmas it has ever known, possibly the best we will ever know. It was all worth it. Best to be off now."

We all groaned as he put on his boots and coat. He pulled a woolen hat down over his head and left. The wind slammed the door shut behind him. We rushed to the window to watch him lumber through the snow towards town.

"Poor Father." Eve said quietly.

"I would rather him tell off Brown than have you marry that man." Mother said.

Eve's jaw dropped open. "You never said that before."

"And don't expect you'll be hearing me say it again Eve Hollis. Now all of you go find something else to do besides cluttering up my kitchen."

Father came home late that afternoon. His face was tired and wind burned. He and Mother, along with Hugh went into the back bedroom to talk. Although my parents told me nothing about the encounter Hugh said that it had gone very badly and Senator Brown was cutting us off socially. Everything to do with the previous business arrangement was to go through Mr. White.

Father said it was time to tighten our belts. We would have to economize from now on. Our parents advised us not to go near the Senator or his house. Father even went as far as to advise that we not look him in the eye if we met him in public.

"And we should probably not attend church for a while." he said. "Reverend Monk is the Senator's protégé after all."

"Is this going to affect your shop Father?" Eve said looking distressed.

"I don't know Eve. I really don't know."

"This is all my fault." she moaned.

"It's really my fault." Hugh said. "But I'm not sorry."

Father sighed. "It's done now."

                              * * *

That spring I turned thirteen. Eve finished school and Scott began his apprenticeship. Father's shop continued to grow despite our estrangement from the Senator. It turned out a lot of people in town didn't like him very much and once word got around that he wasn't going to wed the young girl he fancied they began to see Father in a new light.

The wedding was set for the last weekend in August. It had been sticky and hot all week. Hugh had spent the better part of the last month telling me about the weddings that had taken place in the house. The parlor was the location for all of them including Eve's. Ethan and I had picked flowers from the field down the road, the room smelled sweet and fresh.

Reverend Monk had not been asked to officiate. Father found a judge a few towns over that had a strong dislike for Senator Brown. He was more than happy to do the job.

Saturday morning came at last. Eve married Scott Cooper in the front parlor. All the Coopers were there including their father, Michael, who seemed slightly hung over, but otherwise coherent. Because we lived so far from our cousins and aunts and uncles up north they did not make the journey. Instead they had sent numerous cards and letters of best wishes which Mother stood up on the fireplace mantle.

"Sure was a dandy ceremony." Candy said afterwards.

"Eve is really happy."

"I hope I have a wedding this nice when I get married." She took a glass of punch and swallowed it in one gulp.

"You will Candy. I bet you'll have a wedding twice as big as this."

She laughed and tossed back her hair. "I don't really care about the wedding. I'm more interested in the bridegroom."

"They say you'll know who it is when you meet them." I quoted Eve.

"Oh I know who it is. I just have to convince him. I've got plenty of time though."

"Who is it?"

"You'll find out someday." Candy set her empty cup down and straightened her threadbare dress. It was too small for her, allowing her bony elbows to poke through the fabric. "Are we going to dance?" she shouted. Every redhead in the room turned to look at her.

"Should we?"

"Can we?"

"Let's get our instruments." was heard in quick succession.

"I had no plans for dancing." Mother said nervously.

"What's a wedding without a little dancin'?" Michael Cooper asked. "All my youngsters play. Go get yer stuff."

"Oh boy!" shouted a Cooper boy as the lot of them raced out the front door.

"This is not what we had planned." Mother looked desperately at Father. He merely shrugged and went back to his conversation with Judge Lint.

"Oh Mother it's all right. We're Coopers now." Eve said giddily.

"You may be one but I'm not."

 The Cooper family returned a few minutes later with an assortment of instruments. They took little time in assembling themselves in the corner. Michael Cooper raised a battered fiddle to his neck. Without any discussion they all began to play the same song. The music was bright and merry. Eve and Scott started dancing right away although it was clear Eve had no idea what she was doing. It didn't seem to matter, she laughed and leaned her head on Scott's shoulder as he tried to guide her across the floor.

 The dancing was infectious and soon enough Father had persuaded Margaret to dance with him. Mother looked on and shook her head, but I noticed her foot was tapping. In the middle of the room Candy was leading Ethan around by the arm. He pushed his glasses up and gave me a desperate look. I laughed and was about to join them when I felt a tap on my shoulder.

Hugh was standing behind me. I wondered where he had gone to. He had been drifting in and out all day, with the number of people in the house it was hard to keep track of him. We stepped into the hallway. It was so noisy I felt safe to speak.

"Where have you been?" I asked.

"Oh I've been around. I wanted to let you enjoy the wedding. I like this music. I used to be quite a dancer."

"Prove it."

"Watch this." He put his hands on his hips and started hopping from one foot to another in what I assumed was supposed to be a jig. It was a completely uncoordinated effort that clashed terribly with the music.

I started laughing. "That's it?"

"I would like to see you try this."

"Just watch me." I said copying him. He held his stomach and started laughing.

It was at that moment that eight year old Merrick Cooper decided to wander into the hall. He stopped in his tracks and stared at me. "Why are you dancing by yourself?"

I stopped moving and tried to look like I had no idea what he was talking about.

"Go away." Hugh said.

"I'm telling." Merrick whined.

"There's nothing to tell you dolt." Hugh said.

"I was just being silly Merrick." I said. "Please don't tell anyone."

"You're weird." Merrick stuck his finger up his nose and wiped it on his trousers.

"I'll tell your Mother you just did that."

A look of panic spread across his face. "I won't tell." He ran back into the parlor.

As soon as Merrick was gone Hugh and I looked at each other. "Attic." we both said at once.

Chapter 33

Hugh could still hear the music from downstairs. Emma stopped to catch her breath. She leaned against the attic wall and laughed. "Do you wish you had gotten married?" She sat on the floor.

He shrugged. "Sometimes. I never really met the right person." He sat across from her. "There was a girl once, she was an innkeeper's daughter. I liked her. She was kind and sweet and funny too. I stayed in town six months courting her. That's very dangerous when you're a thief. Normally I would never stay in one place for more than a few days, but Hillary, that was her name, kept me there. I was ready to propose."

"Did she know what you did?"

"Oh yes. She caught me trying to break into her father's strongbox, that's how we met. I went through a strongbox phase, not sure why, anyway I started thinking about how I would marry her and we could set up a little house and so on. I was so stupid." It was amazing how old memories could still feel fresh, like the pale blue of her eyes.

"There's nothing stupid about that."

"No, except she was working with the local sheriff to catch a notorious thief."

"Oh no. So she was pretending to like you just to help the sheriff?"

"Apparently. She was quite happy to testify at my trial. She married the sheriff later that year. I heard years later that they divorced but I don't really know if that's true. Although Doug Cheever, that's the chap who told me, was usually right about such things, he had been working on a farm that year and he saw-"

"What happened at the trial?" Emma asked. She was obviously not interested in learning about what Doug Cheever saw.

"Oh that? Hillary told her story and they convicted me. Of course my brother Patrick was the judge, bit of a shocker there. I hadn't seen him since I was fourteen."

"Is that allowed? Having your brother as the judge at your trial?"

"Probably not." It occurred to him that he would have been wise to hire a lawyer. "Back then people looked the other way about a lot of things."

"What did Patrick say after all those years?"

"I sentence you to a year in jail."

"Oh." Emma tapped her fingers on the attic floor.

"Do you want to go back to the wedding? You can, you don't have to keep me company."

"No. I like it here. I like it when you talk about your life."

"You do? It's so boring."

"No it isn't. Not to me. I haven't done anything."

"You've got a long way to go. Besides how many girls can talk to dead people? That's pretty interesting."

She smiled. "That's true."

Downstairs the music stopped. There was some muffled cheering and rowdy noises which made Hugh a bit nostalgic for the taverns he used to frequent. Before he could get too far into a new memory the music started again. It was a different tempo this time.

"Do you hear that?"

"The music? Yes." Emma looked puzzled.

"It's a waltz."

"So?"

"It's my favorite dance." That wasn't completely true. It was his favorite to watch. He had never actually danced it with someone. There had been many parties in the house over the years and he had learned from observation only. He had practiced by himself more than a few times, although he was not about to tell her that.

"I've never danced it, or anything for that matter."

"Would you like to?" he asked, hoping, praying she would say yes.

"I suppose." she said hesitantly.

Hugh got to his feet before she had a chance to change her mind. Emma stood up, straightened her dress and fixed the ribbon in her hair.

"Just follow me." he said, pleased with how sophisticated he sounded. He arranged her arms, one hand on his shoulder, the other holding his hand. He put his hand on her waist and showed her the basic steps.

The first minute was a disaster. She stepped on his feet, he stepped on hers, and Emma stepped on the hem of her own dress. Hugh thought she was about to give up when suddenly they did three successful turns in a row.

"I think I've got it!" she cried as she squashed his toe. "Oh sorry." But it was a momentary slip. They continued on for another minute or two when suddenly the music stopped. "Oh, we were just getting started." Emma dropped her arms.

Hugh waited. A few seconds passed and the Coopers started playing another one of their confounded jigs.

"That's not a waltz is it?" she asked.

"No. But who needs them? Shall we?" He held out his hand.

To his surprise she eagerly took it. They continued their dance despite the contrasting music from downstairs. Hugh found after a while he didn't even hear the Coopers. The music was in his head, a thousand songs he had heard over the course of the years. He hummed quietly as they turned round and round the attic.

Emma was grinning radiantly. Her brown hair had been curled for the wedding, the curls bounced like springs as she moved. As the afternoon sun streamed through the window it gave her face a rosy glow. Even his own skin had a flush of color thanks to her holding his hand. He was becoming used to feeling alive again. Mika was right, it was addicting.

Chapter 34

Life was different after Eve got married. The morning of the wedding Scott had arranged for a wagon to come and pick up her trunks and a few pieces of furniture our parents had given them. They moved into a little rented house at the other end of town. By the end of the day she was gone.

School started the next week. As usual we walked there with the Coopers. There was a new found camaraderie with them since the wedding. We talked and laughed as we climbed the hill to the school house.

"I for one have been looking forward to this day." Ethan said.

The schoolroom was already full and buzzing with chatter. To my horror I saw that Senator Brown was there talking with the schoolmaster Mr. Burns.

"Brownie!" I heard Candy exclaim behind me. "Oh boy, we're in for one heck of a morning."

I looked at Ethan, he returned my disturbed expression. I had seen Senator Brown exactly once since Father spoke to him. I happened to be coming out of Thalberg's store at the same time he was coming out of Jennings' across the street. Our eyes met for a brief second before I looked away. Even though he had been on the other side of the street I was sure I heard him mutter something. I never told anyone about it except Hugh.

There was nothing I could do but take my seat and wait to see what happened. I slid behind the desk next to Candy. Mr. Burns gently rang the school bell on his desk. Senator Brown stood by with his hands stuck in his coat pockets.

"Boys and girls, I have the pleasure, no make that the honor of introducing our most esteemed citizen here in Fox Cove, our representative in Augusta, and a capital fellow, Senator Hershival Brown." Mr. Burns raised both arms to indicate that we should stand. We got to our feet. Mr. Burns directed us to clap. Reluctantly I joined in the applause while Candy whistled loudly.

"Thank you boys and girls." Senator Brown said. "Thank you very much for that warm welcome. Please be seated." Slowly the clapping waned and there was a loud scuffing as we all sat down.

The Senator cleared his throat. "Now I am sure you are all wondering why I am here this morning. No, I am not going to be your new schoolmaster." He tugged gently at his beard. A couple of people chuckled, one even tried clapping again.

"You see I am here to make each and every one of you an offer. You are probably aware that the development of this town is my primary concern and has been for all my life. Equally important is the education of our youngest citizens." He took a deep breath and turned to face the boys' side of the room.

"Is he still talking to us?" Candy whispered. I shook my head. I had no idea.

"I am making a promise to all of you. The top student in each grade will receive upon graduation a college education paid for most generously by myself." A murmur of excitement rippled through the classroom.

The Senator smiled and rocked back on his heels. "There is a catch however. Once he has completed his education he must return to Fox Cove and use his newfound knowledge for at least five years."

Mr. Burns stepped forward. "This is very exciting, it's a real chance for all of you." he said looking at both sides of the classroom. "Now does anyone have any questions?"

Candy's arm shot up.

"Yes?" said Mr. Burns.

"I want to know if this goes for the girls too. What if I am the top student?" There were numerous giggles in the room. Candy was always at the bottom of the class.

Mr. Burns looked at Senator Brown, who in turn looked at Candy. His eyes narrowed. "Your name young lady?"

"Candace Cooper."

"Don't you think that by the time you leave school Miss Cooper you will be preparing to marry? I doubt you'll be interested in going to college." the Senator said smugly.

"At this rate I'll never get him to propose." Candy said. A couple of the boys started laughing. Mr. Burns slammed his ruler on the desk until they were quiet.

"I am sure you will Miss Cooper." The Senator laughed and started to turn his attention back to the boys.

"But what if I am? And what if I want to go? You promised that you would pay for any top student." Candy said.

Senator Brown tapped his foot on the floor and glared at her.

"I do believe you said *any* student Senator." Mr. Burns said meekly.

"If you are the top student in your class Miss Cooper I will be more than happy to pay." the Senator sneered. He checked his watch. "I really must be somewhere. Thank you all very much for listening." He waved and then dashed out the side door before Mr. Burns could organize standing and clapping again.

"Candy why can't you ever keep your big mouth shut?" said an older girl sitting behind us. She poked Candy in the back with her pencil.

Candy turned around and grabbed the pencil. "I didn't see any of you speaking up. You can thank me later."

The school day settled into its normal routine and by the end of the day it felt as though we had never left for the summer. Candy and I waited for the rest of the girls to leave before we started for home. Ethan was not around, he had been avoiding her since the wedding.

We were just past the cove when I heard the heavy trod of a horse behind us. I didn't bother to look up until I heard my name called. "Emma Hollis!"

I spun around and found Senator Brown riding a large brown horse. He glared down at us from the saddle. "Stop right there." he ordered. He pulled back on the reins and swung down to the ground, grunting as his feet hit the dry dirt road. "I want to talk to you."

My heart was hammering in my ears. I had no idea what he wanted. Father had said not to talk with him at all costs, but I could hardly run away now.

"Yes Senator?" I said shakily.

"I just want to make something clear to you." he said standing uncomfortably close. The sweet smell of syrup drifted through the air.

"Uh huh?"

"That promise does not apply to you. Your family isn't getting another red cent out of me. I thought it best to let you know right away, so there weren't any more misunderstandings."

"All right." I said meekly.

"If she's the best student why shouldn't she get the money?" Candy asked.

"Miss Cooper this is none of your concern."

"Oh yeah?" She dropped her books on the ground and pushed her sleeves up past her elbows. "I'm sick of you bullying everyone in this town."

"Oh really." Brown raised an eyebrow. "And you're going to do something about it?"

"Darn straight I am." She took a step back and kicked the Senator in the shin. He doubled over and grabbed his leg.

"You'll regret that." he gasped. "You're as ill mannered as the rest of your family."

"Thanks. There's more where that came from. And hear this Senator, I will get that money from you." Candy's hands twitched nervously. I wasn't sure if she intended to punch him next.

"Miss Cooper I have full confidence that you will amount to absolutely nothing just like generations of Coopers before you."

"Oh you'll regret you ever said that to me." Candy shouted as she shook her fist at him.

"Let me tell you something you ignorant little donkey, if you think for one minute that you have half the brains to qualify for college then you just go ahead and try. No *daughter* of Michael Cooper is going to amount to a damn thing." The Senator mounted his horse and pointed his finger at me. "As for you, your chance ended when your father turned on me." He pulled up on the reins and his horse whinnied. Its hooves kicked dirt in our faces before it galloped back towards the center of town, taking the Senator with it.

"Boy, that was fun." Candy said picking her books up.

"You shouldn't have kicked him."

"Why not? It felt great. I've been wanting to do that for a while."

"My Father doesn't want me talking to him."

"Lucky you. My Father doesn't give two bits. But I tell you I will get that money from him."

"Candy it takes a lot of work to get to college."

"Oh I'll do it. I'll show him."

"Maybe you should talk to Ethan. He knows lots about studying."

Candy's face lit up. "Oh yeah? Maybe I should. Tell him I will be over this weekend to ask him some questions." She tucked her books under her arm and started skipping towards home.

Chapter 35

"What's this word?" Candy pointed to a sentence in the textbook she was reading. Ethan sighed and looked over his glasses.

"Larynx. It's a part of the throat."

"Oh right. I think I've heard of that." she said scratching her head. She knitted her brow and wrote something in the book.

"Hey that's mine!"

"I know. Thanks Ethan."

Hugh laughed. He was sitting in the corner of Ethan's room watching them study. Emma was downstairs with her mother. Now that Eve had left home Emma was expected to help in the kitchen each afternoon. Accordingly Hugh had taken to spending the afternoon in Ethan's room, it was especially entertaining now that Candy had decided to become a scholar.

Emma had told him of Candy's interaction with Senator Brown on the first day of school. In the months following she had taken to following Ethan home and sitting on the end of his bed asking him a million questions about how to study, what to read, what college was like and what she could learn there. Finally he gave her one of his medical books to read in hopes of keeping her quiet. It didn't work. Candy asked endless questions about the words she saw and the diagrams in the book.

Hugh found it all quite amusing. Candy seemed to make Ethan far more interesting than he actually was. Ethan was less enthusiastic about the whole arrangement, but he put up with it for Emma's sake. He was also putting up with Hugh being in his room. After the first few days he had gone to Emma and complained about having the family ghost lurking in the corner. Hugh was secretly pleased when she defended him.

"He obviously found something to keep himself occupied before we lived here." Ethan said hotly.

"It's depressing for him to sit in a room all alone." Emma replied.

"Can't he read one of those books you bought him? I still can't believe you bought a dead man a Christmas present."

"That was completely unnecessary Ethan." Hugh said.

Emma sighed. "He's read those. That was nearly a year ago. Just let him sit in your room. He won't do anything he shouldn't." She held onto Hugh's sleeve as she spoke. She had a habit of doing that now, he couldn't recall when it had started, but he didn't dare say anything in case she stopped.

"Very well, come in my room if you must." Ethan said looking towards Hugh. "But the minute you make something float in the air I want you out."

"That's just the sort of comment that makes me do bad things."

"Hugh says thank you." Emma said.

"Sure he did."

That's how it started. Now Hugh found himself looking forward to the study sessions. It was obvious that Candy liked Ethan very much, but he couldn't yet tell if Ethan felt the same way.

"What are you getting me for Christmas?" Candy suddenly asked.

"Why should I get you anything?"

"I thought we were friends."

Ethan put his book aside. He glanced towards Hugh as though he could help him. "We are friends. I just didn't think we were the type that exchanged gifts."

"Oh." Candy pushed a stray hair behind her ear.

"Do you want to exchange gifts? I'm not going to have much money, not like last year. I've got a little saved from helping Father in the shop on Saturdays."

"I'm not going to have any, but I'll make you something."

"If you want to." Ethan shrugged.

Hugh leaned back in his chair and smiled. He still thought about last year's Christmas surprise from Emma. He secretly hoped she would do it again, but he couldn't be sure, there was less money to go around now that Senator Brown was no longer in their lives.

He got up and walked through the wall into Emma's room. He had an idea. She had a little desk in the corner with some fancy stationary she had gotten for her birthday. He listened carefully for noises downstairs. He could hear Elsay imparting her wisdom concerning bread making, Emma would be down there for a while. He took a piece of paper and a pen and began to write:

My Dear Ethan,

This letter is from Hugh MacPherson, the dead person, or rather Tormented Soul, who inhabits your house. I know you are not particularly fond of me, but I was hoping you might remember that I have been especially well behaved of late. I have not moved any objects in your room and haven't snapped your suspenders in nearly two years.

Alas, I digress. I have a small favor to ask. I was wondering if you could buy Emma a Christmas present on my behalf. I don't have any money so you'll have to pay for it yourself, but I know you are fond of Emma and I am hoping you will find it in your heart to do me this small favor. I can't ever pay you back, but know you'll be warming the heart of an old ghost.

I was thinking she would like a comb for her hair, similar to what she got Eve last year, but perhaps a bit better quality. I would prefer red or green in color. I also think a bracelet would be nice. Of course I am not opposed to a necklace either. I don't know what kind of variety you have in this town, the last time I shopped here there was just one store, of course I never really shopped at all as you know. I was more on the order of taking back in those days, but I digress again.

Ethan, please write back and tell me if you are willing. I will be forever in your debt, if you need a favor someday I'll be more than happy to oblige if I can. I probably won't be able to help at all, but remember I wanted to.

Your humble servant

Fondly

Hugh C. J. MacPherson

 Hugh folded the letter and put it underneath the box of stationary. Later that evening, after Emma was asleep, he slipped it under Ethan's door. Now he waited.

Chapter 36

It hardly seemed possible an entire year had gone by since we had our Christmas with Senator Brown. I had worked out a deal with Mr. Thalberg. Two days a week after school I came to his store and helped organize and straighten the shelves. In exchange he gave me one book a month and allowed me to pick out a present for each member of my family.

I was planning to pick up the books the Saturday morning before Christmas. I had warned Hugh I was coming home with something, of course he knew what was going on, he had been hinting about having nothing to read for months.

"I can't believe this!" Ethan said at breakfast. He was reading a letter on stationary that looked very similar to mine. "This must be a joke. Of all the nerve."

"What's the matter?" I asked. It had to be from Candy, only she would steal some of my paper and write Ethan a letter.

Ethan looked up. "It's nothing."

"Is it from Candy?"

"What? Oh, yes it is."

"There's nothing to be embarrassed about son." Father said. "Your mother sent me plenty of love letters when we were courting."

"I'll bet she did." Hugh said.

"Edward!" Mother scolded.

"Now Elsay, our children are getting older. Ethan is of courting age, and Emma, well Emma is nearly there. I see no reason why we can't talk in a more open manner. It's the modern age."

"Emma is not even fourteen. I don't think I am ready for her to start courting yet."

"That time will be here before you know it Elsay." Father said.

I glanced at Hugh. I was so embarrassed. "Parents." he muttered sympathetically.

I picked up the books from Thalberg's and hid them under my bed. Christmas was only a few days away. "You cannot under any circumstances look under here." I told Hugh.

"Why not?"

"I am sure you know why not."

"Maybe I do." There was a glint in his eyes I hadn't seen before. "How long will you be at Scott and Eve's on Christmas?"

"I don't know, probably most of the day."

"I'll wait up for you."

"Oh good. I hope you won't fall asleep." I touched his sleeve. I liked doing that. There was something reassuring about knowing he was there. The coldness of his skin seeped through the thin cotton fabric. I couldn't imagine him not being in the house, not being there when I ate breakfast in the morning, not saying goodnight to me at the end of the day.

"I'll try to stay awake." he said smiling.

The winter had been mild so far. The roads were frozen but free of snow as we walked to Eve and Scott's. As we passed the Coopers Candy came running out with something tucked under her arm. She looked quite festive in a green dress with a red sash, she had socks on her feet and her hair was neatly pinned up.

"This is for you." She handed a lumpy package to Ethan. It was wrapped in newspaper.

"Thanks Candy." he stammered. His eyes flicked to my parents and then back to Candy. "I've got something for you as well." He handed her a parcel wrapped in brown paper.

"Can I open it now?"

"Sure." Ethan's face was red, he looked as though he couldn't wait for the moment to end.

Candy tore off the paper and looked at her present. She twisted her face and scratched her head. "What is it?"

"A dictionary. Now when you come across a word you don't know you can look it up and find out what it means."

"Oh yeah, I knew that." She smiled and hugged the book to her chest. "Thanks Ethan. Now open yours."

Ethan pulled off the newspaper and stuffed it into his coat pocket. He was left with a pair of red mittens.

"I made em' myself." Candy said beaming.

"Thanks Candy." He took off his gloves and put on the mittens, they were a good fit.

"You're welcome." Someone shouted inside the house. "Sounds like my Pa's awake. I'd better go. Merry Christmas everyone!" She waved and ran back inside.

"Another Cooper." Mother whispered under her breath. Father patted her hand.

We continued on to Scott and Eve's little house. It was at the top of the hill overlooking the ocean. All the new houses were built there. I felt a pang of anxiety as I saw the most annoying Tormented Soul in all of Fox Cove. It was the bricklayer pacing the sidewalk and lamenting his death.

"Twas a dreadful day when I was bludgeoned to death by a falling brick!" he cried out. "Come ye and hear my tale." He was right in front of Eve's, holding his head and waving his hands dramatically.

"Oh no." I muttered.

Ethan looked up and grimaced. "Can you get by him?"

"I don't know." It was easy for the rest of them, they could walk through him. I could not.

"It twas near one o' the clock when it happened. Oh, the tragedy." He stood in front of Eve's door.

"I'm freezing." Mother said. She passed through the bricklayer and went inside.

"Father-" I began. I planned on confessing my predicament.

"Seers! There are Seers among us! I can feel it in my bones!"

I swallowed hard. There was nothing I could do. He had spotted me, just like Ma Granger. "Father." I said tugging on his coat.

"What is it Emma? I am trying to remember if I brought Scott's gift. I don't think so." He checked his pockets.

"Do you want me to go back and get it?" I asked, hoping for a possible escape.

"No. I mean yes. We will both go, I don't know if you'll be able to find it on your own." He continued to stick his hands in and out of his pockets. "Ethan, go inside and tell your mother that Emma and I will be there as soon as we can."

Ethan agreed and went inside.

Father and I rushed back home. He said very little on the way. When we reached the house he told me to stay put. He ran inside and came back out very quickly.

"Did you get it?" I asked.

"What? Oh yes."

When we returned the bricklayer had moved further down the sidewalk. We went inside and were immediately confronted by Mother. "Edward, where on earth have you been?"

"I forgot something."

"Scott's gift." I added.

"I had it with me." Mother said. "You should have asked before you went all the way back home."

"Oh. I guess I was getting it mixed up with something else."

Mother shook her head and looked suspiciously at me.

Eve and Scott had been married for four months now. They were still giddy and taken to staring at each other across the room. Mother said she had no doubt that Eve would produce a baby by the following Christmas.

The day passed quickly. There were presents to pass around, but not the same as last year when Senator Brown had furnished most everything. Eve made us an excellent dinner and Scott entertained us on his fiddle, a wedding gift from his father. It was dark by the time we left for home, we were all weary and said little as we passed through town. I found Hugh in my bedroom looking out of the telescope.

"Did you look?" I asked, pointing underneath the bed.

"Of course not."

I wasn't sure whether or not to believe him. "Go ahead."

He grinned and pulled the bag of books from beneath the bed. He sat on the floor and eagerly looked through the titles. "Thank you Emma. You don't know what this means to me."

"I didn't know what else to get you." I said sitting next to him.

"This is all I need." To my surprise he put the books back in the bag and shoved them under my bed. "I'll be right back." He sprang up and left the room. A minute later he returned with a small brown paper bag. A smile spread over his face as he put it in my lap.

"What's this?"

"Look inside."

I put my hand in the bag and pulled out a hair comb. It was similar to the one I gave Eve last year, but fancier. It was dark red inlaid with a smooth green stone that was shaped like ivy leaves. It was prettier than anything I had ever owned. "It's beautiful."

Hugh brushed my hair back and pushed the comb in place. I got up and looked in the mirror. "Where did you get this?" I moved my head so the green stones could catch the light.

"There's something else in there."

I looked inside the bag. There was a small paper box at the bottom.

"Open it." Hugh said excitedly.

Nestled on a scrap of blue velvet was a silver star attached to a long, thin chain. I lifted it out of the box, the star spun around and caught the light.

"I don't understand."

"I'll put it on you." He took the necklace from me. "The chain is extra long so you can hide it if you want to." He undid the clasp and brought it around my neck, fastening it at the back. "Do you like it?"

"I love it. I love both. But I don't understand. Are these from you?"

Hugh laughed. "Yes! It's my Christmas present to you."

"But how? Did you find a way out? Did you-?" I hesitated to say the word steal.

"A way out? Of course not. I had a little help though."

"Mika?"

"No! I wrote your brother a letter and asked him to buy something for me."

"You wrote a letter to Ethan?" I asked, thinking back. "So that's what he was reading."

"Yes and then he wrote me back and agreed. I wasn't sure he would. He had to use his own money. I don't exactly earn a living around here."

"I can't believe it. You didn't have to do this Hugh."

He smiled and looked at the comb in my hair. "Yes I did."

"No you didn't. I got you those books because I wanted to, because you deserved something of your own. I wasn't expecting anything in return."

He looked happier than I had ever seen him. "I had to find a way to thank you."

"For what?"

"For saving me. Emma, you have no idea what things were like for me before you came here. There were people who lived here, but I could only

176

watch them from a distance. Can you imagine not speaking to anyone for over one hundred years?"

"But you have Mika."

"You can't really have a proper conversation with Mika. And he's hardly ever around. Emma, before you came I was so lonely, it's all I used to think about. I would have killed myself if I wasn't already dead."

"And now?"

"And now I look forward to every single day. I have a friend in this world. And I wanted to thank you for that." He grinned awkwardly. "So Merry Christmas Emma."

I was at a loss for words. I sometimes felt he regarded me as a pesky little girl he was stuck with. I used to imagine that he would have preferred to have been able to speak to Eve instead of me. She was beautiful and fun, I was just a dull thing who liked to look out a telescope and read books.

"Thank you." I said getting up the nerve to hug him. I laid my face against his cool neck and took a deep breath. "I can't believe Ethan agreed to help you. He's very frugal you know."

"I have his response. Do you want to hear it? He did have a few conditions." Hugh opened my telescope case and took out a folded piece of paper.

"Yes, read it to me."

Chapter 37

Hugh unfolded the paper and paused dramatically making it seem as though what he was about to read would set the world afire. In reality he was recovering from a jolt of Lifeforce he had received when she had so gracefully laid her head on his bare neck. He cleared his throat and began.

Dear Hugh,

Your letter came as a complete shock to me. I really don't know what to say. I can't believe you expect me to find extra money to buy gifts on your behalf. I understand you have no money and cannot leave the house, but is there a precedence for a ghost giving presents to the living?

As you will see from the paper bag I left in the attic I have agreed to help you. I want you to understand I am doing this for Emma, not you.

Hugh, you have completely bewitched my sister. If you hurt her in any way you will have me to answer to. I may not be able to see or touch you, but I can make sure we leave this house and don't come back. That is my warning to you.

Now down to business. I have purchased the hair comb and a necklace for you to give her. As you will see the necklace is in the shape of a star, which I thought was fitting. Her telescope is supposed to be for looking at the stars, not the neighbors.

Now that I have done this favor for you, you can do something for me. I do not want you sitting in my bedroom every afternoon while I study. You can find something else to do with your time. Under no circumstances are you to do anything that would facilitate a courtship between me and a young lady, particularly Miss Cooper. I am merely helping her to study and do not have any romantic interest in her whatsoever.

These are my terms. As I said previously, my sister's happiness is of the upmost importance to me

Sincerely

Ethan Hollis

"That's a bit strong." Emma said. Hugh folded the letter and put it back in the telescope case.

"He's just being a good brother."

"That was really nice of him."

"He did an excellent job." Hugh agreed. "Although now I have to stay out of his room."

"You can come in here."

"I want to write him back, to thank him."

"You can use my desk and stationary." She jumped up and took a couple of pieces of paper from the box on her desk. She opened the bottle of ink and set a pen nearby.

"Right now?"

"Yes, unless you'd rather wait until you're alone."

He sat at her desk and smoothed the stationary. It was pale lilac with little violets on the edges, a bit frilly for his taste, but it was all he had to work with so he couldn't be fussy.

"Can I sit next to you?" She pulled up the dreaded horsehair chair. She sat down and wrapped her fingers around his arm. Her head rested gently on his shoulder as she watched him write.

Dear Ethan,

This is Hugh MacPherson. I am writing to thank you for your kindness. You don't know what it means to me to have you purchase those Christmas gifts for Emma. I know you had to spend extra money this year, but I hope you know I will be forever grateful to you.

I promise I will stay away from your bedroom. As for Miss Cooper I think you should reconsider your position. Sometimes friendship can turn into something else, or so I have heard.

Your humble and devoted ghost

Hugh C. J. MacPherson

"How's that?" he asked.

She smiled and gripped his arm tighter. "Perfect."

Chapter 38

Hugh opened his eyes and looked about. He had not been sleeping, he never slept. But sometimes there was nothing else to do but close his eyes and think of other things. Besides it was rude to stare at someone who was sleeping in the bed next to him.

Emma made a noise and turned over. She pulled the covers up around her neck and sighed. He would have to wake her soon, it was her last day of school. Apparently the teacher made a bit of a fuss when he handed out the diplomas. Hugh wished he could be there. He had never earned a diploma, he had stolen a few.

"Emma." he said softly. He nudged her shoulder and pulled the covers away from her face. He woke her up every morning now. Thanks to his internal clock she was always on time.

"What?"

"It's time to get up." He leaned forward and kissed her on the cheek.

She smiled and stretched her arms out. "Good morning." She giggled and scooted closer to him, her breath came softly on his face. He ran his fingers through her dark hair, it felt like silk.

She kissed him slowly on the lips. His face felt like it was being pummeled by tiny lightning bolts. His skin began to warm as she carefully and methodically moved to his jaw and then to the hollow of his neck and finally towards his chest. Thank goodness he had never tied his cravat that night. She was inches away from his bullet wound when he heard Edward on the stairs.

"Your father." he managed to say. She stopped and put her head back on her pillow. Hugh took a deep breath. His hands gripped the sheets tightly. The places she had touched him burned like a toxin, it was painfully intense and completely intoxicating.

There was a light knock on the door. "Emma?" The door opened a crack and Edward stuck his head inside.

"Yes Father?" she said faking a yawn. Beside her Hugh concentrated on allowing the blankets to pass through him, lest Edward see the lumpy outline of something in the bed next to his daughter.

"I thought I should check on you, in case you overslept. Today is a big day."

"I know Father. I'm awake. Thanks."

Edward nodded and shut the door. He always seemed to be lingering about. Hugh assumed he had nothing better to do. Eve was happily situated with her husband and children in town and Ethan was away at college in Pennsylvania. It was too expensive for him to come home for the summer so he had found himself a job in a grocery store.

"He's always poking his head in here." Emma complained as she pulled back the covers and got out of bed.

"He can't see me."

"I know but it's annoying just the same. I'll be eighteen in a few weeks, I don't need my father peeking in my bedroom every day." She pulled off her nightgown and tossed it on the floor. She filled the wash basin and proceeded to wash her face.

Hugh remained on the bed and watched her. There was no one more fascinating than Emma. He loved the way the water dripped off her elbows at the basin. He loved the way she jammed her big toe into the floor as she stared into the wardrobe trying to decide what to wear. He loved how she still wore the hair comb he had given her years ago, she rarely wore her hair up in one of those infernal knots. Instead she let it slide off her shoulders as she walked, the light picking up golden strands intermingled with the dark.

He loved everything about Emma because he loved her. She had changed his death so completely. When she was younger it had been about her companionship. She listened to him, she made him feel worthy of friendship, of being cared about. He had tried to be as good a friend to her as she was to him. He couldn't really remember when things had changed. It had all happened so gradually. One day she was touching his sleeve, later holding his hand, then one day they just kissed. Not a simple kiss on the cheek, but a real kiss. It had taken them both by surprise.

"How does this look?" She was wearing his favorite skirt and shirtwaist with the tiny pink flowers. Women dressed differently now, everything was covered up and hidden. It was a shame, but luckily he was always around when Emma got dressed in the morning.

"Excellent. Perfect for a graduating lady."

She rolled her eyes and laughed as she leapt onto the bed. "I wish these clothes of yours came off." she whispered in his ear. "You can't imagine what I would do to you then."

"I'd like you to try." The warm burning on his earlobe sent his head spinning. It was a damn shame his clothes couldn't be removed. She managed to slip her hands under his shirt tails and run her fingers across a portion of his stomach and back that lay exposed before the rest of the shirt clung possessively to his chest. His breeches, much to his dismay, were welded on him by some unseen force. It was a shame too for what was contained inside seemed to be in perfect working order.

He slid his hands underneath her skirt, feeling the smoothness of her skin. An absurd pair of muslin under-drawers restricted any further access. "I have to go." She pressed her hands between his legs.

"Emma. Are you ready?" Hugh heard Elsay's sing-song voice outside the door. He had been too distracted to hear her coming up the stairs.

Emma's head popped up as Elsay opened the door. She rolled off Hugh and onto the floor. "Oh."

Elsay looked perplexed. "What on earth are you doing down there Emma?"

"Looking for something." she said pushing the hair out of her eyes. Her face was crimson red.

"Whatever it was you look positively exhausted." Elsay said.

"Yes, well it was hard to find."

"You should really get going. Considering it's the last day of school I think Mr. Burns would like you there early."

"I'll be right down." Emma stood up.

"Very well. Don't be too long." Elsay said. Her eyes quickly swept the room as though she was looking for something. Hugh held his breath even though she knew nothing of his existence. Elsay quietly closed the door, he listened carefully to make sure she returned to the downstairs.

"Is she gone?" Emma whispered.

"Yes."

"What is it with them lately? They're always in here."

"Just be glad they haven't taken one of the bedrooms up here. That could seriously curtail our evenings. Besides, they might find out you talk to yourself." He took her hand and pulled her onto his lap. She wrapped her arms around his neck and squeezed him tightly. His head lay comfortably on her chest, he could hear her heart beating.

"Just think, after today I will be here all the time. You'll be sick of me within a week." She ran her fingers across the stubble on his cheek.

"Not a chance."

"Emma!" Edward's voice came from the foot of the stairs.

"I'm coming!" she yelled. She shook her head and stood up. "I'd better go. I love you Hugh."

"I love you more."

She grinned and whispered in his ear. "Not possible."

Chapter 39

It was a beautiful sunny day. I stepped outside and walked over to the Coopers. Merrick was on the porch scratching his behind.

"Good morning Merrick."

"Candy!" he called over his shoulder. He continued scratching as he stared suspiciously at me. He had never forgotten about catching me dancing in the hallway during Eve's wedding.

"Hi Emma!" Candy cried as she emerged from the house. "Last day of school!" She threw her arms up in the air. Her hair was neatly swept up and pinned behind her head. She had on a white blouse and long red skirt. Her clothes were well worn, but clean and neat.

"Finally." I said as we walked in step.

"Oh I don't know. It was kind of fun these last few years."

"Especially when you were studying with Ethan?"

Candy blushed. We walked past old man Johnson's house. He had died over a year ago and the house was now empty.

My mind drifted back to earlier in the morning. I smiled to myself as I thought of Hugh. I don't quite know when I fell in love. It seemed like I had always loved Hugh, as though he had always been there for me. He was everything I needed in life and being with him was all I wanted.

I was so absorbed in my own thoughts I didn't notice Candy poking me in the arm. "What's up with you lately?"

"What? Oh nothing. I was just thinking."

"I know, but what about? Your face is red."

"What? No it isn't." I said laughing nervously. I took a deep breath. "The air smells fresh today." I was hoping to change the subject.

"If I didn't know better I would say you've been with a man."

"Candy! You shouldn't say that."

"Why not? No one's around. Besides you have the same look on your face that my Ma gets after she and Pa make up from having a fight."

"I'm just excited about the last day of school."

"Are you sure there's not something between you and Mr. Burns?"

"Mr. Burns? I don't think so." I said laughing at the idea.

"You don't like older men?"

I didn't get a chance to answer. Merrick and Nathan Cooper came running up behind us.

"Race you Candy." Nathan said.

"You're on." She and Nathan ran up the hill towards the schoolhouse. Merrick walked beside me for a minute before taking off after Candy and Nathan. The rest of the students were already in the schoolhouse when I arrived.

"Thank you for joining us Miss Hollis." Mr. Burns said as I took my seat at the back. Some of the younger students giggled. "Now I won't keep you too long today. But I have some awards to give out."

The next hour or so Mr. Burns occupied our time by giving out various awards to the younger students. He was a kind and dedicated teacher. Last August, before Ethan left for college, he organized a party for him at the grange hall. Most of the town turned out including Senator Brown who made a long speech about himself and how generous he was.

"Now to the most important part of the day." Mr. Burns continued. "We have five students graduating. When I call your name come up and receive your diploma."

One by one Mr. Burns called us to the front of the classroom and handed us our diplomas rolled up and tied with a red ribbon. Candy's name was called last. She hurried to the front of the room and stood next to Mr. Burns, her face beaming.

"Our final graduate is Candace Cooper." Mr. Burns handed Candy her diploma and shook her hand. "It is also my great privilege to announce that Miss Cooper is graduating at the top of the class."

This was no great surprise to anyone. Candy had been the top student for the last two years. Mr. Burns had her studying out of books he used when he went to college.

"As I am sure you know this means that she will be the recipient of Senator Brown's generous scholarship. You may not know that Miss Cooper has already been offered a place at the Women's Medical College of Pennsylvania."

There was a smattering of applause throughout the classroom. I had no idea Candy was on her way to medical college. From the looks on her siblings' faces they had no idea either.

Mr. Burns dismissed the class shortly afterwards. Candy and I walked out of the classroom together for the very last time. "I didn't know you wanted to be a doctor." I said. "Why didn't you tell me?"

"I really wasn't sure myself. Mr. Burns encouraged me to apply. The more I think about it, the more I like it."

"I've never heard of a woman becoming a doctor."

"Me neither. But Mr. Burns says if a man can do it so can a woman."

"And Senator Brown is going to pay for this?"

Candy smiled and tucked her diploma under her arm. "I am on my way to his house to let him know, just in case he forgot. I'll need you to come with me."

"What? I can't. I'm not even allowed in his house, none of my family is."

"Oh that." Candy said with a wave of her hand. "I need you as my witness. Remember that day on the road when I kicked him in the shin?"

"How could I forget that?"

"That was a great day." she said proudly. "Anyway you were there when he promised if I was the top student he would pay for my education."

"He won't listen to me."

"Just come along anyway. I might kick him again if you aren't around. You always were the sensible one."

I smiled at that. If only she knew what sort of things I was up to at night with the dead man in my house. "I'll come but I doubt he'll let me in the front door."

"Oh he can't still be holding a grudge. That whole business with Eve was years ago. He has a young wife of his own now. Come on." Candy took my arm. We started off for Brown Lane.

Like most annoying people, life had been good to Senator Brown. A year after the debacle with Eve he had married Bridget McLean who was sixteen at the time. Her age had caused a bit of a flap in town, but things soon settled down and nine months after marrying she gave birth to a daughter. Since then they had two more children, both sons, and she was rumored to be expecting again.

It was only a rumor for no one knew much about Bridget Brown. She spent most of her time at home and rarely socialized. When she did come into town she rode in the old enclosed coach with the curtains half drawn. Her maid would go into Jennings' and come out an hour later with a load of goods that would have to be tied down on the roof of the vehicle.

Eve and I were in Thalberg's one afternoon when Bridget's coach pulled up outside. Her maid, a little wisp of a girl, hurried into the store across the street. Through the parting of the curtains we could see a small pair of gloved hands turning the pages of a book.

"That could have been me." Eve said.

"Lucky you."

Eve shrugged. "I don't know. Sometimes I wonder. She's got *everything*."

"Yes, including him." I said, repulsed by the thought.

"Still."

"Are you saying you wished you didn't marry Scott?"

"No, I love Scott, I really do. He's a great husband. It's just that I wonder what my life would have been like." She smiled, I was surprised to see there were tears in her eyes. "Don't rush into anything Emma."

"I won't."

"I mean it. Falling in love is easy. Creating a life around it, that's a whole different story."

Candy rang the doorbell of Senator Brown's house. A few minutes later an older woman answered, probably the housekeeper. "Yes?" she asked, scrutinizing Candy and me.

"I want to see Mr. Brown." Candy said.

"*Senator* Brown is not at home." she said, her eye twitching slightly. Suddenly Ma Granger came walking through the housekeeper. She stepped onto the porch and stared me in the face.

"Been wondering when you'd be back." she said. "He's home all right. He's upstairs fornicating. That's why I'm down here, I've seen enough of that in my time. Used to be pretty good at it myself once upon a time."

"I thought I saw the Senator looking out the window when we were walking up to the house." I said casually.

"Ah that's the way to do it. Can't stand her." Ma pointed to the housekeeper. "She drinks the brandy when he's not looking."

"I will have to check." the housekeeper said coldly. She opened the door and allowed us inside. She brought us to a parlor and had us take a seat.

"Wow, I never knew it was so fancy in here." Candy said gawking at the room.

"Yeah it's fancy." It had been five years since I had been inside Brown Park.

Ma Granger followed us and stood next to my chair. I glanced at her warily, all I needed was another run-in like the last time.

"Don't worry, I'll behave myself. I promised him." she said.

I looked at her questioningly.

"Oh you don't want the redhead to know you see ghosts. Probably a good thing, it's a definite sign of insanity. After I met you I had a visit from a strange being. He lured me up on the roof and told me not to bother you. He was so beautiful, tall black wings and all."

"Emma, what are you looking at?" Candy asked.

I didn't have time to answer. Bridget Brown came into the parlor. She was a small woman with strawberry blonde hair and ivory skin. Her features were delicate, almost doll-like. She looked to be about six months pregnant.

"Can I help you girls?" She folded her hands over her stomach.

Candy stood up. "I want to see your husband."

"He's not available." Bridget said calmly. "Anything you have to say to him you can say to me."

"He smokes a cigar after he's done you know what." Ma said.

"Are you going to pay for me to go to college?" Candy waved her diploma in Bridget's face.

"She's got sass. I like it." Ma said.

"What are you talking about?" Bridget asked. She swatted the diploma away as though it were a mosquito.

"Your husband promised me a college education if I graduated at the top of my class. Now I am here to collect." Candy said, putting her hands on her hips.

"Candy, maybe we should go." I suggested.

"No. I am not going until I see him."

"What is all this noise?" A deep voice came from the hall. A second later Senator Brown strode into the parlor. He put his arm around Bridget. "What do you want?" he said to Candy.

"You know darn well what I want."

"Mr. Burns has already sent me a letter lauding your academic prowess Miss Cooper." Senator Brown said. The scent of maple was noticeably absent.

"You're not going to fool me with those big words. I have a dictionary."

Brown scratched his beard and looked at me. "What are you doing here Miss Hollis?"

"Um, well."

"She's with me." Candy said. "She's my witness, remember that day on the road?"

Senator Brown smirked. "The day you kicked me in the leg?"

"Yeah, that day."

"I remember it like it was yesterday Miss Cooper."

"You promised me an education."

"Yes and I will pay for it. You needn't have brought *her* along." he said glancing icily in my direction.

"I wanted to make sure you were going to honor your promise."

Senator Brown closed his eyes and shook his head. "Miss Cooper there is a vast difference between excelling at a small school in a small town and excelling at a large college out of state. I have no doubt you'll last less than a year." He smiled and patted his wife's stomach satisfactorily.

"Oh!" Candy stamped her feet on the floor. "I will not."

The Senator chuckled. "Now Miss Cooper, there's no need for female hysterics. I will sign the necessary papers. My lawyer, Mr. White, is on his way here right now. Why don't you have a seat and we'll wait for him."

Candy nodded and backed into a chair.

"He's such an old bastard." muttered Ma Granger.

Senator Brown pointed a finger at me. "You can leave this house right now young lady." "You're certainly not welcome." Beside him Bridget smirked.

"Gladly. I'll see you later Candy." I strode out of the parlor and into the front hall. Ma Granger followed closely on my heels.

"You should have told him off." she said as I started to open the door.

"What for?" I said feeling annoyed. I wanted to go home and see Hugh.

"Cause I can't do it. Boy would I love to give that pompous jackanape a piece of my mind. Do you want to know why he used to smell like maple syrup?"

"Yes, but I didn't smell it today." I opened the door. We stepped onto the front porch and I closed the door behind us. She pressed her weather beaten face close to mine.

"I've been just yearnin' to tell someone. You see old Hershival loves pancakes, has em' every morning. He's a slob when he eats, lets the syrup run right down his beard." Ma wiggled her bony fingers in front of her to demonstrate the Senator's syrupy drip. "It gets all stuck in his beard."

"Doesn't he wash it?"

"Him wash? Hardly at all. When he was a bachelor he'd hardly ever take a bath. Day after day the syrup would just run into his beard and stick there. When the new wife came she made him take a bath once a week, and that's whether he needs it or not. Nowadays it takes him a while to build up his aroma."

"So that explains it."

"Yep." Ma said looking quite pleased with herself.

"This, what did you call it, this being who visited you? Did he have a name?"

Ma shrugged. "He didn't say. But oh he was beautiful."

I wondered if it could be Mika. Hugh had never mentioned if he had wings. I would have to ask him tonight.

"Someone's coming. You'd better stop talking or they'll be thinking you're crazy." She walked into the house.

No sooner had she gone than I heard a voice in the distance. "Emma?" I spun around and found Mr. White coming up Senator Brown's front walk.

"Mr. White." I said nervously. He would probably report to the Senator that I was still on the premises.

"Emma Hollis." he said smiling. He was wearing a stylish gray suit with a black and red checked tie. On his head was a soft black fur hat, his sandy hair just showing at the temples. He had barely changed in the six years since we met. "I haven't seen you in so long. I hardly recognized you."

"You're not in town very often."

"No, I have an office in Augusta. I only come down here once or twice a month. Senator Brown called me out here today, he said there might be some trouble after the graduation. Some young woman named Candy Cooper."

"She's in there right now."

He nodded and looked at me, his eyes gliding down to the hem of my skirt. I shifted uncomfortably, feeling like a prized cow at the fair. "I can't believe you're so grown up now."

"I really should be going. Senator Brown doesn't want me here. It was nice to see you Mr. White."

"Oh please call me Jeremy."

"All right" I started down the porch steps.

"Emma."

"Yes?"

He smiled and looked down at his feet. "Perhaps next time I am in town I could call on you? Maybe we could take a walk on the bluff?"

"Sure." I shrugged.

"Excellent! See you soon Emma." He called out as I hurried down the walk. I waved absently and turned towards home.

Chapter 40

Hugh had spent the better part of his day watching Elsay bake a cake to celebrate Emma's graduation. By the afternoon the kitchen was filled with the glorious aroma. It reminded him of how much he missed eating. He had once tried to eat a piece of bread. He quickly discovered that whatever went down quickly came back up. Mika later told him that a dead stomach always remained empty.

Emma came home later than he expected. She had her diploma in her hand. "Is that cake I smell?"

"Yes." Elsay said kissing her daughter on the cheek. "To celebrate."

"Thank you." Emma handed her diploma to her mother. Elsay took the ribbon off and unrolled the paper.

"Very nice. That means every one of our children has finished school." she said proudly. "Can I keep this to show your father?"

"Of course." Emma glanced in Hugh's direction. "Do you need help?"

Elsay looked at her and smiled. "Not today. I'll give you the afternoon off."

"I'll be in my room."

"What on earth do you do up there? You really should be outside more Emma."

"I know. Call me when dinner is ready." Emma said over her shoulder as she left the kitchen and ran upstairs.

Hugh followed her. She was waiting for him as he passed through the bedroom door. She grabbed his shirt and kissed him hard on the mouth.

"I've been waiting all day to do that." she said.

"I've been waiting all day for you to do that." He put his arms around her. "Where have you been all afternoon?"

Emma rolled her eyes. "I had to go to Senator Brown's house with Candy."

"That's too bad."

"It wasn't all bad. He kicked me out which was quite amusing." She reached under his shirt and put her fingers on the bare skin of his lower back.

Hugh's body began to warm. "Why did you have to go there in the first place?"

"Candy asked me to." She sat on the window seat and picked up a pack of cards lying nearby.

Hugh sat next to her. He watched as she expertly shuffled the cards and dealt a hand of Tribute. They started playing.

"Candy had to see the Senator to make sure he would pay for her education." Emma said as she scrutinized her cards. They continued to play while she told him about what Candy and Senator Brown had said, and how rude Bridget Brown was.

"Tribute!" She put down her cards.

"I've taught you too well." he moaned as he scooped up the cards and began a new hand. "Did you see that, what's her name? Ma Granger?"

"Oh yes. I've been saving that for last." Emma said. "When we got there the housekeeper said that the Senator wasn't there. But Ma told me he was upstairs fornicating."

"No one wants to know about that."

"She also told me why he smells like maple syrup." She explained how the Senator's love of pancakes and lack of bathing had led to his distinct aroma.

Hugh laughed as he tried desperately to win. She was getting hard to beat. "So that explains it. One of life's mysteries solved."

"Ma said something else too." Emma switched around the cards in her hand. "She mentioned that a being came to visit her."

"A being?"

"Yes. She said he lured her onto the roof and told her to leave me alone." She set her cards aside and looked at him. "Do you think it could be Mika?"

Hugh was surprised at her question. "Why would Mika be at Senator Brown's house? And what fool would go up on the roof to talk to him?"

"She said he had black wings."

"He doesn't have wings."

"She said he was beautiful."

"He's not."

"Maybe not to you." she said. "I don't know, I guess it wasn't him, it just seemed strange."

"This Ma Granger seems strange enough on her own without bringing Mika into it."

"I wish I could see him."

"You're not missing much."

"Still, it would be nice. And I would like to thank him."

"For what?"

"You." She slid across the window seat and onto his lap. He wrapped his arms around her while she snuggled her head in the crook of his neck.

"You just did thank him. He hears everything." He opened the top three buttons on her blouse. He had always been skilled with his hands, even when using just one. He undid one more button and slid his hand inside, her skin was warm and soft. She moved her shoulder back so that his fingers could maneuver easily inside the constrictive corsets that girls wore these days. His fingertips had just found the soft flesh of her breast when Elsay's voice came through the door like a battering ram.

"Dinner is ready Emma dear."

Emma leapt up. "I'll be right there." She looked down and quickly buttoned her shirt. "I swear they do it on purpose. I really do Hugh."

196

"There's no way they can know."

"They're such busybodies."

"You are the only child left now, they have nothing better to do. I would have given anything to have my parents annoying me at eighteen."

Emma looked at him and sighed. "I forgot about that. You're right, I should be grateful I still have them. I just wish they wouldn't pop in when I'm with you." She grabbed his shirt and pulled him into a kiss. "Let's go have dinner."

Elsay and Edward were already at the table when Emma and Hugh walked into the kitchen. Hugh took his usual place near the window so he could see Emma's face.

"Congratulations." Edward said as she sat down.

"Thank you." She picked up her utensils and started to cut her meat. "Everything looks good."

It was then that Hugh noticed Edward was smiling more foolishly than usual. "I hear you went to Senator Brown's house today."

"Yes. It was for Candy's sake. I had no interest in seeing him. He threw me out in any case." Emma looked strangely at her father. "What's wrong?"

"Jeremy White came by the shop today to pick up my payment for the Senator."

"Oh?"

Hugh was as confused as she was. He had heard of this Mr. White for some time but had never seen him.

"Mr. White? Oh yes he was coming in as I was going out." Emma stuck a forkful of potatoes in her mouth.

"Jeremy said that you agreed he could call on you." Edward said.

Emma coughed and swallowed the potatoes in one gulp, she sputtered and took a drink. "I did what?"

"He said you agreed to a walk on the bluff."

"When did I do that?" She threw her napkin on the table and stared at her father.

"Emma it's nothing to be ashamed of." Elsay said. "Your father and I are pleased."

"Jeremy said he asked just as you were leaving and you said yes."

Emma's face clouded, she wrinkled her brow and then nodded slowly. "He was saying something as I was leaving. I wasn't listening. I wanted to get home to- I wanted to get home. I said yes to whatever he wanted just so I could get out of there." She looked at Hugh, there were tears in the corners of her eyes. "I would never have agreed to that. I have no interest in Mr. White whatsoever."

"That beats it all." Elsay threw up her hands. "You've got to do something with your life Emma. You can't sit in your room all day."

"I can if I want to."

Elsay sighed and looked helplessly at Edward. "Let's talk about it later. I've made a cake and I want us all to enjoy it. Eve said she would try and bring the children over later tonight after supper. Come on Emma."

Emma sniffed and sat up in her chair. "I'd like some cake Mother."

"That's better." Edward said. "Make mine a big piece Elsay." While Elsay was busy at the sideboard Edward turned to Emma and spoke quietly. "When Jeremy does come around you'll have to be the one to explain your lack of interest. He's a good man Emma. You could have a real future with him."

Emma didn't say anything.

Elsay served the cake even though none of them had finished their dinner. The conversation about Mr. White ceased. Hugh stood by the window and watched them. He knew this day would come. It was only a matter of time before the outside world would come calling and take Emma away.

Chapter 41

The next few weeks were some of the happiest of my life. I had nothing to do and nowhere to be. Hugh and I spent nearly every morning in bed talking, laughing and doing other things. In the back of my mind I knew it could not last. I couldn't merely lie about all day in my parents' home when I was a fully capable adult.

But what was I supposed to do now? We couldn't afford to send me to college. I had no interest in getting married. Hugh was the only person I wanted to be with. The only thing left to do was go to work.

I asked Mr. Thalberg if there was anything I could do in his store. He had always been kind to me. His wife was pregnant again and I thought there was a good chance he might need someone.

"Yes, yes." he said immediately. "You can help with the fabric and notions. The ladies always want to know what is fashionable." He shrugged. "I don't know anything about it. My wife reads the magazines. Now you can do it."

"You want *me* to tell people what's fashionable?"

"Why not? You're a woman aren't you?"

"Yes." I was also the most unfashionable girl in town. My clothes never matched and I had no sense of style whatsoever. I wouldn't know a mutton sleeve from a mutton chop.

"You want the job?"

"Sure." I tried to sound enthusiastic.

"Good. Start today." He handed me an apron.

Thus began my job as purveyor of fine fabrics and unsound fashion advice. I had been working a couple of months when the bell on the shop door jingled. I looked up and saw Mr. White step inside holding his hat in his hands. Darn. I had forgotten about him.

"Hello Emma."

"Good afternoon Mr. White."

"Ah that's Jeremy remember?"

"Oh yes. What brings you to Thalberg's?" Maybe he had just come in to buy something.

"I thought I would come and see if I could take you up on that walk?"

Mr. Thalberg looked up from his accounting book.

"Oh well, that's awfully kind of you, but I am quite busy here and I've already had my lunch."

"Emma you can take a break. Go ahead." Mr. Thalberg looked warmly towards Jeremy.

"No I better stay here, it might get busy." The store was empty.

Mr. Thalberg waved his hand in the air. "Nonsense. It's a beautiful day, go and enjoy it."

"It's settled then." Jeremy said. "Shall we?"

I sighed. It was probably best to get it over with. I took off my apron and stepped out from behind the counter.

"Don't you need a hat?" he asked.

"No, I forgot mine this morning."

"Oh." He looked confused. It was a positive sign that he found me utterly unsuitable. He offered his arm and I felt obliged to take it. We walked out of the store all the while Mr. Thalberg was looking pleased with himself.

"I won't be long." I told him.

"Take your time."

Jeremy and I stepped outside. "I thought we could walk up the hill to the new construction. There's something I want to show you." he said.

"Fine."

We strolled up the hill towards the new part of town. The front door of Eve's house was open.

"My sister lives there." I said pointing.

"Do you want to stop?"

I was about to answer when I saw the bricklayer coming down the sidewalk rattling off his usual chant. "I don't think so."

"Twas a black day my friends when a brick came falling from the sky and snuffed me out like a candle. Twas a brick I had laid with my own hands barely an hour before." he cried. "Ah one of the Seers is back. There have not been so many in town since I can't remember when. They can see this here ole' bricklayer in his agony."

We walked in silence. I could not think of a thing to say. Talking to Hugh was easy, we never ran out of conversation. As we walked the silence became uncomfortable. I searched my mind for something, anything. "It's a nice day isn't it?"

"Yes, lovely." he agreed looking up at the clear blue sky. "It was pleasant yesterday as well."

"Yes it was."

"That's when I arrived."

"Are you in town for long?"

"Not this time. But very soon I shall be here all the time. That's what I wanted to show you." he said smiling mysteriously. "Look there." He pointed to a half finished house across the street.

"What about it?"

"That's my new house." He crossed the road dragging me along with him.

"I thought you lived in Augusta."

"I do but I am moving here." He took my hand and helped me maneuver through the piles of lumber and bricks that littered the front yard. We stepped onto the half finished porch. The smell of fresh wood filled my lungs.

"Why are you moving here? What about Senator Brown?" I asked, secretly hoping he might be getting forcibly removed from the state senate.

"He's offered me a job." Jeremy said proudly. "I am going to be the president of the new bank he's building."

"He's building a bank?"

"Yes. Isn't it wonderful?"

I shrugged. Banks didn't interest me, but I was surprised that Father hadn't mentioned it.

"You don't like the Senator do you?"

"No."

He smiled and leaned in close to me. "Truth be told I don't like him much either. But a man has to work."

"You don't like him?" I said hopefully.

"Not really. Surprised?"

"Yes, very. I would have never known."

"I was an orphan. I could never have had the opportunities I've been given without him, and I am grateful. But it doesn't mean I like the man personally. He's a bit odd and he used to smell like syrup."

I laughed out loud. "We used to wonder about that for years."

"I never did find out why. Someone told me he used it like cologne."

"I've heard that one too. Maybe it was syrup from his pancakes dripping into his beard?" I suggested.

"Wouldn't he wash it?"

"Maybe not."

"That's disturbing Emma."

"I know but it could have happened."

"That's a good one." he said laughing. "Do you want to see inside the house? Or at least what there is of it?"

"Sure." We went inside. He described in detail what each room would look like. I imagined, even with my unfashionable brain, that it was going to be very stylish and modern. "How much longer until it's done?"

"They are telling me another two months, but who knows? I can wait, they haven't even started building the bank yet."

"I am glad I got to see it before everyone else." I said taking a last look as we stepped through the front doorway.

"Do you need to be getting back to work?"

"I probably should." I took his arm and we started back towards the shop. The bricklayer was dead ahead.

"Is that your beau?" he called out to me. I tightened my grip on Jeremy's arm.

"Are you all right?" Jeremy asked.

"Can we cross to the other side?"

"So you don't want to walk by the ole' bricklayer eh? Afraid the same fate that befell me will do you in as well? Oh but there not be any bricks falling anymore. Twas a dark day my friends when the brick fell…" He continued his usual lament as we walked down the hill towards the store.

"How long have you worked at Thalberg's?"

"I've been working with the fabrics for the last few months, but I've helped on and off for years."

"That's the first time I've been in there. I am a Jennings' man myself." he said as though it was some kind of badge of honor. I tried not to make a face.

"Just don't ask to buy the wrong thing, he'll put you out on the sidewalk. That's how I met Mr. Thalberg."

"Cole Jennings? I can't imagine." Jeremy looked surprised. "Ah well you never can tell."

"If you've never been to Thalberg's how did you know I was there?"

"Your mother told me. I stopped at your house this morning."

"Oh?"

"You know you still owe me that walk on the bluff." he said teasingly.

"I do?"

"Yes. But when I heard you were in town working I thought it was a great chance to show you the house."

Thalberg's sign was straight ahead. I stopped in front of the store. Mr. Thalberg was gaping out the window at us.

"Looks like we've drawn some attention." Jeremy looked pleased.

I nodded, resisting an urge to stick my tongue out at Mr. Thalberg.

Jeremy straightened his shoulders as though he were about to give a speech. "Thank you Emma for accompanying me. I hope you had an enjoyable time."

His formality startled me. "Thank you." I said automatically. "It was nice to see your house, and talk with you." I surprised myself with my last statement, but it was true, he was not at all like Senator Brown, as I had expected. He was quite likable in fact.

"Then may I call on you for that walk on the bluff?"

"Yes, that would be nice."

"Good day then." he said shaking my hand briskly.

"Goodbye." I turned and ran into the shop. Mr. Thalberg was behind the counter grinning.

"He is a nice boy, no?"

"Yes he's nice."

"When my wife and I began courting we went for walks all the time."

I put my apron on. "We are not courting."

"Does he know that?"

"I don't know."

"Don't you want to get married and have babies?"

"What? Yes, I mean no. That would be nice, but it won't happen."

"How do you know? You are so young to give up."

"I just know." The bell rang on the front door and a customer walked in, ending our conversation. Out of the corner of my eye I saw Mr. Thalberg shaking his head. He couldn't possibly understand.

Chapter 42

Hugh had finally seen the mysterious Mr. White. He knocked on the front door earlier that morning. Elsay had been in the middle of reading a lusty novel when the polite tapping sent the book flying into the air. Hugh, who had been reading along with her from behind the sofa, was equally startled. He had been so engrossed in the story he had not heard anyone approach.

Elsay tucked the book behind the sofa cushions and went to the door. A youthful looking man in an expensive suit of clothes was standing on the doorstep smiling. Hugh immediately took note of the gold watch chain dangling from his vest pocket. He had sandy blond hair, dark blue eyes and a pleasant, boy-like expression.

"Mr. White." Elsay said matter-of-factly. She was rarely pleasant when she answered the door. "My husband isn't at home. You should try the barber shop."

"Actually Mrs. Hollis I was looking for Emma." He looked past Elsay's shoulder as though Emma might magically appear.

"Really?" Her tone suddenly changed.

"Yes I thought we might take a walk. I ran into her a few weeks ago."

"That's right you did. She's not home right now. She's working at that store, Thalberg's. You can find her there. Won't you come in first?" She opened the door wide.

"Yes do come in." Hugh added.

"Perhaps another time, thank you so much Mrs. Hollis." He touched the brim of his hat.

"Very well. Good day Mr. White." She stayed in the doorway and watched him stroll down the road towards town.

Hugh sighed. He had wanted to hate him. He wanted so badly to hate Mr. White but he couldn't. There was no future for Emma and him. He had known that all along, he just hadn't figured out how to tell her.

Elsay shut the door and went into the kitchen. Hugh ran to the window, catching the last glimpse of Mr. White as he rounded the corner and disappeared behind the trees at the end of the road.

He would be good for Emma. Mr. White could give her everything in life Hugh could not. No matter what she said he knew she wanted marriage and children. He could give her none of those, if she didn't move on she would remain in the house with him, missing everything life had to offer.

Hugh had his chance at life. Even though he had spent most of it stealing and ended up a murdered criminal he had still lived more than Emma ever would clinging to him. He would have to let her go somehow. He loved her completely, she was everything to him. When she left he would remain, Tormenting on alone, dead in an ever changing world.

Emma came home late that afternoon. She looked tired and flustered as she managed a smile for him in the darkness of the front hallway.

"Is that you Emma?" Elsay called out.

"Yes." Emma stepped into the parlor. Hugh followed her.

"Did Mr. White pay you a visit today?"

"Yes, thank you very much." she said tartly.

Elsay stopped her knitting. "What was wrong with that? He's a perfectly nice young man."

The front door opened. "Good evening." Edward called out. "It's starting to rain." A few seconds later he appeared looking damp but energized.

"Emma and I were just talking about her day." Elsay said. A knowing look passed between them. They often spoke of Emma in the confines of their bedroom. Hugh sometimes listened in. They were concerned about her, they didn't understand why she spent so much time alone in her room. Elsay was afraid she would become a spinster. Edward's concerns were harder to pin down.

"I heard about your walk with Mr. White." Edward said running his hands through his hair to brush away the rain.

"How on earth do you know about that?" Emma asked. Hugh could tell by her expression that she was getting angry

"Oh, one hears things in a barber shop."

"And just who told you?" Emma turned to face him. Her hair spun like a carousel. She stared at her father, her hands planted firmly on her hips.

"What does it matter who told me?"

"I don't like people gossiping about me."

"Emma, it's a small town, what else do people have to do except gossip?" Elsay snickered. She picked up her knitting and continued with her work.

"That's right." Edward said without much conviction.

Emma's face was turning red. "I want to know who told you."

Edward sighed and scratched his head. "Very well. It was a Mr. Mason. Steve Mason. Are you satisfied now?"

"Who's that?"

"Emma this is ridiculous. You just took a walk with a nice young man. Did you have a good time?"

"He's nice." she said shrugging.

"That's a start anyway." Elsay said.

Emma glared at her mother. "I wish the both of you would just leave me alone."

"Emma Hollis!" Elsay stood up, her knitting tumbling to the floor. "Don't you dare talk to us like that."

"Then stop interfering in my life!" She stormed out of the parlor and upstairs. Hugh remained where he was.

"Let her go." Edward said quietly.

Elsay sat back down and shook her head. "I don't know what's wrong with her."

He rubbed his eyes and sat next to his wife. "Give her time Elsay. She just has to figure out what she wants out of life."

Hugh walked through the parlor wall and into the hallway. He headed upstairs and found Emma in her bedroom crying. She was sitting on the end of the bed with her head in her hands.

"I don't care about Jeremy, Mr. White, whatever he's called." She looked up at him with a tear stained face.

"I know." Hugh sat next to her. He put his arm around her shoulders, he felt the tension and anger leave her body as she wrapped her arms tightly around him and put her head on his chest.

"I hate how you have to stand there and listen to them go on about him. As though I could ever love him." she said hiccupping.

"They want you to be happy Emma."

"I am."

"They want you to have a life of your own beyond these walls."

He felt a change in her. She sat up and wiped her eyes. "What are you saying?"

He hesitated. She was already upset, it wasn't the best time to have this discussion. "Emma, what are your plans for the future?"

"To be with you." she said looking confused.

"I can't marry you."

"That isn't important."

"I can't give you children."

"Why does everyone keep talking about this? I don't have to have children. Eve has enough for all of us."

"I'm dead Emma. My life is over. Your eighteen years old, your life is just beginning."

She jumped up as though the bed was on fire. "What are you saying to me? You don't want to be with me?"

Hugh shook his head. "No, that's not what I am saying. I love you. You know that. I would love nothing more than to spend the rest of time here in this house with you. But you deserve to live *your* life. You deserve everything you want out of life, and no matter what you say, I can't give it to you."

 She shook her head. "You're wrong. I would happily spend every second of the rest of my life here with you."

"You would grow to resent me."

 Her face twisted in pain, tears ran slowly down her cheeks. "What if I died?"

"What?"

"What if I met with an untimely death? Couldn't I Torment with you?" she asked desperately.

"You're not ending your life for me."

"If only you were alive."

"But I'm not." He couldn't say anymore. He had hurt her enough for one day. "Let's talk about it later."

"Or never." she muttered. "Go away."

 He left and sat upstairs in the attic, a place he hardly visited anymore. He could hear her crying in her room. Sometime after midnight the rain let up outside and the clouds parted allowing some moonlight to shine in the attic window. He ventured downstairs.

 Emma was in bed, he couldn't tell if she was awake or not. He hesitated and then gently pulled back the covers and slipped underneath. She turned over and opened her eyes. She watched him as he settled down and rested his head on the pillow. They stared at each other for a few seconds before she scooted closer to him and rested her head on his pillow. Her face was inches from his. Under the covers she took his hand and grasped it tightly.

"Goodnight." she whispered before closing her eyes and drifting off to sleep.

Chapter 43

I didn't sleep much that night. Snippets of our conversation kept swirling through my mind. I woke up a dozen times or more. Hugh came to bed at some point. It was a relief to have him there. I could never sleep properly unless he was beside me.

I hated to think about what he had said. I hated it because I had the same thoughts. He was right. We were from two different worlds. I belonged among the living and he belonged to the dead. We weren't meant to know each other, never mind to fall in love. It was unfair to both of us.

Morning came quickly, the sun shined brightly in my eyes and woke me up. "What time is it?" I mumbled.

"7:36."

I sat up in bed and rubbed my eyes. "I need another five hours."

"Do you have to work today?" He was sitting up with his back against the headboard.

"Yes."

He nodded and ran his hands through my tangled hair. "Are you angry with me?"

"No."

"Emma, I just want you to know that if an opportunity comes up, I mean if someone should ask you something, or want you to spend time with them, you can say yes."

"And what are you going to do?"

"I'll be here, just like always. You can't live for me Emma."

"Can we not talk about this right now?" I turned my face away from him and brushed the tears away from my face.

"It won't go away."

Jeremy didn't go away either. His presence in Thalberg's was as predictable as Mr. Jennings glaring at me from across the street. He wasn't bad company. Once I got over his connection to Senator Brown I found him quite likeable. I never invited him to do anything, but I didn't discourage him either. I didn't talk about him with Hugh. It was a subject we avoided.

The summer passed into an especially cool autumn. Jeremy and I were taking our usual afternoon walk. We were on a narrow strip of sand that served as Fox Cove's only beach. The wind blew hard at our faces.

"When do they start building the bank?" I shouted at him over the wind.

"What?" he said cupping his ear. "Oh, the bank? Any day now." He laughed and tugged at my arm. We stepped behind a large boulder that served as a natural shelter against the elements. "That's better." He let his hand slide down my arm. He tried to catch my hand but I pulled it away. "Emma."

"What?"

He started to speak and then stopped. "Listen, I've been meaning to talk to you about something."

"Oh?"

"You must know what it is."

"No." I *did* have an idea, but I didn't want to hear about it.

"Emma. I want you to marry me."

"What?" I pretended to be shocked.

"You must have known. I love you Emma."

I turned my back on him. I felt like someone had punched me in the stomach. I was supposed to say yes. I could make everyone happy with one word. My parents, Eve, Mr. Thalberg, even Hugh.

"Are you all right?" He put a hand on my back.

"Yes."

"I thought you would be expecting this."

I shook my head no. I couldn't speak. I tried to picture myself in his new house, a banker's wife with a brood of children peeking around the folds of my skirt. It was a pleasing picture, but there was something missing. I tried to imagine kissing him, touching him, but Hugh's face kept popping into my head.

"You need time." he said.

"Yes." I managed to say.

"You can give me your answer later."

I turned around. "I'm sorry. I just need a little time."

"That's fine. I would rather you know for sure."

"Thank you." I said as my voice broke. "I'll let you know tomorrow."

"Very well Emma. I can wait one more day."

When I returned to work Mr. Thalberg was leaning over his counter. "Did he ask you?" It was the same thing he had been saying every day for months.

"Yes." I said bleakly.

He clapped his hands together. "I knew it would happen. I knew the first day he walked in here. Remember?"

"Yes I remember."

"I am going to lose my fashion expert. But I am glad for you."

"I haven't given him an answer yet." I said ignoring the fashion expert comment.

"What? No answer? Why? You're not going to say no are you?"

"I have to talk to someone first."

The walk home seemed longer than usual. It was nearly dark when I came through the door and hung up my shawl. Hugh was in the hallway. I started to motion for him to go upstairs when Mother popped out of the kitchen.

"Emma, where have you been? Your father and I were starting to get worried. Supper is ready." I looked over her shoulder and saw Father at the table waiting patiently for his meal.

"I got delayed." I said vaguely. I followed her into the kitchen and sat in my usual chair. Hugh lingered by the window.

Mother was quick to serve the meal. We ate in silence. Our silverware banged noisily on the china dishes Mother had received from Senator Brown so many years before.

"How was your day dear?" she asked me over a sip of wine.

"Fine."

"Did you see Mr. White?"

"Yes." I said glancing at Hugh. His face didn't change.

"I can't imagine it's going to be long now." Father said with a wink.

"Long for what?"

"A proposal of course."

I shut my eyes and tried to breathe, another minute and I would be crying. I could already feel the tears coming.

"Has he asked you Emma?" Mother said excitedly.

"Let her be Elsay."

I couldn't see Hugh through the tears clouding my eyes. "May I be excused? I'm not feeling well." I bolted from the table and ran upstairs to my bedroom. I slammed the door shut and fell onto my knees, the tears came like a rain shower.

"Emma." Hugh said behind me. He knelt down and put his arm around me. "He asked you, didn't he?"

"Of course, just like you wanted."

"It's not like that."

"Oh, shut up. It is too."

214

"I want you to live a long and fulfilling life. You'll never get that chance with me. It would be like living a half life."

"If you say so."

"Do you love him Emma?"

I pushed him away. "Of course not you jackass. I love you." He fell back on the floor and stared at me.

"You like him though?"

"He's tolerable." I sniffed. "You want me to say yes don't you?" I wiped the remaining tears from my eyes and stood up.

"Yes I think you should. He seems like a good and decent man and he will make a nice home for you. He can give you children and a real life that I can't." He stood up and sighed.

I took a deep breath. I looked at him standing in my room in his wrinkled, untucked shirt with the bullet hole that I hardly noticed anymore. His face was white as a sheet in the darkness. His expression was complacent. I understood what he meant about what I would be giving up to stay with him.

"Do you know what you're going to do?" he asked.

"Yes. I'll give him my answer tomorrow."

Chapter 44

Emma left that morning without saying goodbye. Hugh understood. He heard her go, but he did not leave the attic where he had spent the night. It wasn't until the front door closed that it truly hit him.

He couldn't recall the last time he had cried. It started from somewhere deep down and came bursting out of him. His face was covered with tears, his body convulsed as he sobbed with grief. Emma was leaving him. It was unimaginable, and in his own misguided wisdom he had made it happen. He had convinced himself that marrying someone she found tolerable was better than spending her life with him.

Although he felt no physical pain there was an ache in the pit of his stomach. He was such a fool, such a bloody fool. He had everything he wanted and he had given it away. He fell on his side and let the tears run into his mouth.

"Mika. I need you." He had no one else.

Nothing happened. Eventually the tears subsided and he was left alone with his thoughts. This would be his life again, an empty room staring back at him for an eternity. Maybe she would visit with Jeremy and their children. They would exchange smiles, perhaps a few pleasantries if no one else was around. Things would never be the same.

"Mika." Nothing.

He would have to start seriously haunting the house. He could drive Elsay mad, that would do it. Edward and Elsay had to go. He couldn't bear to see Emma with that man. Jeremy was the best choice for her, but he didn't have to stand witness to it.

"Damn it Mika! I need you! Now!"

"What do you want?" Mika was suddenly standing in the middle of the attic. "I've got others to look after besides you."

"Something terrible has happened." Hugh said desperately.

"If by terrible you mean that girl has gone off to accept his marriage proposal then I say something good has come out of the whole Torment Seer mess." He tapped his fingers anxiously on his leg.

"Why am I not surprised you would say that? You've never wanted me to be happy."

"Don't be so dramatic. And get up off the floor." He tapped Hugh with his foot. "I'm embarrassed to be your Watcher."

Hugh sat up slowly and wiped his eyes. "Has she said yes? Do you know?"

Mika frowned. "Do you think I have time to Watch everyone in this town? I'm busy you know." He grabbed Hugh's arm and pulled him roughly to his feet. "I said get up. You're going to start listening to me whether you want to or not."

Hugh wished he had not called him. But it was too late now.

"You did the right thing." Mika said.

"What do you mean?"

"You encouraged her to spend time with this Jeremy White character."

"And look where it got me."

"Hugh, the living and the dead don't mix. These things almost always turn out badly."

"Then this has happened before?" Hugh asked.

"I didn't say that. Why is there never anywhere to sit down in here?" Suddenly two chairs appeared in the middle of the attic. One was small and covered with red velvet. The other was much larger with a tall back and curved armrests. It was covered in black velvet.

"I didn't know you could do that. All this time I've had to sit on the floor." Hugh said.

Mika shrugged. "You never asked for a chair. I may be a genius but I'm not a mind reader." He took a seat in the large chair and motioned for Hugh to sit in the smaller one.

"Why do you need such a fancy seat?"

"Because I'm special." He leaned back and stared at Hugh. "I'm proud of you."

"Why?"

"Because you stopped thinking of yourself and thought of someone else for a change. I told you the dead and the living do not mix. You've made some progress."

"But you said things like this have happened before?"

"I told you I didn't say that."

"Yes you did."

"Oh, so what if I did?" Mika grumbled. "They rarely turn out well."

Hugh straightened up in his chair. Something Mika said had caught his attention. "What do you mean they rarely turn out well?"

"Just what I said. Why don't you try listening for a change?"

"I was listening. You said they rarely turn out well. But that must mean one time it did turn out well."

"The one time you actually listen- Just forget about it."

"If only I was alive. If only you could make me alive again."

Mika didn't answer.

If Hugh had a pulse it would have quickened. He had hit upon something, he could sense it. Mika stared at him with his ice blue eyes.

"Can you make me alive again?"

"How can I possibly make someone who is dead as a doornail come alive? It's ridiculous." Mika scoffed. He tapped his foot on the floor.

"I thought you said you were special."

"I am. Anyone can see that."

Hugh was about to give up the notion when Mika's expression suddenly changed. There was something in his eyes, as though he wanted to be asked. "Can you bring me back to life?"

"I can't simply wave my hand and you're alive again. It's complicated."

"Who cares? Do it anyway. You said you were proud of me, you said I had learned something."

"So because of one thing you deserve a second chance?" Mika argued. "And what are you going to do if you are suddenly alive again?"

"Be with Emma of course." Hugh said. Mika glared at him. It was the wrong answer. "I'll be the kind of person I should have been. I'll do whatever you want. I'll help the poor and the sick. I'll go to church every day. I'll become a minister, or if you prefer a rabbi. Whatever you want." He was considering getting down on his knees and begging.

Mika suddenly sat up and looked over Hugh's shoulder. "She's left his house."

"How do you know?" He felt the ache in his stomach return.

"I know."

"Then you won't make me alive again?"

"Hugh, it's not that simple. You can't return as Hugh MacPherson, he's dead and gone. You would have a whole new body and a new name."

"But I would still be me?"

"On the inside yes, but not on the outside. I told you it was complicated." Mika looked over Hugh's shoulder again. "She'll be here in three minutes and seven seconds, give or take. She's crying."

Hugh sank down in his seat. He didn't want to see her. He didn't want to hear her say what he knew was coming. She would have accepted the offer of marriage. They probably would have kissed too. His mind filled with the image of Emma kissing the perfect Jeremy White.

"Just wait until she gets here." Mika said softly.

"Do you know what she said?"

"Yes."

"What?"

"I think it would be better if you heard it from her." Mika said.

"Aren't you going to go?"

"Why? Are you sick of me? No, I'd better stay with you."

"But you've never allowed Emma to see you before."

"Who says I'm going to let her see me?"

Hugh couldn't talk anymore. A few minutes passed. He heard the latch on the front door and followed the sound of her soft footsteps up two flights until the attic door burst open. Emma ran into the room, her hair flying behind her. Hugh was surprised to see she was smiling.

"Hugh." she whispered as she locked eyes with him. She stumbled and fell into his lap, burying her face in the crook of his neck. "I couldn't do it."

"Thank God." he managed to say before the tears burst from his eyes. He felt as though an enormous burden had been lifted from his shoulders. A sudden feeling of elation caught him by surprise. He put his arms around her and squeezed her tightly to him. "Thank God." he said again.

"I couldn't do it. I just couldn't Hugh." She smoothed his hair. "It's you Hugh, you forever."

He nodded at her, unable to speak without the chance of bawling again. Emma continued brushing his hair with her fingers. As she did a puzzled look crossed her face. "Where did these chairs come from?"

"Mika brought them." Hugh glanced warily at his Watcher. Mika was passively observing them, it was impossible to tell what he was thinking.

"Mika was here?"

"Actually he's still here."

Emma jumped off Hugh's lap and stared at the empty chair. "Is he sitting there right now?"

"You've got a real bright one there Hugh." Mika said.

"Yes he's there." Hugh stood up. "I wouldn't antagonize him if I were you."

"I'm not going to antagonize him. I just wish I could see him that's all." Emma backed away. Hugh took her hand, his arm began to tingle.

"She's a mere Torment Seer, she could never see the likes of me." Mika remained seated on his elegant chair like a Roman dictator.

"You'll make him angry." Hugh whispered.

"Why? I wish I could see him, just once." She squeezed Hugh's hand tightly.

Mika stood up, he stepped towards them with catlike grace. "She wants to see me does she? How do you like this Torment Seer?" A burst of light illuminated the room. Hugh could hear the glass in the windows rattling. Beside him Emma was shaking.

"You're so beautiful." She wasn't speaking to Hugh anymore.

"Can you see him?"

Emma nodded and ducked behind Hugh. She wrapped her arms around his waist and peered over his shoulder at Mika.

"Stop frightening her." Hugh tried to sound brave.

"I'm not frightening her. She sees dead people all the time. What's one more?" Mika said. "What do you think Torment Seer? What's it like to see something other than a poor pathetic Tormented Soul?"

Emma was squeezing Hugh so tight it was a lucky thing he didn't actually need to breathe. "I, I want to thank you for looking after Hugh." she managed to say.

Mika's mouth dropped open. "You want to do what?"

"I want to thank you for taking care of him."

"And I suppose you're going to take over the job now?" he said coldly.

"No, not at all. I could never replace you."

Mika blinked. It was clearly not the response he was expecting.

"You're the most beautiful thing I've ever seen." she added.

"Thank you. I get that a lot."

"Can't you let Hugh go outside now and then? I know this Tormented Soul, Ma Granger, she can go in and out of the house she haunts any time she pleases and she even went up on the roof once."

"What sort of fool would go up on the roof?" Mika said almost laughing. Hugh sensed a change in his mood but he wasn't sure if it was for the better.

"Couldn't Hugh just walk around the house a bit?"

Mika scratched his chin and stared at Emma. "Maybe we should just get rid of the house and then Hugh could go anywhere he pleased."

"What do you mean?"

There was no time for answers. Hugh was suddenly aware of sunlight on his face. Somewhere nearby there was a loud crack. He looked up and saw the roof of the house was missing.

"Oh my God." Emma cried from behind him.

Hugh assumed she was meaning the missing roof. That was until he saw Mika floating six feet above them. He was being carried skyward by a pair of large black wings edged in shiny silver.

"What do you think? Is that enough room for Hugh?" Mika called down to them.

"You said he didn't have wings." she said in his ear.

"I didn't know."

"That's really not enough room to roam is it?" Mika said. He gently floated down until he was hovering a few inches off the attic floor. Hugh noted there was a slightly deranged look on his face, he wondered if he had once been a mental patient somewhere. Mika laughed and the entire house fell away at their feet. Hugh and Emma found themselves standing on a dusty lot, the house and all its contents had vanished save for the two chairs that Mika had created.

Emma let go of Hugh and looked around at the new landscape in distress. "What about my mother? She was in the kitchen when I came home."

"Don't worry Elsay is safe. Can't you let an old Watcher have some fun?" Mika giggled and the entire town of Fox Cove faded away. All that was left were the grassy bluffs and the sound of the ocean. "That's better. Come on Hugh let's go for a walk."

"What about my family? What about everyone who lives here?" Emma cried.

"Oh stop it Torment Seer. Don't you know it's all an illusion?" Mika said. "I've grown tired of her. Go sit down and don't disturb us."

Emma immediately turned and sat on the small chair. She folded her hands on her lap and stared straight ahead.

"What did you do to her?" Hugh cried. He shook Emma's shoulders. She never blinked an eye but continued to stare ahead.

"She'll soon recover. I'm pretty darn amazing aren't I?" Mika said letting himself bob over the ground as the wind ruffled his feathers.

"You're mad."

"It's quite possible. Now let's take a walk."

Despite the town disappearing and Emma in some kind of trance he found himself wanting to go. Hugh trusted Mika would not harm them. He followed him up the road towards the cove. He winced as the sharp stones of the gravel road cut through his stockings. The wind rustled the trees and blew his hair in his face. It was the most thrilling feeling. Overhead the sun blazed down on him, he squinted and raised his hand to protect his eyes. He hadn't done that for a hundred years or more.

Mika was already strides ahead. Hugh lagged behind watching the dust cloud around his feet as he walked. He repressed an urge to twirl about like a little girl and instead let his fingers skim the tall grasses growing next to the road, the dry edges of the blades tickled his hands.

He walked steadily uphill, turning his ankle several times. He was unused to walking on such an uneven surface. Mika was already at the end of the road waiting for him. It was strange to see Mika out of doors. The sun glinted off the silver tips of his feathers giving them the appearance of sparkling diamonds.

"I only have an eternity." Mika said as he waited for Hugh to catch up.

"Sorry." Hugh walked to the end of the road and up the hill that looked over the cove. There was a strong breeze coming off the ocean, the air was salty and filled with the cries of the seagulls that circled the water's edge.

Mika stood facing the sea. The wind blew at his face, he laughed and stretched his arms out, letting his shirt sleeves flap like a flag. His wings ruffled behind him. Suddenly a gust of wind caught the feathers like a sail and lifted him off the ground.

He rose slowly into the air until he was floating like the gulls down in the cove. He would start to fall towards the ground and then a gust of wind would send him rising up once again. Mika laughed. He was smiling, the dark and moody expression he usually wore was gone. He was joyful.

Hugh watched Mika ride the wind currents. He was playing like a child. "You should really try this Hugh."

"It's a bit tough when I don't have any wings." Hugh shouted back to him. He wasn't sure if Mika heard him, he was quite high in the air.

Mika swooped skyward and then came rushing down to earth. "What did you say?"

"I just said I can't really fly around in the air without any wings."

"I didn't know you wanted wings."

"I don't, I was just saying-"

"I'll give you wings." Mika laughed and kicked off the ground.

"I don't want-" Hugh never finished his sentence. He was suddenly aware of an enormous weight on his back. He felt like he had a small child strapped to him. "What on earth?" The next gust of wind rushed under him, tossing him in the air like a cork. He floated over the ground for a few seconds and then landed face down on a clump of grass.

Hugh could hear Mika laughing from somewhere close by. He turned his head to one side and spit some dirt out of his mouth. As he looked for Mika he realized that there were white feathers hanging over his shoulder. He tried to stand up and found himself stumbling backwards. He fell onto his backside, the feathers curled around his arms. He reached up and tugged on one, it didn't budge.

"You didn't." He glared at Mika who was still bobbing in the air overhead.

Mika laughed and flew to the ground. He sat next to Hugh. "What do you think?" He fingered the edges of Hugh's wings. "I do good work, huh?"

"I think you've had enough fun for one day. Take them off." Hugh said grumpily.

"Those wings are yours forever."

"I don't want them. How am I supposed to walk around with these things?" He didn't know when he had been so uncomfortable.

"They stay closed when you're inside. Who would wear their wings indoors?" Mika sneered.

"Is that why I've never seen yours?"

"Of course."

"How do I get them to close?"

"They close on their own, they know better than to stay open inside."

"I guess I won't have to worry about them."

"Why?"

"Because I will be indoors forever." His skin was starting to feel warm from sitting in the sun. He closed his eyes, he wanted to savor this moment.

"I'll have to put you back inside for a little while." Mika stood up and stretched his arms up into the air. The feathers on his wings braced stiffly against the fierce wind. "I have come to a decision Hugh. I am giving you a second chance at life. I'm going to send you back into the world."

"No! I won't go. I've just received a second chance with Emma." Desperation began to creep into his veins.

"Her? She'll hate you within a year."

"Maybe, but it was her decision. I want to stay here with her." Hugh kicked the ground with his heel. "I love her."

"And I suppose she's madly in love with you?"

Mika was ruining everything. Hugh pushed his fingers into the dirt. He wanted to go home. He wanted Mika gone and most of all he didn't want to be alive again, not if it meant losing Emma.

"I said is she in love with you?" Mika's voice echoed unnaturally in the empty air.

"Yes, I believe so."

"What's that you say?" Mika grabbed him by the arm and pulled him to his feet. "You'll look at me when I'm speaking."

"I know she loves me."

"Then let's see her prove it."

"I don't want to go back."

"That's all you could talk about a half hour ago."

"I know, but now that she's refused him I don't want to go."

Mika smiled and picked at the edges of Hugh's wings. "Don't worry I am not going to separate you from your precious Torment Seer. I am giving both of you a challenge. If you really love each other as you claim you'll have a life together, both of you alive and well."

"And if we fail?"

Mika grinned. "I'll be back later when I'm ready to take you. Take care of those wings. I only make white wings when I'm in a good mood you know."

Hugh suddenly found himself back in the attic. It was like waking from a very disturbing dream. Emma was still staring into space. He touched her shoulder. "Emma?"

She gasped for air and looked at him. "Mika?"

"He's gone. He's put everything back the way it was."

"Mother. I've got to make sure she's all right." She rushed down the attic stairs. He could hear her calling for Elsay.

Hugh sat down. As Mika promised his wings were gone. He put his head in his hands and tried to imagine what it would be like to be alive again. He wasn't sure he was up to the challenge.

Chapter 45

"Mother!" The last thing I remembered was Mika's voice telling me to sit down and be quiet. Before that the entire town had vanished. "Mother, are you all right?"

"Emma?" I heard her voice coming from the parlor. She was sitting on the sofa reading a book. "What on earth is wrong?"

I slumped against the doorway in relief. "Are you all right?"

"Of course I am all right. What's wrong?" She set her book aside.

"I just thought I heard a strange noise. You didn't hear it?"

"No. I didn't hear anything."

"You've been here all the time?"

"Yes."

"Oh." I plopped onto the sofa next to her. I took a deep breath and shut my eyes. The image of Mika floating in the air flickered in my mind.

"Emma, are you all right?" She put her hand on mine.

I opened my eyes and tried to smile. "I'm fine."

"You can tell me anything you know."

"I know." I rested my head on the back of the sofa and stared up at the ceiling. "Jeremy asked me to marry him."

"Oh Emma! I am so happy for you! I knew he would, I just knew it."

"I said no."

She sighed loudly. "Why?"

"I don't love him."

"Emma do you think every woman is in love with the man she marries? Jeremy is a perfectly amiable young man who thinks the world of you. He'll make an excellent husband and father. I think even you know that.

You may not get another chance like this. Sometimes you have to choose what's good enough."

"I'm not going to change my mind."

"Then what are you going to do? Do you want to go to college like Candy and Ethan? I can talk to your father, we'll find the money."

"No. I am not leaving here."

"Then you intend to become a spinster? You're a young pretty girl Emma, there's no reason for this."

"I'm not changing my mind." I was sorry I couldn't say more. I couldn't tell her I was in love with the man upstairs.

She took a deep breath and squeezed my hand. "When your father asked me to marry him I had reservations."

"Did you love him?"

"Yes, but I found out certain things about him that made me doubt whether I could live with him."

"What sort of things?"

Her face clouded. "That's not important now. My point is that I didn't turn my back on him. I went through with it and can't imagine my life without him. I don't want to see you do something you'll regret later."

"I know, but I can't marry him."

"Your father is going to be disappointed."

"I have a job. I can pay for my own things." I said.

"It's not about the money Emma. It's about your happiness."

"I know." I yawned. I hadn't slept much the night before. "I'm going upstairs now."

"Be sure to come down and eat something later." She watched me with a deflated look on her face.

I trudged up to my room. Hugh was waiting for me. He was sitting up in bed. He smiled when I came in the door. My feet felt like lead as I crawled across the bed and collapsed on top of him. He wrapped his arms tightly around me. "Are you all right?" he asked.

"Yes. I just feel so tired now." I put my hand inside the neck hole of his shirt. His skin felt cool and smooth. "What happened with Mika? Did you get to walk outside?"

"Yes." He explained how Mika had taken him down the road to look at the cove. He described the sensation of the sun on his face, the uneven ground beneath his feet, the way the wind rustled his hair. He told me about Mika flying in the air, dipping and swooping over the ground.

"I wished I could have seen that. It sounds fun."

"That's what I thought until he gave me wings."

I sat up. "He gave you wings? You mean real wings?"

"Yes, I mean real wings.

"Where are they?"

"Apparently they close up indoors. It's ridiculous."

"I can't wait to see them."

"That might be a long way off."

"Why? He isn't going to let you go outside again?"

"I don't know." A strange look crossed his face.

"What's wrong? Something happened with Mika, didn't it?"

He looked down and sighed. "Oh you know Mika, he's always saying things to upset me."

"What did he say? Is it about me? I know he doesn't like me."

"It's not important. He's so rude. I don't think he knows any other way."

"He's probably lonely. What does he do besides Watch others live? What kind of existence is that? Who looks after him?"

"Who cares?" There was a hint of bitterness in his voice. There was something he wasn't telling me, but it didn't seem like the time to question him further. His relationship with Mika was closed to me. I had very little idea of what they spoke of. There was a shared history between them, Hugh's former life and his long years of Torment, that I had no part in. "Forget about Mika. Tell me what happened with Jeremy. I thought for sure you were going to say yes."

I smiled at his evasiveness, he wanted to change the subject. "I was planning to accept his proposal when I left this morning. I had every intention of saying yes."

He reached into the front of my blouse and pulled out the star necklace. "I knew you did. What happened?"

I paused. It seemed like weeks ago since I left for Jeremy's house. I had convinced myself I was doing the right thing. He was a nice respectable man with a bright future. Any girl would be lucky to have him. I kept telling myself that over and over again.

The town had been unusually quiet. No one was about save for Mr. Jennings who was sweeping in front of his store. He grunted as I walked by. Thalberg's windows were still dark, I knew what Mr. Thalberg would say anyway. He saw no reason not to become Mrs. White.

"I was sure of myself until I ran into the bricklayer." I intertwined my fingers with Hugh's.

"Is that the dead fool who likes to tell you how he got hit on the head with a brick?"

"Yes."

"What is the matter with him? Who wants to hear about how he died? Do I do that? Please tell me I don't."

"You don't."

"Thank goodness." Hugh said. "How did the bricklayer make you change your mind?"

"First he asked me if I was on my way to see my beau. I said yes and then I realized I was thinking of you, not Jeremy."

"I am your secret beau."

"That's when he said something else. He said, "Hello there Seer! Ah, will be a fine day when you are living up here on the hill near me. It will warm this ole' bricklayer's heart to have a Seer so close by. I'm yearning to have a proper conversation with you.""

"I realized when he said that I was different from the other girls in town. I'm a Seer. I was always so embarrassed by that. I thought there was something wrong with me, like I was some kind of freak. But when he said that I suddenly realized I didn't need to lead a normal life. I didn't have to marry Jeremy just because that's what I should do. I was given the gift of Seeing for a reason, and I think it was to be with you." I kissed the back of his hand.

"It was to save me."

I smiled. "I realized I want to be here with you, no matter what."

"So that's when you made up your mind?"

"Yes."

"How did Jeremy take it?"

"Not well. He doesn't understand. He thinks I am scared of marriage."

"That's what he said?"

"Yes, that and other things."

"What?"

I sighed. It wasn't a conversation I wished to relive. I pictured Jeremy glaring at me. His face was red and angry as he circled around me, shaking his head in disbelief.

"You've led me around like a stray dog all these months." he said angrily.

"I haven't. I never once asked you to come and see me. I never encouraged you."

"You didn't send me away either." He ran his hands through his hair. "I can't believe you are refusing me."

"I'm sorry. Would you rather me accept your proposal only to take it back, or marry you and regret it?"

"I would rather you have rejected me long before this. I took your apprehension as shyness, but now I am not so sure."

"I am your friend Jeremy, I always have been, but I can't be your wife."

"I don't understand. Is there someone else?"

I didn't respond. I didn't want to lie to him. "It's just better this way."

He pointed his finger in my face. "There is someone else, isn't there? Who is it? I've never seen you with another man."

"It doesn't matter. My answer is no." I backed towards the door. "I hope in time you can understand." I hurried outside. He stood in the open doorway watching me. I crossed the street to avoid the bricklayer and raced home.

"He'll get past this Emma." Hugh said.

"I know. He's a really nice man and there's someone out there who is perfect for him. It's just not me. I know you wanted me to marry him. I know you didn't want me to spend the rest of my life locked up in this house with you. But that's what I choose."

"I only wanted you to be happy and have the best life possible. I always wanted you here with me." he said gently touching the side of my face.

"You're stuck with me now." I grabbed his shirt and pulled him into a kiss. I dug my fingers into his back and then remembered that he was a winged soul now. "Why can't I feel your wings?"

"I told you they close when I'm indoors."

"But where do they go?" I crawled across the bed and knelt behind him. I pulled open the neck hole of his shirt and looked at his back. "Um, Hugh, do you know what's back here?"

"No. What?"

"There are wings on your back."

"What?"

"Yes. It looks like they are drawn on with black ink." Inside his shirt were two perfectly drawn wings, one on each shoulder blade. The middle of the left wing was marred slightly by the exit hole from his bullet wound.

"Oh great. Thanks Mika."

I reached my hand in and traced the arch of each wing with my finger. "Thanks indeed." I whispered in his ear as he gasped. "I like them. Now if only this shirt would come off."

"Why didn't I go walking naked through town the night I died?"

"And have you standing in the kitchen next to my mother with nothing on?"

"Might be nice when she walked through me."

"Hugh MacPherson, you naughty boy." I gave him a gentle shove on the back.

He turned around and laughed. "You better punish me then." he said lying back on the bed. He pulled me on top of him. I could feel the hardness growing between his legs.

"With pleasure." I smiled and kissed him. What had I been thinking with Jeremy? This was where I belonged and there was nothing standing in my way of staying with Hugh forever.

Chapter 46

Hugh didn't want to say anything to Emma about his possible return to life just yet. As the weeks wore on without a word from Mika he began to wonder if he hadn't possibly misunderstood the whole thing.

Mika could not have that much power. How could one man be capable of such a thing? It seemed impossible, ridiculous. Mika could manipulate the weather occasionally and even make it appear as though the town had disappeared, but he couldn't possibly take a dead soul and just hand them a new body.

He had most certainly been joking, even though Mika didn't have much of a sense of humor. To be on the safe side Hugh took pains not to call him for any reason or even say his name aloud. He had no reason for Mika now anyway, he had Emma.

It wasn't until February, five months from Mika's last visit, that it became painfully clear what he had meant. Hugh was in the parlor listening to Edward and Elsay talk about Edward's brother Egbert. They had just received a letter from him. He was having an operation on his leg and Edward was worried about it. It was a dull conversation but he liked keeping abreast of family news. Mika suddenly appeared in the corner.

"Are you ready Hugh?"

"Ready for what?" Hugh tried to ignore him and focus on the news regarding Egbert.

"To come with me of course. I told you I am giving you a second chance at life. Don't you remember?"

"What? That? That was a joke of course." Hugh said with a wave of his hand. Inside he felt his fear beginning to grow.

Mika looked annoyed. "I don't make jokes. Giving back life isn't something to kid around about. And why haven't you told the Torment Seer yet?"

Hugh swallowed. Edward was folding Egbert's letter in his hands. "Would you be so good as to make me a cup of tea?" he asked Elsay. "This letter has given me a terrible shock."

"Of course dear." Elsay said gently touching Edward's arm. "You stay right here and I will bring you your tea. And perhaps one of those little lemon tarts you like so much?"

Edward nodded slowly. "Yes that would be nice. Thank you Elsay."

Elsay left the parlor and went across the hallway to the kitchen. He could hear her filling the kettle and opening the tea tin.

Edward slouched down on the sofa and opened Egbert's letter again.

"You should have told the Torment Seer about this months ago." Mika said staring at the back of Edward's head.

"I am not going. I don't want to."

"You don't have a choice. All the arrangements have been made. It's all settled."

"I told you I don't want to go. Emma has made up her mind, she's staying here with me. Forget about what I said."

"The living and the dead don't mix. I've told you this already. I'm giving you a chance to live again and to be with your precious Torment Seer. Of course if you both are up to a challenge." Mika said smiling.

"What are you talking about?"

"I'll tell you but you have to promise not to interrupt."

Hugh glanced at Edward. He was rereading his brother's letter while he reached for the pipe in his shirt pocket. "Can't we go somewhere else?"

"Why? Are you afraid I might give him wings too?"

"Among other things."

Mika snorted. "You really don't know anything do you?"

"No."

"Very well if you're compelled to protect poor Edward then let's go up to the attic." He disappeared.

Hugh rushed headlong up the two flights of stairs and into the attic. Mika was already there sitting on his chair. He was smirking and twirling Hugh's watch in his fingers.

Hugh stuck his hand in his pocket and found it was empty. "Give that back!" He reached for the watch. Mika smiled and jerked it out of reach. "What's the idea? You know what that means to me."

"This old thing? You hardly bother with it anymore."

"I do too. My father gave me that."

"I know. I was there, remember?" Mika looked disgusted. "Since the Torment Seer came you scarcely talk of the past."

"I have a future now, with Emma."

"You have a future all right. Whether it's with that girl is a whole other matter." Mika held the watch in the air and watched it spin around.

"What does my watch have to do with it?"

"Interesting that it should come down to a watch." Mika said idly. "I am a Watcher. I've Watched you all your life. Now this watch will determine the course of things."

"I don't understand."

"Why don't you sit down and listen?" There was something in his voice, a layer of persuasion that Hugh had never heard before. He felt himself sitting in the small chair although he didn't really want to.

"You're really sending me back aren't you?"

"Do you know how many wretched souls out there would give their dead toenails to be in your place?"

"Just tell me what you plan on doing with me." Hugh prepared for the worst news since dying.

Mika closed his hand over the watch and leaned back. "This is such a great chair. It's one of my favorites."

"Get on with it." Hugh muttered.

"Very well. It's a simple plan really. I am shortly removing you from this house and taking you somewhere to be, er, refitted if you will, with a new body. After a short period of time you will suddenly appear in this backwater of a town with a new name, new face, and of course a fake biography."

"And what am I supposed to do? Walk up to Emma and tell her it's me?"

"Of course not. That would be too easy. She will have to figure out it's you."

"How is she supposed to do that when I will look different?"

"You are allowed to tell the Torment Seer that you will be coming back to town in a new guise, all she has to do is figure out which one is you."

"What do you mean which one?" Hugh asked.

"You'll be part of a group. It would be far too easy if one lone stranger rode into town, good grief anyone could figure that out."

"She has to pick me out of a group?"

"Yes. Ingenious isn't it?"

"But I can talk to her?" Hugh asked.

"Naturally, but you can't say anything that would clue her in. I'll still be listening. If you try saying one thing out of line I will banish you to a church belfry and I can tell you that ain't no place you want to haunt."

"This is going to be impossible." Hugh moaned.

"If she really loves you she'll figure it out."

"Why are you doing this? Why are you making it so hard?"

Mika stared at him. "You have to earn life Hugh. You asked me for a second chance and I am giving it to you. But you're not going to get it handed to you."

"Have you ever been in love?"

Mika's face darkened. "You don't get to ask me those kinds of questions."

"Where does the watch come in?"

"Ah the watch." Mika said brightening. "The most ingenious part of the whole plan. I am a genius, did I ever tell you that?"

"Yes, several times. What about the watch?"

"Oh yes. Once the Torment Seer has made up her mind, right or wrong, she is to give your watch to that person."

"So you're turning it over to her?"

"Me? Why should I do it? It's your watch." Mika opened his hands, they were empty.

"What?" Hugh reached in his pocket and found it back where it had always been.

"Pretty clever huh? I could headline in Vegas."

"What is Vegas?"

"Oh sorry, wrong century. Never mind. Anyway, where was I? Oh yes, the Torment Seer gives someone, perhaps you, the watch. If it's you, you can say so and live happily ever after.

"And what if she chooses wrong?"

Mika shrugged. "Then I relocate you to some other place far, far away."

"Alive or dead?"

"Alive of course. I told you I was giving you another chance at life. Mikhail Vernikov doesn't go back on his word. Not anymore."

"I still can't believe that's your name."

"I still can't believe *your* name is Hugh Charles James MacPherson. A little pretentious don't you think?"

"It is a little long." Hugh conceded.

"I've picked a new name for you this time around, and it's really clever."

"I know, because you're a genius."

"I'm glad you've finally noticed. Are you ready to go?"

Hugh leapt to his feet. "I am not leaving now am I?"

"Once you've told the Torment Seer my plan I see no reason to delay. She'll be back from the shop this afternoon. Once you've told her the good news we can get a move on."

"You've got to give me more time. I can't just tell her and leave."

"That's what the last five months were for. I'll give you until tomorrow." Mika said. "I'll be here at eight in the morning to take you whether you're ready or not."

 Hugh hardly noticed Mika leave. He was too busy thinking of how he was supposed to tell Emma it was him, not her, who would be leaving for good.

Chapter 47

Every day I came home and found Hugh waiting for me I knew I had
made the right decision. I could hardly believe that I had considered
leaving him. Occasionally I would see Jeremy out of Thalberg's shop
windows. He walked with his head down, no doubt avoiding the
possibility of accidentally making eye contact with me. They had started
building the bank now and he often met Senator Brown at the construction
site in the morning.

My parents had put away their disappointment. Father made a few
fleeting comments and then the matter seemed to settle itself and life
returned to normal.

It was mid-February and freezing outside. I had what seemed like a dozen
layers of clothes on when I walked home that afternoon from Thalberg's.
It had been a productive day. I had managed to sell two hats and given
some dubious advice on which types of gloves were appropriate for a trip
to Boston. As I came in the front door I pulled my mittens off and rubbed
my hands together. Father was waiting for me.

"Hello Emma."

"Good evening Father." I said kissing him on the cheek. "What are you
doing out here? It's much warmer in the parlor."

"I wanted to tell you that your mother and I are going to have supper with
Eve and Scott. We are just on our way out."

"Oh. All right then." I shrugged out of my heavy coat and stamped my
snow covered boots on the floor.

Mother suddenly appeared in the kitchen doorway. "Did you tell her?"

"Yes dear."

"Eve wants us for supper. Do you want to come Emma?" Mother asked.

"Elsay we are going to be late." Father took his coat from the hook.

"All right Edward. I suppose Emma would like the house to herself. I don't want to stay too long at Eve's. The noise of those children gives me a splitting headache every time. It's the Cooper in them."

"Elsay, those are your grandchildren."

"I know but they are better seen and not heard." They put on their winter things as I took mine off. "And I hope we don't have to go the back way to get there, not in this weather. I always feel like a thief sneaking in Eve's backdoor."

"It's much quicker that way dear."

"Men." she muttered.

They finished dressing and were soon gone. I stretched my arms over my head and smiled to myself. The whole house was mine for the evening. But where was Hugh? I was surprised he wasn't already around.

"Where are you?" I called out. Perhaps he was being detained by Mika. I started upstairs. Maybe I could see Mika one more time in all his ethereal beauty. Hugh was coming down the stairs at the same time. We met on the landing. His face was long as he slumped against the wall.

"What's the matter?" I leaned my body against his. "Was it something Mika said? You can't let him get to you. He's lonely, that's why he lashes out." I wrapped my hands around his waist and tried to look into his eyes. He stared down at the floor.

"He was just here."

"What did he say?"

Hugh sighed. "I need to talk to you about something."

"What's wrong?"

"It's complicated. I think you should sit down."

"You're scaring me." I took his hand and walked him into the parlor. We sat on the sofa.

Hugh shut his eyes. He took a deep breath and looked at me. "Mika is giving me another chance at life."

"What? What does that mean?"

"It means that I will no longer be a Tormented Soul. I will be alive again."

"Are you serious?" I cried. "I've never heard anything so wonderful. When? How? When will it happen?"

Hugh shook his head. "You don't understand Emma. There's more to it."

"Then tell me." I said trying to stay calm.

"I don't know how to tell you this."

"Just tell me. What is it?"

"I won't look like myself. I won't have the same face or body."

"Why not?"

"Because Hugh MacPherson is dead. He can't live again. As I said I will have a new body and a new name too."

I thought about this and shrugged. "I can get used to that. It will take time, but as long as we're together does it matter?"

"It doesn't."

"When does all this happen?"

"There's more Emma."

"Oh."

"Mika has issued us, or rather you a challenge."

"What kind of challenge?"

"To prove if you really love me."

I jumped off the sofa. "How can he say that? If he knows what you do and say all the time then surely he knows how I feel. Why do I need to prove myself to him?"

"Because if you don't you'll never see me again."

I felt the color drain from my face. I sat down before my legs gave out.

"Mika is taking me away, to be, I don't know transformed, remade, whatever he calls it. After a period of time passes he will send me back to Fox Cove. I won't look like myself, talk like myself or have the same name. Your job is to figure out if it's me. I'm not allowed to tell you who I am or say anything that might give you a clue."

"That won't be so bad. There aren't that many strangers who come to town."

"I won't be alone. I'm coming back in a group."

"A group? Who else will be there?"

"I don't know."

"I'm supposed to pick you out of a group? You won't look the same or be able to give me any help and I am supposed to just know it's you?" I could feel the panic rising inside me. It was impossible. "I can't do it."

"You have to. Mika's not changing his mind about this."

"What if I fail?" I didn't want to hear the answer.

"Mika takes me away and we never see each other again."

"I can't do it. I can't. How can I possibly figure it out?"

"You will Emma. I have faith in you. You won't leave me behind. This is for you." Hugh reached into his pocket and took out the watch he loved so dearly. To my surprise he was able to drop it in my lap.

"What happened? I thought this could never leave your body." I turned it over in my hands. The gold was worn and smooth.

"When you've figured out which one I am you are supposed to give this to me. Then I can tell you who I really am."

"If it's really you." I said. "I only have one chance then?"

"Yes."

I looked at the watch. One chance. I was still trying to take in all he had said. I had so many questions but my voice was leaving me. I felt a warm tear roll down my cheek. "I can't do it. I'm afraid."

"So am I. I don't want to leave. I don't want to leave you. I'm afraid to be alive in the world again. Everything has changed."

"How much time do we have? When is Mika coming for you?"

"Tomorrow morning."

"Tomorrow! He couldn't even give us enough time to say goodbye. Damn him."

"It's not his fault Emma. It's mine."

I closed my hand around the watch. "You've known about this for a while, haven't you? Mika told you that day he was here, the day he showed himself to me. That was months ago. Why didn't you tell me then?"

"I wasn't sure if he meant it. I didn't really think Mika could do it." Hugh said, his voice was weak and tired. "And I was afraid to tell you."

"Damn it Hugh! We could have had all this time to say goodbye and now we have one bloody night." I punched him in the shoulder.

"I should have said something. I know that. I didn't know how. Emma, I don't want to leave. I told Mika that. He's not backing down. I'm sorry."

"Shut up. Just shut up Hugh!" I screamed and threw the watch on the floor.

"Maybe I should leave you alone for a while." he said softly.

"Don't you dare." I threw myself on top of him and let out an anguished wail. My body wrenched as the tears came bursting out of me. He allowed me to punch him in the sides as he held me, smoothing my hair and whispering quietly. I had no idea what he was saying. It didn't matter. My face was wet with tears. I gasped for breath as I laid my head on his chest.

We remained like that for a long while. Neither of us spoke. There was nothing more to say. Hugh was leaving. I had spent so much time worrying about Jeremy and whether I could leave our life here, I never imagined it was Hugh who would leave me.

The house creaked and groaned as it settled against the harsh winter outside.

"It's snowing." Hugh said.

"They might have to stay at Eve's for the night." I said hopefully. I didn't want my parents coming back, not yet.

"Maybe."

"How long until you return?" I asked. "A few days, weeks?"

"I don't know. Mika said a short time."

"What's a short time to him? A century?"

"I *will* come back. I promise."

I looked down at the floor, the watch was lying nearby where I had flung it. For the first time I noticed that the chain was different, it had been replaced by a longer one that could be worn around the neck.

I stood up and wiped my eyes. "I have an idea." Hugh raised an eyebrow while I unbuttoned my blouse and took the star necklace off. "Let's switch." I picked the watch up off the floor.

"I don't know if Mika will let me take that."

"If he's going to make me do this stupid challenge then he can damn well let you wear this. And I hope he heard every word of that." I said looping the necklace around his neck. The chain was very long and the star slipped neatly into his shirt. "Now you won't forget me when you're someone else."

"I would never forget you."

"Put this on me." I gave him the watch. He smiled as he opened it one last time. "I was so happy the day my father gave me this. I thought I would grow up to be just like him. Didn't turn out that way did it?"

I pulled my hair out of the way as he fastened the chain around my neck.

"It's a bit bulky." he said. "You don't have to wear it you know."

"I want to. I don't want to decide it's you and then have to run home and get it. Besides I know what I can do." I poked the watch down the front of my corset, the cool metal settled between my breasts.

Hugh smiled. "That could be a real problem when I'm alive."

"What about now?" I didn't want to think of the future.

He reached behind me and loosened the ties of the corset. I raised my arms and he pulled it over my head and dropped it on the floor.

"Ah, there's my old watch." he said tapping the gold cover with his finger.

"I want to go upstairs and forget about everything." I unbuttoned my skirt and let it fall around my ankles. I stepped out of it and kicked it into the corner.

"Are you going to be all right?"

"I can't think about it right now Hugh." I held his hands tightly, trying to remember what they felt like in mine. I wanted to remember every little detail of Hugh MacPherson. I was never going to see him ever again. The Hugh I knew would be gone forever after tonight.

I led him upstairs to my bedroom where I made certain I would recall every inch of his body. Afterwards I curled up in his arms on the window seat, snow gently floated by the window.

"What time is it?" I asked.

"1:57."

"How much longer?"

"Six hours."

"Tell me about yourself." I said. "Tell me everything you ever did, from the time you were born until now."

"Everything? You probably know most of it."

"I don't care. Just don't stop talking. Please."

"Let's see. It all began in 1754 when a most handsome infant came into the world."

"What was his name?" I watched the snowflakes fly lazily outside, there was a light burning at the Coopers. Every so often Michael Cooper would step onto the front porch and lean against the railing.

"Hugh Charles James MacPherson."

I slept a few hours that night, despite my best efforts to stay awake. I had wanted to remember every precious hour we had left. But at some point I must have drifted off. I woke with Hugh gently nudging my shoulder.

"Emma. It's time."

I opened my eyes. We were still on the window seat. The conversation from the night before came rushing back to me. Hugh was leaving, Mika has issued me a challenge, it wasn't all a bad dream.

"No."

"He'll be here any second."

"Why did you let me sleep?"

"You have to sleep Emma." He stood up and straightened his shirt as though he was going somewhere. He was.

Tears started rolling down my cheeks. "I can't do this. You can't leave."

Hugh looked outside. "He's here."

"No." I looked out the window. Mika was standing in front of the house with his hands at his side. His face was placid and serene, as though he had no worries in the world. His black clothes and wings stood out against the crisp white snow.

"He wants me to come." Hugh said. "He's willing me down there."

"Fight him."

"I can't, he's much too strong. We have to say goodbye Emma."

"No I can't, I won't."

"I only have a few seconds left."

This was really happening. I grabbed his face and kissed him. "I love you Hugh. I always will no matter what happens."

He took his face in my hands. "I will come back to you. I promise."

I nodded and tried to take a breath.

"I have to go. I can't resist him any longer." I followed him downstairs. The front door flew open, a blast of cold air assaulted the hallway and went right through my thin nightgown. From the doorway I could see Mika waiting. He was breathtaking. Our eyes met for a split second before he looked away.

"Goodbye my love." Hugh touched my face then walked outside. I tried to follow him but there was an invisible barrier that prevented me from crossing the threshold.

There was a hard snap and then a pair of beautiful white wings emerged from Hugh's back, he stumbled in the snow and then regained his balance. I smiled despite the tears streaming down my face. He turned to face me, our eyes met as he took a deep breath. Mika reached behind him and they both vanished. There was nothing left but the snow.

I felt my legs give out as I collapsed in the doorway. The invisible barrier was gone. I fell forward across the threshold, the side of my face landing in the snow.

It occurred to me later that I had no idea where my parents were. Had they stayed with Eve because of the storm? Had they come home and found my clothes strewn across the parlor floor? Were they around when Hugh left?

All I knew for sure was that at some point Father found me. I vaguely remember him asking what I was doing and then being lifted into his arms. The kitchen swirled by me as he brought me into the quietness of the back bedroom.

I fell into a fever induced sleep. Two days later I awoke, the fever was gone and my entire world had changed.

Chapter 48

Hugh wasn't sure how he had got there. The last thing he remembered was seeing Emma standing in the doorway of the house, her face red from crying, her eyes teary and swollen. Mika had tugged on his wings and everything went black. He had a sense that more time had elapsed since that moment but he couldn't quite grasp how much.

He was lying on a green sofa in a small room with bare white walls and a soft gray carpet that strangely extended from wall to wall. There was a window nearby, sunlight streamed in creating a yellow square on the floor. A door, also painted white, was on the opposite wall.

Hugh's head hurt, which was odd for he usually felt no pain. He sat up and rubbed his eyes. He was surprised to find he still had the same body. His breech covered legs stretched out in front of him. He felt a measure of relief. He was still Hugh MacPherson, he hadn't been turned into someone else yet.

He thought he heard the rustling of leaves outside. He crossed the room and looked out the window. A lush lawn stretched out to a foggy horizon. Directly underneath the window was a bushy oak tree, its leaves rattled merrily in the wind. Where on earth was he?

"Enjoying the view?" Hugh spun around. Mika was standing behind him, his steely eyes seemed to be smiling.

"Where am I?" Hugh managed to say. He felt out of place. The room was so odd, the bland carpeting and lack of decoration.

"It's just a stopping off point. You'll soon be on your way."

"But where am I?" Hugh asked again. "Why do I still have the same body?"

"I am waiting for someone." Mika stepped back and looked at Hugh from head to toe. He smiled and folded his arms across his chest. "It won't be long now."

Hugh stared out the window. He had never felt so nervous, part of him wanted to stay here in this quiet room forever. It was a little like being in his attic. In the attic the world came to him, not the other way around. What if he couldn't work one of the new telephones he had heard Edward talking about? Did he even know who the president was now? There had been a war a few decades ago, what was it about?

"You'll be all right Hugh." Mika said quietly.

"I don't know how to live in this world, everything is so different."

"How do you think I feel?"

"What time do you come from? Can't you tell me now? You're from the future aren't you?"

"I died in 1986."

Hugh's mouth dropped open. "That's almost ninety years from now."

Mika shrugged. "Time is not a straight line."

Hugh struggled to find the right words. "How can- If you were born after me, how can you be dead?"

Mika smiled. "I've been dead for two hundred and forty three years."

"I don't understand."

"You don't have to understand. Some of the souls I Watch are living before I was born and some after. It seemed strange at first, but I am used to it now."

"And you never got a chance to come back, to live again?"

Mika shook his head. "No. It would never happen for someone like me. It's a rare chance for anyone." He looked anxiously at the door. "His Lordship is coming."

"His Lordship?"

"Death."

"Death? What do you mean Death?"

Mika lowered his voice. "I mean the Dark Lord of Death. He's the only one who can give you life."

Hugh swallowed. He didn't want to meet someone called the Dark Lord of Death. Mika straightened up and stared at the door. Hugh wondered if he was preparing to salute, or perhaps a bow was expected. Was *he* supposed to be doing something too? Mika cleared his throat as a warning and Hugh found himself holding his breath as the door opened and the Dark Lord of Death walked in.

Chapter 49

Eve was sitting on the end of the bed. "Emma!" she said squeezing my hand. "Thank God. I was starting to think you'd never wake up."

"What happened?" I murmured. I was in my parents' bedroom. The room was dark, someone had hung blankets over the windows. On the bedside table was an amber colored bottle with some liquid in it.

"You've been really sick." Eve said.

"I have?" I pulled the covers away from my face.

"Yes. You've been sick for days. Margaret Cooper brought this." Eve held up the bottle for me to see. "She makes it herself. I wonder why we're sending Ethan to medical school when he could have just gone next door and learned from her."

"I'll have to thank her."

"You can do that later. You should rest now. I can't imagine what you were doing lying in the snow like that? Did you hit your head and fall?"

"I don't know."

"You'll remember in time." she said patting my hand.

"Eve, has there been any-" I stopped and thought about how to say it. "Has there been anyone new in town?"

She seemed surprised by my question. "Recently? I don't think so."

"No, I mean since I've been sick."

"Not that I'm aware of. What an odd thing to ask." She stood up. "I'm going to get Mother for you. I'm so glad you're awake." She bent down and kissed my forehead.

Within a few days I was up and moving about the house. My parents temporarily relocated themselves in Eve's old room so I wouldn't have to climb the stairs. I was glad to not have a reason to be in my bedroom and see Hugh's books piled in the corner, the playing cards lying about.

Hugh's watch was still hanging around my neck. It seemed odd that no one had questioned it. I had obviously been tended to by my mother and Margaret, why hadn't they removed it? Or at the very least why had they not asked where it came from?

It wasn't until I was strong enough to sit and take broth in the parlor that I found out why. Mother was bustling about tending to the fireplace. Father had gone into town to do a little work at the shop and then to the post office to mail a package to Uncle Egbert.

"You're doing much better now." Mother said poking the fire.

"Yes, I feel better." I looked anxiously towards the hall. I was hoping Father was going to bring word of someone new in town. It was all I had thought about since I woke up.

"You gave me a bit of a scare you know." She brushed soot off her apron.

"I did? It wasn't that serious."

"Not serious? I don't know about that. I still can't figure out how you ended up lying in the snow like that."

"I don't remember." It was partly true. The memory of Hugh and Mika disappearing in front of my eyes was all I could recall, and all I wanted to.

"It was the strangest thing." she said shaking her head. "And then when I saw that watch you were wearing, well I didn't know what to think."

"Oh this." I put my hand to my chest.

"Yes. I couldn't imagine where it had come from. But your father soon set me straight."

"Father did?"

"Yes. He said that Grandpa Hollis had sent it to you."

"Oh yes." I stammered. This was a strange turn of events.

"I don't see why you need to wear it around your neck, it's so bulky."

"I like it." I said cautiously. I heard the front door open. Father came into the parlor wearing his winter coat and boots.

"Edward you're dripping all over the floor." Mother said.

He looked down at his feet and laughed. "So I am Elsay." He was holding a small envelope in his hands. "I don't think you'll be upset for long. I have a letter from Ethan."

"Oh!" Mother cried as she snatched it away. "You haven't opened it yet."

"I thought we could read it together." Father unbuttoned his coat. "Might cheer Emma up." He disappeared into the hallway and hung up his winter clothes. He quickly returned and settled next to me on the sofa.

"Read it to us Edward." Mother said handing it back to him.

Father carefully unfolded Ethan's letter. Mother poked the fire again and sat in her chair. Father cleared his throat.

Dear Father, Mother and Emma,

I hope this letter finds all of you in good health. I have been working at the grocery store and I just started a job as an assistant in the lab here on campus. I am soon to complete the semester and I am glad to tell you I have saved enough money to be able to come home for the summer.

Mother let out a little cry of joy. "At last! It's been too long."

"Over two years." Father added.

I will not be coming home alone. It is my pleasure to announce that I am recently engaged to the most gracious of young ladies. I am anxious for all of you to get to know her. I have arranged lodgings for her in town and she will be accompanying me on my journey. I would expect to arrive at the end of May or beginning of June.

I have missed all of you more than you will know. I look forward to seeing you and introducing you to my fiancé.

Your devoted son and brother

Ethan

"Engaged!" Mother cried. "How can this be?"

"Elsay, the boy is nearly twenty one years old."

"I know, but engaged. Who is she?"

"We shall soon find out won't we?" Father winked at me. He folded the letter and put it in his pocket.

"I don't know about this Edward. I suppose she's some city girl, probably won't know what to make of us."

"Elsay, why don't you just wait and see?"

Mother sighed and wrung her hands. "I know, I know." She stood up and smoothed her apron. "I've got to check on dinner." She hurried out of the parlor muttering to herself.

"She'll be fine. If this girl is good enough for Ethan she's good enough for us." Father patted my knee.

I nodded. I wasn't thinking about Ethan's letter. "Father, I have to ask you something. Why did you tell Mother that Grandpa Hollis sent me this watch?"

He leaned in close. "I've got to thank you for covering for me."

"Covering for what?" Perhaps he didn't understand. "I am talking about this watch." I showed it to him.

"I know."

"I don't understand."

Mother suddenly appeared in the doorway. "And who is this girl staying with? Does she know someone in town? What if it's Brown?"

"Now, now Elsay." Father said soothingly. "You're getting yourself into a state over this." He got up and followed her into the kitchen.

Hugh's watch was still in my hands. I opened the case and looked inside. His name was engraved on the inside cover. How was this connected to Father? Nothing made sense. I snapped the case shut and dropped it back inside my nightgown.

Chapter 50

 Hugh braced himself as he waited for the Dark Lord of Death to enter the room. A few minutes passed before the door opened and someone unexpected came inside. It was a teenage boy with dark blond hair and a slightly dazed expression. He was wearing the most outlandish clothes that Hugh had ever seen. He had on a dark blue short sleeved shirt made of a soft material, there was a large red "B" embroidered on the front of it. His light blue trousers were made of a heavy cotton-like material. He had a pair of thick white shoes on his feet.

"Hugh." the boy said sticking out his right hand.

Hugh shook it. He was obviously some kind of underling.

"Your Lordship." Mika said bowing.

"Hey Mika." the boy answered. "Are you ready Hugh?" He had some kind of thin silver straps on his teeth.

"*You're* the Dark Lord of Death?" Hugh said incredulously.

"Keep quiet." Mika muttered.

"It's all right." the boy said tossing his hair to one side. "I am the Dark Lord. Surprised?"

"Frankly yes." said Hugh. "I was expecting something, someone, I don't know, different."

"I can tell you I am more than qualified for the job."

"Am I allowed to ask how long you've been dead?"

Death smirked. "Actually I just celebrated my three thousand year death anniversary." he said proudly.

"Congratulations."

"Thanks. I can tell you're a real gentlemen, unlike some people." He glanced at Mika.

"It's the way I was raised." Hugh said.

Mika muttered something in what sounded like another language.

"Well I would love to stay and chat all day but every second I stand here the souls are piling up in my office." Death said. "Are you ready Hugh?"

"I think so." This was it. Hugh MacPherson's last moments had arrived.

"All right. Stand still and this will be over in a minute. Oh, and it's a good idea to close your eyes, so I've heard."

Hugh closed his eyes. He felt a slight pressure on his forehead, like the point of a finger. There was a sickening feeling in the pit of his stomach.

"Open your eyes." Mika or Death said, it was hard to tell which.

Hugh opened his eyes and promptly shut them again. He was dizzy.

"Take a deep breath." Mika advised.

Hugh did as he was told. When he opened his eyes again Mika and Death were standing in front of him smiling.

"Not bad." Death said. "Is that what you had in mind?"

"Pretty much." Mika said.

Hugh took another breath as the dizziness began to lessen. He looked at Mika and suddenly realized that he could look him straight in the eye, not upwards as he had always done. As his equilibrium returned he was aware his feet were now bare, the strange grey carpet felt soft between his toes.

It was at this point that he looked down and realized two things. First his body was no longer the one that belonged to Hugh MacPherson, and second he was stark naked. He doubled over and tried to cover himself with his hands while Mika and Death stood by.

"Can't you put some clothes on me?" he said feeling his face flush. He realized he must be alive.

They both laughed. "Do you realize how many times I've seen you naked?" Mika said.

"Maybe so, but can't I have some underpants?"

"Don't you want to see what you look like?" Mika asked.

"Yes, but I was hoping for some underpants first."

"Why don't you take a look at yourself?" Death said. A tall mirror suddenly appeared.

Hugh caught the first glimpse of himself in the reflection. He couldn't believe it, there was not a trace of Hugh MacPherson in the man staring back at him. For some reason he had thought that perhaps there would be some glimmer of his old self. "This is different."

"What were you expecting?" Mika asked.

"I don't know."

"I thought I was quite generous."

"I told you I want some underpants."

"I was talking about your height. You're not short anymore."

"Oh." Hugh said blushing again. "I was never short. When I was alive I was a tall person. Over the years the rest of you grew. I don't know what they feed people these days."

"You're tall again buddy." Death slapped him merrily on the back. "Listen Mika I've got to go."

"Of course your Lordship." Mika said. "Say thank you to his Lordship."

"Thank you your Lordship." Hugh said. "May I have some underpants please?"

Death laughed and tossed his hair aside. "Sure thing." A pair of scratchy underpants appeared on Hugh's new body. He breathed a sigh of relief and went back to looking at himself in the mirror as the Dark Lord left the room.

Chapter 51

I had already begun talking to Mr. Thalberg about returning to work that spring. I needed to get back as soon as possible. Our house was too far from the center of town, a stranger could ride, walk or take a buggy into Fox Cove and back out again without any of us knowing it.

I was reluctant to ask Father anything these days. He had still not explained how he recognized Hugh's watch and what on earth I was covering for him. I wondered if his advancing age, he was nearly fifty five, was causing him to go senile. Eve said she had seen him one day outside of her window talking to himself. When he caught her watching him he bolted down the street before she could get out of her front door.

I was so glad Ethan was coming home. I missed him terribly and I needed a distraction from waiting for Hugh. I sometimes wondered if Mika was playing a trick on both of us, maybe he never planned on letting Hugh return. Perhaps the whole idea of the challenge involving the watch was just a ploy to take Hugh away from me.

I had to believe he would come back. He had promised. Once Ethan was home I could talk with him about it. That was if he could tear himself away from his fiancé. I was just as worried as my mother about this new girl. What if she looked down her nose at all of us? Had Ethan told her we were Seers? There were so many unknowns.

* * *

"Emma! Emma! A wagon is coming down the road. I think it's Ethan." Mother shouted on the last day of May. I left the parlor where I had been reading a book and met her in the hallway. She was wiping her hands on her apron and looking distressed. "Oh, how do I look? Is my hair all right?"

"You look fine." I said opening the front door. A wagon driven by a grumpy looking old man was traversing the muddy road. The wheels skidded and the wagon slid sideways causing the horses to rear up on their hind legs.

The old man shouted a few curse words and snapped his whip. The wagon straightened itself out and rumbled to a stop in front of our house. "That's as far as I go." he grumbled to a dark haired man who was sitting on the back of the wagon.

Next to the driver was a woman, she was elegantly dressed in a white coat with a green belt. Her face was obscured by a green hat with an extra large brim. A white feather jutted neatly from the hatband, matching perfectly with her coat and gloves. I swallowed and thought of my own outfit, a red plaid skirt and a pink blouse. They didn't exactly match and the shirt was too lightweight for early spring. I did have a gray shawl to cover it all, of course it was embroidered with pumpkins. Wrong season. I was a mess as usual.

"Thanks very much my good man." Ethan said. He jumped off the back of the wagon and handed some money to the driver. Ethan hauled off one of three trunks. "The last two belong to the young lady. You know where to take them."

"Yep." said the old man. The woman remained on the driver's seat looking straight ahead.

"Oh a fine one she is." Mother whispered in the shelter of the hallway.

"She's probably shy." I said not really believing it myself. "Let's go out. I can't wait any longer."

Mother took my hand and we stepped out the door. "Ethan!" she cried before giving him a crushing hug. "It's been much too long son."

Ethan smiled. "I know Mother. I've missed all of you so much."

"Let me look at you." She shook her head. "My little boy is gone, who is this handsome man?"

Ethan didn't look like the boy who had left us two years before. He was taller and more muscular. He walked with a self assurance that he never had before. "It's still me Mother, little Ethan with his nose in a book."

I glanced at the young woman on the wagon, she was still looking straight ahead as though we didn't exist. I felt a flicker of anger rise in me.

"Emma, I am so glad to see you." Ethan said hugging me tightly. He smelled good, it was a cologne that we sold in Thalberg's but I couldn't remember the name. I was a hopeless shop girl. "We have so much to catch up on."

"Emma's been very sick Ethan." Mother said. "Take it easy with her."

Ethan looked worried. "Really? I didn't know."

"I'm fine, that was months ago." I said looking at the girl. My temper was really flaring now. She couldn't even be bothered to *look* at us, let alone get down off her perch and be introduced.

"We should get you inside then." he said.

"I'm fine Ethan." I thought I saw the girl's shoulder shake. Was she laughing?

"No, I want you to go inside and sit down. I am practically a doctor you know."

I wrapped my shawl tightly around my shoulders. A cold drizzle of rain was starting to fall. I was not about to go inside. "Aren't you going to introduce us?" I said loudly. The girl's shoulders shook some more.

"You want to meet my fiancé?"

"Yes Ethan, both Mother and I do. That is if she cares to meet us." My voice echoed rudely into the air.

"Emma!" Mother hissed.

Ethan laughed out loud and looked at his fiancé who was doubled over in a fit of laughter. "You'd better come down darling." He reached for the girl's hand. She gingerly stepped off the wagon and held onto Ethan's shoulders. Her boots slopped on the ground. She kept her head down, her face still blocked by the enormous brim of her hat.

"Mother and Emma, may I present my fiancé?"

The girl giggled again and took off her hat. She had bright red hair swept into an elegant chignon. Her face was covered with freckles. There was something familiar in her blue eyes. She laughed and put her hand on my arm.

"Candy?" I said slowly.

"Don't you recognize me? I've only been gone a year."

Beside me Mother made a strange noise. "You look so different."

"I'm elegant now." she said twirling so we could see her outfit. She laughed and gave me a hug. "I told you I would marry him." she whispered in my ear.

"What do you say Mother?" Ethan asked as we walked in the house.

Mother's face was white. "Congratulations Ethan and Candace. Candace, er Candy, your mother didn't mention anything about this to me."

"Oh she doesn't know yet." Candy said as Ethan gently tugged her coat off her shoulders. She looked back and caught his eye. They held each other's gaze for a moment. I noticed Ethan's neck getting red.

I sighed to myself and tried to push Hugh out of my mind. He *was* coming back.

Once free of her coat Candy grabbed my hand. "Let's go somewhere and talk."

We ran upstairs and into my room. I still expected Hugh to be stretched out on the bed waiting for me. The room seemed so empty now. His books lay piled in the corner untouched. I had put the cards away in my desk drawer, there was no one to play with anymore.

Candy shut the door behind us. She looked from corner to corner as though she expected to see someone she knew.

"How did this happen Candy? How did you and Ethan get engaged?" I asked, longing for a distraction.

"Oh never mind that. Where's Hugh?"

I tried to look as though I had no idea what she was talking about. "Who?"

Candy smirked and poked me in the side. "You needn't pretend Emma. Ethan told me all about you two."

"He has?"

"Of course. We have no secrets." She winked and strolled about looking this way and that.

"He's not here."

"Oh. Upstairs then? I always knew there was something going on with you. Remember? I asked you about it once."

"I remember."

Candy grinned and sat on the edge of my bed. "You denied it, but I knew. You really love this Hugh fellow huh? Even if he is dead as a doornail?"

"Yes."

Candy leaned back on her elbows. "Ethan said as much. Of course I understand you couldn't say too much to your brother. Who would talk to him about men? But you've got me now, and I want to hear *everything*."

I felt my face flush. "Everything?"

"Of course. That's what best friends are for."

I wrung my hands.

"Afraid Hugh might hear us?"

"No Candy that's not it. I don't know where to begin." I sat at my desk.

"Just start at the beginning. I've been dying to hear this since Ethan told me you were a Torment Seer. Oh sorry is that impolite to say? You know, the word dying? With a dead person in the house and all."

"It doesn't matter. Hugh isn't here anymore."

Candy sat up and stared at me. "Isn't here? How can that be? Ethan said he was locked in Torment forever.

"Things have changed." I hesitated and then found the whole story pouring out of me. The first time I saw Hugh that day we moved in, the day he taught me to play cards, the year I gave him a Christmas present, the first time we kissed, the night I asked him to stay in my bedroom instead of going up in the attic. It was a relief to get it out, it had been bottled up for so long.

Candy listened intently, interrupting occasionally when she needed further explanation. Her eyes grew wide as I described seeing Mika for the first time, how perfectly beautiful he was, all light and shimmer. By the time I had gotten to the part where Hugh was crossing the threshold into the snow, his white wings outshining the frosty ground, Ethan was stepping through the door.

"What are you two talking about?"

"Be quite Ethan." Candy waved her hand at him. "Then what happened?"

I shrugged and waited for Ethan to take a seat next to her. "Nothing happened. Not yet anyway. I have to wait for Hugh to come back now."

"But you won't know it's him?" Candy asked.

"No."

Ethan pushed up his glasses and looked at me. "What is this about Hugh? I don't see him anywhere."

I told Ethan about Mika's challenge to me and how Hugh was supposed to reappear in town as a new man. He looked at Candy and then me. "When is this supposed to happen?"

"I have no idea. Mika told Hugh a short time, but what's a short time to Mika? A few hundred years?"

"No it won't be that long." Ethan said shaking his head. "Can this Mika character even do such a thing?"

"I don't know."

Ethan wrinkled his forehead. "Maybe he'll come back while we're here."

"Oh yes." Candy said enthusiastically. "I am sure I would know Hugh anywhere."

"You would?" Ethan put his arm around her.

"Of course."

"I see. Got your own secret powers do you?"

"You're just figuring that out?" she laughed.

"I still want to know how this all happened. How did you get engaged? You've always been friends, but when did things change?" I asked.

Candy looked at Ethan and gave him a toothy grin. "What she really wants to say is when did you stop thinking of me as a pesky little girl?"

"I never thought of you that way." Ethan said sincerely. It was interesting how time could make a man forget things.

"Oh really?" Candy nudged him with her elbow. "I had been on campus a month when I ran into him in the library. I was so homesick I couldn't stop talking to him. And being a year ahead of me Ethan had already taken the classes I was just starting."

"Not that she needed my help. She's at the top of her class." Ethan said proudly.

"Really?"

"Don't sound so surprised." Candy said.

"I didn't mean-"

Candy laughed. "Oh Emma it's all right. I would be shocked too, I used to be the most dismal student. What an uncivilized little beast I was."

"I liked that little beast. I hope you don't go completely in the other direction." I said.

"Don't worry, I am still a Cooper. I think I've just learned there's a time and place for everything. For example, maybe I shouldn't have kicked Senator Brown in the leg that day, although it did feel great. What do you think?"

"You kicked Senator Brown? When on earth was this? You never told me." Ethan said.

"It was years ago."

"He's never mentioned it." Ethan said.

"He's probably afraid she'll do it again." I said.

Candy started laughing. "I really wish you had come to college with me Emma. With us." She touched Ethan's knee.

"Really Emma. There's so much out there to experience. It would be so good for you to get away." Ethan added.

"I'm not going anywhere. Hugh is coming back to me. Besides I don't want to be a doctor."

"You don't have to study medicine. There are a lot of other courses. You could study astronomy." he said.

"And what is Hugh going to do when I'm gone?"

"They have correspondence courses, you could do it all from home." He looked over his glasses. "And besides Emma, you shouldn't get your hopes up. Hugh may not come back."

"He will."

"I want him to just as much as you do. I just don't want you to be hurt, to give up on your life if he doesn't return. The whole challenge, the thing with the watch, it all seems a bit unnatural. How do you know it's for real?"

I stood up and looked out the window. "It is unnatural Ethan. It's the idea of a dead man. And what do you know about it anyway? I don't see you chattering away to Tormented Souls and having a Watcher tear the walls of your house down for fun. You weren't there. He is coming back."

"Oh, don't listen to him Emma." Candy said. I heard her whisper something to Ethan, but I couldn't make out what she was saying.

He walked over to the window and touched my shoulder. "Listen Em, I'm just looking out for you. That's my job you know."

"Hugh always said you were a good brother despite being overly serious."

"Is that why he snapped my suspenders? For being overly serious?"

I nodded and wrapped my arms around my big brother. "I'm so glad you're home."

Chapter 52

Hugh couldn't stop staring at himself in the mirror. He didn't look anything like he expected. His thoughts kept creeping back to Emma, how would she ever know that he was in this new body? What if she didn't like what she saw? What if she found him unattractive?

"When do I go back?"

"Go back? Do you even know your new name?" Mika asked. "And are you planning to parade around in just a pair of underwear?"

"No."

"First things first." A pair of navy pants appeared on Hugh along with socks and dark brown shoes. The pants were a heavy material and clung uncomfortably to his legs, especially his calves.

"Ugh, long pants." he moaned. "Do I really have to wear these?"

"You do if you want to look like you belong there. What's wrong with them? You can't tell me that those knee breeches were more comfortable."

Hugh felt affronted. "Of course they were more comfortable. Who wants these ugly things?"

"You'll just have to get used to them."

"Humph. Do I get a shirt?" he asked, admiring his new chest muscles.

"I'm getting to that." Mika said. "I have to show you something first. Turn around and look in the mirror."

As he looked over his shoulder he saw the wings on his back. It was as though someone had used a fine black ink pen to sketch on his skin.

"Once you return to the world of the living it will fade." Mika said.

"Good."

"When and if she manages to discover it's you they'll reappear when you have the watch back."

"I'm delighted."

"You just wait until you die again. Then you'll thank me."

"Why? Why should I thank you for giving me a pair of useless wings and marking up my skin?"

Mika looked insulted. "Do you realize how few souls already have wings when they die? You'll be on the fast track."

"The fast track to what?"

"Oh never mind, you're so ungrateful."

Hugh sighed loudly. He was feeling cranky. The whole process was beginning to tire him, he realized he hadn't been physically tired in ages. He would need to sleep before the day was out. Sleep! He was going to sleep and dream again. He shifted from one foot to another, his shoes pinched.

Hugh looked back in the mirror and found he was wearing a white shirt with a dark bow tie, vest, and jacket. The state of modern clothing was so depressing.

"Oh I almost forgot your hat." Mika said.

A round black hat appeared on Hugh's head. What sort of confounded thing was this? In his day he used to wear a tri-corner hat.

"I can tell what you're thinking." Mika said. "You look perfectly fine. I'll be sending you back with a whole trunk full of these clothes so you better get used to them. Or don't you think that the Torment Seer is worth it?"

"Of course she's worth it. I'd even wear your clothes if it meant I had a chance to be alive and with her."

"Thanks."

"So am I ready to go now?"

Mika folded his arms. "What's your new name? What's your story?"

"Oh that. I thought I would just make something up as I went along."

"Make something up? Oh no. I've got a whole life story for you and the others."

"The others?"

"Yes, we'll get to that. It's all here." Mika produced a white paper out of nowhere and handed it to Hugh. At the top of the page was a name, his new name.

"Not bad huh? Do you get it?" Mika asked.

 Hugh nodded. He got the play on words, it was clever. He would compliment Mika later. He was more concerned with the next line. Occupation. He looked at Mika and shook his head. "There is no way I am doing that!"

Chapter 53

Just as Ethan's letter stated, his fiancé did have arrangements to stay in town. The Coopers' house was currently full of younger Coopers and two fishermen who were boarding in the loft. Candy was to stay in town with Scott and Eve. In exchange for her room and meals she was helping Eve with the housework and children.

One Sunday we were walking on the bluff. "Do you mind taking care of five kids on your summer vacation?" I asked her.

She shrugged. "I've been taking care of my brothers and sisters all my life. Besides, I'll have little ones of my own someday."

"When are you and Ethan getting married?" I held my arms out to keep my balance.

"Not for a while. We're coming home next summer, and then the following summer Ethan and I both will have graduated. Then we'll come home for good, get married and open our office."

"How can you both graduate at the same time? Aren't you a year behind him?"

"I was, but I am taking extra classes to catch up. I'm doing three correspondence courses this summer. I want us to come home together."

"So you won't be married for another two years? That seems like an awfully long time."

"Oh it's fine. It will go fast enough." Candy said distractedly. We were coming up on the side of the church. The service was just ending, townsfolk were filing out of the front doors. We moved a little closer so we could get a good view. "Get down." she whispered. We sunk into the tall grass and giggled.

A crowd gathered outside as people stopped to talk and gossip. Reverend Monk was nearby, his vestments flapping in the wind. He shook hands with a man and rocked back on his heels in laughter at something that was said to him.

Jeremy came out of the door looking sour. He stuffed his hands in his pockets. He was followed closely by Senator Brown and his wife Bridget with their four children. The Senator shook the Reverend's hand and then whispered something in his ear which caused Reverend Monk to nod in solemn approval.

Candy turned to me and made a face. "How on earth did they ever get so many children? Do you suppose she likes doing it with him? Imagine seeing ole' Brown without any clothes on."

I tried not to conjure the image in my mind. Then I had a thought. "What if he comes to you when you're a doctor? You might have to examine him."

Candy stuck her tongue out. "Ugh, what a horrible thought. I'll make Ethan do it. I don't want to even look at that man's toes."

I stifled a laugh and kept my face safely behind the grass. There was little chance of anyone seeing us. The bluff fell away steeply from where the parishioners were standing, unless they walked all the way to the edge of the land and looked down we were safe.

Jeremy took out his watch and checked the time. I couldn't help but feel sorry for him. I had passed him on the street less than a week ago, he looked in the other direction.

"That's the one who wanted to marry you?" Candy asked.

I nodded.

She wrinkled her nose. "I think Hugh is much better looking."

"You've never seen Hugh."

"I know. I bet he'll come back even handsomer. I can picture him on a white horse, in full armor, carrying a sword." She rolled over and looked at the sky.

"Full armor? In the middle of town? This town?" I tried to picture Hugh on a horse. I wondered if he would remember how to ride after all these years.

"Why not? I see him now. Tall, long black hair waving in the breeze. A good profile, Roman nose. Blue eyes." Up on the hill the church door closed. We turned back and found Reverend Monk had gone inside. Jeremy and most of the parishioners had left or were on their way home.

"Oh we missed the Senator leaving. I wanted to see him and his high and mighty wife get into their carriage." Candy said.

"Is this how aspiring doctors spend their time?" said a voice behind us. We sat up and found Senator Brown leaning on his cane. Bridget was nearby holding their youngest. She looked like she had just smelled something foul. Their other three children were too busy pulling each other's hair to notice us.

Candy and I quickly got to our feet. "Senator, what brings you this way?" Candy asked as she brushed the dirt from her clothes.

"As though you didn't already know Miss Cooper, this path leads to my house."

"I knew, and how are you Senator?" she added as though they had just bumped into each other on the street.

"What were you doing here? Spying on decent people who go to church?"

"Yes that's what we were doing." I said.

The Senator glared at me. "I am relieved that Jeremy got wise and didn't marry you."

"She broke it off, not the other way around." Candy said.

"Don't utter such nonsense young woman. If it weren't for that infernal speech I made that day in the classroom you'd be married and living in some shack."

"I have a good mind to kick you in the leg again!" Candy cried as she balled up her fists.

"Candy don't do it." I whispered.

"Quite possibly the most sensible thing you've ever said Miss Hollis."

"Hershival." Bridget touched her husband's arm. "Can't we go now? Why must we stay and talk with *them*?" She wrinkled her nose as her eyes drifted over us.

"Quite right dear. Out of the way." The Senator held up his cane and proceeded to maneuver Candy and I further into the tall grass, allowing them to pass.

"Senator?" I ventured.

"What?" he shouted as he stopped and turned around.

"I was just wondering, since you are so involved with the town and you know so much, would you happen to have heard or know of anyone new moving here?"

The Senator stared at me. "What do you know about that? Who is asking? That Thalberg fellow you work for?"

"No, I am asking."

"Miss Hollis you would be the last person I would tell anything to about *my* town." He turned around and continued the walk home. Bridget smiled smugly at us and pulled her children closer to her as the path narrowed.

"Oh yeah?" Candy shouted after them. "I still say you smell like maple syrup."

"Candy you shouldn't say that. What if he stops paying for college?"

"He won't. You don't need him anyway Emma. Hugh's going to be here any day."

Chapter 54

"This is some kind of joke right?" Hugh waved the paper at Mika.

"No. Why?"

"I'm not doing that." He pointed to the occupation written on the paper.

"You have to."

"Even if I wanted to, I'm not qualified."

"If you would read the rest of it you would find that you are."

Hugh sat on the sofa and read the paper. It was the biography of someone else. This was supposed to be his life?

"See, you are more than qualified."

"According to this paper I am, but I haven't actually done any of this." Hugh said.

"Oh that doesn't matter. You'll manage."

"Manage? I'll probably die the first day."

"Don't be so dramatic."

"Why did you pick this for me?"

"Isn't it obvious?"

"I'm not doing it."

"It's too late for that." Mika said. "Do you realize how much work goes into something like this? I can't just drop you into the modern world. Other things have to happen. Memories and ideas have to be implanted into the minds of the living."

"How do you mean?"

Mika sighed. "Senator Brown has to get the idea in his head that he needs someone like you in town. Once he gets the thought he has to believe it was his own idea. That doesn't just happen Hugh."

"I suppose I will have to talk to him."

"Of course. He's the catalyst to get you there. This is how we give you your new identity and a history in the living world. I've already planted the thought in the Senator's head. It's just a seedling, he's barely aware of it. But it will grow and consume him until he does something about it."

Hugh looked at his life story spelled out on one piece of paper. "When do I get to meet the others?"

"In a few minutes, but first you need to read this. It's their life stories." Mika handed him another piece of paper. It was a list of names followed by a brief description. Hugh shook his head. "This just keeps getting better and better doesn't it?"

Chapter 55

The summer passed quickly and still there was no sign of Hugh. Mother was slowly accepting the idea that Candy was going to be part of the family. She frequently sighed and grumbled. "Emma, if you marry one of those Coopers my nerves may finally give out."

Father appeared less concerned. He puttered about seemingly oblivious to the worries of the world around him. I confronted him one day about how he had recognized Hugh's watch.

"I've never seen this." He put on his spectacles and examined it closely.

"I showed this to you once before and you thanked me for covering for you."

"Upon my word Emma, I've never seen this object before in my life." He looked genuinely surprised.

"But you have, we were sitting right here in this parlor. Don't you remember?"

"When was this?"

"This past winter."

Father nodded and patted my hand. "Ah that's it. You were sick this winter Emma. Probably a memory brought on by the fever."

"No, it wasn't the fever. I remember." I said raising my voice.

Father looked nervously towards the kitchen. "Keep your voice down. Your mother is already in a state over this Candy Cooper business. Do you want her to think something is wrong with you?"

I grabbed the watch and put it in my pocket. "Why are you doing this? Why are you pretending you didn't say it? I'm not crazy."

"I never said you were crazy dear. Just mistaken."

"But-" I stopped talking as Ethan looked in the doorway.

Father leapt to his feet. "Ethan my boy, do come in."

Ethan looked at our faces. "I'll come back later."

Father laughed. "Nonsense! Come in and talk to your sister. I've got to go anyhow. I'm late for uh, something." Father put his spectacles in his pocket and rushed out. A few seconds later I heard the front door close.

"He was in a hurry." Ethan said sitting next to me. "What's wrong? You look upset."

"I don't know." I told him what happened with Father.

"That's odd."

"Do you think his mind could be going?"

Ethan shrugged and scratched his head. "Maybe. Listen Emma, not to get off the subject, but I just saw Senator Brown and there's something wrong with him."

"What do you mean?"

"There was- Oh it's hard to explain." Ethan stopped and tapped his fingers on the back of the sofa. "It's as though he was surrounded, no enveloped in a cloud."

"A cloud?"

"I don't know if that's the right word but as he walked down the road there was a cloud of smoky air following him. I could barely see his face it was so thick."

"So do you think it was something only you could see?"

"Yes. And he's never had it before."

"What did it look like again?"

"It was dark, nearly black. There were these silver specks floating through it too. I've never seen anything like it. It was beautiful really." Ethan took off his glasses and rubbed his eyes.

Mika. I smiled and took Hugh's watch out of my pocket. It was only a matter of time now.

Chapter 56

Hugh felt a strange gurgling sensation in his stomach. He stopped and waited. A few seconds later it happened again. "I'm hungry."

"Really? Already? We haven't been gone that long." Mika said.

"I haven't eaten in over one hundred years, don't you think my stomach might be a little empty?"

"What do you want me to do about it?"

"Can't you make something appear? A roast chicken sounds good right about now." Hugh hoped it would come with potatoes and carrots on the side.

"You think I can just wave my hand and anything I think of appears out of thin air?"

"Yes, and you can tell me about the others while I eat." Hugh suggested.

Mika sighed. A small table appeared. On it was a large plate of roast chicken, potatoes and gravy. There were several kinds of vegetables, none of which were carrots. Hugh was delighted to find a basket with hot rolls and a ceramic dish of butter along with two wedges of pie. Finally there was a pitcher of ale and a pewter tankard, just like the kind he drank out of the last night he was alive. "Will that do?"

"Yes. Thank you." Hugh tore off a piece of chicken and stuffed it into his mouth. He closed his eyes as the glorious taste overwhelmed him. Memories of a dozen different flavors flickered through his mind. He began randomly jabbing his fork at everything and shoving it in as fast as he could.

"Easy there." Mika said. "Don't you remember what happens if you eat too fast?"

"I don't care." Hugh said as he rabidly chewed and swallowed. "Don't you miss this?"

"Sometimes."

"What was the last thing you ate when you were alive?" Hugh mashed a lump of butter into one of the rolls.

"A poisoned drink." Mika said. "Since you intend on stuffing yourself so enthusiastically, I might as well get on with it. I may never get another chance for your mouth to be occupied by something else other than talking."

Hugh made a face but continued eating. The ale was beginning to warm him from the inside and the food started to fill the emptiness in his stomach. He hadn't felt that contented in years.

Mika cleared his throat. "The others, they won't feel the same way you do."

"How so?"

"When I handed you that piece of paper with your new name, occupation and such, you knew it was just a story. You know in your mind that you're still Hugh MacPherson, you have all your memories and experiences from your first life, your Torment, and now your second life. It won't be the same for them. What is on that paper is what they believe their life is. They don't know they've been given a second chance. They don't remember their first life. The only thing they'll bring from it is the way they look, or would have looked if they had grown up."

Hugh put his fork down. "Why don't they remember? Why are you giving them a second chance?" He took a long swig of ale and leaned back on the sofa.

"Hugh, they are my failures. They all died before the age of two. I failed them as a Watcher."

"How can you blame yourself? Infants and young children die all the time. It's just a fact of life."

"It's not like that. Things are different from when you were a boy, children don't die as often as they once did, and these were all preventable. The first died during an argument his parents were having with one another. One of them walked into a lake and drowned. Another one put something in his mouth and choked to death. I failed them." Mika's voice was low. He sat on the sofa next to Hugh and rubbed his eyes. "I hate talking about this. But you have to know. You can't talk to them about me, or what it's like to be brought back to life, they won't understand."

"You shouldn't blame yourself Mika." He suppressed an urge to burp, it didn't seem like the appropriate time. "You told me a thousand times not to steal, but I didn't listen. You told me not to go into the house that night, but I didn't listen to you. You can't be expected to shoulder all the blame. Aren't you just there to guide us?"

Mika leaned his head back on the sofa and smiled sadly. "I don't expect you to understand. When I, when any Watcher finds out a new life is coming into this world it's an incredible feeling. When that new little baby takes its first breath their life is being placed in my hands. It's my job to do everything I can to make sure that they not only survive but make the right choices in life.

"That life becomes so precious to me." Mika continued. "I am with you every second of every day. Even when I'm not beside you I can still hear everything you say and do. I know all of your triumphs and all of your disappointments. When I lose one of you prematurely I take it very personally. This is all I have Hugh, this Watching is all I do. I have no other purpose."

"I'm sorry. I really am."

Mika stood up and the table of food disappeared. "So you understand about the others now. I've implanted their minds with memories from their biographies."

"I won't know what those are."

"You'll manage. If they start talking about something just pretend you remember."

"Manage! That's easy for you to say."

"I'll be there some of the time. I'll coach you."

"I'll still be able to see you? I was afraid- I mean I thought the living aren't supposed to be able to see you." Hugh said feeling more relieved than he cared to let on.

"Yes, you'll see me."

Hugh's stomach made a strange gurgling noise. He giggled. The ale seemed to have gone to his head. "Mika, I think I need to use the privy."

Mika opened the door. "The bathroom is across the hall." Hugh got up and started for the door. "And hurry up, it's nearly time to leave."

Chapter 57

It had been six months and there was no sign of Hugh. I tried not to get discouraged but in the back of my mind I kept thinking of Mika, the way he looked at me the day he took Hugh away, the coldness in his eyes. He didn't care about me. I couldn't help but wonder if it was all a trick.

I had a glimmer of hope when Ethan told me about the smoke surrounding Senator Brown's head. His description of a black and silver cloud reminded me of the first day I saw Mika. There had been an aura of gray-black around him, within the aura were silvery specks of light that shimmered and pulsed. He was the most beautiful thing I had ever seen. I wanted to believe Senator Brown's cloud had something to do with Hugh's return.

The Coopers had a large party for Candy and Ethan the night before they were to begin the trip back to school. The party was held outdoors in the yard between our two houses. Every available Cooper was there with their instruments in tow. After a huge meal cooked by both my mother and Margaret, various members of the family gathered around and started playing their usual jigs and reels. Michael led on his fiddle.

"Your father is looking better these days." I said to Candy as we sat under the oak tree watching and listening. The younger Coopers, including Eve's children, were dancing and hollering at one another.

"He's given up drinking. Mother says he's an awful bore now."

"Really? I thought she would have been happy about it."

"Oh no. Now he's home all the time."

"I wish Hugh was home."

Candy smiled and put her arm around me. "He will be back. I can feel it in my bones."

"I hope you are right." I said. "I miss him so much. It's just not the same without him. I still forget and think to myself that when I get home I'm going to tell Hugh this or that."

"Of course I'm right. When have you ever known me to be wrong?"

I thought for a moment. "Actually never."

"Of course never, I am unerringly right, especially in areas of romance." she said smiling. "That was quite an impressive word for a Cooper wasn't it?"

"Indeed."

In the morning there was a little send off in front of Eve's house for Ethan and Candy. Unfortunately the bricklayer was there muttering about his fate as well as Senator Brown who arrived with a photographer and had several pictures taken with the recipients of his scholarship.

"It does my soul good to know I am helping these two fine young people get a first rate education." he said in-between pictures.

"I'll bet." I muttered to Father who was standing next to me.

"So you doubt old man Brown's sincerity do you?" the bricklayer said behind me.

"Yes I do." I whispered over my shoulder. "And be quiet for once."

"Who are you talking to?" Father asked.

"The Seer wants the ole' bricklayer to be quiet. I wonder what the other Seer wants. Ah, tis a sad day when a poor ole' soul like me can't speak his mind."

"Thank you so much everyone." Ethan said while having his picture taken with the Senator. "Candy and I will be back next summer." He shook the Senator's hand and then made the rounds giving everyone one last hug.

"Take care of yourself Emma." he said squeezing my hands. "I know you'll find what you're looking for."

"I know." I looked at Senator Brown who was having his picture taken with Candy. "Is that black cloud still there?"

"Yes, and it's gotten a bit darker."

"It's time to go Ethan!" Candy shouted from the seat of the wagon.

"Goodbye Emma." he said quietly. He hopped on the back of the wagon as the driver called to the horses and they began the slow climb up the hill.

They waved enthusiastically and shouted goodbye until the wagon rounded the corner and they were out of sight.

"I am going to miss them." Eve said. "Especially Candy, she was such a help around the house."

"Me too." I said, staring at the empty road.

Eve smiled and put her arm around my shoulders. "You look pale Emma. You have ever since you got sick this winter."

"I know, but I'm fine."

"Why don't you come in and have some tea with me? You too Father."

Father was looking nervously from side to side. "What's that Eve?"

"I said why don't you come in and have tea with Emma and me?"

"Oh I've got much too much to do today." He straightened his hat and headed down the road.

"He's getting stranger and stranger." Eve said.

"I know."

"He has his reasons." the bricklayer said. "You'd be the same way if you were in his shoes."

Chapter 58

The bathroom, as Mika called it, was fascinating. Hugh had heard of running water but he had never seen it before. He spent five or ten minutes turning the water on and off, it was interesting that the more he turned the knob the faster the water came out. He experimented with the hot and cold until he had reached what he reasoned was the perfect bath temperature.

There was a knock on the door, Mika's annoyed voice came echoing through. "What are you doing in there?"

Hugh shut off the water and opened the door. "I was just trying things out." he said sheepishly. Mika pushed the door open and looked inside. "You needn't worry about that, there won't be anything like this where you're going."

"Is this what the future is like? Did you have this sort of thing where you came from?"

"Yes." Mika glanced at the privy bowl and pushed down a silver handle on the back. There was a whooshing sound and everything inside disappeared down a hole in the bottom of the bowl, clean water began immediately pouring back in.

"I thought there was a servant to do that." Hugh said, his face burning red.

"It's fine. I need you back in here."

Hugh wiped his hands on a towel and followed Mika across the hall. Once inside Mika shut the door and Hugh was dismayed to see three strangers sitting on the sofa. They stared at him, he reminded himself that they believed Mika's fictional account of their lives.

"Where have you been?" one of them asked.

"Oh just across the hall."

"What's over there?" asked another.

Hugh looked at Mika.

"Listen, we really have to get going." Mika stepped closer to Hugh and whispered in his ear. "They won't remember being here."

"I heard that!" cried one of the strangers, he appeared to be the oldest one. "And frankly I don't recall how we got here." He looked at the others who nodded in agreement. "My mind is a little fuzzy. What about you?" He looked at Hugh.

Hugh nodded vaguely.

"Don't worry, it will all make sense shortly." Mika said. "Stand close to me."

The three on the sofa stood up. Mika held his arm out in front of him. "Now when I count to five I want you to hold onto me." Mika took a deep breath and looked at Hugh. "And I should tell you that when we return it will be four years since you left."

Hugh had no time to react. Mika was already counting. He took hold of his arm and let the blackness envelope him.

Chapter 59

I hadn't given up hope entirely, but with every passing month and year it was becoming harder to believe that Hugh would return. It had been just over four years since he had left. I could never have imagined that so much time would pass without seeing him. I found myself forgetting exactly what his voice sounded like, the precise green of his eyes, the coolness of his skin.

The house felt so empty. Nothing was the same. I no longer turned over in bed in the morning and expected to see him smiling at me. There was a dull ache in my stomach that never quite seemed to go away. Some days I was so lonely I could hardly stand it, other days I could lock it away in the back of my mind.

I searched the faces passing by Thalberg's store less and less. There had been a few new people that had moved to town, but each one was wrong in some way, nothing and no one seemed right. I wondered if I had missed him. Had I walked by him and not even looked him in the eye? What if Mika had thought I was too stupid to even notice and taken him away for good?

These thoughts were running through my head as I stood at my counter in Thalberg's. "What a slow day!" Mr. Thalberg exclaimed from his side of the store.

"Yes." I sighed.

Mrs. Thalberg emerged from the back carrying a small wooden crate. "I'm taking this to the post office."

"I can do it for you." I said, anxious to get some fresh air.

"Are you sure? It's a bit heavy."

"I don't mind."

"Have Emma take it." Mr. Thalberg said. "She's in one of her moods again."

"I am not." I said hotly.

"Oh yes you are. You should have married that fellow who used to come around here. There hasn't been anyone since him. Why? You're pretty enough."

"Elijah stop it." Mrs. Thalberg scolded. "She'll know when the right one comes along. Stop pestering her."

"I am not pestering. I am just saying-" He stopped and waved his hands in resignation.

"Don't listen to him." Mrs. Thalberg said. "He would be lost without you here."

"I just want you to be happy Emma." he said.

"I know." I took the package from Mrs. Thalberg. "I'll be right back."

I hurried down the street trying not to think of the possibility of a lifetime spent alone. The post office was crowded as usual. Much to my dismay I found Senator Brown inside. He was holding court with four or five onlookers. He stopped talking as I stepped inside.

"Hello." I said without much feeling.

"Good day." he said returning the sentiment. He turned back to his audience. There was someone already at the counter so I balanced the package in my arms and waited.

"It was cracking good timing as well." the Senator said behind me.

"When are they coming?" a man asked.

"In a few weeks. The old chap has to get his house in order and then he'll be here."

"Next." Prunella Dickens called from behind the post office counter. I stepped up and put the crate on the counter. She wrinkled her nose and looked at it suspiciously.

"It's for the Thalbergs." I said handing her some coins.

"Uh huh."

"You've done it again Brownie." a man behind me said. I looked over my shoulder and saw him slap the Senator on the back.

"Everything I do is for this town."

"Don't we know it." said the man. The men laughed and grinned up at the Senator in admiration. I was getting curious about what they were talking about, but it appeared the conversation was over.

"Three cents change." Prunella slapped three pennies on the counter. I put the coins in my pocket.

Just as I turned to leave another man came into the post office. His face lit up when he saw the Senator. "Brownie! What's going on here?"

"Oh Jim I was just telling the boys about a letter I received today." Brown said. I stopped and pretended to look at the public notice board on the wall.

"What's the news?" Jim asked, settling into a chair in the corner.

I took a peek at them out of the corner of my eye. The Senator puffed out his chest and put his hand in his pocket. "Well Jim it looks like we're going to have a few new faces in town."

"Really?" said Jim. "What scheme have you got going now?"

I lingered over the public notices hoping the Senator was going to elaborate.

"I've been thinking for a while that there's something missing here in town. And you know what that is?"

"I can't even begin to guess." Jim said.

"A police department of course."

"But don't we have the sheriff?"

"Pish!" cried the Senator. "He's three towns away. When is the last time you've seen the sheriff around here."

"Not recently I reckon, but do we need a whole police department of our own?"

"We most certainly do. We have a bank and quite a few merchants. And I've seen more than my share of suspicious characters skulking about my house."

"Oh, I didn't realize."

"Yes well, I feel crime is going to be a real problem here if we don't do something now. I've been thinking about it for the last few years. In fact I feel a bit like a man possessed." Brown snickered. "This idea has taken hold of me like nothing else. A few months ago I put an ad in a few papers and today I have the acceptance letter from a most outstanding candidate." The Senator took a letter from his pocket and tapped it with his finger.

"So you have someone?" Jim asked.

"Does he? You better tell em' Brownie." said another man.

"I got a response from a most interesting chap. A widower and former military man, he's done a considerable amount of soldiering."

"Was he in the war?" Jim asked.

"I don't know, and I didn't inquire. He has been a firefighter, and now he's working as a policeman in Boston."

"Why does he want to move here?"

Out of the corner of my eye I saw the Senator smile. "That's the best part. He wants to get out of the city for the sake of his children."

"I don't like children."

"Oh Jim don't be such a grouch. They are grown children. Three young men and they are all policemen too. Don't you see? An instant police department."

"Four policemen in this small town? How are we going to pay for them all?"

"Their father, a Mr. Garrett will be the chief, although I prefer the title of Chief Inspector, has a nice ring to it. The boys will serve part of the time here in town and part of the time with the sheriff as deputies. I've got it all worked out. There's no need to worry." the Senator said with a nervous laugh.

"It seems like you waste a lot of this town's money on your own projects." Jim said. "I am sorry Brownie, you're a great friend but I never vote for you."

I tried to suppress a giggle.

"Miss Hollis!" the Senator cried. "Are you spying on me again?"

"No sir. I was just interested in hearing about the new police department. A father and three sons you say?"

The Senator frowned. "I see, thinking of those boys are you? I am afraid every young woman in town will descend on them like vultures when they arrive. You'd better get in line."

"You said their name was Garrett?"

"Yes. You heard every word I'm sure."

"That's another word for attic is it not?"

"Of course it is." he said looking irritated. "Doesn't Thalberg need you back at the store?"

"I am sure he does. Have a lovely day Senator." I said as I rushed out the door smiling.

Chapter 60

There seemed to be a slight gap in his memory. Hugh found himself sitting on a bouncy wagon seat in-between two of the strangers. In the front seat was the other one along with a young boy who was driving the wagon. The boy, who looked to be no more than fourteen, was in command of two brown horses that were pulling the wagon over a frozen country road. The last thing Hugh remembered was standing in that strange room with Mika and the others. Mika had been saying something. What was it?

The words suddenly came flooding back to him. "Four years later! You bring me back four years later!" he shouted aloud. The others stared at him.

"What's the matter with you?" one of them asked.

"Me? Oh, I must have nodded off or something."

"Four years is barely a blink of an eye." Mika said as he descended in the air, his black wings fluttered. The horses whinnied and picked up their pace.

"Four years is too long."

"You're doing it again." said the one up front.

"Careful Hugh they are going to think you are a bit crazy if you talk to things that aren't there." Mika said.

He took a deep breath and forced himself not to respond. Four years. How could Emma have been left waiting all that time? She had probably given up on him by now. How could he have been in that room for four years? Nothing made sense. When he had promised Emma he would return he had imagined it would be no more than a few weeks. She might have moved on, there was always Jeremy White lurking in the background. He looked like the forgiving type. He glared at Mika.

"Why don't you just enjoy the ride Hugh?"

Hugh tapped his foot on the floor of the wagon and tried to take in the view. It had been ages since he was outdoors, not counting that brief stint with Mika a few months back. They were passing through a pleasant stretch of low hills dotted with clumps of pine trees. It was late winter and there were a few inches of snow on the ground, dead grass stuck out through the snow, bland and brittle. Birds called to each other overhead as the sky stretched out clear and cloudless. Hugh thought he smelled salt in the air. "Are we near the ocean?" he asked the young driver.

The boy looked at him over his shoulder. "Of course. Don't you know where you're going?"

"I just didn't think we were that close yet."

"We've been driving since dawn." the boy said.

Hugh nodded. He thought he heard someone snicker. "Carry on."

"Nice one." Mika muttered.

The road continued and began turning to the right. He realized they were on the top of a hill, through the trees he could see the steely gray-blue of the ocean laid out across the horizon. As the wagon turned the corner the road opened up to an orderly row of houses. The terrain was steep, the boy pulled up on the reins and slowed the horses.

Hugh was glad for the leisurely pace, it gave him a chance to look at things. Everything had changed so much, houses looked different now. They had porches, gables and glass panes in every window. The people were just as interesting. The clothes and hairstyles were so different. Hugh realized a bit guiltily that perhaps the Hollis family had not been the most fashionable ones in town.

He was surprised to see that the people on the street were just as interested in him. Many of them stopped to watch the wagon pass, and a few even waved. Hugh waved back, excited to be seen. He supposed now that he was going to have to be a policeman he should know everyone and their business.

As they progressed he noticed a beautiful blonde woman on the sidewalk shaking out a rug. It took him a few seconds to realize it was Eve. She looked up and said something aloud. Three redheaded children ran to her side and watched as the wagon rolled by.

Ahead of them the road took a sharp turn to the left as they descended the hill. Emma had often described the town's layout but Hugh had never fully been able to picture it until now. He looked to his left and saw a sign for Jennings' Emporium, he remembered Emma telling him how she had been asked to leave the store the first year she bought him a Christmas present. Through the window he could see a stout man in a green apron hunched over the counter.

He looked on the other side of the road where he knew Thalberg's would be. There was a reflection on the windows, he couldn't see inside. Emma could be in there right now. He considered asking the driver to stop. As his eyes searched the shop windows Mika came drifting by. "It's not time for that yet. We're expected elsewhere."

Hugh resisted the urge to talk back. The road continued its sharp turn as it wound its way down towards the cove. The topography was vaguely familiar, he had walked that way on his last night alive, he remembered hearing the ocean to his right and smelling the cool salty air.

To his surprise the wagon suddenly turned into a small lane partially hidden by a wide oak tree. As they proceeded Hugh was dismayed to see a sign reading "Brown Lane" swinging in the afternoon breeze. The lane continued upwards before ending at the front steps of a large stone house perched atop a cliff with stunning views out to sea.

A blonde man was on the porch. As the wagon pulled up he stepped onto the snowy lawn. "Welcome, welcome." Hugh recognized him as Jeremy White, the man Emma almost married. The others were already down shaking Jeremy's hand as Hugh jumped off the wagon.

"Glad to know you." Jeremy said shaking Hugh's hand.

"Er, yes. Same here." he mumbled. "What are we doing here? Isn't this Senator Brown's house?"

Jeremy looked confused. "Your family is renting it while you're here in Fox Cove."

"We have to live with Senator Brown?" Hugh said, horrified at the thought.

"No. The Senator has built a new home down the coast." Jeremy spoke slowly as though he thought Hugh had some kind of mental condition.

"You're embarrassing me. Didn't you read that paper I gave you?" Mika said from somewhere behind him.

"Oh yes I remember. I guess the traveling has worn me out."

Jeremy smiled and looked at the others. "We'll soon remedy that. We've got dinner ready. The Senator is waiting for you."

They followed Jeremy inside. The hallway was well decorated. The former thief in Hugh noticed dozens of expensive objects ripe for the picking. They were led into a parlor. The Senator was standing at the fireplace looking important.

"Gentlemen!" he called out. "I've been looking forward to this for some time."

One by one they introduced themselves. Hugh went last and dutifully recited his new name while Mika wandered about as though he had nothing better to do.

It was strange to see the Senator up close. Of course he had seen him before during his Torment, but this was different. Now that they were meeting eye to eye he found himself surprisingly impressed with his presence. He sniffed and tried to detect any signs of maple syrup.

"You chaps are our town's first police force. Make me proud and you'll be handsomely rewarded." Brown said as he passed out cigars.

"You can count on it sir." said one of the others.

"Glad to hear it. Glad to hear it." The Senator lit a match. He held it out so they could all light their cigars. Hugh took a puff and coughed. He hadn't smoked a cigar in over a hundred years, and even then he had never cared for them.

Mika circled around him. "Good luck. I'll be back in a little while. In the meantime you best read that paper again, I put it in your coat pocket."

Chapter 61

The wagon rolled by Thalberg's windows late in the afternoon. I had purposely stayed near the back of the store so I could observe the new police chief and his three sons who were said to be coming into town that very day.

It was all the townsfolk had been talking about for weeks. Since I overheard Senator Brown that day in the post office he had been announcing the arrival of the town's police force any chance he got. He even came into the store to tell Mr. and Mrs. Thalberg about it.

I was trying not to get my hopes up. It could all be a coincidence, three eligible young men with the name Garrett. And then there was the fact they were all policemen, it was fitting for a former criminal to now have to enforce the law. I had counted down the days in my head until the horses and wagon came into view, and then suddenly there they were.

It was impossible to know which one was Hugh. The whole challenge was so daunting that I felt the initial excitement drain out of me as I watched three strangers pass by. I put my hand to the gold watch around my neck.

"Looks like a nice family." Mr. Thalberg said from his seat near the window. "The boys don't really look alike do they? Do you suppose they all have different mothers?"

"Elijah! What on earth would make you say that?" Mrs. Thalberg cried.

"What? Look at them, they don't even look like their father. I am just saying."

I heard the jingle of the front door and straightened my apron. Candy hurried in smiling.

"Hello Dr. Candy." said Mr. Thalberg.

"Oh hello." She ran towards me. "I've got it." she said waving a piece of paper.

"Got what?"

"Everything you need to know about our newest citizens." She was wearing a green wool coat over her white doctors apron, her red hair was swept back with a barrette.

"How did you get that?" I wasn't sure I wanted the Thalbergs to hear all of this.

"Oh I have my ways." she said coyly. "You wouldn't believe the things patients will tell you, especially when they ask to have their bill reduced."

"Candy! You aren't offering patients discounts if they give you information are you?"

"Not exactly." she said grinning. "Anyway I found out their names and ages, that's if you want to know."

"I want to know." Mr. Thalberg said.

"Go ahead."

Candy took her coat off and threw it across the counter. She rolled up her sleeves and straightened the scrap of paper in her hand. "Let's see. We know their last name is Garrett. We have Harold age twenty two, Will age twenty three, and Ryan who is twenty four. You're twenty three aren't you Emma? That puts you right in the middle."

"Yes." I agreed. I could feel the nerves fluttering in my stomach as Candy spoke.

"They were all born in Philadelphia, their mother died after Harold came along. At that point their father left the army to spend more time with the boys. Then they moved to New York where the boys went to school and then onto Boston.

"And none are married?" Mr. Thalberg asked.

"No. Or should I say not yet?" Candy laughed.

They all laughed with her while I tried to imagine which one could be Hugh, they all had the same backgrounds, the same occupation, the same last name. I hoped once I met them it would become clear.

"That's all I've got so far." Candy folded the paper and stuck it in her pocket. "But I'll keep asking around. Are you going to Senator Brown's party tonight?"

"What party?"

"Oh didn't you hear? Ole' Brownie is having a party for all the prominent people in town, you know the who's who. Ethan and I got an invitation a few days ago."

"I got one too." said Mr. Thalberg.

"It's a party to celebrate two things. First of all the arrival of the Chief Inspector and his sons, and secondly I think Senator Brown is announcing his intention to run for governor." Candy said.

"He's running for governor?" Mrs. Thalberg asked.

"Yes. Haven't you heard?"

"Does he really think he can get elected?" I asked.

"Apparently." Candy picked her coat up and slipped it on. "I've got to run, I left Ethan by himself at the clinic. Goodbye." She rushed out the door.

As I left work that evening I walked slowly past Brown Lane. The house was perched on its rocky foundation awash in the last rays of daylight. I squinted and tried to look in the windows, but it was much too far away and the low afternoon sunlight was casting a golden glow on the glass.

My parents were in the parlor when I got home. Father was reading a small card while Mother was knitting. "Emma." he said as I walked past the door.

"Yes?"

"Do you want to go to this?" He held up the card.

"Go to what?" I asked, desperately hoping it was the invitation to the party Candy had told me about.

"Didn't you hear? Senator Brown is having a little soiree for the new police chief and his family. I can hardly believe I got an invitation."

"Maybe he's forgiven you for the past."

"Maybe." Father said looking at the invitation. "Do you want to come with me? Your mother doesn't want to go."

Mother wrinkled her nose. "I don't like that man Edward, I never have. And I have no interest in meeting our new policemen. I don't plan on breaking any laws." she sniffed. "I see no reason on earth why we need a police department here in a small town, that man wastes too much of our money. I hope you don't vote for him Edward."

Father's mouth dropped open. "He paid for Ethan to go to college, and Candy too. How can we not support him?"

"Take Emma. I'm not going."

"Very well." he said. "Put your best dress on Emma, it starts in an hour."

"Yes I will." I rushed upstairs and threw open my wardrobe. I had a few nice dresses that I had got while working at the store. I took a quick look and pulled out a satin crimson. I had never worn it before because the bosom seemed to be cut awfully low, especially for a small town like Fox Cove, but I supposed that situations like this called for more extreme measures.

I slipped Hugh's watch in a black satin evening bag. It seemed unlikely that I would need it tonight, but one could never tell. I took a moment to look in the mirror. I was overdressed for sure, but there was no time to change. Father was calling my name from downstairs.

We walked to the party in the twilight. Father had put on his better suit and was wearing cologne. "You don't think this dress is too much?" I asked him.

"No, no. It's fine." His eyes darted up to the house as we entered Brown Lane. "Now listen Emma, I just want to say you might find me, well let's just say if I disappear for awhile you won't think anything of it."

"Disappear? What are you talking about?"

"I may be required to step out, just go on with the party." he said nervously. "And don't tell your mother about this."

"Father, we have all noticed that you have been acting-"

"Hey there!" Candy suddenly poked me in the back. Father and I turned around to find she and Ethan walking arm in arm.

"We were following you." Ethan said. "Where's Mother?"

"Your mother had a headache."

"Father!" I said jabbing him in the side with my elbow. "She didn't want to come."

Father looked at me calmly. "No dear, she had a headache. You must have misunderstood."

"But-"

"Who cares anyway?" Candy said. "We're missing the party."

"Quite right." Father agreed. "Shall we Candy?"

"Certainly Dads." She took his arm and they proceeded down the lane and into the house.

"I guess you're stuck with me." Ethan said.

"I'm glad. Father just out and out lied. Mother didn't want to go, she never said she had a headache."

Ethan adjusted his glasses. "Let's go in and meet these young men, isn't that why you came?"

"Yes, but-"

"Never mind about Father. He is who he is. I don't know why he says the things he does, but I doubt he's going to change now."

"Do you know something about him? Is he like us?"

"I don't know." Ethan said. "Listen we really should get in there. Candy *and* Father together is not a good combination. Anything could be happening."

"You're right. And Hugh is in there somewhere. I hope."

I took his arm and we hurried up the porch steps and through the open door. A servant led us to the parlor. A partition which divided it from the library had been opened up creating one large room. Everything was

301

aglow in candlelight. There was already a large turnout. People were clustered throughout the room in small groups. Candy and Father were with the Thalbergs who gave us a little wave. Senator Brown was surrounded by his admirers including Cole Jennings.

"There's a very strong presence in this room." Ethan said.

"Maybe it's Hugh."

"No. It's like a force of nature."

"Mika." I said quietly.

"I don't know who it is, but it wants me to leave you alone." Ethan grimaced as though it was hard to catch his breath. "I have to go Emma. I can't resist it." He clutched his chest and walked away. As soon as he left Candy came bounding across the room.

"Have you spotted the boys yet?" She looked about. "Oh there's one, that's Harold, the youngest. He's talking with Prunella Dickens." She discreetly pointed.

I was surprised to see the usually sullen postmistress laughing as a young man with black wavy hair and a ready smile was talking at length to her. He was wearing a navy policeman's uniform with shiny buttons and a silver badge on his chest.

"What do you think?" Candy whispered.

"I don't know. I haven't even met him yet." Prunella said something. Harold replied and they both laughed. "He has a sense of humor."

"Just like Hugh?"

"Yes, but having a sense of humor doesn't mean it's him."

"It's a start. Now let's see, that's Will talking with Jeremy."

"Heaven knows what he's telling him."

Will Garrett was the same height as his younger brother Harold, but otherwise they looked nothing alike. He had blonde hair cropped short, even across the room I could see his bright blue eyes reflecting the candlelight. He was nodding as Jeremy spoke, there was a relaxed air about him as he listened patiently.

"Maybe that's him?" she asked.

"Hugh is friendly and he's a good listener."

"Oh and there's Ryan and his father." Candy said grabbing my arm. "They're against the wall."

In the back corner, near a tall porcelain urn, was the oldest Garrett son, Ryan. He was staring into space, his face void of emotion. His hair was reddish brown and cut longer than his brothers. His father stood silently next to him.

"Someone told me he's a bit of a mysterious character. Very quiet and reserved. Doesn't sound like Hugh at all." Candy said.

I bit my lip and watched him. "I don't know. Hugh's parents were killed when he was just a boy, he is a murder victim, and he was brought back from the dead. He can't always be happy."

Candy sighed. "You'll just have to wait until you meet them."

I was about to answer when I noticed Father coming towards us with a glass of wine. "Hello ladies." he said grinning. "Or should I say lady and doctor." He stumbled, spilling a droplet of wine on the floor.

"Father, are you drunk?" I asked.

"No, but I'm working on it." He looked over our shoulders. "Ole Brownie is coming this way with the boys. He's going to introduce us."

"He is?" I turned to Candy. "Do I look all right?"

"Oh sure, that dress is perfect."

"It's too much isn't it? It's too low, I know it."

Candy shook her head as we turned and saw Senator Brown and the four Garrett men coming towards us. "My mother always says that the more sugar you put out the more bees you get."

"I am just looking for one bee in particular." I whispered.

"Greetings everyone. So good of you to come tonight." the Senator said as he stood before us.

Father raised his glass. "Evening Brownie."

"It appears you've had quite enough already Edward." the Senator observed.

"You're not my wife." Father mumbled."

The Senator cleared his throat and made a motion across the room at Ethan who promptly joined us. "I would like to present our new police force." the Senator said beaming. "First we have Chief Inspector Jason Garrett."

The Chief Inspector stepped forward and made a little bow before shaking each of our hands as we were introduced.

"Next is Officer Ryan Garrett."

Ryan offered his hand and said nothing. I was disappointed he didn't even attempt to make eye contact with me. As soon as the introductions were over he took a few steps back and joined his father.

"Ah yes and here is Officer Will Garrett." continued the Senator.

Will smiled and shook our hands, repeating our names as we were introduced. "It's very nice to meet all of you. I am sure we will all become great friends."

"You can count on it." Candy said.

Will smiled, his eyes were a warm blue. I found myself smiling back until Candy poked me in the side.

"It's too soon to start any of that." she whispered.

"And finally we have Officer Harold Garrett."

Harold came forward and shook our hands. "Greetings one and all." he said grinning. "You must all feel a lot safer now that I am here."

There was an awkward silence as no one was sure what to say. Father hiccupped and finished the rest of his wine.

"I'm joking." Harold said, laughing out loud.

"We knew that." Candy said.

"Of course we did." I added, trying to sound witty.

"Well folks I would like to stay here and visit with you all day but I have an important announcement to make." Senator Brown smoothed his jacket. Bridget arrived and touched his arm.

"You should be getting on with things darling."

"I was just saying so dear." They walked away and joined Jeremy.

"What's all this about?" Harold asked me.

"The Senator is going to announce that he's running for governor."

"Why is he announcing it if everyone already knows?"

"You don't know the Senator very well." I said quietly. The Chief Inspector and Ryan were both watching us. I considered they might be supporters of Brown. "He's big on public displays of his own greatness."

"Oh I see." Harold said.

Jeremy stepped into the middle of the room and cleared his throat. "May I have your attention ladies and gentlemen?" The chatter ceased.

"That's the bank president right?" Harold asked.

"Yes." I side stepped away from the rest of the Garretts and my family. Harold followed me and eventually we found ourselves in the back corner of the room.

"First I want to thank our dear Senator Brown for putting together this lovely party. This is a remarkable day in the history of Fox Cove when we can welcome our new chief inspector of police and three young and capable officers." Jeremy said gesturing towards the new police force.

A polite round of applause rippled through the room.

"But there's another reason we are here tonight ladies and gentlemen and for that I would like to turn the floor over to our esteemed and beloved Senator Hershival Brown." Jeremy's voice rose grandly.

There was thunderous applause as the Senator stepped forward and put his arms out benevolently. He acted as though he was surprised by the adulation. "Thank you, thank you." he said motioning for the clapping to stop. The room quieted to a breathless silence.

"Is he for real?" Harold whispered in my ear.

"Just wait."

"You don't know how much that warms the heart of this old man." The Senator looked meaningfully at Bridget. "I have had the pleasure of serving this town and my district in the state senate for many years now."

There was another round of applause.

"However folks I think it's time for me to move on."

"No!" cried one man.

The Senator chuckled and looked at Bridget again. "Now, now, there's nothing to worry about. I think that I can best serve you and the citizens of Maine in a more prominent capacity. That is why tonight I am announcing that I, Hershival Brown, am tossing my hat into the ring and running for governor!"

The room erupted. Loud clapping and whistling could be heard from every corner.

"Would you vote for him, if you could?" Harold asked.

"I don't think so." I said watching the Senator as he took a deep breath and started to speak again.

"We will make this town the greatest in Maine, the greatest, perhaps if I may dream a little, in New England." His voice lifted inspirationally. The Senator continued, boasting about his qualifications for the job.

"Are you trying to figure out which one is Hugh?" a voice said behind me. I turned around, it was Ma Granger. "Ma Granger knows what's going on here. He told me all about it."

"He who?" I murmured during an eruption of applause.

"Oh you know, don't you dearie? They are all here tonight. That liar I told you about years ago, and the beautiful one, oh he's here all right. He's very close by."

"Mika?" I whispered.

She scratched her chin. "Don't know his name."

"The beautiful one has seen us. I'd better make tracks, he's fixing to do something awful to poor old Ma Granger." She backed away slowly and then turned and walked through the wall. Meanwhile the Senator's speech ended.

"Would you like me to walk you home?" Harold asked.

I was about to agree when I saw Father weaving his way towards me. "No, I have my father and brother." There was no way I could have a real conversation with Harold while Father was drunk and Ethan and Candy were listening.

"Very well. There will be another time I'm sure. Goodnight Emma." He shook my hand. "Oh, I am sorry I mean Miss Hollis."

I smiled. "It's perfectly all right. You can call me Emma."

"Thanks." he said blushing. "Lost my head for a second."

Chapter 62

I woke from a restless night of sleep. My dreams were filled with snippets of conversations from the night before. The names and faces of the Garrett boys swirled in front of me. There was no way I could know which one was Hugh unless I spent time with all of them. I wondered what it was like for him, staring at me with a pair of stranger's eyes. I was older now, four years had passed and I didn't feel like the same girl anymore.

I got out of bed and looked out the window. Merrick Cooper was on his porch smoking a cigarette as he did every morning. I backed away from the window in case he looked up and spotted me in my nightgown. My stomach growled. I got dressed and ran downstairs. Mother was in the kitchen having a bowl of oatmeal.

"Good morning." she said not looking up. I mumbled an answer and helped myself to a bowl from the pot on the stove. "Did you have a nice time last night?"

"Yes. It was quite pleasant."

"Your father came home drunk."

"He had a bit more than usual." I stammered.

"A bit more? He was stinking drunk as Margaret Cooper would say. I was completely disgusted." She pushed her oatmeal- away.

"It's not like Father is it?"

"No it's not." She tapped her fingers on the table. "I suppose you think I am just a nagging wife."

"No I don't."

"You see my own father was a drunk and when he drank--" She paused. "When he drank he was not a very nice person."

"I didn't know."

"Of course you wouldn't, he died long before you were born."

"Have you noticed that Father has been acting quite strange lately?"

Mother sat up in her chair. "What do you mean by strange? I've noticed nothing of the sort."

"You haven't?"

"Of course not. I told you once that your father has some things about him that make him a very undesirable husband. I was close to turning down his proposal."

"Why can't you tell me more? Is he like Ethan and me?"

Her face clouded. "There is nothing about Ethan and you except that perhaps you think too much."

"You know there is Mother, you asked me about it once, remember? When Senator Brown told you the house was haunted."

"That was merely a rumor. I've never found anything wrong with this house except the drafty windows."

"You asked me if I saw anything here. You believe me."

"Maybe I did." Her mouth twitched nervously. "And you said there was nothing. Was that a lie?"

I hesitated. I was tempted to pour out the whole story to her. But I had to see this through on my own. "No, there's no one here." It wasn't a lie anymore.

She poked at the oatmeal with her spoon. "Good."

* * *

The Chief Inspector and his officers were to begin their duties the following Monday. The weekend crawled by with not so much as one sighting of them. I went by the end of Brown Lane more than once hoping to catch a glimpse of them outside. Candy and I even walked the precarious path along the bluff, sneaking within ten feet of the house.

"I dare you to look in the windows," she whispered as we crouched in the tall grass. My heart was pounding in my chest.

309

I was considering her dare when I heard a noise coming from inside the house. We started running back the way we came when we met Amy Jennings and her younger sister Jane walking arm in arm in their best dresses.

"Oh my Emma." Amy said. "You look like you've seen a ghost."

"I was merely taking a vigorous walk." I replied. "Dr. Hollis recommends them." Next to me Candy was breathing hard.

"There's nothing to see at the Browns." Candy said.

"We were just taking a walk." Amy said.

"That's right." Jane added.

"We all know you were trying to get a look at the new policemen." Candy said.

"So were you." Jane remarked.

"*I* am a married woman." Candy sniffed. "Emma and I were merely taking a walk. It's something you girls should take under consideration. You're both pasty white."

"That's the sign of a lady of refinement." Amy countered.

"Is it?" Candy asked. "I wouldn't know about those things would I?" I poked her in the ribs. There was no telling what Candy would say next, and I wanted to leave. "Excuse us." she said shooing Amy and Jane with her hands.

The girls grimaced and stepped aside. Candy and I passed by them and continued back along the bluff, the wind blew hard at our faces. The church was ahead, it was hours past the end of service. We stepped into the churchyard and caught our breaths.

"What a pair, they are." she said tucking her hair behind her ears. "I wouldn't worry about them Emma. They're not competition for you."

I wasn't listening to Candy anymore. I had just spotted Ethan coming towards us with Will Garrett. I tugged on Candy's sleeve. "Look."

Candy squinted. "Is that my husband?"

"Of course it is. Look who's with him." I lowered my voice as they approached. "Do you suppose Ethan has sensed something?"

"Let's find out."

The men quickened their step and met us in the churchyard. "Hello ladies." Ethan said. "Look who I ran into."

"Good afternoon Dr. Hollis. Miss Hollis." Will said making an old fashioned bow.

"Oh please call me Emma." I said, finding myself curtseying back.

"And you can call me Candy. No actually on second thought you'd better call me Dr. Candy. Sounds better. You can call him Dr. Ethan."

"Very well." Will agreed.

"Where are you fellows going?" Candy asked.

"I was just showing Will around town." Ethan said. "Why don't you join us?"

"We'd love to." Candy took Ethan's arm.

"Shall we?" Will said, offering me his arm. I took it and fell in beside him. He smiled and I noticed for the first time the blonde eyelashes framing his blue eyes. We walked behind Candy and Ethan, my hand pressing firmly into his arm. I could feel the muscular tension through the sleeve of his coat. It could be Hugh's arm. The thought of it made me nearly giggle with delight. I stifled myself and what came out of my mouth was more like a hacking cough.

"Are you all right?"

"Yes." I said laughing out loud at the absurdity of getting giddy over a man's arm. If he wasn't Hugh he probably thought I was some kind of lunatic. I tried to compose myself and think of something more serious to say. "Do you start work tomorrow?"

"Oh yes. Bright and early."

"Will you be in town or are you going to be at the sheriff's office?" I asked, quite recovered from my momentary fit of delight.

"Senator Brown wants all of us in town this week, he says it's so we can get to know the townspeople. Next week my brothers and I start taking turns working as sheriff's deputies. I am not looking forward to it."

"Why not?"

"To tell you the truth I haven't been on a horse in a very long time." he said quietly. I wasn't sure why he was whispering, Candy and Ethan were the only ones around and they were too busy chattering away in front of us to notice.

"Really?" I felt myself getting giddy again. Maybe there was a reason I had reacted the way I did.

"Yes. I worked as a policeman on the subway in Boston. No horses there."

"Oh." I said feeling deflated.

"Sorry. That's not very impressive is it?"

"No. I mean I am sure it's interesting work." I was more confused than ever. "I don't know what I mean."

Will smiled and patted my hand. "It's all right. I've always been somewhere in the middle. Ryan is the serious one, Harold is the funny one, and then there's good ole' Will doing the boring sensible job. It's the curse of being the middle child I guess, especially with two brothers."

I nodded in agreement and tried to put it all together in my head. Was he trying to tell me something or was this just a normal conversation? There was no way to know for sure.

We passed by Father's barber shop and the new bank. "Where's your office going to be? Are we building a police station?" I asked.

"Would you like to see? I was just taking Dr. Ethan there now."

"Yes I would."

I tightened my grip on his arm as we continued down Main Street. The street began to make its turn right as it followed the geography of the land. Within the turn lay both Thalberg's and Jennings' stores. We stopped just before Jennings' door.

The storefront next to Jennings' had been empty for quite some time, the windows were covered with brown paper. I had seen a few men coming in and out lately, but hadn't thought much of it.

"This is the new police station?" I asked. Will reached into his pocket for the key.

"For now. It's kind of a strange location. The Senator said he was passing by the windows and the thought came to him like a bolt of lightning." Will jammed the key in the lock and jiggled the handle a few times before the door swung open with a creak.

"Why aren't there any signs up?" Candy asked.

"Oh they're coming. The Senator didn't want anyone to know until this week." Will held the door open while Candy, Ethan and I went inside. Because the windows were still covered it was hard to see much of anything except a few desks and chairs scattered about.

"It's not much right now." Will said as he lit a lamp on the desk near the window. "This will be my father's desk. He calls it his window on the world."

The lamp flickered and cast an orange-yellow glow around the room. Candy peered anxiously into the corners while she held Ethan's hand. Will was right, there wasn't much to see, even with the additional light.

"Is this the lockup?" Ethan asked. He and Candy were at the far end of the room.

"Yes that's it." Will confirmed. There was a large jail cell built into one corner. "This is where the bad guys go."

"How thrilling." Candy said. "I hope I see someone I know in there."

"Candy." Ethan muttered under his breath.

"I am sorry Ethan but I do. There are more than a few people in this town I would like to see locked up."

313

"We will have to see what we can do about that Dr. Candy." Will said. "We had better go otherwise we will start attracting attention and I will be giving guided tours all day."

He blew out the lamp and held the door open as we filed back onto the sidewalk. Next door Cole Jennings was leaning against his store window smoking a cigar. He stood up and stared at us as Will locked the door.

"What are you doing in there boy?" Cole asked, pointing with his cigar.

"I was just showing these fine folks the new police station." Will put the key in his pocket.

"It's going to be right here next to my store?"

"Yes."

"I don't know if my customers will like that, might make them nervous."

"It could prevent them from stealing."

"Hmm." Cole rubbed his plump chin. "I don't know, seems funny."

"Thalberg's store is right across the street. I doubt they'll mind." Will said.

Cole muttered something and gave me a nasty look. He took a last drag on his cigar and tossed it into the street. "If you say so boy."

Will cleared his throat and smoothed the front of his coat. "It's Officer Garrett if you don't mind."

"Certainly *Officer*" Cole sneered before opening the private door that led upstairs to his family's rooms. He slammed it loudly behind him.

"What a grouch." Candy said.

"Indeed." Will offered me his arm again. "Imagine talking to a police officer like that, as though I were a common criminal."

Chapter 63

Hugh's uniform itched. He tugged at the collar and tried to adjust his legs inside the long fabric tubes of his trousers. Nothing worked. He felt uncomfortable and out of place as he stood in his bedroom ready to begin his first day of work. That morning one of the others had laughed at him because he didn't know what a locomotive was. He told Mika about it later when they were alone.

"I can't believe I have to uphold the law now." Hugh moaned. "Me. The greatest sneak thief that ever lived."

"I don't know about greatest ever." Mika said.

"I was damn good and you know it." Hugh snapped. "Now I have to catch the criminals. What if I have to arrest someone?"

"So you'll arrest them. It's happened to you plenty of times, you should know what to do."

"No I don't. Remember this morning? The other one, what's his name? He kept talking about procedure. Procedure this, procedure that. I don't know anything about this job. Why didn't you let me learn more before you sent me here? You gave me half a day and a couple of pieces of paper and that was it. And don't tell me it was because you didn't have time, you let four years pass by. And you always say time doesn't matter to you."

"It doesn't." Mika shrugged. He strolled about with his hands in his pockets.

"Then why didn't you give me a chance to figure things out before I came here?"

"Because it's more fun this way."

"Fun for whom?"

"For me of course."

Hugh felt the anger rising in him. "You really are, oh I don't know what to call you. Emma always said you were lonely."

"A Watcher is alone. You'd better get going. I'll catch up with you at the station."

Hugh still found walking over uneven surfaces difficult despite his new muscular body. Decades indoors pacing the flat floors and precisely built staircases of Emma's house had not prepared him for the soft sand and pebbles of the road. Adding to his difficulties was the biting sea breeze that seemed to blow constantly at his face. He managed an uncoordinated walk with the others to the new police station where Senator Brown was waiting for them.

"Good morning gentlemen." The Senator said as he shook their hands. "It's been a long time coming."

Hugh agreed with the rest that it had indeed been a long time although he didn't mean it. He shifted uncomfortably in his uniform and tried to adopt the look of an authoritative policemen and not a lifelong criminal.

Next door Cole Jennings was looking out his shop window, his sweaty forehead leaving a smudge on the glass. Many townspeople were there, nosy types who wanted to see what was going on. Everyone watched as Senator Brown unlocked the police station door, it creaked open.

"We'll have to get those hinges oiled." the Senator said. The increasing crowd laughed and Senator Brown looked pleased that he had said something clever.

Hugh looked across the street and saw Emma peering out of Thalberg's window. Their eyes met and he couldn't help but smile at her. She smiled back, her gaze drifted to one of the others who was standing next to him.

It's me. I'm right here! He thought frantically.

"Do you think she's figured it out yet?" Mika whispered in his ear. He had suddenly appeared in the crowd looking out of place in his modern clothes and tall black wings. "I'm feeling crowded. They're too close to me."

"Step aside people, step aside people." Hugh said trying to sound bossy.

The townsfolk were not used to a policeman telling them what to do. They looked at one another and didn't move.

"Everyone back up." Hugh shouted. He must have done something right for the crowd took several steps backwards giving Mika plenty of room.

"Thank you Hugh." Mika fluttered the tips of his wings.

Hugh was quite pleased with himself. He had enjoyed that more than he imagined he would, perhaps this wouldn't be so bad after all. He turned to enter the new police station when he found the others staring angrily at him.

"What did you do that for?" one of them said.

"We want to gain their trust, not order them about." said another.

"Stand up for yourself Hugh." he heard Mika say. "They're not Patrick or your father."

Hugh swallowed and looked back across the street. Emma was still at the window. "I am not apologizing for what I do. We are here to police this town and that's exactly what I was doing." He straightened his itchy uniform and walked into the police station to join the Senator, leaving the others standing speechless on the sidewalk.

Chapter 64

My counter at Thalberg's was in the wrong place. I was stuck in the back trying to find an excuse to come up to the window and look outside. Mr. Thalberg was kind enough to find a myriad of reasons to bring me to the front of the store to talk to him. I could then peer out the window whenever there was a break in the conversation.

Unfortunately there wasn't much to see after the Senator had opened the new police station. The following day a sign was put up and the windows painted with the name, *Fox Cove Police* on one, and *Jason Garrett, Chief Inspector* on the other.

"I feel much safer with him there." Mr. Thalberg said as we gazed out the window at the Chief Inspector sitting at his desk.

"Where are the others?"

"Girls." he chuckled.

"What do you mean?" I asked, looking at Chief Garrett. His head was bent over his desk, all I could see was the short gray thatch of his hair.

"You haven't been interested in any man since Jeremy White and now all of a sudden these three boys come to town and you can't stop looking for them."

I blushed and returned to my place. It was true I had been more than a little preoccupied as of late. I had even fallen behind in my correspondence classes to the college that Ethan had suggested a few years ago. It seemed there was nothing else I could put my mind to at the moment.

What was more frustrating was that now that the Garretts were installed as the town policemen they were busy doing their jobs. After the first week the boys had begun taking turns working with the sheriff which meant that they were out of town on most days.

In my mind I had pictured that when Hugh returned it would be a whirl of social events and endless conversations that would make detecting him easy. Instead they were simply too busy working for me to have much of a chance to speak to any of them.

Almost a month after they arrived I was standing at my counter thinking about how I was going to find Hugh when the bell on the front door jangled and Ryan Garrett walked inside.

"Hello." Mr. Thalberg said looking over his glasses.

"Good morning." Ryan stammered. He pulled at his coat collar as he looked about.

"Can I help you find something?" Mr. Thalberg asked.

"Um, yes. Do you have any playing cards?"

Mr. Thalberg glanced at me. "Yes, yes we do. How many?"

"You'd better make it four."

Mr. Thalberg took four packs off the shelf next to him. "Do you like cards?"

"Yes." Ryan said. He looked in my direction but his expression didn't change.

"What games do you like?" I asked as I ventured out from behind my counter.

"We play a little bit of everything."

"Have you ever heard of the game Tribute?"

"Yes I know it. My family plays it sometimes."

I hesitated, not sure how to proceed. His blank expression made me uncomfortable. "Are you good at Tribute?"

He shrugged and pulled at his collar again. "I am a fair player, but hardly the best one in the family."

"Oh. Is there anything else you're looking for?"

"Do you have any books? The selection at Jennings' is terrible."

"Show him Emma." Mr. Thalberg said excitedly.

"We always have books here." I led him to the back of the store where Mr. Thalberg had an entire wall dedicated to reading. "That's how I became a customer here, I was looking for a book for a friend and I couldn't find anything at Jennings'. Actually he tossed me out on my ear, but that's another story." I giggled nervously and looked back at Ryan but he seemed to be barely listening.

"This is quite a selection." he said admiringly.

"Yes, we get new ones every month. Are you looking for something particular?"

"Anything by Wells? H.G. that is."

"Oh yes, I know we got something last week." I searched the shelves and found the book. "Here you are."

A smile crossed his face. "Thank you."

"Do you read a lot?"

"Actually I do, it's-" He stopped, the sound of the shop door opening violently caused him to turn away.

"Ryan Garrett!" called out a raspy voice. Chief Garrett was standing in the doorway. His face was red. "What are you doing?"

Ryan stepped slowly from behind the shelves. "You told me to pick up some cards."

"Yes, when you're off duty. And what is that in your hand?" Chief Garrett tore the book away from Ryan, he looked at the cover and shoved it in his coat pocket. "Ridiculous." he muttered. "How much?" Mr. Thalberg told him the amount owed. Chief Garrett tossed a few coins on the counter. "You are supposed to be on duty. Just because this is a small town doesn't mean you can go shopping while you're at work."

"Yes Father."

"Come along." Chief Garrett hurried outside with Ryan following close behind. They crossed the street and went into the police station.

"I like him." Mr. Thalberg said as he put the coins in the cash register.

Chapter 65

Hugh wouldn't admit it to anyone but himself but he actually enjoyed working. Every morning he looked forward to what his day was going to be like. After decades of wandering the same rooms, he was suddenly free to go wherever he wanted. He had a purpose now, and unlike the old thief who had spent half of his life running from the law and the other half getting arrested, he was a respected member of society.

He had become conventional and he didn't mind a bit. When he walked down the street people smiled and said hello, men tipped their hats to him and a few ladies even flirted. There were no more suspicious glances and people darting furtively to the other side of the street to avoid him.

The only thing missing in his new life was Emma. She was so close. He saw her frequently and had even spoken to her a few times but there was no way to make a connection. He worried constantly that she would pick the wrong one. The others were so easy and relaxed, they had nothing to worry about, they knew nothing. He had to be careful when he opened his mouth, Mika was always listening and if he said the wrong thing it would all be over.

He stopped in front of the window of Edward's barber shop on his rounds one morning and looked in. Edward was busy shaving a man's beard. Hugh tapped on the window. Edward flinched and dropped his shaving mug on the floor where it cracked in two, leaking the hot sudsy water onto the floor.

The customer and Edward both glared at him. Hugh shrugged and continued on his way. He had only wanted to say hello. A few doors away was the clinic that Ethan and Candy owned. Ethan was outside talking to a woman holding a baby. It was Eve. He smiled to himself, he felt like he was seeing an old family member.

"Good afternoon." Eve and Ethan both greeted him using his new name which he was getting used to. "How old is he?" He touched the red haired baby's pudgy little hand.

"Seven months." Eve replied. She hadn't changed much since that day he had locked her and Scott in her bedroom. Her face was slightly weathered and there was a touch of gray at her temples but there was still that fire in her eyes that Hugh had noticed so many years ago.

"How many do you have altogether?" he asked. "That is if you don't mind me asking?"

Eve laughed. "It's hardly a secret. Little Seth here is number six, and he's the last one."

Hugh tried not to let the surprise show on his face. "How very nice."

"Say, do you have a minute?" Ethan asked him. "I would like to talk to you about something."

"Certainly." Hugh imagined it had something to do with a lunatic patient or a dispute over a bill. He followed Ethan into the office, there was a small waiting area just inside the door. Candy was there looking at a stack of papers.

"Oh hello there." she said as they walked in. "Did you ask him?"

"Not yet." Ethan said. "Please have a seat."

Hugh sat down.

"Here it is." Ethan began. Hugh braced himself, he hoped he wasn't going to have to use deadly force. "We're having a picnic at our house and we would like your family to come."

"A picnic?"

"Yes." Candy said. "You haven't really had a chance to meet everyone in town yet. We had that silly party at Senator Brown's but that was really about his announcement to run for governor. It had nothing to do with you. I hope you realize that he used all of you. He's like that. I kicked him in the leg once."

"Candy." Ethan muttered.

"It's true Ethan and I would do it again if I wasn't a highly respected doctor now."

Ethan adjusted his glasses. "What my wife is trying to say is that we are having a picnic at our house this Saturday and we would like your whole family to come. It will be a chance for us to get to know each of you better and a chance for you to meet some of our young ladies."

"I've noticed there are a lot of pretty girls in this town."

"Anyone in particular catch your eye?" Candy leaned forward.

"Actually-" Hugh began. He stopped himself. "Actually they are all so pretty I'm not sure I could pick just one." He had to be careful. Mika was listening.

"So you'll come?" Ethan asked.

"Of course."

"And you'll tell your family?" Candy asked.

"Yes."

"Good then it's settled. It starts at noon. Candy and I live at the old Johnson place, you probably don't know where it is."

"I know where it is."

"And just how do you know that?" Candy pointed her finger at him.

"Senator Brown insisted we learn the layout of the town, you can't be a policeman if you don't know where anything is." he said cleverly.

Her face clouded. "Oh."

He stood up and was about to leave when he heard the door to the clinic open. A man rushed in carrying a young boy in his arms. The boy was barely conscious and moaning. "He fell out of a tree."

Candy dropped her stack of papers on a nearby chair. "Bring him in here." She led them through a door and into a back room.

"I had best be going." Hugh started for the door. Ethan followed him outside.

"You will be there on Saturday?"

"Absolutely."

Ethan folded his arms across his chest and stared at him. Occasionally his eyes flicked just above Hugh's head, as though there was something to look at.

"I should be going." Hugh said. Things were becoming awkward.

"I'll see you later then."

Hugh tipped his hat and continued his rounds.

Chapter 66

"A picnic?" I repeated to Candy as she jumped up and down excitedly in the front hall at home.

"Yes. Why not? It's summer now and what better way to get to know the Garrett boys? Don't worry Emma, just leave everything to me."

"That's what I am afraid of."

"I'm only trying to help." she pouted.

"Oh I know. I'm sorry I shouldn't have said that. Are you sure they'll come?"

"Yes. Ethan and I extended the invitation this afternoon. They'll come."

"Who else is going to be there?"

"Oh anyone and everyone, the whole town is invited. Hopefully Senator Brown will be otherwise engaged." she said with a wink.

"Don't bet on it. If there's a chance of free food he'll be there." I rubbed my temples. I could feel the start of a headache coming on.

"This is really getting to you, isn't it?"

"Yes it is. I haven't a clue which one he is. Every time I talk to one of them they say something that reminds me of Hugh, but it's just one thing here or there. Nothing ever adds up. I know that he can't give me any signs but this is ridiculous. Maybe none of them is Hugh, maybe he's never coming back." The stress of the last few months seemed to bubble up in my throat. I felt my eyes watering.

Candy put her arm around my shoulders. "Don't cry Emma. He's here I know it."

I sniffed and wiped the tears from my eyes. "How can you be so sure?"

"Because Ethan knows who it is."

"What? What are you saying? How do you know?" My heart was racing in my ears.

"You know that look Ethan gets when he sees something? You know something unnatural, ghosts and things?"

"Yes I know the look."

"He gets it sometimes when they're around. It's only for a few seconds, but I've noticed. I think he knows."

"Have you asked him about it?"

"No."

"But then you know which one Hugh is."

Candy shook her head. "No I don't. He looks at all of them that way."

"But you could find out." I said. "If you wanted to."

"I don't want to know."

"Why not?"

"Because if I know I will want to tell you and if I told you or even tried to do something that would persuade you towards one of those boys then that Mickey-"

"It's Mika."

"What? His name is Mika? That doesn't sound right but I guess you would know. Anyway if he gets wind that I gave it away then Hugh will be gone, and who knows what will happen to me. I'll probably meet old Grandpa Cooper at the pearly gates."

I nodded. She was right. My brief moment of hope was extinguished.

"And don't you try and watch Ethan, he only gets that look when you're not around. Most of the time he pretends he doesn't notice anything. He's quite good at it." she said.

"He's had a lot of practice, we both have."

"What's wrong Emma?" Mother was standing in the doorway to the kitchen. It was unclear how long she had been there.

"She's just tired." Candy said patting me on the shoulder. "Did Dads tell you about the picnic on Saturday?"

Mother winced. "Yes *Edward* told me. We shall be there."

"I've invited the Garrett boys too. They are all young and unmarried you know." Candy said.

"I am well aware of their marital status." Mother looked at me. "Emma, are you interested in one of them?"

"All of them." Candy said cheerfully.

"I am glad to hear you are once again interested in the male species, but I would advise you Emma to keep your interest to one member of the family." Mother said. "When I was first courting your father I received some friendly attention from his brother Egbert. But I wisely rebuffed it."

"Lucky!" Candy cried. "I never had the attention of any other man other than Ethan, of course I never wanted anyone else."

"Not all of us can be so fortunate Candy." Mother said. "I am glad to hear this Emma, you've been moping around this house for far too many years."

"I know I have. I've just been waiting for the right time and the right person."

"Let's hope that time has come." Mother said.

"I think it has."

* * *

I arrived early on Saturday. It was eleven o'clock when I found Ethan in the backyard surveying a pile of tennis racquets. I snuck up on him, tapping him gently on the shoulder. He flinched and spun around.

"You scared me half to death."

"Sorry. I wanted to talk to you before everyone arrived."

"It's all right. Let's sit down." We sat on a nearby white wicker couch. He leaned back and waited for me to begin.

I took a deep breath. "Candy says you know which one is Hugh."

Ethan's hands flew up in the air. "What on earth made her tell you that?" He cast an annoyed glance towards the house.

"She said that you look at them like you do when you are Seeing things."

He muttered something under his breath and shook his head. A few seconds passed, the wind rose up and rustled the trees at the edge of the lawn. Nearby two blue jays squawked at each other. "I can't tell you Emma. I don't dare. I am afraid if I do that creature-"

"You mean Mika."

"Whatever. I am afraid he'll take Hugh away. He's very strong you know."

"I know."

"I don't really know anything for sure, it's just that all of them have the same black and silver cloud around them, like the one the Senator had, but not as dense. I can still see their faces. But then one of them is different. He has, oh it's hard to describe. It's like the faint outline of white wings sticking out of his back, but I'm telling you it is very faint. I've never seen that on a living person before."

I sat forward on the sofa. "That's Hugh. I know that's him." I felt the excitement begin to rise in me. "Then he's here, he's really here."

"I can't tell you which one he is, and don't try and look at my face today because I can pretend I don't see a damn thing, you know I can. I'll have to, Mother will be here."

"I don't want you to tell me. Actually I do want you to tell me but I know you can't. I have to figure it out myself. I just don't know how Ethan. I've talked to all of those boys and they all do and say things that remind me of Hugh. How will I know?"

"I've been thinking about that. I think you should forget trying to figure out which one is the most like Hugh and just pick the one you like the best."

"I don't know if I can do that."

Ethan was quiet for a moment. "Emma, when I went to college I met a lot of young ladies. There were some really beautiful girls there. Some came from money, some had prestige, and some were brilliant. And then Candy came to the campus and I didn't give her a second thought. She was my pal from back home, that was it. But as the months went by my mind kept returning to her. I kept seeing these other girls and when I was with them I would be thinking of what Candy would say or do, how she would understand my jokes or what I really meant. One day I just realized that I would rather spend my time with her. And that's what I think you should do. Just get to know them, and one day it will just fall into place."

"And you think that one will be Hugh?"

"Why wouldn't it be? He's still Hugh underneath it all. It doesn't matter what he says or how much in common he might have with the old version. He's still Hugh, he's still the man you love. You'll just know Emma. Trust yourself."

"I love you Ethan. You are the best brother."

"I'm your only brother." he said giving me a hug.

"No competition, huh?" I laughed as I wiped the corners of my eyes.

"Absolutely, your favorite brother forever." His face dropped. "Oh God."

"What?" I looked over my shoulder. Senator Brown, Bridget Brown and their four children were walking across the lawn. "Why is *he* here?"

"Further still, why is he here so early?" Ethan said under his breath.

"Good afternoon!" said the Senator in a jolly tone. He smoothed his beard and shook Ethan's hand.

"I'm glad you could come." Ethan said.

"I know we are a tad early but I think its best. I'd like a chance to greet your guests as they come in, you know get the word out about my campaign for governor." He leaned in close to Ethan. "That is if you don't mind doing a favor for your old benefactor."

Ethan squirmed. "I suppose that will be all right. This picnic is really a chance for everyone to get to know the Garrett family."

"Oh they will, they will." The Senator glanced at me. "I suppose that's why you're here young lady."

"Me? Ethan is my brother, this is a family event." I tried to sound convincing.

"Really Miss Hollis, every young woman in town has her cap set for one of those boys."

"Ethan! I need to see you now!" A voice cut loudly through the backyard. Candy was standing at the back of the house waving.

"I'd better go see what that's about." Ethan said.

"Do you want me to come?" I asked, desperate for a chance to escape the Browns.

The Senator took a seat next to me. "I'd like to talk to you Emma."

"You would?"

"Ethan!" Candy called again.

"I've got to go." Ethan ran across the lawn.

Bridget stood nearby while the four Brown children began playing with the tennis racquets. The youngest child was hitting the three older ones in the back of the knees and knocking them over.

"I should probably see if Candy needs any help." I said.

"Relax Emma." the Senator said. "From the way you are acting I would almost think you didn't want to see me."

"Fancy that."

"Which one of the Garretts are you interested in?" Bridget asked, narrowing her eyes.

"Who says that I am interested in any of them?"

"You ought to know that both of Cole Jennings' girls have their minds made up. That only leaves one for you. And I can name half a dozen other girls who will take him." Bridget said.

"Really?"

"Most people consider the Jennings girls to be the prettiest in the whole town, maybe the whole county. Don't you think so darling?" Bridget looked at her husband.

The Senator nodded and closed his eyes for a few seconds. "Those girls have the biggest-" He opened his eyes. "They are lovely young women and I am afraid Miss Hollis that you don't stand a chance. You should have accepted Jeremy when you had the offer. You and your family fell out of favor long ago when your father betrayed me."

"Oh really? You wanted to marry my sister when she was only seventeen and you were an old man. She hated you, you made her sick, she would have never married you." I turned to Bridget. "Did you know that? He tried to buy my sister from my father."

Bridget shrugged and looked like she might start laughing. "I know all about your family and what they did to Hershival. I'm glad. Your sister is stuck with that carpenter and all those children in that tiny little house and I've got everything I could ever want."

"I don't want you to set your sights on those boys." said the Senator. He leaned in close, his scraggly gray beard only inches away from me. "The Jennings girls will get what they want, and I will make sure that you don't get anything. You don't know the influence I have in this town."

"And you don't know who influences you." I said.

The Senator's face clouded. "What's that supposed to mean? Are you referring to my wife?"

"No. I am just saying that you never know who is watching."

"Ignore her Hershival." Bridget said. "She's trying to agitate you."

The Senator put his fat hand on top of mine. "I promise you that I will make sure you never succeed with those boys."

"We'll see about that."

The Senator looked up. Coming towards us was the Garrett family.

Chapter 67

Hugh clenched his fists as he walked across the lawn. The Senator was leaning suspiciously towards Emma, his stubby hand covering hers. Hugh felt a surge of anger rise inside him. The Senator looked up and caught his eye, he removed the offensive hand. Emma looked over her shoulder and for a moment their eyes met. He loved those moments, however brief they were.

"Good afternoon" the Senator called out. He stood up and started walking towards them. Hugh was forced to shake his hand. "I hope to see you at the polls this November boys. Don't forget who brought you here."

"That would be me you fool." Mika said as he descended from the sky.

"You can count on it sir." said one of the others. Hugh tried to conceal his annoyance. He would say that.

The Senator said something else unimportant and Hugh stopped listening. Halfway across the lawn Emma was standing next to the wicker sofa that she and the Senator had been sharing. She was watching him and the others. It seemed to him she spent far more time looking at them and not him.

Next to her was Bridget Brown. Emma didn't notice but every so often Bridget would look at her with a superior glance. He couldn't imagine what Bridget had to feel so smug about. She wasn't half as pretty as Emma and he doubted she was even a third as smart. All she had was her leering husband and a quartet of unruly children.

"My wife is a beauty isn't she?" the Senator asked him.

"Er, yes." Hugh said. "But Miss Hollis is just as fine."

The Senator looked shocked. "Her? I suppose she has a serviceable face, if you go in for that sort of girl. I wouldn't bother with her though. Her family betrayed me years ago. Horrible people."

"Is that so? That's a shame." Hugh said sympathetically. "But isn't this her brother's home? Aren't you terribly uncomfortable here?"

The Senator stroked his beard and winked. "It's just politics son. Just politics."

"My, you are clever." The Senator looked at him strangely, it seemed the sarcasm was registering when Ethan appeared.

"There's plenty of food inside boys. Who's hungry?"

"I am." Mika said.

"I'm starving." said one of the others. Hugh was hungry too.

They began following Ethan. Hugh looked at Emma, she was still in the same spot.

"Don't worry they'll be plenty of time for visiting." Ethan put a hand on his shoulder.

"It seems our little Common Seer has figured out which one you are Hugh." Mika said.

Hugh swallowed nervously. This was the end. Ethan had blown his cover. He looked back at Mika in a panic, there was no need to hide his emotions now, he was about to be plucked from the earth and sent to who knows where.

Mika met his desperate stare, his icy blue eyes glittered with delight. "Getting scared are you?"

Hugh nodded. Ethan smiled as he glanced at where Mika was walking behind them. He leaned in close and whispered in his ear. "Your secret is safe with me Hugh."

Chapter 68

Candy and her mother had laid out a full table of food. By noontime most of the town had arrived and brought their appetites with them. Lunch was spread out on the dining room table. I could barely get a look at what was being served as the table was swarming with a motley assortment of Fox Cove's hungriest citizens.

On the sideboard was a pile of plates and silverware. I was trying desperately to reach a plate while Merrick Cooper stood in front of me sniffing a chicken leg.

"Merrick can you hand me a plate?"

He looked up from the chicken leg and squinted. "Can't you wait a minute?"

"Yes, I suppose I can." I said listening to my stomach growl. On the other side of the table Will and Ryan were filling their plates, they glanced up at me every so often, maybe if I hurried I could eat with them.

Merrick finally put the chicken on his plate and looked at me. "Are you going to do something strange today?"

"What?"

"Remember when you were dancing by yourself at Scott and Eve's wedding? And I've seen you talking to yourself, a lot of people have." He picked up another piece of chicken and stared at it.

"I don't know what you're talking about."

"Yes you do."

"No, I don't Merrick. And if you aren't going to stop smelling that chicken you can at least hand me a plate so I can have my lunch."

"I'm not done yet."

I was about to respond when an arm reached around me and grabbed a plate from the sideboard. "Here you are Miss Hollis." I looked back and saw Chief Garrett smiling down at me.

"Thank you."

"Not at all." He looked at Merrick. "Young man you've spent far too much time holding up the line, move along." The Chief stepped in front of me and gave him a gentle push on the shoulder. Merrick finally moved. The Chief stayed behind him, nudging him every time he lingered.

"Leave it to my Papa to get things moving. He always was impatient." Harold was next to me grinning.

"Thank goodness. Merrick would have been here all day smelling the chicken." I said gratefully.

"Don't you smell your chicken before you eat it?"

"Not really."

"How uncivilized of you. I am not sure we can be friends." he said picking up a piece of chicken and inhaling so loudly that everyone else around, including Merrick, stopped to look. "A fine piece of chicken if I do say so myself."

"Harold!" his father hissed. "Stop acting like an imbecile."

Harold sighed and put the chicken on his plate. We continued around the dining room table. I stepped onto the back porch and looked for a place to sit down. Most of the extra chairs and wicker pieces scattered on the lawn were taken.

"Don't men give up their seats for ladies anymore?" Harold asked.

"Not when it comes to a picnic lunch. I think the lawn will have to do."

"What about over there?" Harold pointed to a spot on the far end of the lawn near the brook that ran behind the property.

I was about to agree when I noticed Father was there staring and possibly muttering to himself. I wasn't sure I was ready to explain him. "What about under the birches? It will be cool under there."

Harold agreed and we made our way to a clump of trees near the edge of the lawn. A long meadow began and continued towards my house, which was only a short walk away.

"It's so quiet here." Harold said. "And that's your house over there?"

"Yes. When we first moved here I thought it was the ends of the earth. Now I can't imagine living anywhere else."

"You're staying then?"

"Of course."

"What if some dashing young man sweeps you off your feet and takes you away?"

"It would have to be the right man."

"I see."

"And what about you? You can't tell me you haven't noticed how many girls walk by the police station?"

Harold rolled his eyes. "Oh that. They are mostly there for Ryan and Will, not me."

"Really? Are you sure? Senator Brown and his wife warned me this morning to stay away from the three of you. Apparently the Jennings girls consider you and your brothers their property."

"So that's what that was about. I was wondering. I couldn't imagine what you had to say to *him*. He had no right to say that to you. And I do believe the Jennings girls can manage for themselves." He pointed discreetly to a wicker sofa where Jane and Amy were seated, each one with a glass of lemonade perched daintily on their knee. Sitting in front of them on the ground was Ryan and Will. Will said something and both girls laughed with a high pitched whinny.

"I think they've made their choice." he said.

"Are you interested in one of them?"

"Certainly not!" Harold lifted his glass of lemonade in the air. "I propose a toast."

I took up my glass and raised it. "What are we toasting to?"

"To us. Who needs them when we have all the best company right here." he said smiling. His dark eyes caught the sunlight glimmering through the trees.

Chapter 69

Hugh loved to eat. He found himself frequently counting the hours until the next meal. Candy and Margaret's delicious spread was settling nicely in his stomach. He had broken with his company after the meal and was sitting on the edge of the brook listening to the water, reveling in the thrill of being alive.

Mika was nearby floating above the water, his wings flapping gently in the breeze. "Sometimes I forget how handsome I was." he said looking at his reflection.

Hugh made a face. It was fortunate he could not comment aloud. He took a deep breath, the air was sweet and clean. He let his fingers slide between the blades of grass, the sharp ends gently poking at his fingers.

"It's good to be alive isn't it?" Ethan was standing over him. Hugh looked cautiously at Mika who was still admiring his reflection.

Ethan followed his gaze. "There's something there, I can see it. It looks like a big black cloud."

"What an unimaginative description." Mika said.

"Yes he's there." Hugh said.

Ethan sat on the ground. "How are you?"

"I really don't think you should talk to me like this. I'm not supposed to do anything that might give Emma a clue it's me, or else-"

"Or else he will take you away from here."

"You may speak briefly." Mika said empirically. "But I don't want this to become a habit, you two discussing the good old days and Hugh MacPherson. He's dead, remember?"

"He says we can talk, just this once."

"And while you're at it you can tell the Common Seer that if I catch him doing anything to disrupt my plans that I will make him very sorry indeed.

And if anyone can do it, it's me."   Mika floated down from his position over the water and stood at the edge of the brook, his ankles and wing tips submerged underwater.

"What is he saying?" Ethan asked.

"He wants you to keep quiet about me."

"I will."

"I would never be that soft. That was almost polite." Mika complained.

"Tell him yourself then." Hugh said. "I dare you to show yourself."

Mika glared and crouched at the water's edge. "Carry on then, but quickly please. I'm starting to get bored."

"Should I go?" Ethan asked.

"No, he's just grouchy."

"I wanted to know how you are. Candy is making ice cream up at the house and I thought this would be a good time for us to talk."

"Ice cream?" Hugh looked at the house.   He was surprised to find that nearly all the guests were gone. A press of bodies was on the porch looking in the back windows, other than a few elderly women and a couple of dogs no one was about. "What kind of ice cream?"

"Oh will you stop thinking with your stomach. I can create barrels full of ice cream for you. I'm only going to give you one chance to talk like this to the Common Seer." Mika said. "I'll make sure it will take Candy plenty of time for that ice cream to set. "

"I spoke with Emma this morning." Ethan said.

"Does she know it's me?"

"Bad question." Mika said.

"Don't answer that. How is she?"

"She's frustrated. She doesn't know what to do. She's afraid of making the wrong choice."

"I know the feeling. I don't know how to tell her it's me without telling her."

"I understand. I'm not sure what I would do if I was in the same situation." Ethan glanced at Mika. "I just told her that she needs to choose the one that makes her happy."

"Are you kidding? Have you seen the others? They're so perfect. Everything they say and do comes naturally to them. I don't know what I'm doing half the time. Of course she'll choose one of them."

"No she won't. Just be yourself Hugh. Emma fell in love with you, not them."

"How can I be myself when I have to be someone else? I can barely make it through the day sometimes. There are all these modern contraptions to deal with, and there's the language, people don't speak the same way they used to, and there's the money. I don't know the value of anything, and forget history. Did you know we had a civil war in this country?"

Ethan smiled. "You didn't know about that? But you like to read, didn't you read any newspapers during that time."

"When you're stuck indoors everyday for decades the news really doesn't mean much. You know the outside world exists, but it doesn't really affect you."

"I suppose not." Ethan said.

"And on top of everything else I have to be a policeman."

Ethan laughed. "That's so perfect. I love it."

"Thank you." Mika said. "I am a genius."

"I am just glad my brother Patrick isn't here to see this. He always said the law would catch up to me someday, and now I am the law." Hugh said remembering the last time he was in shackles.

Ethan slapped Hugh on the shoulder. "You're going to do just fine Hugh. Just be yourself and Emma will find you."

"But what about-"

Ethan shook his head. "She'll know. Now, guess what we're doing after ice cream?"

"What?"

"Playing baseball. Aren't you excited?"

Hugh looked from Ethan to Mika. "Baseball? What on earth is that?"

Chapter 70

"I've never had such a hard time getting ice cream to set up." Candy said licking her spoon. "It was worth it though, I don't think I've ever made such a good batch."

I let the last drops of strawberry ice cream slide down my throat. We were sitting on the back porch. It was mid-afternoon and the air had turned humid. The rest of the picnic guests were scattered about the porch and lawn, quietly enjoying their sweet treat. The Thalbergs were on a blanket with their children on the far side of the lawn. Eve and Scott had arrived late, their many children were running about playing tag with their sticky fingers. Mother had found her way out of the kitchen and was talking quietly on the porch swing with Margaret Cooper. Meanwhile the Garretts were situated in the middle of the lawn. The boys were stretched out on the grass looking up at the sky while their father spoke to Senator Brown.

The last hour had been a strange one. I had felt oddly compelled to stay in the house while Candy cranked the ice cream maker. The whole time my legs were rigid, as though they were glued to the floor. It felt a little like the day I had first seen Mika, he had made me sit in a chair while he and Hugh walked about. I had known where and who I was, but I couldn't move, as though I was being pinned in place by an invisible hand.

Nearly everyone except for a couple of very elderly ladies had stood motionless in Candy's house and on the porch waiting for the ice cream to set. When it was done we all marched out like obedient soldiers. As I ate the feeling began to pass.

"Guess what we're doing after this?" Candy asked.

"I don't know."

"Playing baseball."

"Baseball? I thought you were setting up for tennis."

Candy shrugged. "I changed my mind. I thought baseball would give you a chance to get a better look at the boys. You know, see their athletic side, see em' sweat a bit."

"Candy you can't plan your picnic around me. And besides maybe they won't play."

"Oh they'll play. I'll make them." She tossed her spoon into the empty bowl. "Ethan! Where are you?"

"I really prefer just to talk with them."

Candy stood up and looked across the lawn for Ethan. "You were talking plenty to Harold at lunch."

"Yes and now I want to talk to Will and Ryan. I doubt Hugh has ever played baseball in his life."

"That's right!" Candy said excitedly. "The boy that plays the worst must be Hugh. Where on earth is he? Ethan Hollis!"

The back door opened and Ethan walked onto the porch smiling. "What? I'm right here."

"How did you get in there?"

"I've been there the entire time. Are you ready to play?"

"Yes." Candy said. "But I want to pick the teams."

"Oh you do? I suppose you have some master plan in mind?"

"As a matter of fact, yes. And save a seat for Emma and I right in front." Candy ran down the porch steps.

Ethan grinned as he watched Candy run across the lawn stopping to talk with every able bodied man. "She's got a plan all right. I'd better get out there. See ya Emma." He patted me on the head before bounding down the steps to join his wife.

* * *

"This is such a good idea." Candy said as we sat comfortably in two wicker chairs on the sidelines of the game. "I don't know why you didn't think of this yourself Emma. Just put them all in a modern situation and watch what happens."

"I don't know how I didn't come up with it." I said taking a sip of my lemonade. So far nothing in the baseball game had happened that was even remotely interesting except that Senator Brown had passed gas loudly when he was up to bat and Candy had giggled loudly at him.

"Will is in line to bat." Candy whispered as her father Michael went up to home plate. "Oh here's Pa."

"Let's see what you've got." Michael called out to Ethan who was pitching. Ethan pitched the ball swiftly at his father-in-law. Michael missed and spun around in a circle.

"Come on Pa!" Candy called out. "His eyesight is shot now that he doesn't drink."

"Does your mother still wish he'd go back to drinking?"

"Of course. He's retired now, not that he ever really had a job and he's been sober for years. Poor Ma." she sighed. As she spoke there was a loud crack from the bat. Michael hit a ball far into the outfield. Harold, who was positioned in center field, ran and started searching for the ball in the tall grass while Michael ran the bases.

"That Harold can't catch a ball. That's a good sign." Candy said. "Oh wait here's Will."

Will stepped up to home plate and flashed a smile to Candy, me, the Jennings girls and anyone else who was looking.

"I think he's the handsomest." she said.

"Really?"

"Don't you think so? The blonde hair and those blue eyes, not to mention his figure."

"Be quiet or someone will hear you." I said looking about. Mother was behind us nodding off in the warm summer sun. Bridget along with Jane and Amy Jennings were sitting nearby on a long wicker sofa. They were whispering to each other and looking at Will.

"Oh I can say things like that, I'm a doctor. I'm supposed to notice what people look like."

I had no intention of agreeing with her but I did enjoy watching Will take a few practice swings before Ethan made the first pitch. Will swung much too late and the ball went flying past the catcher, Chief Garrett. Ethan threw an easy pitch. Will missed it and then the next one. His father pronounced him out.

"Oh this is a good sign." Candy said.

"Better luck next time." Amy Jennings called out as Will tossed aside the bat.

"I'm not letting her get her claws in him." Candy muttered. "Will, why don't you come over here and take a break with us."

Will glanced at Amy who was glaring at Candy. "Thanks, don't mind if I do." He flopped onto the grass in front of us. "That was embarrassing."

"Have you played much baseball before?" I asked.

"That bad, huh?"

"I didn't mean-"

"I know. Actually I haven't played in a long time, and baseball was never really my thing. But if you think that was bad, wait until you see Ryan."

Candy poked me gleefully in the ribs while Ryan took his place at home plate. Ethan sent a slow pitch to him. The ball hit Ryan on the hand.

"Ouch." He muttered as he looked at his father crouched behind him. He shook his hand a couple of times and held up the bat again. Ethan continued his slow pitching while Ryan struggled with each ball, one time he actually made contact and hit a foul.

"You're out!" called Chief Garrett as he patted his son on the shoulder. Ryan joined Will on the grass in front of us.

"Good afternoon." he said. "I'm sorry you had to witness that." He brushed the damp hair off his forehead.

"You can do it Dads!" Candy cried. Father was at home plate rocking back and forth on his heels and grinning wildly.

"Give it all you've got son." he called to Ethan. Ethan threw a fast pitch and to my surprise Father easily hit it into centerfield and started running.

The ball landed straight onto Harold's head and then bounced on the ground which sent him hunting in the grass again.

Will and Ryan laughed. "Poor Harry." said Will.

"I hope we haven't disappointed you ladies too much. I'm afraid none of us spent much time playing baseball when we were growing up." Will said. "I don't even think Ryan knows the rules."

Ryan jabbed Will with his elbow. "I'm afraid the only Garrett that's any good at this is our Papa."

We watched the game for a few more minutes. Father was on second base mugging and making boastful comments about himself and his team. I was grateful to see that Mother was sleeping behind us, oblivious to her husband's behavior. Ryan picked at the grass.

"We got in a new shipment of books at Thalberg's." I told him.

He smiled. "Listen, I never apologized for that time that Papa came into the store shouting, it was completely unnecessary."

"Does he not approve of reading?"

"No it's not that." Ryan said, searching for the words. "He's just all about work. I think it's because-"

"Yes!" Will grabbed Ryan's arm. "Come on."

"Will, you just interrupted me."

"I'm sorry but it's time to change sides. Come on." Will jumped to his feet. "Sorry to leave you like this ladies, but duty calls." Ryan sighed as he slowly got to his feet and the two of them ran into the outfield.

"This wasn't such a great plan after all." Candy said. "They are all so bad. I can't even decide who is worse."

"It's all right Candy. It wasn't a bad idea, you didn't know none of them could play the game."

"I don't know how you're going to do this Emma."

346

"Ethan says I should just pick whichever one I feel the most comfortable around. He says that one of them will be a little different, and that I will just know."

"Easy for him to say, he knows which one it is! Does one of them seem different, is there one you're more comfortable around?"

"I don't know. Maybe there could be."

Candy's face broke into a smile. "Which one?"

Harold was up to bat next. It took only three pitches from Michael to strike him out.

"Emma, tell me who you think it is."

"Not yet. I just need more time. I promise as soon as I am sure or nearly sure I will tell you."

Candy crossed her arms. "No one tells me anything. Oh wait here's the Chief, let's see how great he is."

Chief Garret hit the ball easily on the first try sending it far beyond Will and Ryan who were talking in the outfield. He ran like a trained athlete around the bases, his face flushed and sweaty, but otherwise relaxed. Even from a distance I could see his sharp gray eyes.

"He runs well for a man his age." Candy said.

"Why? How old is he?" Will and Ryan kept looking in my direction and talking. I felt my face reddening.

"Forty three."

"How do you know that?"

"Emma, I am an important person in town. It's my job to know these things."

"Oh I see."

The game went on for several more innings until it was deemed too hot for everyone. The players scattered into groups. Father walked past us and sat next to Mother who was suddenly awoken.

"Were you sleeping during my game dear?" he asked.

"I might have dozed off for just a moment." Mother said rubbing her eyes.

"I've got more lemonade." Candy ran into the house. Will and Harold went over to talk with Bridget and the Jennings girls. Ryan quickly took her place in the chair next to me.

"Hello." he said with a shy smile.

"Hello."

"I'm glad that's over with." He smiled again and I noticed for the first time he had a dimple in his left cheek.

"Who won?"

"Papa's team of course. Was there ever a doubt?" He paused. "So what books did you get in? Anything good?"

"Have you read *The Time Machine*?"

"No. Do you recommend it?"

"Yes and then we have another-"

"Ryan." Chief Garrett was suddenly standing in front of us. "I thought you were going to walk through town this afternoon and keep an eye on things."

"I am. I was just taking a break after the game."

"The criminals aren't taking a break are they? I want you to get out there now."

Ryan looked at me and stood up. "I'll come by the store later this week and pick up that book. On my day off."

"All right. Good afternoon."

"Good afternoon." he said before giving his father a sidelong glance. The Chief watched him leave, his eyes narrowed in the bright afternoon sunlight. As soon as he saw Ryan walking on the road towards town he sat in the chair next to me.

"I'm sorry to take him away from you, but I need him to check on things in town."

"Are his brothers going too?"

Chief Garrett looked at his two younger sons. "They're not going anywhere at the moment. Ryan is the best one for the job. He was an investigator back in Boston."

"Is something wrong?"

Chief Garrett hesitated. "There was a break in last night at Jeremy White's house."

"What?" I cried, nearly coming out of my chair. He motioned for me to sit down.

"It's not the first one." he said quietly.

"Not the first?"

"No. It's the third actually. We've got a thief on the loose."

I couldn't help but smile.

"It's nothing to laugh at Miss Hollis."

"I know. I'm not laughing, not at all. It's just-"

"Just what?"

"It's just odd that's all."

Chief Garrett looked at me strangely and ran his hand over his short silvery hair. "Odd indeed." he murmured. "Do you open the store by yourself in the morning?"

"Yes sometimes. But the Thalbergs live upstairs."

"Maybe so, but I wouldn't go in there alone if I were you."

"I won't. Do you think he's dangerous?"

Chief Garrett shrugged. "I hope not, but one can never tell. I'll be coming by the store tomorrow to talk with the Thalbergs."

"Thank you." I regretted I had been smiling earlier when it was so obviously a serious matter. "It's nice to have all of you right across the street. Mr. Thalberg says he feels safer just seeing you in the window."

"Thank you."

"Emma I need your help with this lemonade." Candy called from the back porch.

"I had better go." I said. "Thank you for warning me."

The Chief nodded. "Don't tell anyone else about this right now."

"Why not? I thought you were coming to the store tomorrow to tell the Thalbergs."

"I am. I'm going to all the merchants in town. But I don't want to scare people."

"I won't say anything." I agreed. "You're the expert after all."

"Thank you. You'd better go help Dr. Hollis, she's looking a bit steamed."

Candy was standing on the back porch with a half empty tray of lemonade. Her hair was sticking out at all angles, her face reddened by the heat.

"Wilted is more like it." I said. "Goodbye."

Chapter 71

"I don't mind telling you I feel like my privacy has been completely violated." Jeremy looked at the empty wall above his fireplace where an expensive painting had hung until three days ago when his home had been invaded by the thief that was on the loose.

"Did you lock your doors that night?" Hugh asked as he scribbled notes on a small tablet of paper he kept in his pocket.

"The front door yes, but the back door, I'm not sure. I don't generally check it." Jeremy said anxiously. "You know one of your colleagues already asked me these questions."

Hugh tapped the pencil lead on the paper and tried to keep his temper in check. "I am aware that you have already answered these questions but now *I* am asking you. You do want this fellow caught don't you?"

"Of course I do. But I don't understand what's taking so long. How hard can it be to find one man when there are three of you, well actually four of you on the case?"

Hugh sighed and put his notes away. "Mr. White, first of all you don't know it's just one man. He may be part of a group. These scoundrels often work together. Secondly, not all of us are working on this. I am sure you know the sheriff requires our help in other matters. And finally, you underestimate how clever these types of criminals are."

"Oh really? If they are so clever what are they doing stealing for a living? Why don't they get a job like the rest of us?"

"Maybe circumstances forced them into that life."

"Horsefeathers. I was dirt poor but I didn't let that stop me from making something of myself."

"But you had help from the Senator."

"How do you know that?"

"I thought it was commonly known." Hugh stammered.

"I haven't talked about that in years."

Hugh shuffled his feet. "I think the Senator must have mentioned it, he does enjoy talking about himself."

Jeremy stared suspiciously at him. "Yes, I suppose that's it."

"I should be going."

"Do you think there's any chance of getting my things back?"

"It's doubtful, these types usually sell everything they take, but if we can catch them before they leave town we might find something."

"Thank you." Jeremy shook Hugh's hand. "I know I've been difficult. I'm just concerned, especially about the bank."

"I understand. Thank you for your time." Hugh began walking towards the front door. Jeremy followed close behind.

"Did you enjoy the picnic this weekend?"

"Yes, it was most agreeable."

"I saw you talking with Emma Hollis." Jeremy paused and looked briefly out of the window. "I once thought there might be something between us. I actually proposed marriage." He laughed nervously.

"Really?" Hugh tried to sound surprised.

"Yes. But she turned me down."

"I'm sorry."

Jeremy nodded absently. "I was angry for a long time."

"Naturally."

"But I think it was for the best. Emma is a really sweet girl, but I don't know, she's a bit of a dreamer. She's looking for something or someone who I don't think exists. I just thought I should warn you."

"I was simply talking to her."

"It was written all over your face. I could tell that from clear across the lawn."

"I don't think *she* noticed." Hugh said thinking back to his conversation with Emma.

"That's my point."

* * *

Hugh returned to the police station, glad to be done with his interview. He ventured a quick glance at Thalberg's but didn't see anything except Mr. Thalberg sitting behind his counter reading a book. That was one thing Hugh missed, ever since starting to work he had little time to read, and now this cursed thief was taking more time out of his day. One of the others, his favorite one, stood up when he came in.

"What did you find out?"

"Nothing new, but we've got to get people to start locking their doors. I think we should either post a public notice or go door to door and warn them." Hugh said.

"That will scare the devil out of them. These people aren't used to this sort of thing. They've never had a policeman come to their door and warn them about a potential crime. It isn't like it was in Boston."

"If we don't warn them this bandit will be all over town. He's walking into houses while they're asleep, and he'll keep doing it until we stop him."

"He'll move on in a week or two." the other said.

"In a week or two? We need to find him now before he hurts someone."

"How do you propose we do that?"

"Night patrols. If we each take a different part of town at night we might catch him in the act."

The other one rubbed his chin. "Night patrols? It might work."

"It will work."

"Let's try it before we start posting public notices. Agreed?"

Hugh agreed. He was sure he could catch this thief in the act. No one in Fox Cove was more qualified for the job than him.

Chapter 72

On Monday all of us in the store found ourselves looking up more quickly when the door opened. Chief Inspector Garrett had been there in the morning to warn us about the thief that was roaming the town at night. He was talking to all the local businesses but did not want us to tell anyone else.

"Why not?" Mr. Thalberg asked. "Do you want them to be robbed?"

Chief Garrett shook his head and rested his hand on his night stick. "Of course not. We've discussed it and I don't want to scare people unnecessarily. We're starting night patrols and I wouldn't be surprised if we had him in a day or two. Meanwhile I want you to be extra careful. If you see anyone unusual let me or Ryan know."

"We will." said Mrs. Thalberg. "Thank you."

The Chief touched the brim of his hat. "Good day." He started to leave and then turned back to me. "And don't forget, don't come in here alone."

"I won't. I promise."

"Goodbye." he said as he hurried out the door.

"I don't like this." Mr. Thalberg said. "This is why we left the city."

"I have faith in the police." Mrs. Thalberg said.

Later that day, just before closing, Ryan came into the store with his hat in his hand. "Good afternoon." he said quietly.

"Good afternoon." I was aware that the Thalbergs were listening intently.

"I was wondering if you still had that book."

"Yes of course." I led him to the back of the store. "Here it is." I pulled a copy of *The Time Machine* off the shelf and handed it to him.

Ryan grinned. "Thank you."

"You're welcome." I looked into his brown eyes, trying to see Hugh.

"Did you enjoy the picnic?"

"Yes of course, and you?"

"I did. I'm sorry I had to leave so suddenly, it's just that Papa had other ideas."

"He said you were an investigator."

A blush came across his face. "Actually I was a detective. Burglary is kind of a specialty of mine. I'd like to imagine I know how these fellows think."

"The thieves you mean?"

"Yes."

"Oh I see."

He looked towards the front of the store. "I should go." He took a few steps and then stopped. "I wanted to ask you something. Papa is having a dinner a week from Saturday and he said each of us can invite someone. Would you, I mean if you aren't otherwise engaged, like to come?"

"Yes of course."

"I think there may be cards after dinner. It's quite a passion in our family." His face began to turn red.

"I love cards, but I only know one game."

"Tribute wasn't it?" he asked.

"Yes, how did you remember?"

"Not many people play that anymore, it's such an old game."

"Yes I know, but I learned it from someone quite old." I said hoping for a reaction.

Ryan looked only mildly surprised. "Dinner is at seven, but you can come early if you like."

"Thank you." I said trying to suppress an excited giggle.

"I really should go. We start night patrols this evening."

"Do be careful."

* * *

I walked home from work that afternoon engrossed in thoughts of the dinner party. It was a beautiful summer day, the wind off the ocean was gentle, bringing with it the sounds of the gulls swooping and diving on the dock and a crisp salty taste in the air. For the first time in years I was beginning to feel hopeful about things.

"Lovely day isn't it?" said a voice behind me. I stopped and turned around. Will was standing there in plain clothes smiling.

"Yes it is."

"On your way home?"

"Yes."

"May I walk with you? I happen to be going that way. We are starting our night patrols and I'm going to be stalking around your house."

"My house?" I took his arm. "Why there?"

"Your house and the two others on that road are quite isolated from the rest of the town. It's a perfect opportunity for a certain type of rogue." The wind blew his blonde hair.

"It sounds dangerous, what if he's carrying a pistol? You could get hurt."

Will shrugged. "Oh it's nothing. I am sure he's just some deranged loner looking for money. Don't worry about me."

I nodded but I wasn't feeling nearly as confident as he was. We started down our narrow little lane towards home. The trees above cast a dark shadow over the road.

"Say, I wanted to ask you something." he said as we passed Ethan and Candy's house. "My father is hosting a dinner a week from Saturday, to thank your brother and sister-in-law for the picnic. They are to be the guests of honor. Us boys are allowed to invite a guest and I thought you might like to be mine, my guest that is. What do you say?"

I smiled in the dim shadow of the trees. "I'm afraid your brother Ryan already asked me this afternoon, and I accepted."

"What?" Will said angrily. He pulled his arm away.

"I really have to get home." I started to walk away.

"No wait. I'm sorry. I shouldn't have reacted like that. It's just that I had planned on asking you. Can you forgive me?"

"Of course."

"Thank you. The last thing I want is for you to be angry with me."

"I'm not." My house was straight ahead. "I'll still see you at the dinner."

"I know." he agreed with a trace of annoyance in his voice. He looked at my house and sighed. "Don't forget to lock your doors tonight."

"I will. I'll check myself before I go to bed."

"Good. An unlocked door is just an open invitation for a thief. Isn't that what happened the last time?"

"What?" I spun around, but he was already gone.

Chapter 73

Hugh couldn't see a thing. He was standing under a tree in the middle of the night waiting for this nuisance of a thief to show his face so he could arrest him. He had been outside for three hours and all that had happened was that two cats had strolled past him and he had given a warning to an old man for urinating on a rose bush.

It had been a full week of night patrols with no results. He had been all over town but the darned fool never made an appearance. Tonight he was in the center of town, the others were each stationed elsewhere. He yawned. He could have gotten more accomplished sleeping in his bed than standing outside in the middle of the night.

Another few minutes passed when he heard the unmistakable sound of footsteps not more than a few feet away. He held his breath and put his hand on the butt of his pistol. What if he had to shoot somebody? Maybe they would just go away.

He waited and listened, the footsteps came ever closer. Hugh slowly took out his pistol. He swallowed hard and tried to resist the urge to run away. In front of him the bushes moved. There was an uneasy silence. Finally he got up the courage to speak. "Come out where I can see you or I'll shoot."

The bushes moved again and he felt for the trigger, a black figure emerged in front of him. "Shoot me if you want to but I doubt it will do any good." Mika said with his hands raised.

Hugh put the pistol away. "Oh you. What's the idea of sneaking up on me like that?"

"I just wanted to see if you were paying attention. Did you notice how I made those footsteps? I can walk in silence or I can make a sound."

"Yes I know, I was dead once too. You don't have to explain the technical details to me." Hugh grumbled.

"And you don't have to be such a grouch."

"I'm sorry but I'm tired, we've been out here for a week and this stupid thief hasn't shown his face yet. Why did you send him here?"

"Me? I am not in control of everything in this town. You are a policeman, he is a criminal, seems pretty natural to me." Mika folded his arms across his chest.

"It's an awfully big coincidence that he shows up in town just after I do."

Mika shrugged and stared up at the starry sky. "Too bad you can't sprout your wings, it's a nice night for flying."

"A darn shame."

"You are so ungrateful. By the way, nice job at the picnic. I am sure the Torment Seer was very impressed." Mika said.

"This is taking a lot more time than I expected."

"I have all the time in the universe."

"I don't and neither does Emma. How much longer is it going to be?"

"How should I know? Although I think the Torment Seer is starting to notice a certain someone."

"Do you mean me?" Hugh asked anxiously.

"Maybe and then again maybe not. I don't concern myself with the doings of lower Seers."

"You're impossible." He looked up and saw one of the others, his least favorite, coming towards him in the gloom of the night.

"I say he must have left town by now. We've been at it for a week. I think we should go home." the other one said.

For once Hugh agreed. "I think you're right. Let's go."

"What a break for our thief, he's got the town at his mercy again." Mika said as he flew up into the night sky. Hugh watched as Mika disappeared into the darkness and then took the short walk home and to bed.

Chapter 74

There was no news about the thief, it was a commonly known secret in town despite Chief Garrett's desire to keep it limited to a need-to-know basis. Father and I had done a decent job protecting Mother from the truth. He said that she had a strong aversion to crime and the less she knew the better.

My mind was more focused on the dinner party at the Garretts. The picnic had proved less than insightful, but I had a good feeling about this party. I was pondering what to wear as Father and I walked into town one morning. The party was just a few days away and I was trying to think of what might actually look fashionable. Father was beside me muttering to himself and looking over his shoulder.

It was early and there were few people about. We had just passed the cove. Father's barber shop was only a few hundred feet away when I saw a young man squeeze out from between two buildings. He looked from side to side and then froze when he saw us.

"Father, look." I said grabbing his arm. "Who's that?"

Father squinted as the boy stared at us. For a second our eyes met, there was a look of terror in his. He couldn't have been more than sixteen years old. He hesitated and then squeezed back between the buildings and out of sight.

"We need to follow him." I said starting to run.

Father caught my arm. "Emma you can't go running after that boy, he might be the thief."

"I know. I want to see where he goes."

"Go to the police station."

"All right. We'd better hurry."

"You go yourself." Father said nervously. "I have to open the shop."

"But you saw him too."

"You'd better hurry Emma." he said giving me a gentle push. I stood for a minute with my mouth open and then hurried into town leaving him standing in the middle of the road.

As I rushed past the darkened storefronts and houses I imagined at every turn the boy leaping out and grabbing me, pulling me into the dim light of the narrow passages between the buildings. I was relieved to see a pale glow coming from the police station. I pushed open the door and found Chief Garrett sitting behind his desk.

"Miss Hollis." he said as he stood up.

"I, I-" I slid into a chair to catch my breath.

"Are you hurt?"

I shook my head. "No. Father and I saw a boy this morning. He came out from between two buildings."

The Chief sat next to me. "Have you seen him before?"

"No never." I described what happened. "I don't know, maybe it's nothing."

"Maybe not, but I want to check it out. Where did you see him again?"

"Between the feed store and Mr. Coster's house."

"Very good. I'll start there." He stood up and opened his desk drawer. He took out a pistol and slid it into an empty holster on his hip. "I want you to stay here until I get back." He opened the front door and shouted for Harold. "Harold will stay with you while I'm gone. He's right around the corner."

I felt a nervous quivering in my stomach. "Are you going to shoot him?"

He flashed a smile and his steely gray eyes softened. "Well I'm certainly not going to let him shoot me."

The door opened and Harold came running in. "What is it?"

"I want you to stay with Emma. She saw a stranger this morning and I want to check on it."

"I can go to Thalberg's." I said.

"No. You'll stay here. Harold, I don't want you leaving here until I return."

"Yes sir."

Chief Garrett hurried out the door. I looked out the window and watched his flinty silver hair shine in the morning light until he disappeared.

"I don't know that I saw anything." I suddenly felt like a fool running into the station just because I saw a strange boy.

"It's a good lead Emma." Harold said. "And it's the only one we have to go on."

"I hope your father is all right."

Harold smirked. "He'll be fine. He was a soldier you know, and a prison guard too. That's what I used to do."

"You were a guard?"

"Yes. It's a bit boring sometimes, always being in the same place. I was happy when we came here and I could see more than the same four walls every day."

"I guess it would be."

Neither of us spoke for a few minutes. I found myself frequently looking out the window. Harold grinned nervously and looked at the floor. "I hear you're coming to dinner on Saturday."

"Yes."

"As Ryan's guest."

"Yes."

"I would have asked you myself if he hadn't beaten me to it."

I saw a flash of silvery hair, it was just Mr. Taylor walking with his dog. I sat down and sighed.

"There's nothing to worry about. Now about the party-" Harold began.

To my relief Chief Garrett was walking on the other side of the street carrying a rumpled bag. A few seconds later the door opened and he came inside.

Harold and I jumped to our feet. "What happened?" We both said at once.

"I didn't see anyone, but I found this hidden underneath a pile of rags behind the feed store." He set the bag on his desk, a metallic clanging came from inside. "You boys should have found this." he said looking warily at Harold. The Chief opened the bag and pulled out an empty silver picture frame, a pair of candlesticks, a pewter mug, and a small roll of cash.

"Who do these belong to?" Harold asked.

"How should I know? Do you recognize any of this Miss Hollis?"

"No, not at all."

He closed up the bag and handed it to Harold. "Show these to the victims and see if they belong to anyone."

Harold took the bag. "I'll see you on Saturday Emma."

The Chief sighed heavily. "Get going Harry. There will be plenty of time for socializing."

"Yes sir." Harold said before hurrying away.

"Do you really think that boy was the one you're looking for?" I asked once Harold had left.

Chief Garrett sat at his desk. "I think there's a very good chance it was. That was really quick thinking on your part."

"My father saw him too, but he didn't want to come here."

"I'll talk with him later. Some folks are uncomfortable dealing with the police." He scratched a note on a piece of paper. "As for you, I want you to be extra careful, especially at night."

"Why? Do you think he's dangerous?"

"I don't know. But you've seen him and that might make him nervous. You never can tell with these types, you never know what you're dealing with."

"He looked awfully young."

"They start earlier and earlier these days Miss Hollis." He sighed.

"I'll be careful." My stomach felt like I had swallowed a stone. I took a deep breath.

"We'll catch him. Don't worry." he said reassuringly.

"I know."

"I hear you'll be at my party this weekend." He leaned back in his chair.

"I'm looking forward to it."

"Yes Ryan told me he had invited you." he said with a note of curiosity in his voice.

"He did. Is that all right?"

"Of course it is, it's just that-" He glanced out the window and stood up. "What on earth?" The door opened and Mr. Thalberg walked in.

"Emma, are you in trouble? You've been in here a long time, are they holding you for something?"

"If she was in trouble she would be locked in that cell." The Chief pointed. "Now go back to your store and leave the policing to me."

"I'm sorry." Mr. Thalberg said. "I didn't know."

"Thank you Miss Hollis. I'll see you later."

I rose and took Mr. Thalberg's arm which was shaking. We left the police station and walked across the street.

"I wouldn't want to cross him." Mr. Thalberg said as he opened the shop door for me. We both looked back across the road, Chief Garrett was watching us. It wasn't until we were inside the store that he finally sat down and resumed his work.

Chapter 75

Officially Hugh had not been to many parties. His parents used to have them often enough, but he was always too young to attend. He and Connolly were usually confined to the staircase landing, peering through the rails while Patrick and his sister Laura talked and drank wine with the adults.

Once he was dead he attended his fair share of occasions as a ghost. They held a certain enjoyment, especially walking through people and listening to private conversations. But no one ever talked to him, or even knew he existed.

Since coming back to life and returning to Fox Cove he had experienced exactly two parties. One was nothing more than an excuse for Senator Brown to announce his candidacy as governor and the other a picnic lunch at Ethan and Candy's home.

The picnic had not gone exactly as he had hoped. He didn't know if he was really making an impression on Emma. And then there was that baseball game, he didn't understand what was going on during that entire episode.

But now the Garretts were hosting a dinner at their house. The two weeks between the picnic and the dinner had felt like an eternity. At last the evening had come. He was quite impressed with his own reflection despite his modern clothes. He was growing used to his new body, sometimes it was hard to remember what the old Hugh MacPherson looked like.

He joined the others as they welcomed their guests in the parlor before dinner was served. Senator Brown had left his servants in place when he rented the house to them. Hugh secretly enjoyed having a butler to answer the door, a maid to serve drinks, and a cook preparing the menu. He had always had servants growing up although he had never told Emma because he didn't like anyone, even her, to know how wealthy he had been.

The guests of honor were Ethan and Candy. They arrived first, along with Emma. She was smiling brightly in a yellow dress with sprigs of green. Her hair was curled and flowed down to the middle of her back, it was held in place with the hair comb he had given her years ago. He did not approach her immediately. She was so beautiful to look at, he wanted to savor the moment for just a few seconds.

"Good evening." Ethan said shaking his hand.

"Good evening." Hugh repeated as he watched Emma approach.

"Hello." she said to both of them.

"Good evening." he answered. With a gloved hand she pushed a stray hair from her face. He found himself having to keep his hands to his sides. He longed to touch her.

"So I hear we are to play cards tonight." Ethan said.

"What? Oh yes."

"I love to play cards." Emma said.

"I do believe I've heard that about you."

The rest of the guests began to arrive. Jane and Amy Jennings walked in with their hair done up in a most unflattering style. Hugh was appalled to see they were wearing makeup. Back in his day only ladies of a certain profession dressed like that. But he supposed he was being old fashioned and they were certainly game for anything they were invited to. Right behind them was Miriam Blanchett, a recent widow who had just gone back into society.

"Excuse me, I want to talk with Mrs. Blanchett." Ethan said. "Do you mind?"

"Of course not." Emma said. "Will you play Tribute tonight?" She asked after Ethan had gone.

"If you like. Although I don't know if everyone will know how to play."

Emma turned around and looked at the Jennings girls. He was amused to see her frowning at their choice of wardrobe. "They can learn."

"So are you any good?" he asked.

"Oh yes, I'm a splendid player. I would be worried if I were you."

"I'll have to make sure I keep my eye on you."

She laughed and for a brief second rested her fingers on his arm. She quickly pulled her hand away. He held his breath. Did she know? Was she going to take the watch from her bag right now? Her face was reddening. "I'm glad to see Mrs. Blanchett here. I haven't seen her since her husband was lost."

"Oh yes. It's very nice indeed."

She blinked and began staring at something in the far corner of the room. Hugh couldn't see anything but a gaudy vase.

"Is everything all right?" he asked, leaning close. He caught the faint scent of roses and his head spun.

"Um, well not exactly." she said still looking into the corner. "Actually I am feeling a bit lightheaded. I think I need some fresh air."

Hugh looked again but saw nothing. Emma had told him once that the house contained a tormented soul, a Ma Brewster or something like that. He had never noticed any ghostly presence, but then it was he who usually did the haunting, not the other way around.

"Let's go out on the porch." he said offering his arm. To his delight she took it. They left the parlor and went through a pair of French doors that opened onto the porch. Hugh heard a gossipy whisper from one of the other guests as they passed by. The sea air was a refreshing change from the stifling parlor. The moon was rising, casting a shimmering reflection on the dark ocean waves below. "This should make you feel better."

She leaned against the porch railing and took a deep breath. "This was just what I needed, thank you. I saw, I mean I see. Never mind, I don't know what I am saying." She laughed and took his arm again. He put his hand over hers and was about to say something romantic and witty when he noticed something in the corner of his eye.

Mika was leaning against the house watching them. "Make your excuses Hugh. The Torment Seer and I need to talk."

Chapter 76

The fresh sea air felt so good. I opened my mouth and breathed it in, tasting the saltiness. The house had been so stuffy. Ma Granger had been making strange faces at me. I was afraid of what she might do. It was a relief to be outside and away from everyone else.

I felt a happiness welling up inside of me that I hadn't felt in a long time, a feeling of unexplained elation. I found myself starting to giggle although I wasn't exactly sure why. "If I lived here I would be on this porch every spare minute." I said to him.

His face was caught in the shadows and I couldn't see his expression. "Do you mind if I leave you here for a moment? There's something I have to check on." His voice was flat and unemotional.

"Of course." I said taking my hand from his arm. I was glad for the darkness, he couldn't see my disappointment.

"Thank you." he muttered. He turned and went back inside.

I looked back at the sea. Was I acting too silly? It must have been something I said or did. I felt my mood sink. I stared out at the water and wondered how long it was until dinner. A few minutes passed when I began to perceive I was not alone. Slowly I turned my head and saw Mika.

"Good evening." he said.

"Good evening."

"I want to talk with you."

"Me? Why me? I've done something wrong haven't I?"

"Someone is just a bit paranoid, aren't they?" He took a step forward. He shimmered luminescent in the night air.

"What do you want to talk about?" I asked, resisting an urge to curtsey. There was something beautifully magnificent about him, as though I should bow in his presence.

"I thought we could talk about you and Hugh, and maybe me." He stepped closer. "Let's go somewhere else though. This place smells like maple syrup."

"All right." I said uneasily. "The beach is right down these steps."

"I was thinking of somewhere higher up. Put your arms around my neck."

"What?"

"I said, put your arms around my neck."

I did as he asked. His skin was ice cold, like Hugh's used to be. He put his hands on my waist. I became covered in goose pimples. My heart was hammering in my ears. I had never been so close to a man I hardly knew, let alone an extraordinarily beautiful creature like him.

There was a gentle rustling as my feet lifted off the ground. The cool night air crept around my ankles and up my skirt. "What are you doing?" I cried as the second story windows passed by us.

"Flying."

"Where are we going?"

"Not far." We glided upwards, past the third story windows and across the roof. Much to my surprise there was a wooden platform built across the peak of the roof. On it were two chairs, one large and ornate and one small and plain.

We floated towards the platform and landed with a gentle tap. "There we are." he said letting go of my waist. I looked down to make sure my feet were on a solid surface before I released my grip.

"What a strange place." I said looking around. "Who built this?"

"I did."

"It's cold up here." I murmured as I rubbed my arms.

"Oh sorry, I forget sometimes." He sat in the large chair, his wings framing his shoulders.

As he stared at me a rush of warm air, like an invisible fog, swirled around me. I felt like I was being wrapped up inside a quilt. "Thank you."

"Sit down."

I sat on the small chair which was not as uncomfortable as it looked. "What am I doing here? I'm missing the party."

"The party is of no consequence. I wanted to talk to you. This will be the last time you'll ever see me."

"I'm sorry to hear that."

"Why? Because you love me so much?" I could barely see him in the deep of the night. His usual glow was diminished and he could almost pass for anyone on the street. I looked out at the horizon and could just make out the shadowy outline of a ship passing off shore.

"Actually I do love you. You gave Hugh his life back."

"I didn't do it for you."

"I know."

"I did it for him."

"I'm glad you did. Even if-" I stopped and tried to collect my thoughts. "Even if I fail at this challenge I am glad you did it. Hugh deserved to finish the life he started."

"How noble of you."

"I'm not being noble. I've just had time to think over the last four years. I want to find Hugh more than anything. I love him. But I want him to be happy too, and if that means he and I go our separate ways then I will have to learn to live with that." I had never spoken those words aloud, I felt relieved to have said them.

Mika muttered something I couldn't hear. He shifted in his chair but it was impossible to tell if he was looking at me or not.

"Why do you hate me so much?" I asked.

"I don't hate you."

"You certainly make me feel like you do."

"I don't hate you." he repeated. "I'm jealous of you."

"Me?" I said letting a gust of wind take my voice with it.

Mika was silent. The wind died down and the night became deathly quiet. I could not hear a sound from the house below. It was as though we were the only two beings in the universe. It was difficult to determine how much time passed before he spoke again.

"When you're a Watcher like me you are with the person you Watch from the first moment they take breath until the second they see their last light of life, and even beyond that. Every second is spent making sure that that soul makes it in life.

"I have known Hugh since his birth. I have seen everything that happened to him good and bad, and believe me there wasn't much good. I was there when the fire started. I was the one who told him to get out. I was there when he first began to steal. It was my idea, I told him to do it because he was starving and wearing rags. He was fourteen years old. What else was he supposed to do? I didn't mean for him to continue the rest of his life. How did I know he would be so damn good at it?

"When he was killed in your house that night it was because of me. I failed him. I couldn't get through to him. He wouldn't leave. So he was left in Torment. I would come in and say something superior, keep him company now and then. I felt useful, I was doing something for my Watched, that's what I am meant to do. And then you came along."

"And you were no longer needed?"

"Something like that. A third wheel is what they would call it in my time. I was not a very nice person when I was alive. I have a special gift and I used that to my full advantage. There was no one I wouldn't hurt, betray, or abandon just to get what I wanted. When I was killed-"

"How did you die?" I interrupted.

"Poison, but that's not important."

"Who did it?"

"I don't know."

"Do you mean they never found out who killed you?"

"They may have. It's not my concern." Mika said. "You'll understand when you're dead."

"I don't want to think about that."

"No one does until they meet their Watcher. Now can I get back to what I was saying?"

"Yes. I was just curious."

He took a deep breath. "As I was saying I was a terrible person and when I died I was made into a Watcher so that I could help someone else avoid making the mistakes that I did."

"What happened?"

"My first Watched died at one year because of my carelessness." His voice became small. "I was devastated. I have a son that I haven't seen since he was ten days old. I barely got to be a father. My Watched belong to me. I have no access to my son or his mother, no friends or family. I've had all that taken away from me. So when you stepped into that house and you started making Hugh happy all I could think was that he was mine."

"No wonder you don't want me to succeed."

"I do. I have to want what's best for Hugh. My feelings don't matter. They can't. That's why I wanted to talk with you. I am afraid you're going to make the wrong choice."

I sat up in my chair and tried to peer through the darkness. "What are you saying? Do you know what I am thinking? Who I am thinking of?"

"I can't read your mind, but I don't think you've really been paying attention."

"I have been. I have listened to everything those boys have said. They all sound like Hugh at different times. How am I supposed to do this? How am I supposed to figure this out? Why did you have to make up such a stupid game?"

"Because you can't get everything handed to you, you have to work for it. I've learned that much." he said.

"I can't do it."

"Then why not give up? Just hand the watch over to the next one you see and be done with it." he said coldly.

"You know I won't do that."

"Then use all your senses. Don't make your choice just yet. Wait a little longer."

"Can't you give me a hint? Anything? Point me in the right direction. Please."

"Absolutely not." Mika said. "You have to find him on your own. Trust your instincts."

"I will."

"Hugh will need you once I'm gone."

"Gone? Where are you going?" I asked.

"If you're successful then I have to leave."

"Why?"

"Because a person who is truly alive doesn't see their Watcher, my job is an invisible one."

"Does Hugh know this?"

"No, but it won't matter to him."

"Yes it will." I said. "More than you realize."

"You'll have to take my place."

"And where are you going?"

"Back to where I started, the voice in the back of his mind."

"He won't see you anymore?" I asked.

"No. Not until he dies again."

"But he'll remember you?"

"Of course. I can't erase memories."

"But you make people do things, you can manipulate them." I said. "How else could you remove me from the party? Won't they be looking for me?"

"They'll never know you were gone. But now that you mention it I should get you back there, something exciting is about to happen." he said rising from his chair.

"You said this is the last time I will see you."

"Yes. You shouldn't be able to see me at all. Are you ready?"

I stood up. "I am. But can I ask you something first?" I wanted to spend just a few more minutes in his company.

"What?" he asked with a tinge of impatience.

"Where are you from? Your clothes are strange looking, and you talk a little different."

"I could say the same thing about you." he said. "I was born in 1943, I died in 1986."

"I knew it. I just knew you were different. What's the future like?"

"I am not going to stand here and give you a history lesson for the next ninety years, you're not that old, you'll live to see most of it."

"Can't you tell me just one little thing?"

He paused and looked up at the sky, a sliver of moon was peeking out from behind a cloud. "The moon."

"Yes?"

"Men will walk on it."

My mouth dropped open. "Are you sure? How? How can that possibly happen?" My mind was reeling.

"That's all I'm saying. Now come on, put your arms around me."

I complied and we lifted into the air. His black wings moved slowly as we glided across the roof, down the back of the house and onto the open porch. "One more thing." he said just before my feet touched the floor. "If you tell Hugh anything about this conversation you'll be very sorry. Goodbye Emma."

He let go of me. There was a brilliant flash of silver and green light. I put my hands up to shield my eyes, a second later the light was gone leaving me in the dark night air.

"Are you ready for dinner?" Ryan asked. He was standing next to me holding out his hand.

"Yes." I said unsteadily. My mind was racing with everything Mika had said. I couldn't even begin to understand the part about the moon. Maybe he was lying. I might never know for sure.

I took Ryan's hand and followed him into the dining room where the rest of the party was already seated. Ryan pulled out my chair and then took his seat across from me. I looked carefully at each of the Garrett boys. Mika said I had to trust my instincts. My eyes came back to one face in particular.

Chief Garrett rose and tapped his wine glass with his knife. "I would like to thank everyone for joining us tonight. Especially our guests of honor Dr. Ethan Hollis and Dr. Candace-" He stopped. There was a flurry of voices coming from the front hallway. The butler burst in followed by Virgil Wentworth who was panting heavily.

"Someone just busted in on my tack store." He leaned on the back of Candy's chair to catch his breath.

"What happened?" the Chief asked.

"I was upstairs having a right proper dinner with my wife and son when we heard glass breaking downstairs. I rushed the boy and the missus into a closet, got my axe and went down to the store to confront to him." Virgil coughed and wiped the sweat from his forehead. "He was just a young thing Chief, not much older than sixteen. He had his fingers on the cash register."

"What did you do? Did you chop him in two like a piece of firewood?" Candy asked excitedly.

"I raised my axe and I hollered at the top of my lungs and he ran out as fast as could be."

"Did you see which way he went?" Ryan asked.

"Nope. By then I was down on my knees thankin' the good Lord above for sparing me and my family." Virgil put his hands together in prayer.

"We need to go." Chief Garrett said. "Boys get your pistols." Ryan, Will and Harold stood up.

"But we haven't even had dinner yet." Jane whined.

"You all may stay and have dinner if you like." the Chief said. "If this fellow is on the loose this may be the perfect time to catch him. Ethan, I trust you can make sure the ladies get home safely."

"I will." Ethan said. "Be careful. All of you." Ryan glanced at me and then followed his father and brothers outside.

"Some party." Amy moaned. "I wanted to play cards."

"I'll second that." I muttered to myself.

Chapter 77

Hugh was annoyed. He had been looking forward to that dinner all week long. Just as Emma seemed to be noticing him he was pulled away to chase after a lunatic burglar. He had a new respect for all the sheriffs, policemen, deputies, and ordinary men who had tracked him all those years ago. What occasions had he disrupted in their lives?

He had just taken a walk through the cove, opening up every fish shack and lobster hut he could find. He had been yelled at by more than a few fishermen as he used his baton to overturn piles of debris and look under porches. A cat had flown out at him and scratched his face as he pulled up an old canvas tarp.

He sighed loudly as he trudged up the hill, the smell of fish guts slowly drifted away. Mika was nowhere to be found. He could have really used him at a time like this. He was trying to do a job he knew nothing about. He stopped at the top of the hill to catch his breath.

"This is ridiculous." he muttered aloud. The town of Fox Cove lay to his left, to his right was the short wooded lane that Emma lived on, along with her brother and the Coopers. He hoped Ethan had escorted her home safely. She should be sleeping peacefully in her bed. He could picture that room in every detail, it had been his room once. That seemed like a lifetime ago.

He rubbed his eyes and tried to think of what to do next. From somewhere close by he heard a snap, like a twig breaking underfoot. He held his breath and listened, the night was so still and quiet, it was almost deafening. All was silent for a moment and then he heard the faintest of footsteps on the road to Emma's house.

Hugh's heart started beating so loud he couldn't hear a thing. He forced himself to calm down. He had him. He knew he had him. There was something familiar in the deliberately slow steps. It was how he would have done it. Careful and quiet.

He waited until the footsteps were barely audible before he started to follow. If this fellow was anything like he was then he would be listening for signs of pursuit. The entrance to the lane was covered with overhanging branches. Hugh let them be his cover while he peered into the darkness. A lone figure was walking down the center of the road. It was a man, but beyond that it was impossible to tell anything else. It could be one of the Cooper boys getting in late.

Hugh took a few steps forward, being careful to stay in the dark shadows of the trees. The man walked past Ethan's house without as much as a glance. Hugh continued a few more feet and then crouched behind a thick oak tree. The stranger continued by the Coopers and straight on. He felt the panic rising in him. He made sure his pistol was still in its holster. He had shot a rifle once when he was thirteen, he hoped it would be enough practice.

The man reached the Hollis' front door and put his hand on the door latch. Hugh could tell from the way his arm jerked that the door was locked. A feeling of relief swept over him. He waited, ready to attack as the thief walked back up the lane. But instead he looked into the parlor with his hands cupped around his eyes. He jiggled the window, it slid up easily. With practiced ease he jumped over the sill and disappeared into the darkness.

Hugh leapt from behind the oak tree and started running. He was trying to formulate a plan in his mind, but all he could think of was Emma and this man creeping around inside her house while she slept. He considered briefly getting Ethan or even Michael Cooper, but this was his task to perform.

Hugh approached the house as quietly as he could. He ducked under the parlor window and tried to listen. There was nothing but the sound of the wind blowing through the trees, an owl hooted somewhere in the distance

He pulled himself up onto the sill with considerably less skill than his adversary and swung his legs into the parlor. Edward's desk, which was behind the sofa, was open. A few papers were scattered on the floor. He waited and listened. The house was deathly quiet. Suddenly he heard someone in the hallway.

A boy entered the room stuffing a biscuit in his mouth as he walked. He stopped. A look of panic flickered across his face. He swallowed the biscuit and stared defiantly at Hugh.

"You're coming with me." Hugh slowly lifted the pistol from its holster. He had pinned his badge on his shirt before he left the house. The boy's eyes glanced at it shining in the pale moonlight.

"Are you going to shoot me copper?" He looked to be barely sixteen. His clothes were worn and patched and Hugh could tell by the way his belt was tied around his waist that his pants were probably stolen, or he didn't get enough to eat.

"Just come with me, give yourself up and I promise I'll recommend leniency. You don't have to live like this." It was something Patrick had told him once.

"Ha!" the boy snorted. "What do you know about it?"

Hugh wasn't sure what to do next. He raised the pistol and pointed it at the boy. "Put your hands in the air and turn around."

"Shoot me instead. I ain't got nothin' to live for."

"Do you have any family?" Hugh asked. His legs felt like jelly. He hoped in the darkness of the room the boy couldn't see his hands shaking.

"What's it to you?" He took a step forward, his chest was only inches from the barrel of the pistol.

"I understand what you're going through."

"A cop? I doubt it."

"Put your hands in the air and turn around." Hugh said firmly. He needed to take control of the situation.

The boy slowly turned around, raising his hands as he did.

Hugh reached for the handcuffs in his back pocket. As he fumbled in the dark he lowered the pistol slightly, it was at that moment that the boy spun around and Hugh saw a flash of metal. The boy thrust his arm forward and Hugh let out a gasp. The pistol dropped to the floor as a white hot pain coursed through him. Hugh looked down and saw the blade of a knife slicing into his side. He heard himself struggling to breathe as he looked at the boy. There was no emotion on his face.

"Sorry copper, it was you or me."

Hugh fell to the floor. He was no longer aware of the boy or anything else except a tearing pain. He gasped for air as the light in his eyes dimmed, he was going to die again, it had all been for nothing. He closed his eyes and let himself fall into the darkness.

Chapter 78

I awoke Sunday morning still thinking about Mika and the aborted dinner party. I dressed and hurried downstairs. Mother was in the kitchen having a cup of coffee.

"Good morning."

"Good morning." she answered sleepily.

"Is Father in bed?"

"Goodness no. He's gone into town to find out if they caught that man. I certainly hope so. I can't sleep at night knowing there's a stranger lurking about." She had found out about the thief a few days before, Candy had let it slip.

"Don't worry, I triple checked the door last night, it was locked."

"I know." Mother smiled. "I checked it twice myself."

I stretched and yawned, the clock in the parlor struck ten. Outside the window Scott and Eve were walking down the road followed by their children. As they approached the Coopers Stephen, Sarah and Saul ran onto the porch and started banging on the front door. I laughed as Michael stepped out in his bathrobe, his hair uncombed. The children let out a whoop and rushed past him and inside the house.

There was a quick knock on our door and then voices in the hallway. "Good morning!" Eve called out as Sally and Sam, the two middle children, ran into the kitchen.

"Grandma!" they cried as they clung to Mother, burying their reddish blonde heads in the crook of her arm.

"Where's Granddad?" asked Sam.

"He'll be here soon. In the meantime you can help me with breakfast."

"I want to stir the oatmeal." Sally cried.

"No, I do." said Sam.

It had become something of a tradition for all of us to get together for a late breakfast on Sunday mornings. Eve and Scott usually came straight from church and were in their best clothes. My parents and I had not attended church since we were asked to leave years before by Senator Brown. Ethan and Candy went occasionally. Candy said it was important for the town doctors to be seen.

Eve handed baby Seth to me. She smiled and fixed a red curl on his head. "Emma, when are you going to get married and have babies?"

I felt my face getting red. "I don't know Eve. Maybe I never will."

"Oh come now. I've never heard of such a thing."

"Candy is the next one to have a baby." I said holding one of Seth's pudgy hands.

"What about those policemen? They are all handsome, especially Ryan." Eve said with a sparkle in her eye.

"Let her be Eve." Scott said. "She doesn't need your meddling. Besides if she is going to pick any of them it should be Harold. He's the nicest if you ask me."

I sighed. Seth giggled and waved his arms in the air.

"Girls." Mother said. "A little help please."

"Yes Mother." Eve and I said in unison. We helped her with breakfast while Scott looked after the baby. Sally and Sam soon got bored with preparing the meal and wandered off to play elsewhere.

"Everything is done and Edward is still not here." Mother said glancing out the window. "Not to mention Ethan and Candy."

"They might have had an emergency, let's start without them." Eve said. "I'm starving."

"I suppose we could." Mother said.

"Sally, Sam, where are you?" Scott called out.

A few minutes passed before the two children came running, their faces were red.

"What have you been doing?" Eve asked.

"Trying to wake the man up." Sally said.

"Wake who up?"

"The man in the parlor." Sam replied.

Mother shook her head. "If Edward is napping in there-"

"It's not Granddad." Sally said. "I don't know who it is. He's sleeping on the floor, someone hurt him I think. There's blood on the floor."

Mother's face turned pale.

"I'll go." Scott handed the baby to Eve. He was gone for less than a minute. When he returned he looked as though he had seen a ghost. "Eve take the children and your mother to my parents."

"What?"

"Just do as I ask. I'll explain later. I'm going to get Ethan. Emma, stay with him until I get back."

"Stay with whom?" Mother asked. "What's going on?"

"I don't have time to explain." Scott said as he rushed out the door.

"This is very strange indeed." Mother said.

"I think we should go." Eve took Sally's hand. Mother took Sam's hand and they all went outside.

I waited until they were gone before I dared step into the parlor. At first I saw nothing except that Father's desk had been disturbed and there were crumbs on the floor. I held my breath and took a step forward. Lying behind the sofa, unconscious with a knife sticking out of his side and a pool of coagulated blood around his torso, was Chief Inspector Jason Garrett.

Chapter 79

Hugh was having the strangest dream. He was walking through a field of tall grass. Ahead of him was a thicket of pines. They reminded him of the trees that used to surround his house when he was a boy. The sun was at his back, it felt warm through his shirt.

Grass waved in the amber colored sun, the feathery tops billowing this way and that. At the edge of the trees he could see distant figures, they were watching him. He squinted but he couldn't tell who they were, he was too far away.

Presently he came upon the foundation of a house. Inside the foundation weeds flowered between patches of sand and rubble. Hugh stared for what seemed like hours. It was his house. This was where his home had once stood, now it was nothing but a ruin.

He looked up and found the strangers at the edge of the woods were strangers no more. He could clearly see their faces. His father, his mother, Patrick, Laura, and Connelly were all there. It was his family. They were just as he remembered. He felt himself smiling as he ran towards them.

"You shouldn't be here." Laura said.

Hugh stopped. He was confused. In the back of his mind he had a feeling something had happened to him, but he wasn't sure what it was.

"Where have you been Laura? Did you survive the fire?"

She looked at him but didn't answer.

"You don't belong with us Hugh, not yet." his mother said.

"Of course I do. I'm your son." There was something nagging at the back of his mind, like a name he couldn't remember.

"It's not your time Hugh." his father said.

"You need to fight." Connelly told him. Hugh noticed he was wearing a sash around his waist. The Scarlet Highwayman.

"You have to go back." Patrick said. They had always looked the most alike, he and Patrick, but now as he looked at his older brother he felt different. Something had changed. "Fight Hugh."

"Fight for what? I want to stay here. This is where I belong."

Patrick shook his head. "Don't you remember who you are Jason?"

Jason. That was his name now. He looked at them standing proudly in the sunny field where they had once all lived together. "I'm dying again, aren't I?"

Chapter 80

The house was deathly quiet. There was no one there except Jason Garrett and myself. "They're coming to help you." I said quietly. I knelt down, my knee sinking into the puddle of blood on the floor.

The knife stuck out of him at a ghastly angle. Was he dead? Hesitantly I touched his hand, his skin was clammy but not cold. He looked like he was sleeping, his eyes shut gently, the slightest trace of a rise of his chest indicated he was still breathing. I stroked his forehead and waited.

"What happened?" Ethan cried as he burst into the parlor. I stood up and moved aside. Ethan opened his bag. "Damn it Jason!" he said as he knelt on the floor. Candy arrived with Scott following close behind.

"Someone needs to find the boys." I said. "I can go look for them."

"No Emma." Ethan said. "I want you to stay here. Scott can go."

"But I know them better than he does, they're my friends."

"No. You need to stay here in case- He's in bad shape. Scott, can you please go?"

"Sure." Scott agreed. "Don't worry Emma I'll find them." He hurried outside.

"He's in shock." Candy said.

"We've got to get that knife out, but I don't want him to start bleeding again. I don't know Candy, he's lost so much blood." Ethan said.

"We have to do it right now." she said. "Emma, go and start boiling as much water as you can."

I ran into the kitchen and began filling a pot, my stomach was in knots. My mind kept skipping to Ryan, Will and Harold. Only the night before we all had been enjoying the party. Now everything had changed. I looked out the window in time to see Mother coming to the front door.

"What are you doing?" she asked as she walked into the kitchen.

"Candy needs me to boil water. I imagine it's to sterilize their tools." I said as I lugged the heavy pot onto the stove. Some of the water slurped over the sides and onto the floor.

"Are you telling me they are going to treat that man right here in my house?"

"Yes. They can't move him yet, he's bad off. I think he's dying."

Mother made a face. "That's too bad, but has anyone asked what on earth he's doing here in the first place? A man was stabbed in the middle of the night in our house Emma."

"Honestly Mother I haven't given it a thought." I said as I struggled with the water pump. "We can figure that out later, right now we have to concentrate on saving his life."

"I certainly hope they don't think I had anything to do with it."

"I doubt it." I said as the water began to gush.

Ethan opened the parlor door and joined us in the kitchen. His sleeves were rolled up to his elbows and his face was red and damp.

"How is he?"

"I don't know Emma. He's bad. We have to get that knife out and stitch up the wound." He opened his bag and began laying surgical instruments on the table. "Candy is going to do it. Her hands are steadier than mine right now. Will you sit outside and wait for the boys to arrive? It might take a while and I don't want them bursting in on something."

"Of course."

"Ethan, can't you take him to your clinic, or at least your house?" Mother asked.

Ethan looked appalled. "He's dying Mother. There isn't time."

"I know." She folded her arms across her chest. "It's just the thought of a policeman under this roof." She shuddered and wandered into the pantry.

"I don't understand what's gotten into her." I said.

Ethan shook his head. "I really don't care right now. Just wait outside, please."

"I will."

"I'll call if I need you in there."

I stepped outside and sat in a wicker chair that Father often used. All was quiet. The Coopers seemed to have disappeared as the midday sun rose high in the air. Chickadees chirped and darted past as the minutes crept slowly by.

From inside the house I could hear the muffled voices of Candy and Ethan. I wasn't sure how much time had passed when I saw Ryan and Will come into view at the top of the road. I stood up as they raced towards me.

"Is he all right?" Ryan cried. They ran in the front door.

"Wait!" I called out.

They turned around and came back outside. "Is he dead?" Will asked, his eyes pleading with me.

"No. He's in pretty bad shape though."

Ryan took my hands. "What happened to him?"

"He's been stabbed, he's lost a lot of blood."

"Did he say anything?" Will asked.

I shook my head. "He's unconscious. We don't know how long he's been here or how he even got here."

Ryan let go of my hands. "I can tell you how. That damned thief. He's not just a burglar anymore, he's a murderer."

"Papa is not going to die." Will said.

"When I get my hands on that bastard I'll kill him. I really will." Ryan said. "We've been looking for Papa everywhere, he never came home last night."

"Scott is still looking for Harold." Will added. "What if something happened to him too?"

"Harry is fine Will." Ryan said. "He has to be."

"I'm so sorry." My words sounded hollow, but I couldn't think of anything else to say. "I'm sure Ethan will be out soon to tell us something."

They both looked at me but didn't say anything. Time dragged by. Margaret opened her door at one point, looked at Ryan and Will, and went back inside.

After what seemed like an eternity the front door opened and Candy stepped outside wearing a bloodstained apron. She looked exhausted. "I should have taken this off." she mumbled.

"Is he alive?" Ryan asked.

Candy nodded. "He is. But he's lost a great deal of blood. When we removed the knife he began bleeding again. His body is in shock and he's developed a fever."

"But you can make him better can't you?" Will asked.

"We're going to try. But I have to be honest with you, I don't know if he can survive this. I'm sorry."

Will turned his back and walked a few paces away. Ryan watched him and then looked at Candy. "Can we see him now?"

"Yes. Of course you can." she said softly. She opened the door and Ryan followed her inside the house.

"Do you want to see him Will?" I asked.

Will turned around, tears were running down his cheeks. He quickly wiped them away. "I'm sorry you have to see me like this."

"Why are you sorry? Your father is gravely ill."

"He's all we've had since our mother died, none of us remember her, not even Ryan."

"Do you want me to go in with you?"

He smiled sadly. "Thank you."

"Will!"

We both looked up and saw Harold running towards us. His feet skidded to a halt on the gravel. "Where's Papa?"

"Inside." Will answered.

Harold looked at me. "Is he?"

"He's alive, but he's very ill."

"I want to see him."

"I was just taking Will in now." As I spoke the door opened and Ryan came out.

"Harry! Thank God you're all right."

"We were just coming in to see your father." I said.

"I'll take them in." Ryan said. As they went inside Ethan came out.

"How are you doing Emma?" He flopped into the wicker chair and let out a sigh.

"I feel helpless."

He grabbed my hand and squeezed it. "So do I." He pushed his glasses on top of his head and rubbed his eyes.

"Do you really think he'll live? Honestly?"

"If he has something to live for."

"He does. His sons."

Ethan nodded and shut his eyes. "Yes, he has that too."

Chapter 81

"Yes they do, more than you know." his father said. "They are praying for you. If you die they will never be the same Jason."

"I'm Hugh MacPherson."

"You have people who love you Jason, your three boys and Emma." Laura said.

Emma. At hearing her name a flood of memories came rushing back to him, her face, her body, her voice, and their years together. How could he have forgotten? He was in her house that night, chasing a thief like himself. He had been stabbed. The pain in his side intensified. His knees buckled and he fell limply to the ground.

"Get up and fight Jason. You have to fight harder than you ever have. Don't give in to death this time." his mother told him. She broke away from the family and knelt at his side. She took his hand, her skin was warm and soft. He realized that he now looked older than she did.

"I've missed you." he said. "It's been so long."

Her eyes crinkled as she smiled at him. "I'm sorry I had to leave you. I'm sorry you had to fend for yourself."

"Do you know what I became?" The pain in his side was becoming stronger. He was starting to remember the hot tearing of the knife.

"Yes I know. That's all over now. You have to go back. The game is not yet finished."

Hugh tried to think. What game? Why couldn't he remember anything?

His mother stood up and returned to her place next to his father. They watched him as he lay on the ground, his side throbbing. He wanted to get back to Emma, but he couldn't quite figure out how.

The light in the sky seemed to dim. He could feel a darkness surrounding him, like a blanket wrapping him up. It would be so easy to give in. He could stay here and close his eyes, his family surrounding him.

Emma didn't even know who he was. Every time he had tried to talk to her, she didn't seem to notice him. She would give that watch to one of his sons. The watch, his watch. That was the challenge.

He bolted upright. "Where's Mika?"

Chapter 82

Ethan and I sat outside the house while the Garretts were in with Jason. We were both quiet. There wasn't anything left to say. A fly buzzed around my head while Ethan tapped his foot nervously on the ground.

In the distance I heard someone whistling. I looked up and saw Father walking jauntily towards us, he was carrying an apple in his hand. He waved. "How goes it?"

Ethan and I looked at each other. "Come in and I will tell you about it Father." Ethan said.

"Oh I can't stay. Do you know I can't find one police officer in town? I have a bit of information for them."

"They are all here." I said.

"What's that?" Father asked.

Ethan explained what had happened that morning. I was surprised to find his voice breaking as he spoke. I had not realized how close he had been to Jason.

"You don't say?" Father said. "The scalawag must have stabbed him, the one they've been looking for. He's left town, ran out of here last night. He was last seen tearing up the road past Jeremy's house."

"How do you know that?" I asked.

"Oh I heard it from someone in town." he said vaguely. "That's what I wanted to tell our policemen."

"But who told you?" I said. "Are you a Seer?"

Father smiled and patted my cheek. "Emma, do you really think this is the place for such a discussion? What if your mother heard you? You know how she feels about the subject. Remember you don't see dead people, it's all in your head."

Ethan ignored Father's response. "I've got to get back in there. Father, will you help me bring down my old bed? I'm going to make the parlor into a sick room."

Father agreed and we went inside. Mother was in the kitchen muttering to herself. The door to the parlor was still closed. I stood against the wall, afraid to knock.

A few minutes later Ethan and Father came lurching slowly down the stairs with Ethan's old mattress, their shoulders bumping loudly against the wall. The commotion caused Mother to come out of the kitchen.

"What is going on out here?" she asked, her hands on her hips.

"I am bringing my bed down for Jason, he can't sleep on the floor." Ethan said.

"Why should he sleep here at all?"

Ethan dropped his end of the mattress on the stairs. "He's far too ill to be moved. The wound could open and start bleeding again."

"My home is not a hospital for recovering police officers." she sniffed.

Ethan ignored her comment. "I want that door opened up too, the one that connects Eve's bedroom to the parlor."

"Whatever for? Don't you remember when Eve snuck Scott Cooper up there?"

"How long ago was that? Ten years?"

"Do you want Emma inviting one of those boys upstairs?"

Ethan smiled. "Those boys as you call them are staying in Eve's room tonight."

"Edward, tell Ethan this is ridiculous." Mother looked desperately at her husband.

"There's nothing to fear Elsay." Edward said from the back end of the mattress.

She sighed and smoothed the front of her skirt. "I suppose it will have to do."

"Yes it will." Ethan snapped. "I don't know if he's going to make it through the next few hours at this point."

The parlor door opened. Ryan and Will emerged red faced followed by Candy who had her arm around Harold. I looked inside. Jason was lying on the sofa covered in a blanket, his face was gray and pale.

"Oh good, you're bringing in the bed." Candy said. "Why don't you boys go outside for a minute while we get the room set up. I'll let you know when you can come back in."

Ryan nodded and the three of them walked past me and out the front door. I followed close behind, not knowing what else to do. They collapsed on the grass outside. Harold let out a long sigh while Will laid on the ground and closed his eyes. Ryan wrapped his arms around his knees and looked at me.

"Can I get you anything?" I said. "A drink? Something to eat?"

"No." he said looking at his brothers. "We're not hungry."

I watched as a hummingbird flew determinedly in and out of the morning glories growing around the front door. Time passed slowly.

"He's not going to make it is he?" Harold finally said.

Will sat up and slapped Harold's leg. "Of course he is. Why are you talking like that?"

"Because it's true. He's dying."

"Shut up Harry." Will said.

"I don't want it to happen. God knows I don't. But he's not trying, he's not fighting. Is he Ryan?" Harold asked.

Ryan looked at his brother. "No, he's not fighting. You're right Harold. It's like he's somewhere else entirely."

Chapter 83

Mika was gone. Where had he been when Hugh was stabbed? Nowhere. Hugh felt angry. What a useless Watcher, he could have warned him against going into the house that night. This time he would have listened.

As he sat on the ground holding his side he noticed a man walking towards him. Hugh didn't remember ever seeing him before. He was tall and lanky with long dark hair to his shoulders. He was wearing brown trousers and a plain white shirt.

The stranger was smiling as he approached. "Hello Hugh." His hair blew romantically in the breeze. Hugh thought with some amusement that he looked like a hero out of a book.

"Hello." Hugh managed. The pain in his side was becoming unbearable. In the back of his mind he thought he heard hushed voices.

"How are you?"

"Who are you?"

The man smiled and brushed his hair off his shoulders. "I'm Charlie Winslow. You and I were killed by the same bullet."

Memories of that night came rushing back to him. The damp smell of the house, the drunken state of his own mind, the smooth wood on the staircase railing, the look of horror on Charlie's father's face as he realized he had killed his own son.

"You need to stand up and fight for your life." Charlie said.

Hugh wanted to laugh. "How can you say that? I cost you your life. I deserve to die."

"I forgive you."

Hugh stared in disbelief at Charlie. He looked like he had just had a pleasant meal at a tavern, his expression was happy and satisfied. "How can you forgive me?"

"Do you forgive my father for killing you?"

"I deserved it."

"My father struggled for a long time. Not just because I died, but because you died too. He would pray every night for you. I was there by his side, he just couldn't see me anymore."

Hugh propped himself up on his elbow. The pain had subsided slightly. "Really? He prayed about me?"

Charlie smiled. "Yes. He had killed an unarmed man. That haunted him. He thought about that night over and over again."

"So have I."

"I know. But you don't have to anymore."

"But your life was cut short."

"Yes." Charlie agreed. "But I am still here, just in a different way."

Hugh sat up. "Then you really forgive me?" The voices in his head grew louder.

"Yes. Now you need to fight to stay alive. You have your sons and Emma to live for."

Hugh thought he heard someone somewhere say his name.

"I have to go now." Charlie extended his hand. Hugh took it and Charlie pulled him to his feet. "Goodbye Jason."

"Goodbye." Hugh said. Charlie nodded and started walking back the way he came. Hugh watched him until he disappeared into the trees. He looked at Patrick. "I don't belong here."

"We'll see you again someday Hugh."

"Are you ready?" he heard a voice above his head. He looked up and found Mika floating above him in the air.

"Where have you been?"

"Right here."

Hugh looked back at his family, but they were gone. There was nothing but a clump of weeds where they had been standing. The voices in his head became louder. He could hear other sounds too, the scraping of furniture, the banging of pots and pans, the opening and closing of a door.

"Open your eyes." Mika said.

Chapter 84

The house was quiet that morning. I was in the kitchen washing the dishes and pans from breakfast. The late summer sun streamed in the windows. Outside the two youngest Cooper girls were playing tag in their tattered dresses, they had just a few days before school started again.

It had been three days since we had found Jason Garrett lying on the parlor floor with a knife in his side. He had got no worse, but no better. Ethan said he was lingering, as though he couldn't decide whether to stay in this world or move onto the next.

As I dried the pans with a towel I thought I heard a noise from the parlor. I put the pan aside and tiptoed across the hallway. Jason was lying in Ethan's bed, the covers pulled up to his neck. Sunlight created a patch of light on the blankets.

He groaned and moved his head. I took a step closer and watched him. At first nothing happened, then I saw his eyelids flutter for half a second. I sat on the chair next to his bed and leaned forward. He moaned and slowly opened his eyes.

"Chief Garrett?"

He smiled weakly. "My name is Jason."

"I'll get Ethan."

"No." His voice was raspier than usual. "Wait a minute."

I stood up and put my hand on his forehead. "You're cool."

"I know." He ran his hands over his short hair and rubbed his eyes.

"How do you feel?"

"Not bad considering that boy tried to slice me like a piece of bread." He pushed the covers aside and tried to push himself up. He cried out in pain.

"I'm getting Ethan."

"Oh give me a little reprieve will you? Once he gets here he'll poke and prod me the rest of the day. Help me sit up."

He put his arms around my neck while I set a couple of extra pillows behind his back. I felt my face turning red as his whiskery chin brushed my cheek.

"There you are." I said as I helped him lean back slowly. "Now I really should get Ethan."

He winced. "Give me another minute, I might go back to sleep again."

"Do you remember what happened to you?"

"Yes. I saw that good for nothing thief come in the window. I followed him inside and before I could arrest him he pulled a knife on me."

"They haven't found him yet."

"I shouldn't think so, it only happened last night."

"Last night? You've been here for three days."

"Three days?" he cried. "I've been out for three days?"

"You've been terribly ill. You had a very high fever, and an infection. Ethan said you didn't seem to know which way you wanted to go."

"I didn't. I thought it was my time to die."

"Did you see your wife?"

"My what? Oh, yes I saw my family."

"And you wanted to stay with them?"

He closed his eyes, thick blonde lashes cast a shadow on his face. "I thought I wanted to stay there. I had forgotten how much I had to live for."

"Your sons?"

"Something like that."

"They've been awfully worried about you."

"Really?" He seemed surprised by the notion.

"Of course. They've been worried sick. Harold is just outside, he's been here all morning. If you had died they would have been devastated."

"That's what they told me, when I was asleep I mean. They kept telling me I needed to go back, that I needed to fight for my life."

"Aren't you glad you did?"

He nodded and put his head back on the pillow. "I suppose you think I'm crazy talking like this, delirious from the fever."

"Not really. I believe the dead walk among us, in fact-" I stopped and looked down at the floor.

"In fact what?"

"I don't know what I was going to say." I said, amazed that I had nearly disclosed that I was a Seer.

"Maybe it was just a dream I was having."

"Maybe." I said not believing it.

"What's this?" He held up his arm. He was wearing one of Father's old shirts, the sleeves were at least two inches too short.

I started to laugh. "That's my father's shirt. He's a bit shorter than you."

"Yes, I am tall. But why am I wearing his shirt?" He stretched his arms out as far as they could go. He winced and shifted his weight.

"Your shirt was covered in blood."

"My sons didn't bring me any of my own clothes?"

"Apparently not." I said giggling.

He smirked. "Am I wearing his trousers too?" He started to lift up the blankets.

"Chief Garrett!" I cried, my face turning red. I had no idea if he had anything on his bottom half.

"I told you my name is Jason." He looked underneath the covers. "I do believe I see my ankles and several inches of my leg." A strange smile spread over his face. "That was some party I had the other night wasn't it?" he said, suddenly changing the subject.

"The dinner party? A smashing success. Although I was disappointed that we didn't play cards."

"Oh yes, we were going to do that. You've told me more than once that you're an excellent card player, but I have yet to see any evidence of it."

The secret door opened and Ethan appeared looking excited. "You're awake."

"I know I should have gotten you right away Ethan it's just that-" I began.

"I wouldn't let her." Jason said. "I needed a few minutes to get my bearings."

"It's fine." Ethan said as he checked Jason's pulse and stuck a thermometer in his mouth. Jason mumbled something. Ethan swiped the thermometer out of his mouth and looked at it.

"Normal. You're normal, I don't believe it. I have to look at the wound." Ethan said. "Emma, why don't you go and tell Harold."

"Oh yes, Harold." I said guiltily. I had forgotten about him. I stepped outside and closed the door behind me. The Cooper girls were still playing there. "Have you seen Harold Garrett?" I asked.

"Has his Pa died?"

"No, he's much better."

"Shucks." Olive Cooper pointed towards the woods.

Long ago, when Hugh was alive, the road had continued past our house and went on for another few miles. There had been a fire that had wiped out all the houses and stopped burning just before it reached our place. All that was left of the old road were two ruts in the grass. I followed them as they wound their way along the shore. To my right, through the trees and scrub, I could hear the ocean pounding the sharp rocks below.

I only had to walk a few minutes when I found Harold sitting on the trunk of a felled pine tree. He looked up as he saw me approaching. "He's dead, isn't he?"

"No. He's awake and his fever is gone."

He let out a cry of joy and kissed my cheek. "Come on, what are you waiting for?" he cried as he grabbed my hand and raced back to the house. I hung on as we hurried past the Cooper girls and inside. Ethan was just opening the parlor door.

"You can go in. He's much better."

Harold rushed inside with me following close behind. "Papa!" he cried as he flung himself on top of his father, burying his face in his neck. Jason let out a groan and somewhat reluctantly put his hand on Harold's shoulder.

"Take it easy son."

"Oh I'm sorry Papa, did I hurt you?" Harold said getting off the bed and taking a seat.

"I've been picked at by the doctor like a Christmas turkey. I'm just a little sore."

"I'm so glad you're awake. I, I was so afraid you were going to die."

Jason scrutinized his son's face. "You were really afraid?"

"We all were."

Jason's face softened. "Harry."

"Should I fetch Ryan and Will?" I felt I was intruding on a family moment.

"Yes please." Jason's face shone as he looked at Harold.

I left the house and ran into town. As I passed Father's barber shop I was tempted to tell him the good news. I looked inside and saw he wasn't there. His assistant was working. He waved at me as I walked by. I continued up the street and around the corner to the police station. Ryan and Will were inside playing a game of checkers. Their faces were drawn and tired.

"Oh no." Will said as I shut the door behind me. Ryan stood up and straightened his jacket.

"It's good news. He's awake, and he's doing much better."

Will's face lit up. "Are you sure?"

"Yes, I've talked to him myself."

Ryan let a long sigh of relief.

"Can we see him now?" Will asked.

"Of course, Harold is with him."

Will dashed outside and ran down the sidewalk.

Ryan looked at me and took a deep breath. "I could not have watched my brothers go through that. If he had died-"

"But he didn't."

He took a step forward and put his hands on my shoulders. His brown eyes were warm and moist. "I can't thank you and your family enough for what you have done for us these past few days."

"We were happy to help."

"You have helped me more than you'll ever know." He leaned in close and kissed me tenderly on the mouth. "Thank you Emma."

He grabbed his hat and hurried out of the police station. I watched him run down the street, his hair glistening red in the midday sun. Across the street Mr. Thalberg was in his window watching me. As our eyes met, he gave me a big smile.

I stepped back into the shadows and wondered why I didn't feel more elated that I had just been kissed by the man I believed to be Hugh MacPherson.

Chapter 85

It was hard to believe he had been asleep for three days. The encounter involving his family and Charlie still floated through Hugh's mind even as his two oldest sons rushed into his makeshift room.

"I'm so relieved." Will said as he sat on the end of the bed. Ryan pulled up a chair next to Harold.

"You can't get rid of me that easily boys." He guessed they weren't so bad after all. He had always liked Harold. He supposed because he was the youngest Hugh could relate to having bossy older siblings. Will had never given him any trouble, other than being handsome. But for some reason Ryan had rubbed him the wrong way from the start. Maybe he reminded him of Patrick, or maybe it was because Emma seemed to notice him more than the others.

He glanced into the hallway and saw her lingering outside the parlor door. She was biting her lower lip and looking anxiously from one to the other. Every so often she would meet Hugh's gaze. She was furiously thinking, he could tell that much. Every time she looked at Ryan a strange expression crossed her face.

"We'll find him Papa." Will said. "The man who did this to you."

"He was nothing but a boy, and I doubt you'll find him."

"He nearly killed you." Ryan said. "He has to pay for that."

Hugh shrugged. "It doesn't matter."

"How can you say that?" Will asked.

"I'm just grateful to be alive. If he's meant to be found he will be."

"This doesn't sound like the Papa I remember." Ryan said.

"Ryan, when a man has been through what I have he's bound to have a change of heart."

"Let's just be thankful that he's all right." Harold said.

"Of course we're thankful." Will said. "We love you."

Hugh found himself breaking into a grin. "You do?" He was surprised to feel a wellspring of happiness bubble up inside of him. He had never imagined he would have any feelings for this motley assortment of boys, and yet he found himself thinking that these were his sons, and he liked how that sounded.

He heard a noise in the hallway, a second later Candy arrived. "Everyone out, I need to examine my patient. You can come back later."

The boys reluctantly stood up and filed outside, Emma disappeared from view as they left.

"Hello there Chief." Candy said poking him in the arm.

"Where's Ethan? Shouldn't he be the one to do this?"

"He's having something to eat." Her red hair was tumbling out of her barrette. "What's wrong with me? Don't you think a woman can handle the job?"

"No, it's just that-"

"Who do you think took that knife out of you?"

"You know Ethan already examined me today."

"He did, huh?" Candy shrugged and sat on the chair next to the bed. "You don't look forty three."

"I don't?"

"No." she said. "How long has your hair been silver?"

"A while."

Candy nodded. "Were you a blonde like Will?"

"Say yes." he heard Mika's voice beside him.

"Yes."

"I see." Candy looked at him for a few minutes. "I should be going." She stood up and started towards the door. "I'm going to recommend that you stay here for a few more days. We could probably move you to your house, but-"

"But what?"

Candy smiled. "It really annoys my mother-in-law having you here." She left the parlor, closing the door behind her.

"Having fun?" Mika asked.

"Thank you for letting me see my family."

"Maybe that was a dream."

Hugh shook his head. "I was dying, wasn't I?"

"Death is a natural occurrence."

"How could you let that happen to me? Where were you when I was chasing after that boy?"

"I was busy."

"You're supposed to protect me."

"You lived, didn't you?" Mika said angrily.

"Yes, because my family made me see that I had something to live for, because Charlie Winslow forgave me."

"Then I have done my job."

"How can you always be right?"

Mika laughed. "Come on, how can you even ask that? Just take a look at me." He stretched his arms out to show off his magnificence.

"Were you like this when you were alive?"

"Oh no, I was much worse. I'm practically sweet now."

"I hadn't noticed."

Mika laughed again. "I was right though, as much as you hate to admit it. You who couldn't understand why I brought you back as a forty three year old father of three. Now do you see? I've given you a second chance at life and people who love you, not just the little Torment Seer, but three children who think the world of you."

"I am beginning to understand." Hugh grumbled.

"You would have been miserable as one of those boys."

"It wouldn't have been all bad. Emma noticed them right away didn't she? Not their gray haired father."

"Of course she did, she's young. But you have qualities that those boys can only aspire to." Mika said. "Hugh you're not young, if we want to get technical you're over one hundred years old. You've had decades to learn about life, you can't put someone like that in the body of a boy. You're compassionate and kind, you're patient and loving, and you're even funny on occasion."

"I'm all that?"

"Yes. And you're good hearted."

Hugh winced. "I wouldn't have liked to be called that back in my time. I was a pretty rough character you know."

"Just because I said you had a good heart doesn't mean you weren't a scoundrel."

"That's right. I had a fearsome reputation."

"Fearsome is a bit strong." Mika said. "But if it makes you feel better, you were a bad apple."

Hugh laughed. "I can't believe I am a policeman with three children. I'm so legitimate."

"Just be yourself Hugh. You have everything you need to make the Torment Seer notice you."

"If she notices."

"You are hopeless. Jason Garrett is far more attractive than that short, skinny, brown haired Hugh MacPherson."

"I was never short!" Hugh cried. "And there was nothing wrong with Hugh MacPherson. I got plenty of compliments back in my day, and plenty of offers too."

"I know, I was there. And those offers weren't exactly from people I would call ladies."

"What do you know? I think there was a lady once, and anyway those were hardworking girls. Just because they-" Hugh stopped talking as the parlor door opened.

Edward looked in curiously. "Just wondering if everything is satisfactory in here? I thought I heard you talking."

"Oh yes I'm fine Mr. Hollis. Sometimes I like to talk to myself, it's a good exercise for the mind." Hugh said feeling embarrassed.

Edward nodded. "I do it myself all the time."

"I bet you do." Mika said quietly.

"You can call me Edward by the way. Old friends need not stand on ceremony."

"Then call me Jason."

Edward nodded and stroked his beard. "Jason it is then. Jason Michael Garrett, a fine name indeed. Toodles." Edward said making a little bow before he backed out of the parlor and shut the door behind him.

"How does he know my middle name?" Hugh turned to ask Mika, but he was already gone.

Chapter 86

The Garrett boys sat once more outside the front door of the house, but the mood was much different than the past few days. I brought out a pitcher of lemonade and they toasted to their father's health.

"And to the Hollis family." Will said raising his glass.

"To the Hollis family." Ryan and Harold repeated. My mind was still replaying the kiss Ryan and I had shared just an hour or so before. It should not have surprised me, it was what I had wanted up until just a few days ago. I had been so convinced that Ryan was Hugh, but now I wasn't so sure. Mika had cautioned me to wait, to give it a little more time. In the back of my mind something told me he was right, but I couldn't put my finger on exactly what he meant.

The front door opened and Candy came bounding outside. "Emma." She grabbed my hand. "Can I talk to you somewhere private?" She dragged me behind the house. "I have to tell you something."

"I have to tell you something as well."

"You do?" She looked surprised. "What is it?"

"Ryan kissed me."

Candy's face lit up. "He did? How was it? Is he Hugh?"

"I don't know. It wasn't what I expected."

"What do you mean?"

"I don't know. I thought I would feel more, I thought I would know right away, but I didn't."

"He didn't kiss like Hugh?"

"The kiss was fine. I don't know, something just doesn't seem right. I can't really say what."

"Maybe it's not him." Candy said.

"I was so sure up until today. I really like him and he is a lot like Hugh."

"But is he?"

"I don't know." I said shaking my head. "Maybe I am thinking about it too much. What did you want to tell me?" I was eager to talk about something else.

"Oh yes. I think that I might be-"

"Emma, I need to see you." Ethan shouted from the corner of the house. "What are you two doing?"

"We were just talking." Candy said.

Ethan looked annoyed. "You can do that later. I have to talk to Emma."

"Me?" I asked. "It seems everyone wants to talk with me today." I met him at the corner of the house.

"Emma I need to ask you a favor." he said. "I am trying to work out a schedule for Jason. I was wondering if you would be able to come home during your break at Thalberg's and make lunch for him. I know you usually stay in the store, but Candy and I have to be at the clinic and-"

"I would be happy to."

"You would?" He seemed surprised. "It's just that I don't think Mother will come home until he's gone and I don't trust Father to be able to cook a meal."

"Ethan I don't mind. You don't have to try and convince me."

"Oh. In that case thank you. Sorry to interrupt." He went back inside.

Once he was out of view I turned back to Candy. "What is it you wanted to tell me?"

"You look happy."

"There's nothing wrong with being happy." I replied. "Now what is it you wanted to tell me? Something about Jason?"

"*Jason?*" she said. "Never mind, it can keep for now. I'll see you later Emma." Candy turned and left me in the backyard wondering what on earth that was all about.

Chapter 87

The next morning Mr. Thalberg could barely wait until we were alone in the store to start talking about what he had seen through his window the day before.

"Emma." he began as soon as his wife had gone upstairs. "I couldn't help but notice what happened in the police station yesterday."

"Chief Garrett is out of the woods. I came to tell Ryan and Will." I said looking down at my counter.

"I know you think I am a nosy old shopkeeper, but I have known you since you were just a little girl and I am happy for you. Ryan is a nice young man, a little quiet, but nice all the same. He's not who I would have picked for you, but there, it's done and that's all I will say about it."

"Nothing has been done. I haven't chosen anyone." I said defensively.

"Oh. I just thought-"

"And what did you mean that he would not have been your choice?"

He shrugged. "What do I ever mean Emma? What do I know about choosing a boy for you? If my wife heard me talking this way she would be furious."

"It's all right. I know you mean well. Who would you have chosen?"

He shook his head. "It doesn't matter. You know better than me."

"I'm not sure I do." I muttered as a customer walked into the store.

At lunchtime Mr. Thalberg was surprised that I would not be joining him and his wife upstairs as I had done for the last few years.

As I was leaving Will was coming out of the police station. He crossed the street and joined me. "Are you going to cook lunch for Papa?"

"Yes."

"Oh good. I think I will join you." he said. "If that's all right."

"Of course it is."

"I should say congratulations to you."

"Congratulations for what?"

"Ryan tells me. Oh I don't know quite how to put this." Will paused and then began again. "He's says you have an understanding between the two of you."

I stopped in the middle of the sidewalk. "What do you mean an understanding?"

Will raised his eyebrows and looked about, several people were staring. "I am just repeating what Ryan said."

"I know of no understanding." I said hotly.

"I'm terribly sorry."

Walking towards us was Senator Brown. He was striding along in his usual arrogant manner. "Oh wonderful." I said under my breath.

"Good gracious how are you young people on this fine day?" He shook Will's hand.

"Excellent Senator." Will said. "My father expects to make a full recovery."

Senator Brown nodded and stroked his beard. "Good news, glad to hear it my boy."

"He's staying with us right now Senator, I am sure he would love a visit from you." I told him.

The Senator leaned back on his heels and narrowed his eyes. "I think I shall wait until he's in his own home Miss Hollis. It sounds as though he will have a lengthy recovery."

"Oh that's a shame, we were all looking forward to seeing you there." I said. "I will let him know that you send your regrets."

The Senator tapped his foot and stared at me.

"That's where we're going right now." Will said. "Emma is going to make him lunch."

"What a delight." Senator Brown said insincerely. He looked at Will. "Actually young man I was coming into town to look for you or one of your brothers."

"Oh?"

"I need one of you to escort me on the campaign trail. I'm going up north, Godforsaken country, and I don't know what I will find."

"Do you expect it to be dangerous?" Will asked.

"I don't know. I just don't know my boy. I haven't been that far north before, not sure what I will find. Might get attacked by a bear." He laughed nervously.

"I don't know anything about bears." Will said. "I'm a city boy."

The Senator's mouth twitched making his beard swivel back and forth. "Young man I am a gubernatorial candidate. I think as the local policeman it is your duty to escort me into a potentially dangerous situation. And seeing that your father is out of danger I see no reason that you should not do your duty, after all it is because of me that you are here in the first place."

"How long is this going to take?" Will asked.

The Senator stamped his foot on the ground. "It will take as long as it takes to convince everyone that I am the best choice to lead this state. And when I am elected governor I promise you will not be forgotten William."

"Please give Papa my best." Will said to me. "I think I had better go."

"That's more like it." said the Senator.

"I'll need to leave Harold a note at the station."

"Let's go then." the Senator said brushing past me.

Will shrugged and looked back as he and the Senator walked away in the opposite direction.

I sighed and continued towards home. Thoughts of the Senator were soon forgotten, but I could hardly forget what Will had said. Ryan and I had an understanding. It had just been one kiss. Had I been willing things in that direction all along? I had never been so confused in all my life. I took a deep breath as I opened the front door to the house, now was the time to shake off all the muddled thoughts and half baked theories that were swirling in my head.

Jason was sitting up in bed reading a book. "Hello."

"Are you hungry?"

"Always."

I smiled, relieved that I could spend an entire hour not thinking about Hugh.

Chapter 88

Hugh leaned over the edge of the bed to watch Emma disappear into the kitchen, the wound in his side smarted and he was forced back onto the pillow. "I'm sure I could have managed to find something."

"Nonsense." she called out. "I don't mind at all." She came back to the parlor. She held up a can of beans. "I'm afraid it's these and a sandwich."

"That's fine."

"Just give me a few minutes. The fire is on so it shouldn't take very long for these to heat." She turned away. The midday light was streaming in the windows, it touched the ends of her light brown hair. Hugh tried leaning forward again but the pain was too much and he slumped back on the pillow.

"How are you feeling?" she asked. He heard a heavy pan being set down on the stove.

"Not bad. I really should be getting home though."

There was a pause before she answered him. "Why? You're no trouble."

"I can't just lay here in your parlor. Your mother moved out because of me."

"She didn't move out, she's just staying with my sister for a bit." Emma said. He heard more clangs and bangs from the kitchen. He closed his eyes and tried to picture her moving efficiently about the room. "Are you sleepy?" Hugh opened his eyes and found her standing next to his bed. She was wearing an apron with snowflakes embroidered on it.

"No, I was just resting my eyes."

She was holding a piece of cheese in her hands, she broke it in two and handed him one half as she sat down. "What are you reading?"

"Oh just something Ryan gave me." he said picking up the book.

Emma's eyes widened. "*The Time Machine*! What do you think of it?"

"I just started it this morning, but I am most intrigued."

She popped the cheese into her mouth and leaned her elbow on the edge of the bed. "I can't imagine what it would be like to travel to other times. If you could go anywhere, to any time, what would it be?"

"I don't know." He had seen plenty of changes in the course of his life and death, but there was that privy closet, the one he had used when he was waiting to come back as Jason. That he would like to see again. Would he live that long? "I don't know. Where would you want to go?"

She smiled and picked absently at the bedcovers. "I heard this thing. Someone told me, I really can't say who, but someone mentioned to me that someday men might be able to walk on the moon."

"Walk on the moon? How is that possible? I've never heard of such a thing, whoever you talked to is obviously a lunatic."

Emma smiled and then laughed. "Yes, they probably are. But I would like to find out for myself."

"I would like to know what sort of fool goes around saying these things." he said eating the cheese.

Emma laughed again, her eyes sparkling. "Oh wouldn't I love to tell you, but I am afraid it's a secret. Keep reading though, it gets even better."

"I will. I haven't anything else to do."

She hesitated. "What else do you like to do?"

"Besides keeping law and order?" Hugh said heroically.

"Yes, although that probably takes up a lot of your time."

"It does. But I'm a terrible homebody I'm afraid. There was a time when I used to dream of getting away. But not anymore, I look forward to getting home every night. I can't think of a better place."

"I'm the same way. I'm sure people think I'm boring."

"You're not boring to me. But-" He hesitated, unsure how far he should take the conversation.

"But what?"

"It does get lonely in that big house. I know I have the boys, but they have their own lives, and-" He stopped. "I'm sorry, you don't want to hear about this."

Emma was watching him. There was a strange look on her face. "I understand, more than you probably realize."

It took everything he had not to jump up and announce who he was. Damn Mika. Emma had been left waiting for four years. But he couldn't say anything about that. He could acknowledge the way she felt and how he felt too. "It's funny how you can have so many people around you and they never really know how you feel inside."

A sad smile spread across her face. She reached her arm out as though she was going to touch his hand and then quickly withdrew it. Outside the window a pair of goldfinches flew by. Slowly Emma lifted her brown eyes and looked at him. It was not as she had viewed him before, as the chief of police or some handsome boy's father, but as Jason. He was about to say something profound with a hint of humor and a dash of romance when she suddenly jumped out of her chair.

"Oh my beans!" She ran out of the room. "They're just about done." she shouted. "As soon as I make the sandwiches I'll bring everything right in."

"I can come in there."

Emma came running across the hall. "Should you be up?"

"Of course. I can't lie in bed all the time."

"Are you sure Ethan would allow it?"

"Absolutely. I'll need a little help though." He pulled off the covers and winced.

"You're in pain."

"No, I am just lamenting having to wear your father's trousers." He looked down at his bare ankles. "I'll have the boys bring me something from home." With considerable effort he swung his legs off the bed, his side pinched and he took a minute to breathe.

"I can get something for you, the boys are all busy at the moment."

"What do you mean?"

"I'll explain it to you in there." she said. "If you insist on eating at the table that is."

"I do." Much to his delight she helped him to his feet. He draped his arm across her shoulder and held onto her hand, leaning a bit more than he really needed to. As he stood Edward's small shirt rode up and he grinned as she had to put her other hand on his bare skin. He glanced at her face and thought he detected the slightest of blushes.

They walked awkwardly into the kitchen. Emma helped him into a chair and set about making two ham sandwiches. She put one in front of him and spooned out a bowl of beans from the pot on the stove. Once a second bowl was filled she put them on the table and sat across from him. She picked up her spoon. "I'll get you some things from home today."

"Just ask Fred."

"Fred?"

"Yes, my butler."

A broad smile spread across Emma's face. "Your butler?"

"Yes. I don't see what's so funny about that."

"You and Senator Brown are the only people I know who have butlers."

"A butler is very useful." Hugh said taking a spoonful of beans. "I had one growing up."

"I shall seek out Fred then."

"Very good. Now what's this about the boys? You said they were busy."

"Oh yes, Will sends his best. He was going to come with me, but we met up with Senator Brown on the way here and he wants Will to come up north with him while he campaigns."

"To do what?"

Emma shrugged. "Protect him from bears I guess."

"Or a rampaging moose." Hugh said eagerly eating his sandwich.

"I think he'll be gone for at least a few days. Ryan is on duty with the sheriff, so that leaves-"

"Harold. Harold is patrolling the town?"

"Yes, he's quite capable."

"I know I just don't like him being on his own." Hugh said. "He's so young."

Emma's face softened. "You know, I had you all wrong."

"What do you mean?"

"When you and the boys first came to town you were so serious."

"I'm not."

She shook her head. "No, not at all."

"It was a lot to take in, a new town, new job, new people. I don't make friends easily, it takes time. Of course when you're stabbed in the side and dependent on others to take care of you that speeds up the process."

"You've had a lot of pain in your life, haven't you?"

"How do you know that?"

"I can see it in your eyes. You have an old soul."

He suppressed a giggle. She was noticing him, she was finally noticing him. "I have had a lot happen to me."

"It must have been hard losing your wife and having three small boys to raise."

"It was. But I think I did a good job." He was beginning to believe Mika's story about himself.

"You did. Do you ever think you'll marry again?"

Hugh's heart was beating fast. "Possibly."

She nodded and took a spoonful of beans. Was she interested in his marital status or was she just making conversation? "You said you had a butler growing up. Where was that?"

Hugh paused in mid chew and tried to remember. "Uh, Pennsylvania."

"Oh. And do you have any brothers or sisters?"

Why was she asking him these kinds of questions? "No."

"Ryan said you were orphaned and raised by your uncle."

They had been discussing him. He wasn't sure if that was good or bad. Had she been curious about him or just looking for ways to draw out his son? "You spend a lot of time with Ryan."

He saw with dismay Emma blush. "Yes. We have a lot in common."

What about him? He had everything in common with her. "I'm glad he's made friends here."

"You have too." she said pushing away her lunch.

"Not really."

"Ethan was devastated when we found you."

Good old Ethan. "He is a friend, and Candy too."

"And me." She stared at him. "I should probably get back to work. I'll stop by your house and ask for Fred."

"Thank you." he said gratefully. "Can you help me back to the parlor? I'm tired." She helped him across the hall. He was feeling weary and the lunch in his belly was making him sleepy.

He managed to get into bed by himself. His side was hurting more than it had all day. He winced. Emma shook her head. "You should have stayed in here." She pulled the covers up around his shoulders.

"I know."

"I'll bring you some of your clothes tonight when I get home from work."

Without thinking he grabbed her hand. "Thank you for lunch and keeping me company."

"You're welcome. Now I think you should sleep. I'll see you tonight."

"Goodbye." he said yawning. She wasn't gone for more than a minute before he was asleep.

Chapter 89

"Fred?" I asked timidly as an older man with a stoop and a balding head answered the door at Brown Park.

"Yes Miss?"

I had seen him before when Senator Brown lived there and after the Garretts moved in, but I never knew his name. "I'm here to get some of Jason's, I mean Mr. Garrett's clothes, he's staying with us right now, that is I mean he's staying-"

"I am aware of the arrangement Miss Hollis. I have already prepared a bag for Mr. Garrett. I have been waiting for his sons to take it to him." Fred coughed. "Won't you come in?"

He opened the door and I followed him into the house. I glanced inside the parlor, Will was there looking into a large blue bag.

I stopped in the doorway. "I thought you were going north."

He looked up. "I am. I'm just on my way out in fact. It took some convincing to make the Senator realize that I might need to pack some clothes."

"How long will you be gone?"

"About a week."

Beside me I heard Fred clear his throat. "Good luck Will."

"Thank you. Take good care of Papa for me."

Fred cleared his throat a little louder. I gave a little wave to Will and followed the butler upstairs stopping at a large door at the end of the hallway. "The bag is on the bed, if you would kindly make sure I haven't forgotten anything."

"You want me to go in there and look?"

Fred smiled and turned the doorknob, the door swung open, creaking slightly. "I'll be downstairs if you need me." He turned on his heel and walked away.

I tiptoed inside feeling as though I was trespassing. There was a large bed in the middle of the room, on top of the quilted bedspread was a canvas bag.

"Want to know what's in there?" a voice said behind me. I spun around and found Ma Granger leering at me.

"Why do you have to sneak up on me all the time?"

"What else have I got to do? There's lots of interesting things in that bag."

"Like what?"

"Undergarments."

"I don't want to see those."

"Oh don't you then?"

"No. I am just doing the man a favor. I have to be getting back to work."

"You don't want to visit with your old Ma Granger do you?" She scratched her bosom.

"I don't have time." As we spoke I began to look around Jason's bedroom. I had never been upstairs in Senator Brown's house before. It was a large room with an arched window that looked out towards the sea. I was surprised to see there was a telescope on a tripod in front of it.

"What's this?" It was brand new, all the fittings were shiny brass.

"It's a telescope, ain't you never seen one before?" Ma asked.

"Is this Mr. Garrett's?"

"Yep."

"Does he use it?"

"Yep."

Around the room bookshelves rose halfway up the walls. I quickly scanned the spines. I recognized many of the titles, some I had even recommended to Ryan. "Are these his books?"

Ma looked at me and squinted. "Yes indeed. Are you feeling all right? This is his room you know."

"I know. I am surprised, that's all." Above the bookshelves were several awards and commendations in black frames, they were from various military and police organizations. On the other side of the room was a bureau covered in framed photographs.

"You sure are curious today." Ma said as she followed me.

The pictures were of the boys at various ages. A large photo near the back of the collection was of Jason and his sons in front of the police station here in town. They were standing with their arms around each other.

"I remember this. I was watching from Thalberg's window. Jason was shouting at everyone to step back." I said pointing to the picture.

"I wouldn't know about that, there's black magic in pictures like that."

"No it's just science, you see-"

"I would hush up if I were you, someone's-" Ma never finished her sentence.

"What are you doing in my father's room?" Ryan's voice was suddenly behind me. I threw my hands up in the air. My purse, which I had been carrying, flew out of my hands. I had not bothered to close it and the contents rose up as though being carried by a strong wind. My wallet, keys to the store, and most importantly Hugh's watch sailed into the air before landing with a thump on the wood floor. The watch ended up a few inches from Ryan's toes.

My heart was pounding in my ears. I bent down to pick it up when I heard another voice. "Emma, don't."

I looked up and saw my father standing in the doorway. Ma Granger slapped her thigh and grinned. "Edward Hollis, you old dog! It must be my lucky day."

Chapter 90

Hugh was just starting to get into a deep sleep when he felt someone poking him in the shoulder.

"Are you asleep?"

He opened one eye. Mika was sitting next to his bed. He shut his eye and was just beginning to slip back into dreamy unconsciousness when he felt himself being poked again.

"Hugh, wake up."

"What? Believe it or not I am trying to sleep."

"I know."

"Then what is it?"

"I'm bored."

Hugh groaned and opened his eyes. "That's not my problem. Don't you have others to Watch?"

"Yes I'm doing it right now. One of them is taking a bath, another one is in school, and she's taking notes just like I told her to."

Hugh sighed and sat up. "Can't you just let me sleep?"

"Oh you can do that any old time."

"That's because you don't remember sleeping. I used to feel that way, but not anymore." He yawned. Maybe Mika would just go away.

"You know Ryan thinks he's in love with the Torment Seer."

"I suspected as much." Hugh said. He more than suspected it, he had heard the boys whispering about it in the days before he was stabbed.

"What are you going to do about it?"

"What can I do? I'm not going to fight my own son for her. I'm being myself just like you told me to. Didn't you think we had a nice lunch today? I thought I was quite witty."

"You were delightful." Mika said. "Nice bit with having her help you into the kitchen."

"That was a mistake, she was right I wasn't ready to move, my side hurts like hell."

"That's a shame. But do you think that she feels the same way about Ryan?"

Hugh hesitated. This was possibly his least favorite conversation of all time. He had watched for months while Emma had slowly grown closer to Ryan. He had tried everything he could think of to get her attention, he even convinced Mika to make him a baseball phenomenon in order to impress her, but she hadn't even looked his way. In the back of his mind he knew she believed that Ryan was him.

"Why are you asking me this?" he grumbled. It had been a glorious day so far, the last thing he wanted was Mika ruining it.

"Because right now the Torment Seer is at your house retrieving your clothes, and she's just dropped your watch on the floor, right at Ryan's feet."

Hugh struggled to understand what Mika was trying to tell him. "And?"

"And if Ryan picks up that watch it's all over for you."

"Even if it's by accident?"

"Yes, even so. Ryan merely has to touch it and you are-"

"Somewhere I don't want to be." Hugh said. "Then why are you here? Why don't you do something about it?"

"I have actually. I've sent one of my favorite people over there to straighten things out." Mika said brightly.

"Who's that?"

"Edward of course."

"Edward Hollis?" Hugh cried. "What can he do?"

Mika smiled wickedly. "Oh you have no idea what Edward is capable of."

Chapter 91

I stood motionless. Hugh's watch was at Ryan's feet, the chain snaking its way around his shoe. If he touched it there would be no going back. I couldn't be sure that even if he accidently stepped on the chain it wouldn't count. I was playing by Mika's rules.

"Mr. Hollis, what are you doing here?" Ryan looked perplexed.

Father stared anxiously at the watch and then cleared his throat. "Ryan don't move a muscle." His voice echoed and was unnaturally loud.

I looked at Ryan and then realized what had happened. He was standing perfectly still, as though he was frozen in time. His eyes were looking at Father with a glassy blankness, it reminded me of a china doll I used to have when I was a girl. I touched his arm, his muscles were taut and unyielding.

"What have you done?" I cried. Father's eyes shifted towards me, there was a strength and power in them I had never seen before. It was frightening.

"Emma, pick up the watch. Be very careful it doesn't touch him, especially the chain."

I hesitated. "What did you do? How? What are you?" I looked at Ma Granger who was standing off to the side with one hand on her hip while she used the other one to pick at her teeth.

"Emma just pick up the watch. I will explain everything to you later." Father said. There was a note of authority in his voice I found hard to resist. I bent down and dragged the watch across the floor, away from Ryan's foot, before picking it up.

"Very good, now pick up the rest of your things and put them back in your purse."

I did as I was told. "Now are you going to tell me what's going on?"

"Later." He licked his lips nervously. "Ma, how are things looking downstairs?"

"You can see her?"

Father ignored my question. Ma Granger stuck her nose in the air and sniffed like a hunting dog. "Nothing to worry about Edward. No one's coming. Don't worry I'll let ya know. You don't think your ole' Ma Granger would let you down?"

"You *can* see her. Why didn't you ever tell me?"

Ma snickered. "I told you there was a liar, didn't you ever suspect it was your own Pa?"

"No I didn't." I had a million questions tumbling around in my head.

"Never mind that now. " Father said. "I'll explain everything later, but right now you have a chance to give Ryan the watch, if you want to."

"What?" I clutched my purse. "You just told me to pick it up."

"Yes because I wanted it out of harm's way. Now that we have the situation under control you can decide."

My mouth dropped open. "Then you know about Hugh? You know about the watch, the challenge. You must know about Mika too."

"Of course I do. All you have to do is put the watch into Ryan's hand, when I bring him around he'll have it and if he's Hugh you'll know. This could end today."

I hesitated. I could feel the watch through the leather of my purse. There was a part of me that was tempted to do it. I could risk it all and just make my choice. Ryan and I were similar, we had similar interests, and he was a little like Hugh.

"You were sure it was him just a few days ago." I heard Father saying. "When did things change?"

"The night of the party." I said. "You know that dinner party that Jason gave, the one that never really happened?"

"The beautiful one came to see you." Ma said.

I smiled at her. "Yes Mika came to see me and he told me not to make a decision yet, to give it more time. And then he, I mean Jason, was hurt and

I haven't really had time to think about it. And part of me is glad of the distraction because I can't figure it out."

"Then he's not Hugh?" Father asked.

I looked at Ryan, his expression was still frozen in the shock of seeing my father. It would all be so easy. It could be over in a matter of seconds.

"Emma, is he Hugh?" Father asked.

"I, I don't think so. Part of me wants him to be Hugh, but the other part-"

"The other part what?" Ma asked excitedly.

I looked at Father. "Do you know? Do you know which one he is?"

"That is irrelevant Emma."

"No it's not. How come everyone knows except me?"

"It's not exactly everyone." Father replied.

"Yes it is. Ethan knows, Ma knows, and now I find that you do too. I can't even begin to understand how, and of course there's Mika-"

"I don't think he really counts on your tally." Father said. "And besides what does it matter if we know? It's what you think that matters. And this young man isn't him?"

"No." I said regrettably. I liked Ryan, he was interesting and smart and I even liked the way his auburn hair hung over his brown eyes. But he wasn't Hugh, something inside me, or maybe my own Watcher told me so. There was a nagging thought in the back of my mind. I couldn't quite put my finger on what it was.

"Very well then." Father said. "Shall we bring him back?"

"We? Shouldn't that be you?"

"This is one of my favorite parts." Ma said. "I love the look on their face when they've realized something has happened but they don't know what."

"Has he done this before?"

Ma eyed Father and laughed. "Oh sure, did it to the old Senator once."

I looked at Father in astonishment. "Once we leave here you have to tell me what's going on."

"I will. Move back to where you were Emma." I returned to where I had been standing. He nodded his head and Ryan snapped back to life as though he had just been woken up. "Good afternoon." Father said jovially.

"Hello Father. I was just picking up a bag of clothes for Jason. I think he's getting tired of wearing your things." I said trying to laugh, my voice sounded nervous and false.

Ryan looked at Father and me in bewilderment. "I thought." His voice trailed off as he looked at the purse tucked neatly under my arm.

"Is everything all right my boy?" Father asked.

Ryan pushed his hair off his face. "I don't know."

"Ah well, I think there's something going around." Father said. "Maybe you've caught it, you'd better get your rest son."

"Perhaps so." Ryan said. "So you're here to pick up clothes for my father?"

"Yes, they're in that bag on the bed."

"I'll take them to him right now."

"Are you sure?"

He blinked and took a deep breath. "Yes. I think I need some fresh air." He picked up the bag and started for the door. Suddenly he turned back and looked at me. "I hope I'll see you later Emma. I would like very much to talk to you about something."

"Oh, all right."

"Goodbye Mr. Hollis."

"Good afternoon." Father said tipping his hat genteelly.

"I bet he's going to propose to you." Ma said clapping her hands together.

"Don't say that."

"Ladies, I think my work here is done." Father turned and started to walk out of the bedroom.

I grabbed his arm. "Don't you dare walk away from me Edward Hollis. You owe me an explanation and you're going to give it to me right now."

Father looked surprised. "You don't expect me to tell you right here do you?"

"Yes I do. You are not getting away with this anymore. I want to know what's going on with you."

"Very well. If you *must* know I'll tell you. Let's go somewhere else though."

"Fine." I said angrily.

"I've never seen this side of you before Emma."

"Just tell me what's going on." Behind us I heard the swish of Ma Granger's skirts.

"Are you sure you want to hear this?" she whispered in my ear. "You might not want to know about the other one."

I stopped and looked back at her. "What other one?"

Ma's wrinkled face broke into a smile. "The one that follows Edward. He's ever so gruesome, looks a lot like my first husband." She laughed and put her bony hand on my shoulder.

I looked at Father. "What is she talking about?"

"I'll tell you about it when we get out of here." He picked up his pace and we rushed downstairs and outside. Ma Granger followed us onto the porch, cackling all the way.

Chapter 92

Hugh couldn't sleep after Mika left. What if Emma gave Ryan his watch? It could all be over. He heard the front door open. Ryan was suddenly in the parlor. Was he coming to announce that he and Emma were in love?

"I've brought you some clothes from home." Ryan said.

"Oh? I thought Emma was getting those for me."

"She was. I just saw her at home. It was so odd, her father was there too."

"Oh?" Hugh tried to look surprised. "Did, did Emma give you anything?"

"Give me anything?" Ryan frowned. "No, why?"

Hugh breathed a sigh of relief. Whatever Mika had sent Edward there to do it must have worked. It wasn't over yet.

"Something happened there." Ryan began. "I don't know. It was strange, have you ever had, have you- Oh never mind."

"What is it?" Hugh asked. He was beginning to get curious. What sort of odd behavior had Edward unleashed this time?

"I just felt like I lost time or something. It was as though I went to sleep for a few minutes and when I woke everything was as it appeared, but it felt like something had happened that I didn't know about. I'm not making any sense I know." Ryan's face was pale.

To his own surprise Hugh found himself putting a hand on his son's forehead. "Maybe you're coming down with something."

"Maybe."

"Thanks for bringing my clothes."

"You're welcome. Do you want me to help you change?"

"No, I'll do it later."

"What do you think of Emma Hollis?" Ryan asked suddenly.

The house was quiet except for the steady tick of the mantle clock. "She's a nice girl." he said with a shrug.

"She's a lot more than that." Ryan said. "But I suppose you hadn't noticed. You're so much older than she is."

"That's true. Does she feel the same way about you?"

Ryan's face turned pink. "I think so."

Hugh tried to keep his expression calm. Inside his stomach felt like jelly. "What are you going to do about it?"

"I'm not sure."

"Not sure? I thought you said she felt the same way." His heart was banging loudly in his ears as he spoke, he was surprised Ryan couldn't hear it.

"Sometimes she seems really interested in me, and then other times I'm not so sure."

"Really?" Hugh tried not to sound hopeful.

"There are times she looks at me as though she expects me to take a mask off and turn into someone else."

"How odd."

"I think she's not sure how she feels."

"Probably."

"What should I do Papa?"

Hugh sighed and allowed his pulse to return to normal. He brushed Ryan's hair off his forehead and smiled. What a relief to not be that age anymore. "Just be yourself Ryan, if she loves you she'll let you know. That's all any of us can do."

Chapter 93

"Don't you have to go back to work?" Father said as we stopped at the end of Brown Lane. "Isn't this your lunch break?"

I had forgotten about that. "Yes but-" I couldn't think of anything else to say.

"But nothing. We both have to get back to work. I'll talk with you tonight."

"No you won't, you'll pretend none of this happened. You'll tell me it was all in my head, or I dreamt it."

Father smiled and patted my hand. "Emma, I promise I won't. You've seen too much here today for me to deny anything. I'll answer all of your questions. But right now you'd better get back to Thalberg's."

I sighed. He was right. "Tonight then."

Father nodded. "Tonight. Your mother is still at Eve's so we can talk without her hearing."

"All right. You promise you'll be there?"

"Yes. Now you'd better get going."

I set off for work not quite believing him. When I got to Thalberg's the store was already reopened after our lunch break.

"I'm sorry I'm late." I said as I rushed in and shoved my purse underneath the counter.

"It's not a problem." Mr. Thalberg said. "How is Chief Garrett?"

"He's doing fine."

"He is a nice man, no?" He looked over the top of his newspaper.

"Yes he is." My mind was still reeling from Father's display of talents. He was obviously some kind of Seer, but what kind?

"I like him." Mr. Thalberg was saying.

"Who?" I asked. How was Father able to control Ryan?

"Chief Garrett of course. You are distracted this afternoon."

"Oh yes him. I'm sorry I am more than distracted. But Jason, yes he is very agreeable." I smiled as I thought of our lunch earlier in the day. "Actually right now he is the one person I look forward to seeing."

Mr. Thalberg set his paper down and smiled. "Is that so?"

"Yes, he's the only person who isn't full of complications. He's just himself."

The day dragged by, when it was finally time to leave I hurried home. Father's barber shop was dark as I passed. He wasn't going to be there, I just knew it. I was already forming a plan in my head, if he wasn't home I was going straight to Eve's and then door to door if necessary until I found him. He wasn't going to get out of it this time.

I ran the last few steps, flung open the door and rushed into the kitchen panting. Father and Ethan were setting the table for dinner.

"Good evening Emma." Father said.

"Hello." I said cautiously. "Did you forget our meeting tonight?"

"Of course not."

"Really?" I asked suspiciously. "You're going to explain what happened this afternoon?"

"Yes, I told you I would. I asked Ethan here precisely for that reason."

"And I'm checking on him." Ethan said pointing at the half open parlor door with a fork.

"I want the truth this time."

Father chuckled. "Oh Emma you are a delight." He shook his head and continued to set the table. There was a pot boiling on the stove, it smelled like some kind of stew.

"Now I know what I can give Jason for lunch tomorrow. How is he?" I was thinking I might pop in for a second.

"He's sleeping right now. I've given him some medicine for the pain, but he's doing much better. He's a fighter that's for sure." Ethan said.

"Now children, let's have dinner and I will tell you all about myself." Father said. He spooned out the stew while I found half a loaf of bread in the pantry along with some butter. As we sat down and waited for our dinner to cool Father looked up in the air, his eyes darting back and forth. "Where to begin, where to begin?"

"Why not tell me what you did to Ryan this afternoon?"

"What are you talking about?" Ethan asked. "What did he do?"

Father scratched his beard. "I'll get to that but first-"

I wasn't waiting any longer for the truth. "You're a Seer aren't you? Don't deny it this time. I know you are, you can see Ma Granger and you could see Hugh and Mika too."

"What?" Ethan cried.

Father shrugged his shoulders and smiled innocently. "I am what is known as a Seer."

"And?"

"And what?"

"And what kind of Seer? Why haven't you told us this before? You used to take a switch to Ethan and me when we were younger. I got punished for seeing Aunt Linda's dead son, you took me to her house and I had to apologize and tell her I was making it up, you could see him all the while couldn't you?" I said pointing my finger.

Ethan's mouth dropped open. "Is this true?"

Father grimaced and stirred his stew nervously with his spoon. "So many questions."

"Start answering."

"I, I am what's known as an Uncommon Seer." he said loosening the knot in his tie. "Apparently it's very rare, at least according to Mika. He's the same kind. When Senator Brown showed me this house. I saw Hugh first and then outside I met Mika, he introduced himself to me."

"Right in front of the Senator?" Ethan asked.

"He was able to control the Senator. Brown never knew what happened."

"Just like you did to Ryan this afternoon?"

"Yes." Father said tapping his spoon on the bowl. "I didn't want to, but I had to, it was for you Emma."

"Mika told you what kind of Seer you were?" Ethan asked.

"Yes. He was quite interested in me." Father said proudly. "He said he had never met another Uncommon before. We talked for quite a while, comparing notes, life stories, that sort of thing."

"How did he know you were Uncommon?" I asked.

Father shrugged. "I'm not sure. Mika is extraordinarily gifted, far more than me. But then he's had a lot more years of experience than I, and he is dead, a definite advantage." Father swallowed a spoonful of stew and seemed to relax. "It might be of course because of Henry Gage."

"Henry Gage?" Ethan asked. "Wasn't that the name of Mother's father? He's dead, isn't he?"

Father put down the spoon and wiped his mouth with his napkin. "Yes that's him, this is where I need to go back." He sighed and scratched his nose. "Like you children I had always been different growing up. I could see dead people. I could talk to them. I could see other things too, beings that were not human. I found I could tell them what to do too, but I never liked to, it didn't seem right. You see my father was a Seer too."

"Grandpa Hollis?"

"Yes. But unlike both of you I never had to hide, we were very open about it in my family. Most of us have gifts. My brother Egbert introduced me to your mother. There might have been something between them, but I am afraid when I saw her I fell completely in love. She was the most perfect girl I had ever met, still is." Father closed his eyes and smiled wistfully.

"Egbert is like you Ethan. He sees shapes and shadows." he continued. "He told Elsay about it. I don't think she really believed him, but soon she began seeing more and more of me and less and less of him, it was a wonderful time then. She brought me home to meet her family, and that's when I made a disastrous mistake."

"What happened?"

"I walked into her house and found there were dead people Tormenting there, a man and a woman, they had been hung. I could tell by their crooked necks. The woman told me that Elsay's father was not a very nice man." Father took a sip of water. "You see Henry was exceedingly cruel, he used to do things to your mother and your aunt Linda, unspeakable things. When I was alone with Elsay I asked her about it."

"What did she say?" Ethan asked.

"She denied it of course, and then she wanted to know who had told me this. I told her about the dead man and woman and you know your mother, she got very upset. She said there were no such things as ghosts. She threw me out of the house. I didn't speak to her for a month. But I kept coming back at night. The man and sometimes the woman would come to the basement window and tell me about what was happening inside."

"So what did you do?" I asked.

"I killed him. I killed her father."

Ethan dropped his spoon on the table. "What did you say?"

"I went to see Henry when he was alone, it was hard to do because there were always others at home, but the dead ones helped me. I told him I knew what he was doing, he denied it of course, but I persisted in my own way and made him confess. There was a struggle and I picked up something, a marble bookend I believe, and bashed him over the head. He died right then and there." Father said coldly. "I would do it again if I had the chance."

"You killed him? But you were never in prison." I said.

"I know. I was never caught. The dead ones helped me bury him in the cellar. That was no easy task. Of course I thought it was over, but it turns out I had created a Tormented Soul out of him, but instead of haunting the house he died in, he haunts me."

"What do you mean he haunts you?"

"He follows me around and talks to me, mostly cursing. I can't blame him, I did crush his skull." Father said matter-of-factly.

"Is he here right now?"

"He's outside. But he still follows me when I leave. Mika showed me how to keep him out of the house. I told you he's remarkably gifted. Henry can't hurt you Emma, he was a deplorable human being but all his anger is directed at me now."

"Is that why you're always looking over your shoulder and muttering to yourself?"

"Yes, it's mostly because of him, but I see other things too."

"But what about Mother? Does she know what you did?" Ethan asked.

"Yes. Of course, she and her family noticed right away that Henry was missing. No one had any idea what happened to him. After a few months passed I took a chance and called on her. She was much changed, she was happier than I had ever seen her. I knew then that I had done the right thing. We began to pick up where we left off, it was then that I made the mistake of telling her what I had done and that her father was haunting me. I've never seen her so frightened in all my life. She realized that wherever I was, so was her father. I thought I would lose her that day."

"How could she marry you knowing all that?" I asked.

"Because she loved me."

I found myself smiling. "I knew you loved each other, but I guess I really never thought it was like that. Mother told me once that there was something about you, something she had to decide if she could live with, that was it."

Father nodded. "Yes it was. Now can you understand why she doesn't like to talk about ghosts and dead people coming back to haunt the living? Every time that she hears you talk like that it reminds her that Henry is nearby, a man that she hated, a man that took so much from her. I prayed that when we had children you would not inherit the family gift, we had five in total, three of you lived. Unfortunately Eve was the only one spared."

"But you beat us." Ethan said.

"I know, I know." Father said looking down. "I regret that, I should have told you the truth, but your mother was so adamant, she didn't want Seers in her house. She was so frightened that you would be able to see him, that somehow he could hurt you."

"But why can't I see him? He's a Tormented Soul, isn't he?" I asked.

"I didn't know why until I met Mika. He says Henry and I are locked together in our own special sort of Torment. His punishment is now and immediate, mine will come later. He says you can't see that sort of thing Emma."

"Can you see him Ethan?" I asked.

"I've thought from time to time I've seen something, but what I see is so indistinct, there are no definite forms, nothing recognizable. I can't tell where one being begins and the other one ends."

"Are you scared of when you die Father?"

"Do you mean because I will have to pay for what I did? I took a life and I will deal with the consequences then and there. I don't regret it, I never will. Your mother and her sister didn't deserve that life. Mika says my Watcher probably told me to kill him."

"Then you know about Watchers?" I asked.

"Yes. I know about everything."

A thought struck me like a blow to the head. "Oh God, you came into my room one morning and Hugh was in there-" I felt my face turning red. "He was in my, I can't say it. Oh God. You heard everything we said."

Father smirked. "Yes I am afraid I heard and saw a few things a father shouldn't have, it's the plague of being a Seer. What's the harm Emma?"

"The harm is that you saw me and him. Oh God. Why didn't you tell me?"

"I wasn't concerned. Hugh is a nice enough fellow. I thought he was a fine choice for you, expect for the dead part. His former profession isn't exactly admirable, but I'm not in a position to judge people."

"But you wanted me to marry Jeremy."

"Yes, because I thought you had no future with Hugh. But now everything has changed."

"How come Hugh didn't know you could see him? Or did he?"

"I think he suspected something from time to time, but remember when you came here you were twelve years old, a novice. I arrived at the age of forty three and I had had a lot more time to perfect my skills at *not* Seeing."

"But-" Ethan stopped. "I have so many questions I don't know where to begin. Does Mother know about Hugh and Mika?"

"No." Father answered. "She doesn't want to know. She knows the rumors about this house, that it is haunted, but she doesn't want to know if it's true. It's better for her that way."

"Is that how you know so much about what is going on in town?" Ethan asked.

"Yes. There are more beings in this town than you can imagine. Of course one of my best sources of information is someone I call Mr. Mason."

"You've mentioned him before, who is he?"

"That bricklayer up near Eve's house."

"The bricklayer! He never tells me anything except how he died." I said.

Father smiled. "It was a brick of his own making."

"I know."

"I have ways of making them tell me what I want to know. I don't like to use beings like that, but I will if I have to. He's the one who told me that the boy who stabbed Jason had left town. He'll let me know if he comes back."

"Ma Granger said you've controlled the Senator." I said.

"Once or twice. Sometimes I just can't stand listening to that man talk. I give myself a little break, look around the house, maybe have a glass of wine, that was years ago though."

Ethan and I were silent, our dinner barely touched. Father leaned back in his chair and glanced at the window. I turned around and looked outside. "He's there?"

"Yes. He's always out there looking in." Father stood up. "Now children let's get these dishes washed."

Chapter 94

Hugh kept as quiet as possible in the darkness of the parlor. He could not believe what he had just heard. Edward was an Uncommon Seer, like Mika. They were so completely different, it didn't seem possible.

He had always suspected that Edward could see him. There had been too many coincidences over the years. Edward had always made a point to not let Hugh walk through him, and there had been the time that Hugh had locked Eve and Scott in the bedroom. Edward had not believed they were trapped until Hugh said aloud what he had done.

It all made sense now. He pulled the covers around his shoulders and closed his eyes. He wished he could stay in this house forever. He smiled to himself, he had been trapped inside for decades, wanting nothing more than to get out, and now he longed to stay.

After Edward finished talking Hugh heard the dinner plates being cleared. A few minutes later Ethan crept into the parlor. "Did you hear all that?" he whispered.

Hugh laid perfectly still and said nothing.

"I think you're awake."

Hugh kept quiet.

"I hope you heard every word." Ethan said as he slipped out. Hugh heard the front door open and close.

He looked at the dull floral wallpaper in the hallway that had been hung years before. From the kitchen Edward said goodnight to Emma. Hugh held his breath, a second later she emerged from the kitchen. She lingered for a moment and then stepped into the parlor.

Because he was in a darkened room he knew he could keep his eyes open and she would not see he was awake. Part of him wished she would jump on the bed, tear off the covers and then his clothes and do what she wanted with him. The chances of that happening were slim, but he enjoyed the thought anyway. She stayed a second longer and then backed away, shutting the door quietly behind her.

Chapter 95

I was still thinking of everything Father said while I was at work the next day. My mind kept reviewing things that had happened over the years, every unexplained event in our family suddenly made sense. There was so much I could have shared with him. I refused to think about what he had heard or seen between Hugh and myself. I knew that he had looked in our room while Hugh was in bed next to me.

I sighed and looked at the clock. It was just past ten. I sighed again, it was hours until lunch time. I found my mind constantly jumping ahead, thinking of what I would say to Jason. It would be such a relief to see him and forget about everything else.

"Is everything all right?" Mrs. Thalberg asked. She was dusting a display case.

"Yes. I am just jittery today."

She smiled. "You are like that a lot lately."

"I know."

"I was like that when Elijah was courting me." She glanced at her husband who was helping a customer at the front of the store.

"I'm not being courted."

"No?" she looked surprised. "I thought Ryan Garrett was your beau."

"No he's not." I tapped my fingers on the counter. "I thought he might have been at one time, but not anymore."

"Oh that's understandable. I liked another boy before Elijah, sometimes it just takes a while."

"Too long." I muttered.

"Are you going home to make lunch for the Chief today?"

"Yes."

"He's feeling better?"

"Yes, he's getting better. He's so lucky, he was on our parlor floor for hours before anyone found him. Candy said it's a miracle he lived."

"Is that so?" Mrs. Thalberg said. "He is a lucky man then."

Thankfully the store got busier and time passed quickly. Mr. Thalberg locked the front door after I slipped outside for my lunch hour. I looked across the street and saw Harold at his father's desk. His head was bent over some papers. I briefly considered inviting him along, there was a chance he was Hugh, but somehow I couldn't make myself walk across the road.

I continued on my way. As I passed by Father's barber shop I glared at him through the front window. He waved at me with his razor. When I arrived home I found Jason in bed reading his book.

"Hello." I said.

He set the book aside. "Hello." He turned on his side and leaned on his elbow, wincing.

"Don't hurt yourself."

"I won't. Dr. Candy was here earlier, she put that stew on the stove for you."

"She did? That was nice of her."

"I was thinking of getting it myself."

"You will not. I saw you make that face just now, you're still in a lot of pain, aren't you?"

He bit his lower lip, his gray eyes hooded by his thick lashes. "I suppose I am hurting just a little."

I took my sweater off and went into the kitchen. Last night's stew was simmering on the stove. I put some in a bowl and brought it to him. "Be careful it's very hot." I said grabbing one of Mother's fancy little pillows to put underneath.

He set the bowl in front of him and stirred it with his spoon. I went back across the hall to get myself some. I returned to the parlor and sat next to him.

447

"There's bread too." I offered.

He shook his head. "This is enough. I don't do anything, you can't work up an appetite when you're stuck in bed all day."

"It's that boring, huh?"

"Yes. I love to read, but it's hard to concentrate in here. I need fresh air. It reminds me of-" He stopped and looked at me.

"When you were a prison guard?"

"A what?"

"Harold told me that you worked at a prison once."

"Oh yes I did. I had nearly forgotten. I was thinking of something else, but that is a fitting analogy."

"I didn't realize how much you liked to read until yesterday, your bedroom is full of books."

He smiled and took a spoonful of stew. "So Fred let you upstairs?"

"Yes. I am not sure why, he had the bag all packed. But I'm glad. Your room was very interesting, not what I expected."

"Did the maid forget to make the bed?"

"You have a maid too?" I asked. "Do you ever have to lift a finger?"

"Preferably no." he said with a smirk.

"The bed was made. I was talking about the books and the telescope."

"Oh that. It makes a useful tool when you're the chief of police."

"It's for looking at the stars, not people. And besides, you had it at the window overlooking the water."

"Maybe I like to look at the lobsters."

I laughed and dug into my stew. We ate for a few minutes in a pleasant silence, the spoons gently dinging the bowls. Outside the leaves rustled and a chickadee sang its staccato call.

"That was delicious." Jason said.

"You can thank Margaret Cooper." I took his bowl and Mother's frilly pillow.

"I will."

I brought the dishes into the kitchen. When I returned he was sitting up with the covers partly pushed off. I hoped he didn't need to use the chamber pot.

"What's the matter?" I said feeling nervous.

"Can I ask you a favor?"

"Yes."

"It's rather silly." he said, his face turning a shade of pink.

"I like silly things."

"Would you read to me from *The Time Machine*, just a few pages?"

"Of course I would."

I grabbed the book from the table next to him and sat down. I opened to where he had folded a corner of the page and began to read.

"I'm sorry." Jason interrupted. "But I can't really hear you that well. Can you move a little closer?"

"Really?" I thought I had been speaking clearly. I pulled my chair closer towards him. "Is that better?"

He wrinkled his nose. "Maybe just a tad more?"

I scooted my chair nearer. I was so close I was forced to rest my elbows on the bed. "How's that?"

"Oh much better. I can hear you perfectly now." He leaned back and closed his eyes.

I continued reading until the clock struck the hour. "It can't be." I said glancing at the mantle. I closed the book. "I'm afraid I have to go."

"I know. But thank you Emma. It was so nice to listen to your voice."

"Really?" I stood up. "I could read some more to you after supper."

"If you don't want to-"

"But I do." I said. "But now I have to fly. Goodbye Jason."

"Goodbye." We both stared at each other and I was aware of an uneasy silence hanging in the air.

"See you later." I mumbled as I rushed outside. I was going to be late again. I hurried into town. I had only a few hundred yards to go when I saw Ryan coming towards me. He smiled and gave me a little wave.

"Good afternoon."

"Yes, hello." I answered. "I'm late for work."

"Oh you had to make lunch for Papa today, didn't you? He can be so demanding." he said catching my arm. I looked up the road and saw a customer entering Thalberg's. Late two days in a row.

"He's not demanding." I argued. "He's perfectly agreeable."

"Oh really? I see he's charmed you."

I didn't answer him.

"I was hoping we could have that talk soon."

"What talk?" I couldn't imagine what he was referring to.

"Yesterday when you were at my house, I told you I wanted to talk to you. Don't you remember?" He looked hurt.

"Oh yes." Yesterday felt like a thousand years ago. I had completely forgotten until now. "I'm really late for work Ryan."

"I know. I'll let you go. But I want to see you as soon as I can. I want to talk about the future."

I swallowed hard. "I'll have to get back to you on that. Um, listen I've really got to go. I'll see you later." I ran towards the store without daring to look back.

Chapter 96

Hugh picked up his copy of *The Time Machine* and flipped through the pages. He set it aside, he wouldn't read any further until she got back tonight. He closed his eyes and tried to hear her voice in his head. When he had been dead Emma would sometimes read to him in the attic.

He smiled to himself as he replayed his little trick of pretending to not be able to hear in order for her to come closer. There was some risk involved, she might think he was infirmed, but it had been worth it. It was all he could do not to pull her into the bed next to him.

There was more to come tonight. He wondered if he should change into something more formal than the dull white shirt and brown trousers he was wearing. He so hated the current fashions. The long pants clung uncomfortably to his legs, especially in bed, and the shirts were course and plain. He sighed, he supposed there was no going back to the proper clothing he grew up wearing.

He was thinking of getting up and trying a walk around the room to stretch his legs when he heard the front door open. He looked hopefully into the hallway. Elsay came around the corner.

"You're still here I see." she said.

"Yes."

She made a noise and scratched her nose. "This is my parlor you know."

"Yes I know. I can't thank you enough for letting me recover here Mrs. Hollis."

"You seem much improved."

"I am better, but I'm still in a lot of pain. Would you like to see my wound? It's quite dreadful looking." Hugh asked, flinging off the covers.

"Certainly not!"

He pulled the blankets back on. "I'm sorry, I was just trying to make conversation."

"If that's what they call conversation in the city then I'm glad I live here in Fox Cove."

"I really am sorry."

"It doesn't matter Mr. Garrett." Elsay said. "I believe you are well enough to finish your recovery at home."

"Oh?"

"Yes. I've been in touch with Senator Brown and he has sent for another doctor. A gentleman from Augusta that the Senator has known for many years, he's been hired to be your personal physician. He'll be staying with you at your home until you recover."

Elsay flashed him a triumphant grin. He remembered Edward's story from last night, she had experienced great pain in her life. He now understood why she lashed out at people, she was going to conquer them before they could conquer her. He understood, but he didn't have to like it.

"So I take it you would like me to leave now?" he asked. "Shall I walk home then?"

"Mr. Garrett, I know you are hurt. I am not without my sympathies, but you cannot continue to occupy my parlor indefinitely, if my husband and son had their way you would never leave."

Hugh suppressed a smile.

"And then there's the matter of Emma." Elsay continued.

"What about her?"

"Why should she have to come home every day and make your lunch when you have three capable sons? And I don't think it's proper for you, a grown man, to lounge about with a young girl in the house."

"I'm sorry you feel that way, but your daughter is hardly a girl. She's the same age as my son Will."

"Precisely." Elsay answered. "Dr. Jonas, that's your doctor now, is coming this afternoon in a buggy to take you home."

Hugh took a deep breath. "Thank you so much Mrs. Hollis for your consideration. I will be ready."

"Not at all Mr. Garrett. I knew you would understand. I'll put your clothes outside." She picked up the bag Ryan had brought him only yesterday.

"You can call me Jason if you like." Hugh said. "Everyone else in your family does."

Elsay shook her head. "I don't think so Mr. Garrett. I don't believe we should become that familiar." She left the room. He heard the front door open and the sound of a thud as his bag was unceremoniously tossed on the ground.

Chapter 97

The sun was still shining as I left work that afternoon. I considered taking a shortcut into the alley behind Main Street to avoid a chance run in with Ryan. I was being such a coward. After months of staring and flirting how could I suddenly tell him I was not interested? I couldn't put it off forever, but I could put it off one more day.

In the end I chose to take my chances on the main road. The alleyway tended to attract some less than savory characters. Luckily I saw no one of interest until I was passing by the picket fence in front of Ethan's house. Candy was behind the fence cutting the dead blossoms off her rose bushes. Her head popped up as she heard me walking by.

"Hello Emma. You're in an awful hurry."

I stopped and looked behind me. "I'm trying to avoid someone."

"It's not me, is it?"

"No, of course not. It's actually Ryan Garrett."

Candy's face lit up. "Oh I've got to hear this. Why don't you come in?"

"I can't stay too long. I've got things to do at home."

"That's all right. Come on." she said taking off her gloves. I opened the gate in the fence and followed her inside. Ethan had spent a lot of money refurbishing the old Johnson place. Candy said the décor was very modern. I had to take her word for it, I never could follow trends.

We sat in the living room on a long sofa upholstered in green leather. "Do you want tea or coffee?" Candy asked. They had recently acquired a cook and Candy was always keen to put her to work.

"No. I told you I can't stay long." I breathed a sigh of relief, safe in the confines of Candy's house, unable to be spotted by Ryan if he happened to walk by.

"Now tell me what's going on. Why are you avoiding Ryan? I thought you liked him. I thought you thought he was Hugh."

"I did, but not anymore. I told you he kissed me."

"Yes."

"A week ago I would have been happy for it to be him, but something is missing."

"Then it must be Harold or Will."

"I guess so."

"But which one? It's down to two now, it should be easier."

"I suppose."

"But which one do you like better?"

"I don't know Candy. Harold is funny and sweet, Will is pleasant and well mannered. How should I know which one he is?" I snapped. A part of me wished I hadn't come in and started talking about this.

"What's the matter? Are you getting tired of Mika's challenge?"

I nodded. "I am so weary of it. Every day I wake up and wonder if this is the day I will figure it out. And then I go to bed every night realizing I'm not any closer to Hugh. He's been gone for four and a half years Candy. I'm worn out." I put my head in my hands. I hoped I wasn't going to start crying.

I felt Candy's hand on my shoulder. "I'm sorry Emma, I really am. I wish there was something I could do to help."

"I know." I wiped the corner of my eyes. "I've just got to keep going, that's all I can do. I'm not giving up, sometimes I just need to not think about it. That's what I like about going to make Jason his lunch. I have an entire hour where I can just relax. I am almost glad he was stabbed, I know that's terrible to say. I can just sit back and talk with him and laugh, he's really funny you know, and I don't think about anything else. Today I read to him and tonight-"

"Emma." Candy said staring at me.

"What?"

"I wish you could see your face right now."

"Why? Is it dirty?" I put my hands to my face. I had once gone all day with a smudge on my nose and no one had told me.

Candy laughed. "It's not dirty, your face was beaming when you talked about him."

"Who was I talking about?"

"Jason."

"Oh." I said feeling oddly happy to hear his name.

"You like him, don't you?"

"I told you, he's very nice. I like talking to him."

"Emma stop it, you know what I mean."

I felt my face getting hot. I considered getting up and leaving. "I don't know what you mean Candy. I do like Jason, but he's not Hugh."

"How do you know?

"Because he is obviously one of the three sons."

"Why? Why not Jason?"

"Because he's old enough to be my father."

"But he's not your father and besides who says he has to be one of the boys?" Candy asked.

"Hugh told me before he left that he would be part of a group, the group has to be the three boys, they are all similar in age, in occupation and they all have parts of Hugh's personality. See how alike they are? That's the point Candy. I have to find him among the group. Jason isn't like them, he doesn't fit the pattern."

"Is it that you don't find him attractive?"

"Have you not heard anything I just said?"

"I heard you. So you don't find him attractive?"

"I didn't say that." I looked at my watch. I would have to make an excuse and leave.

Candy tapped my hand to get my attention. "Then you do find him attractive."

"I suppose I might."

"Might? Emma, I was his doctor and let me tell you that underneath his clothes he is-"

"Candy, do you really think you should be talking this way about your patients?" I got to my feet.

"It's just for your ears Emma. Don't you want to know what I was going to say?"

"No I don't, with any luck that man will be my father-in-law someday. Do you think I need a mental picture of what he looks like without his clothes on?" I started for the door.

Candy followed me. "You might not need a picture, but do you want one?"

"I have to go."

"Why are you getting upset?"

"I like being with him because I don't have to think about all this, that's all. If I start thinking about him I'll lose sight of Hugh."

"I'm sorry. I was just trying to help." Candy said.

"I know you were. But I have to figure this out myself."

"You're right."

"I know I am. Now I really do have to go." I left the house and hurried home looking behind me to make sure Ryan wasn't there. I opened the front door and peeked into the parlor. The bed was stripped, all that was left was the pillow. Mother was there dusting.

"Where's Jason?" I asked. "Is he taking a bath or something?"

Mother smirked. "He's gone home."

"What? What do you mean?"

"Senator Brown arranged for a doctor to stay with him at his own house. He left about an hour ago."

"But why? He was comfortable here. What about Ethan and Candy? They saved his life."

"This has nothing to do with Ethan and Candy. That man belongs at home, not here in our parlor. It was high time he left. I was worried sick leaving you in the house with a strange man, and I can see it's come to no good. You've taken a liking to him."

"What's wrong with liking him?"

"He's a policeman. I don't trust the police, never have. They are always so nosy, always looking into things that don't concern them, things that happened years before."

I suddenly understood what she meant. She was afraid for Father, he had never been caught for killing Henry. She was afraid he would be taken away from her.

I looked at the empty bed. At the corner of the pillow I noticed something. I lifted the pillow and found *The Time Machine* underneath. I slipped the book in my pocket without her noticing and ran upstairs.

Chapter 98

Hugh was in a sour mood. Not only had Elsay tossed him out without so much as a goodbye but now he was trapped in his bedroom with Dr. Jonas, a wrinkled old man with wiry white sideburns and a frequent habit of burping in-between sentences. To make matters as awful as they could possibly be Senator Brown was there with his uppity wife Bridget.

"I am sure you'll find this much more accommodating than a parlor." the Senator said.

"I thought you were up north campaigning." Hugh replied. Dr. Jonas poked him in the side. "Ouch that's where the knife went in, be careful."

"I'm just taking a look." Dr. Jonas belched.

"I was, but come to find out that up there they hadn't even heard of me." the Senator answered.

"I can't believe it." Bridget said as she fiddled with the eyepiece on the telescope.

"Be careful with that." Hugh told her.

Bridget pouted and put her hands in her pockets.

"You're in a foul mood Garrett." the Senator said.

"I am not. Ouch. Will you stop it?" he said to Dr. Jonas who was still poking him.

"He's an ornery one, ain't he?" said the doctor.

"Please continue Dr. Jonas." The Senator said. "I am afraid Mr. Garrett has been through a trauma."

Hugh ignored the last comment. "If you're back then where is Will?"

"What's that?" the Senator asked, cupping his ear.

"I said where is Will? My son?" Hugh shouted. "Ouch."

"Oh William. Yes I know who you mean now. I'm not sure." The Senator rubbed his beard and looked into the distance as though he was trying to remember something.

Hugh began to panic. "What do you mean you don't know where he is?"

"Calm down, calm down. We started out on the campaign trail, but I could soon tell it wasn't going to be a successful trip. It still shocks me to realize how many people don't know the name Brown. Unimaginable really."

"Why didn't you keep going? Meet people, let them get to know you." Hugh asked.

The Senator looked at Bridget and smiled. "Because just before I left my little wife here told me something. Can I tell him dearest?"

"I suppose." she said wrinkling her nose.

"I'm going to be a father again Garrett." the Senator said patting his stomach.

"That's great, but what about Will?"

"Oh yes. After I decided to go home I let him and my other men go their separate ways."

"Then you don't know where he is?"

"Not exactly." the Senator said. "But I am sure he'll turn up. He's a capable young man."

Hugh tried to get out of bed. "I have to go look for him." He was surprised at his own desire to find Will. A few months ago he wanted nothing more than for all three of the boys to leave him alone.

"Oh no you don't." Dr. Jonas put a hand on his chest.

"Don't be ridiculous Garrett, let one of your other boys go look if you insist. He'll turn up in a day or two. He's young, remember what it was like at that age?" He winked as though he and Hugh had a secret between them.

"Your concern is overwhelming." Hugh snapped.

Dr. Jonas put a fist to his own shrunken chest and hiccupped. "Something didn't go down right."

"What do you want him to do? You're so ungrateful." Bridget said suddenly. "Hershival has given you this beautiful house to live in and seen that all three of your sons and yourself have employment. He gives and gives to this town and no one ever thanks him."

"Dearest Bridget." The Senator took her hand. "I'm sorry Garrett, my wife sometimes gets ideas."

"She can speak her mind if she likes. But I want it said that I pay rent for this house. And I alone applied for the job here, it was your husband's idea to hire my entire family. And now my son is missing and God only knows where he is or what has happened to him. I would like, Bridget, for my senator to show a little more concern for the whereabouts of my boy."

Bridget looked at her husband. The Senator nodded. "I'll speak to the sheriff first thing in the morning."

Hugh was so angry he felt as though his head might explode.

"I'll ride over tonight if that would make you feel better." the Senator offered.

"It would, thank you. Ouch." He turned to Dr. Jonas who was looking at his side again. "If you don't stop poking me I swear I will punch you right in the nose."

The doctor scratched his nose with his bony hand and looked back at the Browns. "Ain't he got a temper on him?"

Chapter 99

I put Jason's book in my bag that morning. I wanted to give it back to him and apologize for Mother making him leave our house, but there was still the danger that I would run into Ryan. I didn't know if I was ready to talk to him. I was almost to the store when I met Harold coming out of Brown Lane.

"Good morning." I looked cautiously about to make sure that his brother wasn't behind him.

"Morning." Harold mumbled. He looked as though he hadn't slept at all.

"What's wrong?"

"You haven't heard?"

"Is it your father?" I asked, grabbing his arm.

"No, it's Will. He's missing."

"Missing? How?" Harold explained how Will hadn't returned home after Senator Brown disbanded his campaign trip.

"Does he have friends up north he might be visiting? Or a girl?"

Harold shook his head. "No, he doesn't know anyone. It's not like Will to just vanish, he wouldn't do something like this."

"I'm so sorry. Is there anything I can do?"

"Ryan and the Sheriff are out looking for him. I wanted to go but Papa insists I stay here."

"Someone has to keep order here in town."

"That's what Papa said, he's made me acting chief." Harold pointed to his father's gold badge which was now pinned on his jacket.

"Your father left his book at my house. I was going to bring it to him at lunchtime, maybe I should give it to you. I doubt he's in the mood to see anyone."

"No, I think you should give it to him." Harold said. "He really likes your company."

"Really? He said that?"

Harold smiled. "I can tell." He looked at his watch. "Is that the time? I've got so much work to do. I'll walk you to the store." He offered his arm and we walked the short distance to Thalberg's. "Don't forget about the book." He crossed the street and unlocked the door to the police station.

News spread quickly about Will. Everyone seemed to have a theory about what had happened. Most thought he was just a young man who found something better to do than come home to his father and brothers, but a few had more ominous predictions.

I went to the Garretts' house at lunchtime. Fred the butler answered the door. When I told him who I was calling on he frowned. "Mr. Garrett is recovering upstairs in his bedroom."

"I know. Well I don't know, what I mean is that I am not surprised, that is I would like to see him anyway, if that's all right." I stammered. "He left something behind at my house."

"I can give it to him Miss Hollis."

"Ah yes, that's awfully kind of you, but I would prefer to give it to him myself."

Fred blinked and then motioned for me to take a seat in the hallway. "I'll have to ask Mr. Garrett and his doctor. Please wait here."

I watched as he slowly climbed the staircase. Maybe it was the wrong time to come here, they were having a family crisis after all. They didn't need me barging in to return a book, it was not as though Jason would be reading, his son was missing.

"What are you waiting for?" Ma Granger said as she emerged through a wall.

"I'm returning a book to Jason. Fred is checking to see whether or not I can go up."

Ma waved her hand in the air. "Just go anyway."

"I can't just walk into the man's bedroom."

"Why not? I used to do it all the time back in my day." Ma chuckled. "Got a bit of a reputation if you know what I mean, but I had a lot of fun doing it."

"I think I should wait." I said picturing myself sashaying into his bedroom unannounced.

"Suit yourself. He's just sitting upstairs in his pajamas and a bathrobe, nothing you can't see. He's got this old crow for a doctor, might be older than me." She laughed and scratched herself. "The butler is coming."

Fred appeared at the top of the stairs. I hoped he hadn't heard me talking to the air that contained Ma Granger. He walked downstairs and through Ma, who sighed contentedly. "Mr. Garrett will receive you."

"Thank you." I went upstairs with Ma following close behind. "You don't need to come with me." I whispered over my shoulder. "I am just returning a book."

"How are you going to stop me?" She grinned with her blackened teeth. "You ain't your father dearie." She drifted through the wall.

I considered giving the book to Fred and getting out of there. I knew what Tormented Souls were capable of, especially ones with too much time on their hands. But Jason was expecting me. I had just been announced by his butler. I couldn't run away from everything.

I knocked on the door. It was opened by a wizened old man with a scraggly beard and bushy sideburns. "Who are you?" He made a face and burped loudly.

"I'm Emma."

"Oh yeah, come in." he said holding the door open. "Sorry I forgot, my mind is not what it used to be."

"Thank you." I stepped inside. Jason was on a sofa near one of the windows that faced the ocean. He was wearing a blue bathrobe. He smiled and gave me a little wave. Standing behind the sofa was Ma with a delighted look in her eyes.

"I'm Dr. Jonas." the old man said. "Better not tire him out young lady."

"I won't."

"Come in Emma." Jason said. "You can leave us Dr. Jonas."

"What's that?" the doctor asked. "You want me to leave, eh?"

"Yes."

"Get out of here old man." Ma said.

The doctor mumbled something I couldn't make out and left.

"I've brought your book." I took it from my bag and handed it to him.

"Thank you. I did forget this, didn't I?"

"Sure he did." Ma muttered. "Why don't you sit down dearie?" She put a hand on my shoulder and shoved me onto the sofa next to him.

"I hope you don't mind."

"I was just going to invite you to sit down."

"I'm sorry to hear about Will."

"I'm worried sick about him. I don't know where he is and I'm stuck in this damn room. I can barely walk. I certainly can't ride, all because of that cursed thief. He comes into this town, has everyone scared out of their minds, tries to kill me, and he gets to go onto the next job leaving our lives turned upside down. How does someone like that have the right to be so selfish?"

"Harold told me this morning that Ryan is out looking for him. You said he was an investigator, surely he can find him."

"It's just so frustrating sitting in this room doing nothing. Not to mention having to listen to Dr. Jonas."

"He's an old tin horn." Ma agreed.

"I just have to believe Will is all right. I can't even think of the alternative." Jason said.

"I wish there was something I could do to help."

"Actually, you are helping. I don't really have many friends in this town. It's nice to be able to talk to someone."

"I'm sorry my mother made you leave. None of us wanted it, she's very, how can I say this?" I hesitated. "She's very sensitive."

"I understand. It must be difficult having a strange man lying about in your parlor."

"It's fun though." Ma said.

"You look much more comfortable here."

He looked down at his bathrobe, a pair of striped pajamas peeked out. "I guess this is a step up from your father's clothes. It's not really my style though."

"This conversation is so boring." Ma grumbled. She poked me in the back of the head causing me to lurch forward.

"Are you all right?" he asked.

"Yes." I said pretending to cough.

Ma poked me again which made me have to create a fake coughing fit.

"Are you sure you're all right? Should I call Dr. Jonas?"

"Please don't." I said turning around to glare at Ma who looked pleased with herself. "Maybe I should go."

"Do you have to?"

"I'll stay if I can keep my coughing to a minimum." I stared straight at Ma.

"I'll behave if you'll talk about something more interesting than clothes." Ma said. "And move a little closer to him, he doesn't bite."

I had forgotten how annoying Tormented Souls could make themselves. I pretended to have to stand up and fix my skirt, when I sat back down I was an inch or two closer.

"That's better, but I would be a lot closer than that. Heck, what am I sayin'? I'd be in his lap." Ma said. I tried not to giggle.

"Are you sure you're all right?"

"Yes I'm fine." Out of the corner of my eye I saw Ma take a few steps back.

Jason looked like he was about to say something and then stopped. He thumbed through the pages of *The Time Machine*.

"I would imagine it's even more difficult to sit here and wait for news about Will with your wife gone."

He looked surprised. "Um, yes, that's true."

"I would say you are closer to your boys than a lot of fathers. They adore you."

"They do?"

"Why are you always so surprised at that?"

"I don't know. I guess I never really thought about it before."

"They've all told me how much they care about you."

"You really like my boys, don't you?"

"Yes."

He hesitated. "Ryan especially though."

I swallowed. Had Ryan put him up to this? Was his own father going to have the talk with me? "I like Ryan." I said meekly.

"It's not my place to interfere but-" He stopped. "It's not my place."

"I like all your sons equally. We're all friends."

He opened his mouth and then closed it. He slowly stood up and groaned. "It hurts if I sit too long in one place."

"I'll help you." I stood up. He put his arm around my shoulder and I held onto his waist. His whiskers, which had been growing since he was stabbed, were shaved away and he smelled of some type of spicy soap. "Where do you want to go?"

"I'll stretch out on the bed." We walked slowly. He must have been very tired for he leaned heavily on my shoulder. I took his other hand and eased him onto the bed.

"Thank you, you're quite a good nurse you know." he said still holding my hand.

"Not at all." I said not letting go.

"This is getting boring again." I heard Ma say behind me. I felt something on my back as she gave me a hard push. I lost my balance and fell straight towards Jason. He toppled backwards as I landed on top of him.

"Ouch." I heard him say as our eyes met.

"Oh God." I struggled to get up. My foot got wrapped up in the bed skirt and I fell on the floor. "I'm so sorry." I said as I got to my feet.

He was still lying on the bed with a strange look on his face. "It's perfectly fine. It was just an accident. Are you all right?"

"Oh I'm fine." I said glaring at Ma. I brushed the hair out of my eyes and tried to take on the appearance of a normal human being. "Do you want me to get your doctor?" I was afraid to go near him with Ma still lingering nearby. "Did I hurt you?" I could feel my face burning red, my heart was racing in my ears.

"Not at all."

"I should go."

"You should get some rest I think."

"Yes I will." I said nervously. "Goodbye."

"Goodbye and thank you for bringing my book. You'll come again?"

"What?" I backed into the sofa nearly falling over it. I grabbed my purse and stuffed it under my arm. "Oh yes I'll come back." I said, not knowing why I was agreeing after what had just happened. "Goodbye."

"So long Emma. You'd better come by again, this was fun." Ma cried.

I rushed out, shutting the door behind me. Dr. Jonas was in the hallway smoking a cigar. "Hope you didn't tire him too much young lady."

Chapter 100

Hugh leaned back on the pillow. He wasn't sure what had gotten into Emma that afternoon, she was acting very peculiar, but he hadn't minded. He kept replaying the last few minutes in his head. He could still feel her lying on top of him, her breath on his neck, her knee brushing between his legs. Their eyes had met for a brief second and he thought she had recognized him but he still couldn't be sure.

"Had a good afternoon?" He heard a voice near the window. Mika was standing with his hands in his pockets.

"Yes." Hugh said, still day dreaming.

"That nuisance of a Tormented Soul was interfering in business that doesn't concern her, but I've seen to it that she won't do it again."

"Do you mean Ma Granger? Was she here?"

"Of course."

"What did you do to her?"

"I told her to mind her own business, what do you think? I can be very persuasive when I want to be." He smirked.

"Do you think Emma is starting to realize it's me?"

Mika shrugged. "How should I know?"

Hugh sighed and stared up at the ceiling. He was feeling tired, not just because he was injured, but because he couldn't stop worrying about Will. "Can't you at least tell me if Will is all right?"

Mika looked at him unconcerned. "It's not for me to say."

"I wish you cared. This is my son."

"You've become quite the father you know."

"I know. I don't really know how it happened. I just began thinking of them more and more as mine." Hugh said. "And they like me, I don't know why. I've never been very nice to them."

"Their minds are filled with memories of you. I did give them a rather wonderful childhood, the one I should have had if I had been normal." Mika turned away from the window. "I have a son you know."

"You do?"

"Yes. I haven't seen him since he was an infant. But he's out there, and I'll find him again someday."

"You never told me you were a father."

"There's a lot I haven't told you. It isn't your place to know things about me."

"When you tell me these things I suddenly understand why you make the choices you do." Hugh said. "Sometimes I feel like you're working against me."

"Everything I've done is for you. I'm on your side, I always have been. The doctor is coming. Goodbye Hugh."

A second later the door opened and Dr. Jonas crept in. "Talking to yourself again, eh? You might want to get your head checked out someday."

Chapter 101

As soon as the store closed I went to search out Candy. I spent the afternoon in a muddled confusion, replaying the events of earlier that day. The way Jason looked and smelled, the way his firm, muscular body felt underneath mine. Nothing was turning out as I imagined it would. Why was I suddenly feeling this way?

I hurried into the clinic, the bell on the front door announced my arrival. Ethan was in the waiting room sorting through a box of glass medicine bottles. "Hello Emma." he chirped.

"Where's Candy?"

"Are you all right? You don't look so good."

"I'm fine. I just need to see Candy."

"She's out back. Are you sure there isn't anything I can help you with?"

"No, I'm sorry Ethan. I don't think you're going to want to hear this. It's kind of a woman's issue."

His face turned pale. "Oh, in that case you'd better see her. Last door on the right."

I hurried down the hall. When I opened the door Candy was sitting in a chair reading a stack of papers. "Emma, what are you doing here?" She threw the papers aside.

"I need to talk to you. I've got a huge problem."

"You're not pregnant, are you?"

"No, I am not!"

"Oh good. I've just had two unexpected pregnancies today, and one of them, oh well I guess I'm not supposed to say." She looked disappointed at not being able to share what was obviously going to be the next piece of gossip making its way around town. "What is it?"

"I like Jason Garrett."

Candy smiled. "I told you that the other day."

"I know you did. But I thought it might have been just a momentary fondness because he had been staying in our house and he was hurt, but now I'm not so sure."

"What happened? Did you see him today?"

"Yes." I proceeded to tell her about how Ma Granger had poked me in the back of the head and then forced me to sit closer to him. How she had pushed me on top of him when I was helping him into bed.

"I like this woman." Candy said. "I used the ole' fall on top of him routine with Ethan. I pretended to trip and pushed him right on the ground. I kissed him while he was down there. Why should men have all the fun?"

"I didn't kiss him."

"But you wanted to?"

"I don't know why I am feeling this way. I never expected to. I spent so many months ignoring him, sometimes he would try and make conversation with me and I would just say something to be polite and then talk to one of the boys. I never even thought about him until-"

"He got stabbed?"

"No, actually it was at the party he gave, we were talking and I just found myself suddenly having fun, he was so engaging. I wanted to stay with him but then Mika came and I was suddenly up on the roof. Maybe Mika was trying to warn me off him, maybe he saw I was starting to like him and he didn't want me to make the wrong choice."

"Maybe." Candy said. "Or maybe Jason is Hugh."

"I want him to be." I hadn't really admitted that to myself until that very moment.

"Then give him the watch."

"What if he's not? Then Hugh is gone and I'll never see him again."

"Let's go over this. What do you like about him?"

I took a deep breath. "He's funny and clever. I don't know, when I'm talking to him he just seems to understand what I'm saying. He likes some of the same things I do. I just like being with him. When I'm with him I'm happy."

"You like the silver hair?" Candy asked.

"Among other things."

Candy grinned. "You really like him Emma. I thought it was just a flirtation but I think it's more than that."

I didn't answer her.

"You have to give him the watch Emma."

"What if I'm wrong? Just because I want him to be Hugh doesn't mean he is."

"At some point you're going to have to take a chance. I know you only have one try at this but you can't put it off forever, and don't you want to know? Stop thinking about it. How do you really feel?"

"I think I love Jason."

"Give him the watch first thing in the morning."

"First thing? I have to work in the morning."

Candy rolled her eyes. "Honestly. I'll go to the store and tell them you're sick."

"There's a big shipment coming in, loads of parcels. I should be there."

"Really Emma sometimes you are impossible. Go and see Jason after work then. If I were you I would be there right now, but I know how you are. Just promise me you'll do it tomorrow."

"I will."

"It will be all right." she said hugging me. "Just think tomorrow at this time you'll be with Hugh."

Chapter 102

Hugh was stuck in his bedroom despite the fact that he was feeling better. He had asked Dr. Jonas that morning if he could go downstairs, he was immediately denied.

"You'll stay here until you're good and healed. Do you want that wound to open again?" Dr. Jonas waved his bony finger in Hugh's face.

Hugh longed for company. He wondered how he had managed to get along all those years before Emma came along, he had once gone five entire years without speaking to anyone, even Mika. As the lunch hour approached he held his breath expecting to hear Emma's footsteps coming up the stairs, but the time came and went and there was no sign of her.

He had thought he was really making progress, he was beginning to believe that she had taken a liking to him, but now he doubted himself. She probably just saw him as an old man, like Senator Brown, maybe she was disgusted by falling on top of him yesterday.

He was working himself into a black mood when he heard a commotion downstairs. There was a rabble of voices, doors opening and closing and furniture being moved. Fred came rushing in looking flushed.

"Mr. Garrett sir, Ryan is back, they found Will."

Hugh jumped off the bed. "Oh God."

Fred saw the look on his face. "No sir, it's good news, he's alive, he's downstairs right now."

Hugh exhaled. It felt as though he had been holding his breath for a week. He rushed past Fred and out the bedroom door.

"Sir, sir!" Fred cried behind him. "Let me get the doctor."

Hugh ignored him and hurried down the stairs. His side began to ache as if Dr. Jonas was poking him again. He would worry about that later.

He ran into the parlor only to find it empty. He crossed into the adjoining library and found Will sprawled out on the large sofa in the center of the room. Surrounding him were Ryan, Harold, and Dr. Jonas.

"Papa." Will said trying to smile, his upper lip was scabbed over. His right eye was blackened and swelled. The rest of his face was covered in purple bruises. His blonde hair looked as though it had been hacked off with a butcher's knife. There was a long cut across the top of his scalp, slicing across his left ear.

"My God Will." Hugh fell to his knees and wrapped his arms tightly around his son.

"Careful there, you don't want to suffocate him." Dr. Jonas said.

Hugh didn't care what the doctor said. He had to squeeze Will as tightly as he could to make sure he was really there. He hadn't realized how lost he had felt up until that moment, he released his grip and held Will's face in his hands. "I love you son."

"You haven't said that since we came here." Will looked at his brothers.

"I know, but I'm saying it now." Hugh looked back at Ryan and Harold. Ryan's face and clothes were dirty, he looked exhausted. Harold was grinning, the chief's badge shining brightly on his chest, how proud he had been when Hugh gave it to him. "I love all of you."

"Enough of this." Dr. Jonas said. "My Pa never talked to me like this and I turned out just fine. Used to give me a good slap right across my backside and it did me a world of good too. Whole blasted world's gone soft nowadays, back in my day you didn't tell em' you loved em'. Heh, modern life. Mr. Garrett, you should be in bed."

"He's right Papa, you're not well." Will said.

"I'm not going anywhere. What happened to you? Where have you been?"

"You'd better sit down Papa, it might take a while."

Ryan and Harold sprang into action and pulled a chair close to the sofa. They helped Hugh into it. They then got their own chairs as did Dr. Jonas.

"I don't think we will be needing you right now doctor." Hugh told him.

"What?" Dr. Jonas leaned forward in his chair. "Why can't I hear? Seems like it will be a damn good story."

Hugh looked at Will who nodded. "All right you can stay, but don't interrupt."

"I ain't the interrupting type."

"Of course not." Hugh turned his attention back to Will. "Now tell me what happened. Who did this to you?"

Will cleared his throat. "I started out with Senator Brown and a group of politicians. We were going up north to campaign, we rode for a couple of days, stopping in the towns along the way. It turns out most of them hadn't even heard of the Senator and they weren't very interested in finding out about him. The Senator was very low, a few days into the trip he gathered us together and told us he was going home. His wife was expecting another child and he wanted to be with her. Of course it was really because the trip wasn't going well."

"So he just left you?" Hugh asked.

"Yes. He told us to go our separate ways, we had all rode our own mounts, so it wasn't that difficult. Most of the men left immediately. I was hungry so I asked around and found a little place that served lunch and drinks. It was a pretty rough place, but I wasn't bothered. While I was eating I overheard three boys at the bar talking. One of them was bragging about stabbing a policeman the week before. I listened for a while and then I approached the boy, he couldn't have been more than sixteen years old."

"He wasn't."

Will took a deep breath. "I asked him to tell me about what he had done. I pretended I was really interested, made him think I admired him. I wasn't wearing my uniform so they didn't know what I was. He told me how he had been working in this town near the coast, how he had broken into houses and stole things, and how the police were inept and couldn't catch him. He said on his last job the police chief had followed him inside some house and before the cop could fire his pistol he stabbed him and left him for dead."

"You don't know for sure it's the same one who hurt me."

"No?" Will put his hand in his pocket. He pulled out a long silver chain, on it hung the star necklace, the one that Emma gave him the night before he left. It had been missing since the night he was stabbed, but he had been afraid to tell anyone about it because he was afraid it would somehow reveal his identity to Emma. "It's yours isn't it?" Will asked.

"Yes." Hugh said fingering the tiny star. "He must have taken it when I was unconscious."

"What did you do then, did you kill the bastard?" Dr. Jonas asked.

"I pretended I was really impressed with him, congratulated him and started to leave. I was planning to find the sheriff, I had no authority to arrest him. I got my things and went outside. I was getting ready to leave when they confronted me, they wanted to know why I was asking so many questions. I tried to talk my way out of it, but then one of them shoved me and he felt the badge in my shirt pocket. Once they saw that it was all over." Will stopped and looked at Harold. "Can you get me some water please?"

Harold left the room while Will rubbed his jaw and looked down at the floor. Hugh knew he was coming to a part of the story he was reluctant to relive. He reached out and patted Will's hand. They waited silently until Harold returned with the water. As Will took the glass Hugh noticed his hand was shaking, he took a long drink and then handed the empty glass back to his brother.

"As I was saying, they figured out I was a cop. They started hitting me, it didn't take much to knock me out, they were well practiced. When I woke up I was in a small cabin tied to a chair. The boy, the one who stabbed you Papa, was there. I was so angry, so furious at what they had done I started yelling and cursing at them. I told them I was your son and how I had nearly lost you, and what worthless bastards they were.

"They didn't take kindly to my description of them, so they kept me there in that cabin for the next two days." Will stopped and looked at Hugh. "It wasn't enough just to kill me, they wanted to have a little fun." He shut his eyes and grimaced. "Ryan can take it from here."

Ryan looked at Will for a few seconds and then began. "I followed the route that Senator Brown had taken and started asking around, it turns out more than one person had seen Will being taken, they knew who had done it as well.

"The three of them are brothers, kinda strange, isn't it? They are well known around those parts and there were a few places they used as hideouts. I got hold of the sheriff up that way and we raided all their usual spots until we found Will."

"Were they arrested?" Hugh asked.

"Absolutely, with what they were doing to Will-" He stopped. Out of the corner of his eye Hugh saw Will shaking his head. "They have enough to put them away, but you may need to ride up there and identify the one who stabbed you."

"I'll do that." Hugh said. "Listen boys I think Will is getting tired. Let's help him upstairs."

"In a minute." Will shut his eyes.

Hugh turned and motioned for Ryan, Harold and Dr. Jonas to leave. They left the room. He waited until he was sure the door was shut before he spoke again. "I'll help you when you're ready."

"How are you going to do that? You're still recovering." Will said.

"I'm doing much better now, especially now that you're home."

"I got him for you."

"Who?"

"The boy who tried to kill you."

"You didn't have to do that Will."

"Yes I did. Although I didn't think it would be this hard."

"Will, I want you to know that you can tell me anything. Whatever happened up there, if you want to talk about it you know you can."

"I know. Do you want this back now?" Will held up the necklace.

"Why don't you keep it for a while? You've earned it." Hugh put it around Will's neck.

Will smiled and tucked it inside his shirt. "I'm tired. Can you help me up?"

Hugh stood up and with a bit of difficulty helped Will to his feet. The two of them hobbled out of the library and into the parlor where Harold and Ryan were waiting. Without saying a word, his other sons took Will and helped him upstairs. Hugh followed them. Once inside Will's bedroom Ryan and Harold started tugging at his clothes.

"No." he said quietly. "I only want Papa to help me." Ryan and Harold looked at each other and left.

Hugh helped Will off with his clothes and into a clean nightshirt. He tried not to react when he saw the bruises and cuts across his son's body. There were splotches of dried blood on his legs and feet. "Do you want to have a bath drawn?"

"Not now. I want to sleep." Will crept slowly into bed. Hugh pulled the covers up to his chin and kissed him on the forehead.

"I love you Will."

A smile spread across Will's face. "I love you too Papa."

Hugh patted Will's cheek and turned away. He felt as though he had heard the most beautiful words ever spoken, he repeated them to himself in his head over and over again. A surge of happiness filled him like never before. He felt as though he might burst. The emptiness he had carried inside of him was nearly gone, he was someone's father and it made him happy to think so. His new life was nearly complete, there was just one thing missing. Emma.

Chapter 103

Candy was waiting outside that evening as I left work. "Are you going to see Jason?"

"Yes." I said nervously. I had thought of nothing else all day. I felt for the thousandth time in my pocket to make sure the watch was still there. It was going to seem strange not to have it with me any longer. I had been carrying it for so long it felt like it belonged to me.

"What's going on here?" Candy said as we approached Brown Lane. From the end of the road we could make out at least half a dozen wagons and buggies parked haphazardly outside the house. Horses were randomly tied on the porch railings or left to graze on the lawn.

As we walked towards the house a group of men stepped outside and began to light cigars. "Something's happened." Candy muttered. The men stared at us as we rushed up the porch steps. "Why are you here?" she asked them.

"Haven't you heard? William is home, they found him up north."

"Is he dead?" Candy asked.

"Hell no." another man said, taking a puff on his cigar. "He's bad though, they beat and tortured him something awful."

"We'd better get in there." Candy opened the door and walked into the house without knocking. There were a few people hanging about in the hallway. From the parlor I heard Senator Brown's voice. I looked inside and saw him leaning on the mantel smoking a cigar and talking to a group of admirers, a photographer was nearby taking his picture.

"What's he doing here?" Candy whispered. Fred walked by carrying a tray of drinks.

"Fred!" I called out. He stopped, the drinks sloshing in the glasses.

"Yes Miss Hollis?"

"I need to see Mr. Garrett, that is Jason Garrett."

"Oh I am sorry but Mr. Garrett is resting now, he's had a very trying day."

"I won't bother him. I just have to give him something."

"I'll take it and give it to him when he wakes up." Fred offered.

"No, I have to do it in person."

"She's got to see him *now*." Candy said.

"But-" Fred began.

"What's the trouble Fred?" Senator Brown said striding towards us.

"This young woman wants to see Mr. Garrett sir. But I told her he's sleeping, the doctor doesn't want anyone to bother him."

"I'll handle this." the Senator said quietly. "You serve the drinks to these fine folks." The Senator looked in the parlor. "Just a moment folks, a little personal business to attend to." He turned back to me. "What do you want?"

"I want to see Jason."

"Since when are you on a first name basis with a man twice your age?"

"He is not twice her age." Candy said. "That would make him forty six and he's only forty three."

"Dr. Hollis, your mathematical analysis is not necessary. I want to speak only with Emma. Now what business do you have with him?"

I took a deep breath. "It's personal."

The Senator narrowed his eyes. "I've never trusted you or your family."

Candy muttered something next to me. I poked her in the side with my elbow.

"You can't stop me from seeing him." I said.

"That's right." Candy added.

"Watch me." He grabbed each of us by the arm and dragged us to the door. A man opened it and the Senator proceeded to push us outside.

"I'll get you for this Brown!" Candy shouted. "I'll sue you for everything you're worth. You should be ashamed, treating women this way."

The Senator merely shrugged. "Gentlemen, see that these ladies do not come back inside. And Emma?"

"What?" I shouted.

"There's no need to be angry. I was merely going to say you can come back another day when he's feeling up to company from a little girl." He smiled. The men on the porch chuckled at his cleverness.

"Why are you doing this? You don't even know why I want to see him, it's important."

"Emma I could care less about you and your trivial life. Your father should have thought twice about crossing me all those years ago."

"My father could run rings around you. And by the way, everyone calls you maple drawers behind your back." The Senator's face dropped as he disappeared into the darkness of the house, slamming the door behind him.

Chapter 104

"Mr. Garrett sir, you've got to wake up." A voice interrupted his sleep. Hugh turned over and found Fred shaking his shoulder. He put a hand to his eyes as the morning sun streamed in the windows.

"Why are you waking me? Is Will all right?"

"Yes, he's fine. It's Senator Brown sir." Fred replied. "He's downstairs waiting for you."

Hugh sat up in bed. "Waiting for me? Why?"

"He wants you to ride up north to identify the boy who stabbed you. He said you were willing to do it."

"I am, but right now? Will just came home."

"I know sir, but the Senator said that the district attorney won't press charges for attempted murder unless you identify the boy."

Hugh rubbed his eyes. "I was willing to let him go. I know what it's like to be young and desperate, but now that he's hurt my boy-"

"I understand sir." Fred nodded. "I had a son once, he was killed in the war."

"I'm sorry to hear that. It must have been awful."

"It was sir. Now you'd better hurry, the Senator is not fond of waiting."

"But I can't ride yet."

"He's got the carriage out."

"I suppose I should feel honored."

Fred nodded and went about getting Hugh's uniform out of the wardrobe. He was pleased to see it again as he liked how he looked in it.

"What was going on last night?" Hugh asked as he began to dress. "It sounded like a party downstairs."

"Oh that was the Senator, he had a few people in. I'm afraid he's going to take credit for finding Will. It's all part of the campaign you know."

"I don't care if he takes credit as long as Will is all right. But did anyone ask for me by chance? A young lady perhaps?"

Fred frowned and stared into space. "A young lady? It was so busy. I can't remember."

Hugh sighed. "I'd better get downstairs." She wasn't coming back, she was obviously disgusted by what happened last time they were together. He would have to start all over again.

He finished getting dressed and hurried downstairs. As he was going out the door Fred handed him a leather satchel and a small lunch pail. "I've packed some breakfast for you sir."

"Thank you Fred. Please look after Will and tell him I am doing this for him."

Fred watched Hugh and Senator Brown depart in the Senator's fine carriage before shutting the door. It was then that he realized what he had been trying to remember all morning.

"Oh dear. It was that Miss Hollis that came to call on him last night, she wanted to give him something. Oh Fred you've done it again, Mother always said you had a memory like an old tramp's sock." he said aloud. "That's how I got fired the last time. Oh dear. Hopefully it wasn't anything important."

Chapter 105

The next morning I was determined to see Jason. I didn't have to work at the store. As soon as I had my breakfast I left. The night before I found a small box for the watch. I wrapped it in some fancy paper that we used in the store and tied it with a ribbon.

I had pictured over and over again in my head what the scene would look like. Jason would unwrap and open the box and then suddenly confess that he was Hugh. I loved Jason, and if I loved him then he must be Hugh. It all made sense to me now. My mind was made up as I walked into town.

I ran up Brown Lane and rang the doorbell three times. Fred answered and gave me a funny look. "Miss Hollis."

"Good morning. I want to see Mr. Garrett, remember I have something for him." I said determinedly.

"I remember. Please come in."

He opened the door and I stepped into the hallway. My stomach was starting to feel fluttery. I expected Fred would leave to tell Jason I was here, but instead he just stood by nervously wringing his hands. "I'm afraid Mr. Garrett is not at home."

"Not at home?"

"No, he left this morning with Senator Brown. They are heading up north so that Mr. Garrett can identify his attacker."

Father had explained to me the night before what had happened to Will. "Is he well enough to travel?"

"Apparently so." Fred said.

"When do you expect him back?"

"Not for a few days."

"Oh." The nervous excitement drained from my body. "Did you tell him that I came to see him last night?"

"Oh, now that-" Fred began.

"Hello Emma."

I looked up and saw Ryan standing in the parlor door smiling at me. Oh dear. "Ryan, I hear you're quite the hero these days."

He shook his head. "I'm not a hero. I just did my job. It feels like I haven't seen you in such a long time."

"I know." I said trying to maneuver towards the door.

"Do you have some time this morning? I'd like to talk to you."

"Oh yes, you did want to talk."

"Yes."

I took a deep breath. I had to get it over with sometime, it might as well be now. I followed him into the parlor. He closed the door behind us. "Emma, I don't know how to say this."

"Ryan I think you're a really wonderful person but-"

"Please, I have to say this to you."

"Go ahead then." I said preparing myself.

"I know I kissed you that day in the police station, but I shouldn't have done that. I really, really like you Emma, you're one of the nicest girls I know but-"

"But?"

"I met someone up north."

"You did?" I said hopefully.

"Yes, you see I was working very closely with a sheriff's deputy and he has a daughter, Rose is her name, and when I met her, I don't know something happened. I don't know how to explain it." Ryan stopped, his face was glowing.

"You fell in love?"

"Maybe, but I hardly know her."

"But you want to?"

Ryan's face broke into a giddy smile. "I do. But you Emma, I let you believe that- No, I take that back. I really do care about you, it's just that-"

"You don't love me?"

"I thought I did. I'm so sorry Emma."

"Ryan, I think you should know something."

"Yes?"

"I don't love you either."

"You don't?"

"No. I didn't know how to tell you so I've been avoiding you for days." I said. "I've been avoiding a lot of things lately."

He laughed nervously. "You don't know what a relief it is to hear those words."

"I do actually."

"Do you want to see Will?"

"Yes, if I can. Is he well enough?"

"I think so. Just try not to act too surprised by what you see, he looks different."

"I won't. Where is he?"

"In the library. He insisted on coming downstairs this morning, just as stubborn as Papa."

He opened the door and we found Will sitting up at a small table shuffling a deck of cards. Ryan was wise to warn me. Will's appearance was so altered I felt my mouth gaping open. He looked at me through his bruised and swollen eyes.

"Hello Emma. I'm a sight for sore eyes, eh?" He laughed and dropped the cards on the floor. "Oh damn." He leaned forward in his chair to pick them up.

"Will stop trying to do everything yourself, you should be in bed." Ryan said as he knelt down and began picking up the cards.

"I can do it." Will was wearing a pair of green pajamas topped with a white robe. As he leaned over to pick up the cards I noticed a silver chain working its way out of his collar. There was a small pendant hanging from it. I blinked when I saw it was a silver star, my silver star that I had given to Hugh so many years before.

It felt as though all the air had been sucked out of the room. I sat down on a chair in stunned silence. Meanwhile Ryan finished picking up the cards. Will looked down and noticed the necklace, he slipped it back inside his pajamas.

"I'm sorry you have to see me like this Emma." Will was saying.

I had betrayed Hugh by falling in love with another man. How could it have happened? I had been so careful, taken so much time and still I had failed. I loved Jason. I wanted to be with him, not Will.

Hugh had come back to life to be with me and I had turned my back on him. I had obviously ignored all the signs and gone blindly ahead. It had been four and a half years since I had been with Hugh, maybe I didn't love him anymore. Or maybe I didn't know him as well as I thought. Even as I sat and watched Will, knowing who he was, I didn't want to be with him.

"Are you all right?"

My face felt hot. "Yes."

"Maybe you shouldn't have come in here." Will said. "I know I look awful."

I shook my head. "I'm sorry, I'm just a little overcome." Through my purse I could feel the small box I had wrapped Hugh's watch in. I couldn't put it off any longer, if Candy were here she would have told me to go ahead.

I could not abandon Hugh. Underneath Will's bruised exterior was the man I loved, even if I couldn't see it now. I would give him the watch and once we were married I would insist we move away so I would see as little of Jason as possible.

"Do you want me to walk you home?" Ryan asked.

"No." I said shaking my head. My legs felt like jelly. I would never be able to walk anywhere. "I would like to speak with Will alone if you don't mind."

A strange look crossed Ryan's face. "All right then. Just ring the bell if you need anything Will."

"I know." Will watched his brother leave. After the door was shut he leaned forward in his chair. "I suppose you want to know what happened to me."

I opened my bag. "Actually I have something to give you." I took out the box. I straightened the ribbon and handed it to him.

Will's face lit up. "You didn't have to get me something."

I supposed he still had to play along until he had the watch in his hands. "I wanted to. I heard you had been through a lot." I hadn't heard any details, but it was obvious by his bruises and the way his hair had been hacked off that something awful had happened.

Will set the box in his lap and sighed. "Never in a million years did I imagine anything like this would ever happen to me."

"I'm sorry, I really am." I reminded myself that this was Hugh and he had been through a traumatic ordeal. I was going to have to help him through it. "If you need someone to talk to-"

"I know." he said tugging at the ribbon. "I never knew humans could be so cruel to one another."

"Did they do that to your hair?" The ribbon fluttered to the floor.

"It's amazing what sort of a haircut you can get from a bowie knife." He ran his hand over his blonde head. He tore at the wrapping paper. "I love presents."

I tried to smile, my stomach felt like I had swallowed a boulder. "I hope you like it."

"I'm sure I will." He set the wrapping paper aside. His face showed no signs of the impending reunion. "I got a present yesterday."

"You did?" He lifted the top off the box, my heart was hammering in my ears. In another minute it would all be over and I would have Hugh back again. I should be elated, but instead all I felt was a mounting sense of trepidation. I hated myself for feeling that way, this was Hugh, and now I dreaded facing him again.

I had covered the watch with a layer of tissue paper, that was all that stood between me and Hugh. Will paused and looked at me. "Yes, my father gave me his necklace yesterday. I couldn't believe it. Now let's see what this is." He put his hands on the tissue paper.

Something inside my mind snapped to attention. I jumped to my feet. "What did you say?"

"Papa gave me his necklace." Will fished the chain out of his collar and showed it to me. "He said I deserved it for what happened to me."

"He did?"

"Yes." Will's hand was still poised on the tissue paper. "The boy who stabbed him took it as some kind of trophy. But I got it back, and yesterday he said I could keep it. I was really surprised because he never takes it off. Now let's see what's in here."

I snatched the box out of Will's hands, my other hand grabbed the lid and jammed it back on. "You can't have this."

Will looked astonished. "What do you mean? You just gave it to me."

"I know but as it happens it's just like the necklace you're wearing."

"Just like this?" Will said looking down at the star. "But the box felt heavier than that. Let me see."

"No."

"Emma, it isn't very nice to give someone a gift and then take it away before they even have a chance to look at it."

"I'll get you something else."

"Can't I at least see it?" he said reaching for the box. He took one corner and nearly pulled it out of my hands. Sensing his strength I held onto the opposite corner and for a few tense seconds we were locked in a tug of war. Our eyes met and I could see the determination in his. I gave a hard pull and managed to get it out of his hands, stumbling backwards as I did. Will looked stunned and hurt.

"I'm sorry. I know you don't understand. Please forgive me."

"I think you should go now."

"Yes I think so." I dropped the box in my bag and started for the library door. I turned back to look at his bruised face. "I really am sorry Will."

Ma Granger was on the other side of the door looking worried. "It was a bad scene in there, eh?"

"I didn't see you."

"I stuck my head through the wall behind you. The beautiful one was there too."

"Do you mean Mika?"

"He looked mighty angry."

"It wasn't my fault. I didn't ask about the necklace, Will volunteered the information. I would have never asked, I know better. Is Mika still here?"

Ma shook her head. "No, he's gone."

"He can't take Hugh away now, not after all this." I said realizing that I had been right after all. I hadn't betrayed Hugh. I had fallen in love with him all over again.

Chapter 106

Hugh hadn't travelled in over a century. When he was eight years old he had accompanied his father to London on business. He remembered being fascinated by the bustling city with its strange smells and sounds. That was so long ago, he couldn't imagine what London looked like now. He suspected it was a far cry from the Maine wilderness that was buzzing by Senator Brown's carriage.

He stuck his head out the window as they rode alongside a freight train. Hugh had read about them but had never seen one in person. He was amazed by the power of such a machine. The ground shook as it roared next to them, the wheels and gears turning together, black smoke billowing overhead.

"I would swear you've never been anywhere." Senator Brown said. "I would have thought four days on the road would have tempered your curiosity."

"I like travelling that's all." Hugh leaned back on his seat. He did not want to appear unsophisticated.

They were on their way home. Hugh had identified the young man who had stabbed him and given a sworn affidavit accounting what had happened that night. He had once been sympathetic to the boy, but not after what happened to Will. He gladly cooperated with the prosecution. He had enjoyed the irony of it, he had once been the defendant, witnesses pointing their fingers at him. Now the tables had turned.

The carriage lurched along the rutted roads, outside the foliage was just turning to shades of gold and red. Senator Brown was on the opposite seat staring at him.

"I hear that you and your wife are expecting another child." Hugh said, desperate for something to say.

"I'm the one who told you." The Senator grumbled. "But, yes indeed, number five. I can still keep up with the younger men if you know what I mean. My wife has no complaints."

"That's nice."

The Senator leaned forward and licked his lips. "In fact I think I wear her out sometimes. I haven't lost my appetite for it."

"That's nice." Hugh repeated. He shouldn't have said anything.

"Speaking of which, is there something between yourself and Emma Hollis?"

"What do you mean?"

The Senator started to speak when Mika suddenly appeared next to him. "Go to sleep old man." The Senator's eyes rolled back as his head flopped on the cushioned seat back, a few seconds later he began to snore loudly. "I have to talk with you Hugh. One of your sons has tipped the Torment Seer off about you. That's unacceptable."

"I don't believe it." Hugh began to panic. "How could they? They don't know who I really am."

"No they don't. But you gave that cursed necklace to Will and he in turn has told her that it is yours. I have made it perfectly clear that she is to have no help from anyone."

"But Will would not have known that." Hugh couldn't believe how foolish he had been to let Will keep the necklace. "Emma asked him about it?"

Mika glanced at Senator Brown whose mouth hung open as he slept. "No, actually she didn't. I am surprised to say she's quite smart, she knows better than to ask. When she saw it she was under the impression that Will was in fact you."

"I should never have given it to him." He was embarrassed to admit he had not even thought of it at the time.

"No you shouldn't have, but after some confusion Will set her straight, and thereby confirmed that you are indeed the one she's looking for. My rules have been broken." Mika said angrily.

"You can't take me away, not now, not after all this time." Hugh begged. "It's my fault not hers."

"I can take you away anytime I like." Mika's eyes were cold.

Hugh said nothing, he had brought it upon himself. As usual he did things without thinking of the consequences, he hadn't changed one bit from his old life. One necklace was going to tear everything apart.

"There's only one problem." Mika said.

Hugh remained silent. He had no interest in anything else Mika had to say.

"The Torment Seer was going to give you the watch before Will said anything."

"What did you say?"

"Try listening for once in your life. She loves *you*. Somehow that girl figured it out all on her own. Will only confirmed it. I hate technicalities."

Hugh started laughing with joy. He had done the impossible. He had managed to reach Emma through the body of someone entirely different, without help from anyone else. "So what is she doing right now?"

"Waiting for you to come home."

Chapter 107

"What do you get for a man that you tried to give a present to and then took it back before he could look at it?" I asked Mrs. Thalberg as I walked around the store looking for something suitable for Will.

"That sounds complicated."

"It is." It had been three days since I nearly chose Will, leaving him bewildered after I snatched the watch out of his hands. I had to make it up to him somehow, the only thing to do was to send him a real gift and a letter of apology.

"We have those nice cuff links we just got in." she offered. "I could send them out to be engraved, what letter would you want on them?"

I smirked at her. "Is that your way of finding out who they are for?"

Mrs. Thalberg looked guiltily at me. "Yes in fact. Lately you seem as though you-" She stopped and looked at her husband who was staring out the window.

"Like I can't make up my mind?"

"Yes, that's it."

"I know, but I've made my decision now."

"You have? Who?"

I didn't have a chance to answer her. Mr. Thalberg was waving at me from the front of the store. "Emma, come quick! It's the Senator's carriage."

Coming around the bend in the road was Senator Brown's carriage, lacquered in red with gold lettering on the side announcing the owner. The driver pulled up quickly on the reins as three red haired children ran into the street, they were Eve's.

"He must be bringing the Chief back." Mr. Thalberg said.

My knees started shaking. I strained to catch a glimpse of Jason through the windows as the carriage began to move again. Suddenly the Senator's head popped out and shouted something at the driver. The carriage lurched to a stop, rocking back and forth in front of Jennings'. The Senator appeared on the sidewalk. He said something to the driver and disappeared into the store.

"Go and see if he's in there." Mr. Thalberg said tapping me on the arm.

"What?"

"Go and see if the Chief is in there before the Senator comes back."

I looked at Mrs. Thalberg. "I would. That is who you're looking for isn't it?" she said.

I smiled at her. Was I really so obvious? "Yes."

I ran out the door, a blast of cold autumn air hit my face. I should have worn a shawl. I went across the road to Senator Brown's shiny carriage and rapped on the door. Above me the driver stared down suspiciously. My heart was beating fast.

The door slowly opened. Jason was seated inside grinning. His gray eyes were mischievous. "You knocked?"

"Yes. I saw the carriage and wondered if you were in here." He was wearing his navy blue uniform, the brass buttons glinted at me. He looked impossibly lovely.

"Come in. The Senator is in the store." he said offering his hand. I took it and he pulled me inside the carriage and shut the door, blocking out the world.

I sat next to him. He smelled woodsy, a mixture of pine and earth. "Jason."

"Yes?"

"I, I-" I couldn't finish my thought. I couldn't think of anything else except him. I lunged at him and kissed him on the mouth, he moaned and pulled me on top of him. My head hit the roof of the carriage. We stopped momentarily and looked at each other.

"I've wanted this for a very long time." he said.

"Don't talk." I said kissing him again. I could feel his hands sliding up the bare skin of my legs. Thank heavens it was still too warm for long underwear.

My mouth slid down his neck, the stubble on his chin brushing my face. "The Senator will be back any minute now." he whispered in my ear.

I sat up and ran my hands through his short gray hair. "I couldn't resist you any longer. I have to talk to you."

"You do?"

"Yes. It's important."

He glanced out the window. In the back of my mind I was vaguely aware of the people walking past on the street, unaware of what was transpiring inside. "He will be back any minute."

I followed his line of vision and saw Senator Brown standing at the counter in Jennings'. He was leaning confidently on his walking stick and talking as usual. "Why is he always lurking about?" I muttered as I turned back to Jason. I stroked the side of his face. "I love you."

There were tears at the corners of his eyes. "I have waited so long to hear that. I love you too Emma." he glanced outside again. "He's coming."

"You don't think he should find us this way?"

He laughed. "Probably not. Although I would love to see the look on his face."

I quickly moved, banging my head once again. I took my place next to him on the seat, resisting the urge to hold his hand.

"Your skirt." he mumbled.

I looked down and realized my bare legs were showing. "Oh, Mr. Garrett. I can't imagine what you're thinking."

"Can't you?"

I was pulling on my skirt, trying desperately to appear as though I had been up to innocent pursuits when the carriage door opened and Senator Brown came inside.

"Miss Hollis you do turn up in the oddest places." He looked at me and then to Jason. A frown appeared on his face. "What is going on here?"

"Miss Hollis just stopped in to say good morning." Jason said.

Senator Brown looked at me as though he knew every detail of what had just taken place. "You're obviously still desperate to see this fellow. Does your mother know what kind of daughter she has?"

"That's not fair-" Jason began.

"Do you still have whatever it is you wanted to give him? Why don't you just hand it over? I would love to know what was so important that you had to come see him before we left."

"You didn't tell me that she came to see me." Jason said. The Senator shrugged.

"I don't have the item with me right now. It's merely a token of my appreciation for the fine work of the police."

"Is that all?" the Senator scoffed. "We are on our way to the bank right now for an important meeting."

"I'm buying the Senator's house." Jason said. "We are signing papers this afternoon."

"Really? I'm happy for you."

The Senator cleared his throat. "Don't you have work to do at that store?"

"I'm going." I turned to Jason. "May I come and see you later this afternoon? We can have that talk."

"Yes."

"He's going to be busy." the Senator said.

"No I'm not."

"Yes you are. I've just been speaking with Jane and Amy Jennings. They are giving a little concert in William's honor this evening."

"You're joking." Jason and I both said at once.

"Certainly not. Jane and Amy Jennings are accomplished singers, and young ladies of the highest quality. A rare quality these days." The Senator glared at me. "Garrett, you are expected to be at your son's side tonight."

"Very well, I'll invite Emma as my guest." Jason took my hand.

"You will not." the Senator said.

"I can invite whomever I want to my own home."

"If you invite Miss Hollis I won't sign the papers and I'll make sure you never get a house in Fox Cove."

Jason leaned forward in his seat. "Are you telling me that you would prevent the sale of your home, and any other, over whether or not I invite Emma to a ridiculous concert? Have you nothing better to do with your life than to be a twisted, bitter old man?"

"I vowed the day her father betrayed me that I would do everything to make him and his family miserable. I was denied what I wanted. I can at least return the favor, even if it is temporary."

"What the hell were you denied?" Jason shouted.

"You don't know anything about it."

"I know all about it. Is this because of Eve? Because you didn't get to bed her? You didn't care about her, you didn't give a damn about her. You just wanted to have her, just because you could, to appease your appetite as you call it."

"I am accustomed to getting what I want."

"Jason." I said quietly. "I'll see you another time."

He turned and looked at me, his face softened. "I want to have that talk with you."

"I do too. But it can wait a little longer. I want you to have a home of your own, one that belongs to you. You go along and sign the papers. I'll see you another time."

He looked at me and took a deep breath. "All right."

I turned my attention to the Senator. "As usual it's been a real pleasure Senator. I always enjoy our meetings."

"I don't appreciate humor Miss Hollis."

"I know." I opened the carriage door. "Goodbye Jason."

"Goodbye Emma."

"Don't forget he's not inviting you to the concert." the Senator warned.

"I understand completely Senator. Do give your lovely wife Bridget my regards." I shut the door and the carriage rolled on towards the bank. I looked at the store and found Mr. and Mrs. Thalberg watching out the window. They smiled enthusiastically at me. I motioned to them that I needed one more minute and then walked down the sidewalk and into the police station.

Harold was inside still acting as the chief. He stood up when I walked in. "Good afternoon Emma, what can I do for you?"

"Harold, I need a huge favor. Can you invite me to a concert at your house?"

Chapter 108

It had been a productive day. Hugh had purchased a home and experienced the most fun he had ever had in a carriage. He replayed Emma's surprise visit in his mind over and over. He liked that they had a secret together. She knew it was him and he knew she knew. He smiled to himself at such circular logic as he strode up Brown Lane, maybe that should become Garrett Lane.

Hugh unlocked the front door of his house and stepped inside. He stood in the front hall and took a deep breath, smelling the timber of the wood floors, the faint scent of the polish Fred used on the banister, his dinner cooking in the kitchen.

This was his home. He had never owned anything before, let alone a house. He had once thought all there was to life was taking what others had, now he knew better. He would continue being a policeman until his new mortgage was paid. He was making his own way in life now, not by taking but by earning. He was proud of himself for the first time ever.

"Papa?" He heard Will's voice from the parlor. Hugh stepped inside and found the room had been transformed. The partition between the parlor and library had been folded back. Every chair in the house had been lined up in neat rows. At the front of the room was the piano, a small wooden platform sat nearby.

"What's this for?" Hugh pointed to the platform.

"It's where the girls are going to stand when they sing." Will said.

"For heaven's sake. I didn't think he meant a real concert."

"Since when does Senator Brown not mean what he says?" Will asked. He was seated in the front row in his pajamas. He looked well rested. The bruises on his face were fading. He slowly stood up and gave Hugh a tight hug.

"You look much better." Hugh said.

"I feel better." Will's choppy hair had been cut short leaving him with little more than blonde fuzz on his head. "Mr. Hollis came and fixed my hair."

"I like it. Maybe I should get mine done that way."

Will laughed and sat back down. "I missed you Papa. I wished you didn't have to leave right after I came home."

"I know, but I had to identify that boy." He took a seat next to Will. "It's done now." He put his arm around Will's shoulders. "Did Dr. Jonas take care of you?"

"Oh yes." Will said rolling his eyes.

"Papa!" Ryan called out as he ran into the parlor. "I've missed you."

Hugh smiled at the warm reception he was getting. "I have something to tell you boys. Where's Harry?"

"He's coming." Ryan said. A few seconds later Harold bounded into the room.

"I want you to all sit down." Hugh said. Ryan and Harold sat on the other side of Will. "I have an important announcement." The boys looked at each other. Hugh waited a moment, relishing the building anticipation. "I bought this house."

One by one the boys' mouths fell open. "Are you joking?" Ryan finally said.

"Of course not."

"But this is a big house." Harold said.

"I can afford it." Hugh said, liking how it sounded.

"Then we are going to stay here in Fox Cove?" Ryan asked.

"I am." Hugh said. "You boys are grown men. I can't stop you if you want to leave, but I hope you'll stay. I love being your father you know."

The boys looked at each other again. This time Will spoke. "You were so different when we came here. It was like you became a whole other person. All those years we had this wonderful, loving father and then you turned into a stranger. We thought you hated us."

Hugh sighed. "I know. I wasn't myself and I wasn't always nice to you. When we came here I had a hard time adjusting. Everything was so different, life seemed upside down."

"And now?" Ryan asked.

"I'm happy. I have everything I ever wanted. I am so sorry I treated you that way. I love you boys so much. I would give my life for you and-" Hugh stopped.

"And who?" Ryan asked.

Harold stood up. "Papa I need to talk with you."

"What is it Harry?"

"I need to speak with you privately."

"Oh, very well." Hugh said with a shrug. Harold grabbed his arm and dragged him into the front hall, shutting the parlor door behind them.

"What's this all about?" Hugh asked.

"I think you should know that I invited Emma Hollis to the concert tonight."

"You did?"

"Yes." Harold said seriously. "We are just friends, there's nothing more to it."

"Why did you have to drag me out here to tell me that?"

"Because I didn't want you to think I was trying to take her away from you."

"What makes you say that?"

Harold looked at him as though he couldn't believe what Hugh was saying. "Papa it's been quite obvious to me since we moved here that you've had your eye on her."

"I have?" Hugh said coyly.

Harold looked annoyed. "Oh stop it. You know you have."

"She's much younger than me."

"I don't think she notices that anymore."

"But wasn't there a time when you were interested? Didn't you want her to come to that disastrous dinner party I hosted?"

"I did. But only for your sake."

"But why would you do that?"

"Because you haven't looked at another woman in all the time I've known you. I never knew Mother, remember?" Harold said. "I know you gave all that up to raise us. I was just an infant, you could have easily given me away."

"I wouldn't do that."

"I know. I just want to do something for you. So when Emma asked me to invite her-"

"She asked you?"

"Yes."

Hugh patted the side of Harold's face. Emma had found a way around things as usual. He would have to take a bath before the concert. And there was his wardrobe to consider, something to catch her eye and preferably easy to remove if the occasion called for it.

"Thank you Harry." Hugh said as he ran upstairs. He had a concert to get ready for.

Chapter 109

Father and I waited for Harold in the parlor. Mother was busy preparing dinner in the kitchen. I could hear her humming as I looked out the window.

"I'm going to give Hugh the watch tonight." I said checking to make sure it was still in my bag.

"This is it then?"

"Yes."

"Nervous?"

"Yes." I admitted.

"Are you sure you've got it right Emma?"

"Yes. I got a little help though. I'm afraid Mika won't like it, he may still take Hugh away."

Father shook his head. "He won't. He can't do anything, you already knew days before that slip of Will's."

"You really do know everything don't you?"

Father shrugged.

"Harold should be here soon." I said anxiously. I was going to do it tonight no matter what, even if I had to stand up in the middle of the concert and announce it to the whole room.

"Don't worry about your mother." Father said quietly.

"What do you mean?"

"I'll make an excuse for you if you should come home late, or not at all."

"Thanks." I mumbled as my face grew warm.

"Emma!" Mother called out from the kitchen. "There's a young man coming to the door, one of those policemen. I can't tell which one, they all look alike to me."

Father and I exchanged looks as I went into the hallway and opened the door. Harold was standing outside dressed in a navy blue suit with an olive green plaid tie.

"You look handsome." I said.

"Are you surprised?"

"No." I turned back and gave Father a final look. He nodded confidently. I took a deep breath and stepped outside. Harold offered his arm. "Thank you for inviting me to this."

"Oh you're perfectly welcome. I was going anyway, it's at my house." he said with a laugh.

"Why isn't it at the Senator's house? It's his party."

"The travelling would be too hard on Will, even for a short distance."

"And your father will be there tonight?"

"Of course." Harold said grinning. "He wouldn't dream of missing it."

The house was brimming with guests by the time Harold and I arrived. The autumn air had turned cool and consequently the porch was empty. We hurried inside, to my relief Candy and Ethan were there. Candy let out a little cry and rushed towards me.

"Emma, Jason is here tonight. Oh sorry." she said looking at Harold.

"It's all right Dr. Hollis." Harold replied. "I do understand."

"You do?"

"Yes, I do." Harold looked around. "The Senator is coming our way. Let's get this over with."

The Senator stopped and glared at me. "Miss Hollis what are you doing here? Do you not recall the conversation we had this afternoon? I told Chief Garrett not to invite you."

"Papa didn't invite her, I did." Harold said beaming.

"Young man that was not my intention."

"But Senator you merely stated that Jason could not invite me. When Harold asked it never occurred to me that you wouldn't like it."

The Senator tapped his foot on the floor. "You've become very sarcastic lately. It's quite unbecoming for a young lady."

"This isn't your house anymore." Candy said.

The Senator frowned. "If you weren't one of my protégés Dr. Hollis you certainly wouldn't be here. Where's my wife? I believe I am developing a headache and only my dear Bridget knows how to comfort me."

"Your protégé?" Candy began.

Ethan put a hand on her arm. "I think I saw Bridget in there talking with Jane." He pointed towards the parlor.

The Senator nodded and brushed past us, his face looking paler than normal.

"I'm not his protégé." Candy lamented. "And I do know what that word means."

"Never mind him." Ethan said adjusting his glasses.

"Emma, can I get you some punch?" Harold asked.

"Yes thank you." I searched the faces around me. After Harold left I turned to Ethan and Candy. "I'm going to give Hugh the watch tonight."

"Finally." Candy said. "You should have done it days ago."

"Are you sure of your decision?" Ethan asked.

"Yes."

"Here we are." Harold returned with two glasses of punch.

"Thank you."

Ethan put his arm around Candy's shoulder. "We should mingle a bit."

"Good luck Emma." Candy squeezed my hand and the two of them set off towards the parlor.

"Shall we go in too?" Harold asked. "Everyone is there."

"Everyone?"

He smiled. "Yes everyone."

I took his arm. "Oh God, is Will in there?"

"Of course he is."

"He's mad at me."

"You mean about giving him a gift and then snatching it out of his hands before he could look at it?"

"Yes that."

"He'll get over it." Harold said with a shrug. "Now come on, we're missing everything."

We entered the parlor and I saw that we were indeed missing everything. It looked as if the whole town was in attendance. At the front of the room, near the piano, were Jane and Amy Jennings. Despite my lack of fashion and taste I did observe they both looked incredibly pretty, beside me Harold noticed too. He flashed both of the girls a smile.

Bridget was standing next to Senator Brown who was sprawled in a chair. She was putting a wet rag on his forehead and holding his hand. The Senator looked up at her thankfully, he suddenly seemed small and dependent. His bold presence was diminished, he was just another face in the crowd.

The parlor and library had been opened up, dozens of chairs were lined up in rows. In the front row looking somewhat recovered was Will. I ventured the tiniest of waves. He nodded curtly and looked away. A few rows back was Cole Jennings. He tugged at the collar of his formal suit and said something to his wife who nodded and patted his hand.

My eyes continued their search until they came upon a head of silver hair at the back of the room. I stopped and waited until he looked up. I could feel myself grinning. A nervous energy invaded my body. I felt like I could sprout wings and fly to him.

Harold pulled his arm away. "I'm going to have a word with Jane."

"Uh huh." I said staring at Jason. He set his cup of punch down and started walking towards me. I wondered how I hadn't noticed him for all those months. He was certainly the most handsome man in the room, and indeed in the whole town. He was wearing a black suit with a white shirt and black and white pin-striped tie. I caught a flash of his gray eyes as he moved.

I took a step forward and then realized someone was in front of me. "Jeremy!" I cried as I collided with him, my glass of punch sloshing onto the floor. "Oh no."

"Not a problem Miss Hollis." Fred said appearing out of nowhere. "I'll get it." He crouched down and wiped the offending punch from the polished oak floor.

"I've haven't talked with you in a long time." Jeremy was saying. Behind him Jason had stopped and was leaning against the wall looking amused.

"It's been a long time." I agreed. We had nearly been engaged once. I supposed I owed him a few minutes of meaningless conversation. "How have you been?" I looked over his shoulder at Jason.

"Quite well actually." He leaned back on his heels as though he planned for this to be a lengthy meeting.

"That's nice."

"The bank is doing well."

"Great."

He rubbed the beard he had recently grown. "Emma I've been meaning to say this to you for a while. I think you were right all those years ago when you turned down my proposal."

"It wasn't you-"

He shook his head. "You don't have to explain. I was pretty angry back then, but now I realize that you were right all along. The past few years I've watched you struggle. You've been looking for something. I wanted to be that something for you, but I know I'm not."

"Jeremy-"

"It's all right Emma. Recently I have noticed-" He looked over his shoulder and then back to me. "I see I am keeping you."

"I just wanted to give my regards to the Chief Inspector."

Jeremy smiled. "Yes, I'm sure you do. I'm happy for you Emma." He kissed me lightly on the cheek before walking away.

I hurried towards the back of the library where Jason was waiting.

"Tough room." he said. I resisted the urge to kiss him.

"I hoped you had some time for that talk." I took his hand. "Is there somewhere private we can go?"

"Yes, but the problem is the whole thing is about to start."

"What? Now?"

"Yes, and it goes on forever. I was here for the rehearsal this afternoon."

"That figures." I groaned. At the front of the room Senator Brown was asking people to take their seats.

Jason smiled. "Listen I have to sit through at least part of this thing for Will's sake. I am going to be right up front, when it's almost over I will get up and leave. You wait about five minutes and then meet me upstairs in my bedroom."

"Are you suggesting Mr. Garrett that I go to your bedroom un-chaperoned?"

"Absolutely. You know you didn't have a chaperone in the Senator's carriage this afternoon-"

"And look what happened."

"I know. Can you imagine what would have happened if he hadn't been so rude as to interrupt?"

"Ladies and gentlemen, let's take to our seats." the Senator was shouting.

"I'll wait for you to take your leave then." I said.

"Please, let's be orderly about this." the Senator was saying.

I let go of Jason's hand. Harold was waving at me. He was standing next to a chair in the row behind Will. "I saved you a seat."

I sat down and soon found myself crowded in on either side by people I didn't know very well. I leaned forward and tapped Will on the shoulder. "Are you feeling better?"

He glanced over his shoulder. "Yes." he said coolly before returning his attention to the front of the room where Amy and Jane were standing.

A few seconds later Jason arrived through the entrance from the front hallway. He looked at me, his face turning a shade redder, and then took his seat directly in front of me.

"Now ladies and gentlemen." the Senator began. "Tonight is a special night for so many reasons. It was in this very room that I had a magnificent thought."

Ryan looked back at me and rolled his eyes.

"I had a vision of a new police force to keep law and order in our sleepy little town. When Chief Garrett wrote to me about how he and his sons were all officers of the law how could I say no?" The Senator stopped and looked eagerly at his audience, a few people in the back clapped.

"As the months have gone by this group of strangers have become our friends. William is recovering from a most trying time." The Senator was interrupted by a hearty round of applause. Will stood up and shyly acknowledged the crowd. "And we have caught the young hooligan who nearly killed our Chief Inspector." Another round of applause began.

Jason stood up and turned around. He was clearly enjoying the attention. He waved and smiled at various people in the room. He was proud of himself, it was something I had never seen in him before. Hugh had always hung his head, he was forever ashamed of his life and how it ended, but not Jason. He was confident and pleased with himself.

"Yes that's fine." the Senator said as he waited for Jason to sit down. "Now I would like to turn your attention to our fine young ladies who have volunteered their time in order to put on this concert in honor of William."

There was more clapping followed by a detailed summary of Jane and Amy's qualifications and an introduction of the man at the piano. As

Senator Brown rambled on I saw Ma Granger out of the corner of my eye, she was walking through the rows of people, a look of supreme pleasure on her face.

"Ah, I haven't been able to do this for a long time." she said. "I feel like I'm at the devil's door I'm so warm." She finished walking through the guests and stood in front of the Senator, she put her hands through his beard and cackled.

"Before I turn the room over to the girls I have to remind each of you gentlemen that if you want to see your humble senator here become leader of this great state, you need to get out there and vote. Ladies, imagine what life will be like with me at the helm of this sturdy ship we call Maine. Men, vote for Brown!" The Senator held his arms up as though he was conducting an orchestra, half the room exploded in excitement while the other half clapped politely.

"Thank you, thank you. Now without further ado I give you the angelic sounds of Jane Jennings." The Senator hurried to his seat in the front row. Jane took a deep breath and looked at the piano player. She began to sing.

Jane had a pleasant voice. Ma Granger began twirling about to the music, her skirts billowing around her. Any other night I might have enjoyed Jane's singing and Ma's dancing, but as the song progressed I found myself distracted by Jason who was seated in front of me.

His silver hair was cut short in the back, it tapered to the nape of his neck which was peppered with gray and blonde hairs. Just above his collar was a distracting patch of bare skin. I stared at his neck for what seemed like hours. I had stopped listening to the music. More than once I had to stop myself from leaning forward and kissing that little patch of skin.

It was as though everyone in the room had disappeared and it was just the two of us. Up front I could see Amy and Jane alternating songs, sometimes singing together, but I couldn't hear a thing. Ma was still twirling and walking through the occasional person but my mind was elsewhere.

How could I have not seen it? He was so obviously Hugh. The boys couldn't hold a candle to him. It boggled my mind. How could I have been so blind? I felt shallow and foolish that I had been only looking at the outside. The boys were young, but Hugh was not young. It all made sense now.

Amy hit a high note and I was brought back to my senses. In front of me Jason whispered something to Will and then stood up and walked out of the room without looking back. My heart started beating fast in my ears. I looked at my watch, five minutes was going to feel like an eternity.

Around me people started clapping. I joined them although I wasn't sure exactly what for. Amy and Jane joined hands and took a bow. Jane looked at the piano player and said something which was impossible to hear over the applause. In front of me Harold was cheering enthusiastically.

I looked at my watch again, barely two minutes had passed. I could take it no longer. I stood up just as the girls launched into another song. The man and woman on either side of me looked up in annoyance, it soon became clear that the perfect seat Harold had saved for me, the one directly behind Jason, had left me trapped.

"Excuse me." I whispered to the woman next to me as I attempted to navigate my way out. My fellow guests looked on with barely disguised contempt as I forced them to either swivel their knees to one side or stand up to let me pass. "Sorry."

The last chair in my row was occupied by a large woman in a sparkly satin gown. My toe caught the hem of her dress causing me to trip loudly. I looked up and found the entire audience glaring at me. "Sorry." I mouthed. I rushed into the hallway, stopping for a moment to catch my breath. Fred was standing at the bottom of the stairs.

I took a deep breath as I approached him. "Now listen Fred, it may seem strange but I have to go upstairs for a minute, actually more than a minute, possibly much longer."

Fred raised one eyebrow and looked at my purse which I was clutching to my chest. "Mr. Garrett already informed me of your visit. I've been waiting for you. Mr. Garrett doesn't want anyone else going up, lest you be disturbed." He raised his eyebrow again and I felt as though he knew exactly what was going on. I brushed it from my mind and ran upstairs.

Jason's door was closed. I paused and tried to calm my breathing. Slowly I opened the door and stepped inside. He was standing at the window looking out of the telescope.

"It's a good night for stargazing." he said looking up. He seemed amazingly calm. My legs felt like rubber as I shut the door. "You'd better lock it too. In about ten minutes Fred will have forgotten why he's standing at the bottom of the stairs and they'll all be traipsing up here."

I nodded and locked the door, putting the key on a nearby dresser. When I turned around Jason was standing in front of me. He brushed the hair from my eyes and kissed me. "I've waited all night for that."

It would be so easy to become distracted as I put my arms around him. "Wait a minute." I pushed him away.

"Ouch." He touched his side.

"Oh no, I forgot about your wound. Are you all right? You should have said something this morning in the carriage, I was practically mauling you."

He smiled. "It's fine unless someone pokes me there. But I can handle the pain, even when I'm getting mauled."

"I have to talk to you."

"I know. This must be pretty serious. What is it?"

"I, I have a present for you." I opened my bag and took out the dented box. I handed it to him.

He turned it over and smirked. "Nice wrapping."

"Sorry, it got a little damaged."

He took the lid off. "What on earth can this be?" He removed the tissue and looked up at me in surprise. "What's this?"

I opened my mouth but no words came out.

He took the watch out of its nest of paper and held it up to the light. "What a curious object. Is it an antique?" He flicked open the cover and looked inside. "Hugh Charles James MacPherson. What an absurdly long name. Sounds like some rich twit." He ran his fingers over the watch case, a smile spread across his face. "I do believe that was my name once upon a time." Jason looked at me. "Hello again."

"Hugh." I buried my face in his neck. I squeezed him so hard it was a wonder he could breathe. Nearly five years of worrying and wondering and near misses had led to this moment. I felt as though a heavy weight had been pinning me down for all those years and now it was gone. I was overwhelmed with emotion, it began to fill me up until I couldn't breathe.

"Hugh." I repeated. I let go of him and fell to the floor, hot tears poured over my face. My breaths came in hard gulps, my whole body heaved. I wanted to speak but I couldn't.

"Emma." I heard him say. "It's all over now." I opened one eye and saw a watery image of his face in front of me. "You did it. You did it all on your own."

He sat next to me on the floor, stroking my hair and speaking in a low voice. I couldn't understand what he was saying but it didn't matter. I took a deep breath and wiped my eyes. "Are you really Hugh?"

"Yes." he said taking my face in his hands.

"Prove it. Tell me something only Hugh would know."

"Let's see. I was born in 1754, died in 1784. I was killed on my thirtieth birthday, murdered in the house that you live in. I had two brothers Patrick and Connelly and a sister Laura."

I wiped my eyes again. "I didn't believe I could do it Hugh. I've waited for years. What took you so long?"

"I never knew that Mika planned on bringing me back four years later. For me it's only been eight months since I left."

"I had nearly given up on you."

"I told you I would be back."

"I want to see your wings."

"I can't exactly make them pop out. You have to be dead for that to happen."

"I know, but I want to see them. You said that when I chose you they would be visible. I have to see them, then I will know it's really you."

"You still don't believe it's me?"

"I do. But I have to see them."

"Very well." He got to his feet. I stood up and helped him off with his jacket, he started unbuttoning his shirt but I pushed his hands away and did it for him. I untucked his shirt and let it slide off his shoulders and onto the floor. He had a scar forming on his side where he had been stabbed.

"Turn around." I said, running my fingers over his soft skin. He did as I asked and there was the final proof I needed, his wings etched like ink into his back. The edges were tinged in white with a hint of gold. I looked up and saw the patch of skin on his neck I had been looking at during the concert. I stood on my tiptoes, for he was taller now, and put my lips on his bare skin. My hands slipped around his waist, my fingers looking for his belt buckle.

"We have a lot to catch up on." he said turning around.

"I know. But we can do that later."

He smiled and caught his hand around my waist. "I love you Emma."

"I love you too Hugh. I've never loved anyone else."

"It's Hugh only in this room."

"I know." Downstairs I heard one of the girls hitting a high note, the concert seemed like a distant memory. I removed his belt and pulled the button off his trousers. I tossed it on the floor.

"Oh really?" he said with a smirk. "How would you like it if I pulled the buttons off your clothes?"

"I would love it." I said taking his arms and walking him towards the bed. "I've waited a long, long time for you." I pushed him onto the bed and crawled on top of him. "Those trousers come off, don't they?"

"It all comes off now." He rolled on top of me, desperately trying to pull his trousers down.

"Hurry up." I felt myself begin to slide off the bed. A second later I was on the floor. Hugh landed on top of me with his face between my breasts.

"Not bad." I heard him say. I poked him in the shoulder and started laughing. He looked up and smiled. "I've waited over a century to get these damn things off and I still can't. I'm hopeless."

"I love you Hugh. I don't know how I ever survived all these years without you."

"You don't have to worry about that ever again. Now help me get these off. Ridiculous long pants, it's no wonder birth rates are declining."

Downstairs Amy and Jane sang their hearts out to thunderous applause. Upstairs I had Hugh all to myself.

Chapter 110

It had been a long time since Hugh had been on a horse. He had only ridden a few times since he had been returned to life. Now he found himself atop Tar, Ryan's black quarter horse. He was riding back into town with his wife seated in front of him.

He was keenly aware of the stares they were receiving as the horse sauntered down the main road. He tipped his hat to the various onlookers, he was after all the chief inspector, an important member of society.

"I don't think they expected to see Emma and Jason together." he whispered in her ear.

Emma looked back at him, her eyes luminous. "They'll have to get used to it."

"Indeed." He pulled at the reins. The horse came to a stop in front of Eve and Scott's house. Hugh dismounted and helped her down.

"Thank you Mr. Garrett."

"You're welcome Mrs. Garrett."

Emma went into Eve's house. Hugh waited, idly nuzzling the horse's face while he watched the front door. A man passed by him and nodded. "Morning Chief Garrett."

"Good morning."

Emma came skipping out of Eve's door. "They're coming." she said excitedly. She took hold of the saddle. "Up please." He lifted her up and swung himself back on the horse. She took his right hand and wrapped it around her waist while he picked up the reins with his left.

"Make sure to go slowly past Jennings'." she said.

"Why?"

"So Jane and Amy can get a good look at my husband."

"I don't think they ever considered me to be husband material."

"Fools."

The road began to curve towards the coast. On the right was Thalberg's. In the window Elijah Thalberg was reading the newspaper. He looked up and stared out. Hugh and Emma waved at him. Elijah briefly turned away, a few seconds later his wife Sharin smiled at them.

"I think they're pleased." Hugh said.

"They always liked you."

On the other side of the street there was nothing to be seen at Jennings' except Cole standing on the sidewalk smoking a cigarette. He looked at the two of them but seemed unimpressed. To Hugh's relief the police station was empty. He wasn't sure how the boys were going to take his news, especially Ryan and Will.

Emma made two more stops that morning, one to the barber shop to talk with her father and finally a visit to the clinic to see Ethan and Candy. "They are all coming."

"I've never been to a family meeting before." Hugh said.

"Neither have I. But I don't know how Mother will react. It's better to have everyone around. Now you'll be at the house in an hour, right? And remember don't come in until I tell you to."

"I'll be there. Maybe we can go upstairs to your bedroom? I have many happy memories from that room."

She smiled and reached up to kiss him. "Behave yourself and I might even take you up to the attic. I'll see you later Jason." She jumped off the horse and started towards home.

Chapter 111

There was no telling what kind of reaction my announcement was going to have with the family. It was the reason I had called a family meeting. I looked down at my hands and slipped my wedding ring into my pocket. I opened the front door and went inside. Mother was in the kitchen muttering to herself as she rolled out a pie crust, her arms and face were dotted with flour.

"Oh this crust." she said looking up. She shook her head and tossed the rolling pin on the table. "I need a break. How was the concert?" She wiped her hands on her apron.

"Fine."

"Why did you stay at Ethan's last night?"

"I was really tired." I wasn't sure exactly what Father had told her.

"Oh? It's just a few more steps here."

"Actually I wanted to stay up and talk with Candy."

"It's so strange of you Emma, not to come home."

"I know." I was eager to change the subject. "I've called a family meeting this morning."

Mother's eyes widened. "A family meeting? What on earth is that?"

"It's where a family gets together and talks about things."

"And what do we have to talk about?"

"It shouldn't take very long." I said.

"I suppose I will be expected to serve lunch."

"No, that won't be necessary."

"Who's coming?"

"Eve, Scott, Candy, Ethan, and of course Father."

Mother pulled out a chair and sat down. "I don't like the sound of this. I'm nervous."

"It's good news. Really."

Within an hour everyone was assembled. Scott was wearing his carpenters apron and smelled like sawdust. Eve followed him, she looked at me curiously as she took a seat in the parlor. Ethan and Candy arrived fresh from the clinic. Candy poked me in the arm and grinned. The last to show up was Father, as soon as he came in Mother ran to him.

"Oh Edward something dreadful has happened."

"What is it?" He looked alarmed.

"Emma has called a family meeting."

Father smiled and patted her cheek. "There's nothing to fear Elsay. Come have a seat and let's see what this is all about." She sat next to him and took his hand. I smiled as I watched them. I had never given their relationship much thought as I grew up. I assumed they loved each other, but I didn't think of them as being in love until recently.

"So what's on your mind Emma?" Candy said loudly.

I looked from face to face and wondered how to begin. Obviously I couldn't start at the real beginning. *Once upon a time there was a ghost in our house named Hugh.*

"I wanted to tell you all-" I stammered and looked down at the floor. I took a deep breath. "I wanted to tell you that this morning I got married."

Eve and Scott looked at each other, their jaws gaping open. Ethan smiled satisfactorily while Candy screamed with delight and stamped her feet on the floor.

"Married?" Mother cried. "How is that possible? You don't have a beau." She looked at Father in desperation. "How can this be Edward?"

"Now Elsay, let Emma finish. I'm sure she'll explain it all."

"Married!" she cried again. "Are you joking Emma?"

"No, I'm not actually. We rode over to Groverstown this morning and got married."

"Have you gone mad?" Mother jumped to her feet.

"Who is he Emma?" Eve asked.

"Indeed. Who is he? What sort of nefarious character has tricked you into this?" Mother grabbed my shoulders. I could see the panic in her eyes.

"Jason Garrett."

"Swell!" Candy cried.

"Who on earth is that?"

"You know who that is Mother." Eve said. "He's the police chief." She looked at me. "I didn't even know you were friends with him Emma."

"A policeman!" Mother cried. "And an old one too."

"He's only forty three."

"Forty three? He's twenty years older than you. Twenty years!" She looked at Father who merely shrugged. "Why couldn't you have married one of his sons? They are all tolerably handsome and more importantly your own age."

"I don't love them."

Mother wrung her hands and looked at Father again. "What are we to do Edward? A policeman in the family."

"Doesn't sound like there's much we can do Elsay. Emma is a grown woman and free to make up her own mind."

"I suppose I will have to get used to it. I've done it before." she said with a glance towards Scott and Candy.

"Thank you Mother. I know this is hard for you." I looked out the window and saw Jason waiting under the oak tree. "Can I bring him in now?"

Mother looked outside and then turned to Ethan. "This is your fault. You left him here in that condition and made Emma get his lunch. Throw two people together like that and trouble is bound to happen."

Ethan didn't say anything.

"Mother I would have married him anyway, no matter what Ethan did. I love him." Outside Jason looked up and smiled. I waved at him to come inside.

I heard the front door open. A second later Jason was standing in the parlor. "Good morning."

Father stood up and offered his hand. "Congratulations, Emma has just told us."

Jason smiled. "Thank you Edward."

"So you really are the one, eh?" Candy asked.

"Yes."

"Thank goodness. If Emma had picked one of those other boys I would have just died." Candy began. "Not literally, but you get my idea. Oh yeah you really do don't you? Heh, that was a pretty funny thing to say. Of course you're no boy. I mean that in a good way though. Heck, I was your doctor and everything and there's nothing wrong-"

"Candy that's enough." Ethan said. He shook Jason's hand and then unexpectedly hugged him. "I'm so glad it all worked out."

"Mother?" I looked at her.

She timidly shook Jason's hand. "Welcome to the family Mr. Garrett."

"Thank you, but you may call me Jason."

"Very well. You'll have to excuse my shock. Quite honestly sir you are the last person I would have ever expected her to marry."

"I am a bit older than Emma."

"A bit?" she muttered. "Actually it is your choice of profession that worries me."

"I don't plan on investigating you, or your husband."

Mother's face softened and a look of relief came into her eyes. She was still worried about Father being arrested for murder. "Welcome to the family Jason. I suppose you are appealing in your own strange way."

"Thank you."

Candy cleared her throat. "Listen, since we are making announcements I was wondering if I might say something too."

"Edward, why all these sudden announcements?" Mother whined. "I'm just getting used to having an old policeman as a son-in-law."

"I'm sure it's nothing to worry about Elsay." Father said soothingly. "Go ahead Candy."

"Thanks Dads." Candy took Ethan's arm. She started to speak and then looked at Ethan. "You tell them. I talk too much don't I?"

Ethan smiled and touched her face. "You do talk too much, but I wouldn't want you any other way." Candy laughed and put her head on Ethan's shoulder. "Candy and I are expecting a baby."

"Now this is too much." Mother said swaying on her feet. "I've got to lie down. A policeman *and* another Cooper in the family."

"Sorry children I'm afraid we've overwhelmed poor Mother." Father said as he guided her out of the room.

The rest of us congratulated Candy and Ethan before calling an end to the meeting. Everyone had to return to work. On the way out Candy grabbed my arm and whispered in my ear. "So it's really Hugh?"

"Yes."

"How was it?"

"What?"

"You know when you gave him the watch." she said. "And afterwards. You stayed at his place didn't you? Remember I am a doctor."

"Candy, honestly must you know all the details of my life?"

"Of course."

"I'm happy for you." I said touching her stomach.

She looked down and smiled. "I'm not going to go like my mother and have one right after another. I'm a modern woman you know, a career woman at that."

"I know.

"If it's a boy maybe I'll name it Hugh."

"You wouldn't."

"Why not? It's my baby. Ethan did have a part in it, but if I'm pushing it out of you know where then I'll give it a name. Maybe I'll name it Hershival after old Brownie. Or better yet Maple. Good for either a boy or a girl."

"Candy, don't ever change." I said. "I'll see you later."

She ran outside to join Ethan. I shut the front door and found Jason lingering on the staircase landing. The house was quiet.

"I was standing right here, in this very spot when I was killed." he said. "And there is where Winslow stood." He pointed at the top of the stairs. "And Charlie was here behind me. It seems like a lifetime ago."

"It was."

He took my hand. "The meeting went pretty well."

"I suppose. Mother is going to take some time."

"Don't worry. I'll grow on her."

"Oh I forgot." I reached into my pocket and put my wedding ring back on.

He put his arm around me and kissed the top of my head. "I thought you were going to show me that attic of yours. I've been very, very good."

"You have, haven't you?" I unbuttoned his coat and slipped my arms inside. "You are such a good boy."

"You'd better show me that attic now." He fingered the buttons on my dress.

"Right this way sir." I grabbed his hand and brought him upstairs. The attic was just as it always had been, except for the extra boxes that had accumulated over the years. I had only been up there a few times since Hugh left.

He stopped at the top of the stairs and looked around. "This was my whole world once. It was so lonely until you came along."

"You won't be lonely anymore." I said wrapping my arms around him. "You know there were a few things we could never do up here before."

"Emma."

"What?"

"Mika is here. He says he needs to talk with me alone."

I remembered what Mika had told me on the roof this past summer. I smoothed the front of his jacket and went downstairs leaving them together for the last time.

Chapter 112

"Are you happy Hugh?" Mika asked. He was standing at the far end of the attic with his hands in his pockets. His face was unemotional.

"Of course I am. You know that."

He took a step forward. "You've made something of yourself."

"Yes I know. I used to scoff at people like me, or at least pretend to. Of course I really just wanted what they had."

"And what's that?"

"A home, a family, to be respected by other people." There was something different about Mika. He was starting to look transparent. "What's the matter with you?"

"I'm leaving."

"Are you going away for a while, like you used to?"

"No. I'm going away forever."

Hugh didn't understand. "You can't leave, you're my Watcher."

"I'm still your Watcher, but I can't allow you to see me anymore."

"But I want to."

Mika smiled sadly. "How many living people can see their Watchers?"

"I don't know." Hugh argued. "What does that matter?"

"I'll still be here. It will be just like before you died."

"I didn't know about you then." He wished he had a chair to sit down on. There was a strange ache in the pit of his stomach.

"I thought you didn't like me."

"Sometimes I don't. But you were the only one I had for all those years, my only company. Mika, you're my best friend."

Something in Mika's expression changed. For a brief second he returned to normal before he started to fade again. Within the transparency there were shimmers of green, silver and gray. "I'm a Watcher. I have no friends."

"I'm your friend."

"You have the Torment Seer now. She's your wife, you don't need me."

"It's because of you that I have her. It's because of you that I have my sons. You've done everything for me and I've done nothing for you." Hugh realized for the first time how often he had taken Mika for granted.

"It's not your place to do anything for me. I have merely fulfilled my duty."

The air around Mika began to swirl strangely with what looked like sparkly pieces of dust. Hugh wondered if this was how Emma had seen him. He suddenly felt Mika's presence like never before. "You are beautiful. I never realized it until now."

"Of course I am. You'd better remember this moment, the next time you see me I'll look like regular old Mika again."

"Why is that?"

"Because you'll be dead again."

"But you'll still be here now? While I'm alive? I just won't be able to see you anymore?"

Mika nodded. "As usual I'm repeating what I have already said. Yes, I will still be here. But this time listen to me. Listen to your instincts. You'll still hear me harping at you, you just have to be open to it. Don't ignore me."

"I won't. I promise. I want to thank you for everything you have done for me. I promise I will do everything you ask me to. I will be the best person I possibly can."

"Don't get dramatic Hugh. You worry about the small things and I'll handle the tough stuff."

"All right."

"I'm going now. It's going to be pretty impressive so get ready."

"Goodbye friend." Hugh offered his hand.

Mika paused and then put his translucent hand in Hugh's. Hugh felt like he had stepped into a blizzard. A blast of cold air surrounded his body. The attic disappeared and for a brief moment he was standing in a damp field, voices and images were flashing in the back of his mind, blurring together. He found himself getting dizzy.

Mika let go. "Goodbye Hugh. I-" He paused for a moment and then grinned. "You can thank me for the wings when you're dead." A blast of white light filled the attic. Hugh closed his eyes. He was blown against the wall. He slid to the floor and pulled his knees up to his chest. When he opened his eyes he noticed the air was shimmery, sparkling particles twirled in the midday sunlight, winking at him as they floated by.

"Goodbye Mika."

He wasn't sure how long he sat there. The attic was deathly quiet, he felt for a moment as though he were the only person left on earth. Then he heard Emma's footsteps on the attic stairs.

"Jason?" she called out as she reached the top step. "Is he gone?" The air had cleared, the particles gone.

"Yes, Mika's gone." Hugh said. "He's been part of my life and death for so long. I just never thought he would leave."

Emma reached out her hand. He took it and she pulled him to his feet. "Jason." she said stroking his cheek. "He's not gone. He's still there. You just have to believe. I learned something about that lately."

"I know."

She smiled. "Now let's go home."

He took her hand and together they left her house and stepped into the autumn air. The leaves furnished a canopy of red and gold as they walked up the narrow lane. In the trees chickadees flew busily about while on the ground a chipmunk darted nervously back and forth. Hugh took a deep breath, the cool salty air refreshing him. He saw the roof of his own house ahead of him, he turned and looked at Emma and felt gloriously alive.

<u>about the author</u>

Mary Swift lives on the coast of southern Maine. When she's not writing she enjoys travelling.

<u>for more information and other stories</u>

www.amazon.com/author/maryswift

www.facebook.com/maryswiftwriter

Made in the USA
Monee, IL
07 September 2023

42356894R00312